THE NIGHT-BORN SISTERS

ALESSANDRA WOODWARD

RENAISSANCE CREATIVE BOOKS

Book Cover Design by TK Palad

Edited by Iulia Marin

A Renaissance Creative Book

ISBN: 978-1-777-5979-4-8 (Paperback)

ISBN: 978-1-777-5979-5-5 (Ebook)

THE TAPESTRY OF SWORD AND FLAME

THE DEFENDER'S THRONE

THE NIGHT-BORN SISTERS

THE LAST HEARTH QUEEN (2024)

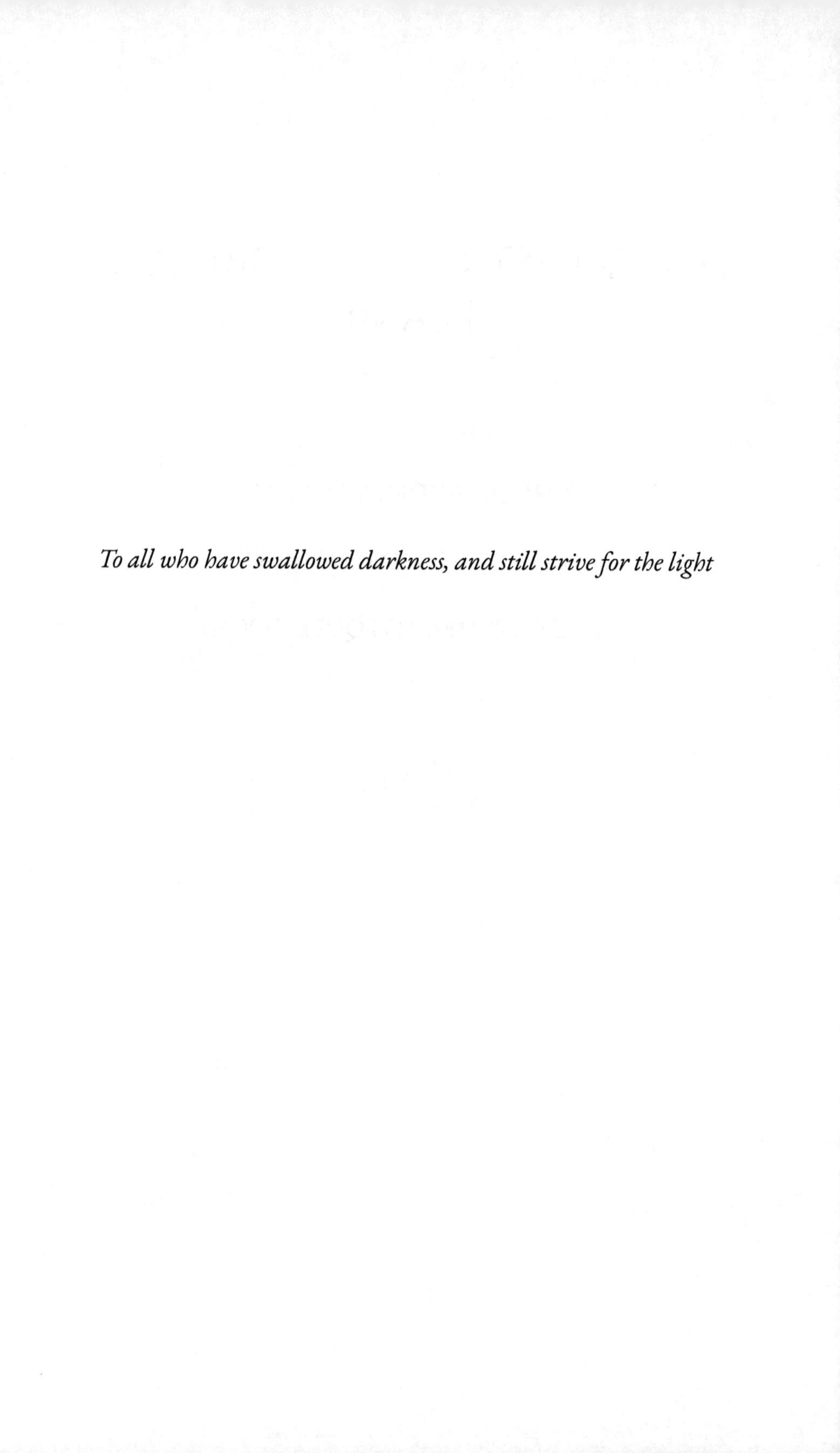

To all who have swallowed darkness, and still strive for the light

This book contains subject matter that may be triggering, including but not limited to: graphic violence, sexual assault, death, and pregnancy loss. Please be kind to yourself and read at your own discretion.

MOONS

Wolf/Quiet Moon-January
Ice/Storm Moon-February
Wind Moon-March
Seed Moon-April
Hare Moon-May
Horse Moon-June
Buck/Mead Moon-July
Sturgeon Moon-August
Hazelnut Moon-September
Blood/Harvest Moon-October
Dark Moon-November
Cold/Oak Moon-December

Prologue: The Vow

Somewhere in the Rhodope Mountains, Ancient Bulgaria, 1216 BC

And Night bore hateful Doom and black Fate and Death, and she bore Sleep and the tribe of Dreams. And again the goddess murky Night, though she lay with none, bare Blame and painful Woe, and the Hesperides who guard the rich, golden apples and the trees bearing fruit beyond glorious Ocean. Also she bore the Destinies and ruthless avenging Fates, Clotho and Lachesis and Atropos, who give men at their birth both evil and good to have, and they pursue the transgressions of men and of gods: and these goddesses never cease from their dread anger until they punish the sinner with a sore penalty.
~Hesiod, Theogony, 8th Century B.C.

She was not permitted to say goodbye to her father. Her mother insisted there was no time, that the shadows grew deep and the woman who would hear her vow had little patience. So they left, at first on horse, as she expected, but then on foot, like beggars and tinkers. They left no tracks. Penny's mother was the best hunter in the land, and therefore the most skilled tracker; she knew how to move through copse and wood, bracken and field, without leaving a trace, and how to seek out her prey before they could take cover. Though they moved quickly, it took three days of walking to find the cave. Penny did not know where they were when they finally stumbled upon the cragged entrance, the carved lintel stone twice as high as her head. She knew only that she was cold, and a little hungry, and more than a little afraid that she had made the wrong decision in agreeing to come to this place and swear this vow, even if it meant she could be queen.

She already missed her father.

The cave was damp, and cramped with shadows. Penny had already heard all sorts of tales of this place—how the young came away with new lines spidering their eyes, new fears in their hearts. How the old sometimes did not come back at all. Her own father had told his own story by the heat of many fires, his rich, deep voice practiced in telling tales, his arms squeezing her ribs at just the right time so that she squealed with fear, while the creatures in his fanciful story appeared to come alive in the flames. He had told her of the vicious Erinyes, the agents of the Moirai, who sought vengeance on wrongdoers. He had warned her how the snake-infested creatures would visit their punishment upon her if she did not keep her promises. Sometimes, she dreamed of those Furies, felt their malevolent eyes watching her every move, threatening her, so she made sure she did not break her promises, even the little ones, and she knew she could not break this one, either. She promised her mother she would swear this vow, despite how it terrified her. Still, she had not understood the true reason of why she should be afraid, until she saw the woman.

The hag's face was withered and pale, like ice, the eyes just as clouded and cold as the frozen lake at the valley's bottom. Trepidation dragged sharp nails down her spine, and Penny peered over her shoulder at her mother, searching for reassurance. Antiope's face was set in familiar lines. There was no allowance for hesitation. Penny was being pressed forward in the same manner as a rebellious mare, with her mother's words squeezing her ribs the way a rider's heels dig in for speed.

"You must," Antiope said, pressing the goblet into her hand and giving her a firm nudge on her shoulder blade. "Remember, say *everything* as I have instructed. It will be all right."

Penny advanced into the shadows, clutching the cold metal cup between both hands, the smell of honey teasing her nostrils. The opening of the cave and the silhouette of her mother's tall frame disappeared in the night behind her. The old woman in front of her was hunched over a stone table, her crooked hands weaving threads that seem to be made of the very shadows she sat within. A stub of beeswax candle was the only light—or heat—in the stone walled room.

"What do you want?" a croaking voice demanded.

"I have come to...to swear my vow."

Penny knew she must do this strange thing, knew how important it was to her mother, though she couldn't understand why. When she completed this task, they would leave for her mother's home, for the place where Penny would one day be queen, but her mother had insisted this must be done before Penny could enter that place. She had not said why, but Penny knew better than to question her mother.

"A vow, you say." The old woman stopped her fiddling with shadows, turning curious blank eyes toward Penny. "Children do not swear vows to me, or my sisters."

"I—" Penny did not know what to say. Her mother had only told her this must be done, told her this woman was the one who must receive her oath. She had not prepared for resistance.

"Say it, then. What you have been sent here to say by that devious one you call mother."

Penny could not untie the knot that tightened her tongue. Devious mother? Irritation flared, loosened her tongue, granted her courage. Her spine straightened. Her chin lifted. She removed her dagger from her belt, fumbling to hold the small cup upright with fingers that suddenly shook. She did not hesitate when the blade met flesh. Blood welled on the fleshy base of her palm, dripped into the chalice. Once the words, repeated back to her mother a hundred times over in practice for this moment, finally began, she could not stem their flow, and let them join the red blood mixing with honey in the cup.

"I swear upon my own life, upon the blood of my children, upon my soul's rebirth in the Otherworld, that my legacy shall be to only create life, never take it. To only raise up, never cut down. To welcome all, and harm none. This is my vow, and may my death be swift and merciless, may a curse descend upon me and my blood, should I ever break it. From this day until my last day, I shall be a refuge of safety for all, a mother to the wounded, and a true image of the Matar's abundance, as Her Spirit made flesh. This I do swear."

She poured three drops of sweet red blood onto the bare earth, onto the Mother's flesh, then drank the rest. It tasted metallic and warm, but the sweet honey helped her swallow it down. Penny did not know if it was her mother's breath she heard sucking in from far behind at the cave's entrance, or the crone's rasping lungs in front of her, but there was a long silence which drained the newly found confidence from her. Had she said something wrong? Had she missed something?

"You do not know what you say, girl," the crone finally said.

Was it anger in that autumn grass voice? Penny frowned, frustrated. This was not part of the rehearsal. She tried again. "I vow to only create life, and never—"

"I heard you the first time. Cease your prattling."

Penny's mouth snapped closed and she shrank back, fingers clenched around the cup. Her father's tales of vicious Erinyes loomed in her mind, but her mother's insistent blue eyes crowded out any thoughts of fleeing.

"I have heard your vow. This is a heavy burden you would take on, child, and a great sacrifice. If you break a blood-sworn oath sealed with honey from the Mother's own mouth, do you know what happens?"

Penny nodded, whispering, "Furies."

The woman grunted. "What do you want in exchange for this sacrifice?"

"What do I want?"

"That is what I asked. What do you want?"

Penny didn't know, hadn't been prepared by her mother for this part. She wished she could ask her father, who didn't even know she had come here. A very important secret, her mother had insisted.

Devious mother, the crone's words echoed once more, and Penny shivered. She said the only thing she could think of, and hoped it was enough.

"I want to be a good mother, when it is my time. A good Hearth Queen to my people. And...I want my mother to be proud of me."

A long silence was her only reply. It stretched out for so long Penny thought she would not receive one, when she heard the hag say, her voice full of regret,

"I have heard your words. Now go."

Penny turned to leave, but the old woman was not finished.

"Remember, child, that sometimes what you seek is already with you, and sometimes it is as far as the stars from the earth, or the dead from the living. When I see you again, you shall know the truth of what I say."

PART ONE

THE BREAKING

1

BEES

Themiscyra, Northern Pontus (Present day Turkey).
Three days before the Sturgeon Moon, 1206 B.C.

"All honey comes from the hive of the moon," Penny said, breaking off a small piece of honeycomb and passing it to her wide-eyed, eager companion. Leandra licked her rosebud lips in anticipation of the sweet treat. "So all the stars you see in the night sky are the bees pollinating the dark with Kubileya's nectar, which shines golden as the sun when the day comes. That same light is what we tend in the Sacred Flame, which burns eternal. That way, we know She is with us even in the dark." She watched Leandra's tiny pink tongue lick the sweet comb, and smiled. "How does it taste?"

"Good," Leandra said, thinking carefully about this new information, the honeycomb dripping sweet syrup over her fingertips. Then, "I thought the Flame burned so we would be safe. And Mama says bees get honey from flowers. How does the honey get from the moon into the flowers?"

Penny wound a bit of rough rope over her hooked thumb, wrapping it around her elbow and back again, coiling it neatly for storage under the new hive. "That, my dear, is a mystery only the queen knows, and a secret only she can pass on to her daughters, one of whom will one day be queen. And yes, as long as the Flame burns in the tower, you can be assured that Kubileya will keep Themiscyra safe. While it burns, She is with us. This is Her promise."

Leandra's eyes crossed as she inspected the honeycomb pattern of the sweet mass, without removing her tongue from its edge. "So the bee queen has Ishassaras, too?"

Penny scrunched her lips thoughtfully, then shrugged. "I suppose you could say she has Ishassaras, yes. A queen gives birth to many potential new queens, but not all of them will be suitable for the role. She whelps hundreds of baby bees. Maybe thousands."

"She has hundreds of Ishassaras?" Leandra asked, incredulous. A new light gleamed in her eye. "And they all have to fight over who rules the hive?"

Penny shook her head, chuckling. "You are so like your mother, Leandra. Always ready for a tussle. But no—not every bee is born to rule. In fact, not all are daughters. Some will be sons, some workers, some fighters, but only one will eventually become queen. When the old queen dies, a new queen is chosen by the others, and she will then be the sole birther of new queens." Penny leaned down, speaking conspiratorially. "However, if any queen bee doesn't do a very good job making new babies, she will be destroyed."

"Destroyed?" Enormous blue eyes stared up at Penny, widening in dismay. The small section of honeycomb pinched between Leandra's fingers became a secondary concern as she digested this new fact, though there were plenty of sticky crumbs around the girl's mouth to occupy her tongue between questions.

"It is the way of things," Penny said with appropriate soberness, straightening. "The hive must have new daughters, and new workers. If she does not first die from disease or old age, she must be replaced by one of her daughters who *can* continue to provide more daughters, and more workers."

Penny smiled and moved closer to the open hive as Leandra's mouth rounded into a honey-ringed "O" of fascination. She listened to the steady buzz of the new swarm, pleased with its size and their vigor. It was a fine swarm to capture at the start of harvesting season. Sylviu had been helping her mark out the paths each of the Xanharaspas would use in tomorrow's Trials when they stumbled upon the treasure of the sluggish, disoriented bees. Upon their return to the orchard with the swarm, Sagitta had found them, begging them to watch her daughter and keep her out of mischief while the ha-mazaan finished her own preparations for the Trials. The seductive prize of fresh honeycomb had been enough to keep Leandra content with Penny and Sylviu for a short while, but the girl was not one to sit idle for long, and the impromptu lesson on beekeeping was now distracting Penny from the work she needed to finish, including her own preparations for tomorrow's celebration feast, when the Xanharaspas would finally graduate to Savaran.

"What about the male bees?" Sylviu's voice came to them through the veil of leaves under the ancient apple tree. One round, nearly ripe fruit hung so close to his head that he had to duck to see past it, his hazel eyes twinkling with mischief, though his face was properly solemn. "What do the boys do?"

"They work," Penny answered archly, and looked pointedly at the brush in his hand. Sylviu's lips twitched, but he went back to the task, his hands swishing the willow bristles with brisk efficiency against the tight inner weave of the basket.

Leandra's curiosity was immediately piqued by the idea of boy bees.

"Is there a bee king? Like my grandfather? Does the king bee have to die, too, when he makes no more babies? How do you tell the boy bees from the girl bees? They all look the same."

"There is no bee king," Penny assured her. "Just like there is no king here in Themiscyra, and never will be. And boys do not make babies, you know that. But you can tell they are boy bees because they don't have a stinger. Only the female bees can sting you."

"Like boys don't have swords. Only ha-mazaans have swords," Leandra said with all the certainty her four summers could give.

"Yes, sort of like that," Penny smiled.

"Well, the boys do *help* make babies," Sylviu put in, sounding properly affronted, though he did not look up from his task to see Penny's dampening frown. "Besides, boys may leave their 'stingers' at Themiscyra's gate, but we have them at other times. In our own homes, for example, or when we travel, or when we go to battle. However, the lovely Ishassara is right about one thing," he looked up, winking at the girl, "boy *bees* don't have stingers."

"But why not?" Leandra asked him, then turned to Penny without waiting for Sylviu's answer. "Do boy bees have to live separately from the girls once they're old enough, like he does?" She pointed at Sylviu, but the avalanche of questions could not be stopped just for the sake of an answer. "Are the boy bees killed if they try to hurt the girl bees? Is that why they don't have stingers?"

Leandra's questions flowed faster than the Terme, her voice a high-pitched accompaniment to the music of the bees, and Penny could barely keep up, though there was no pause for her to give answers, even if she knew them.

Why did the hive have only one queen, and yet the ha-mazaans had two? Why did Marpe spread honey on ha-mazaans' cuts when they weren't careful with their weapons? Was it true she couldn't eat the honey from the bees far on the western ridge, where the wild rhododendrons grew, without stumbling and seeing scary visions, and getting super sleepy and maybe, as her mother kept warning her every time she begged to taste it, possibly even dying? Honey can't kill you, can it? Do boy bees help choose a new queen when the old one dies? Does Matar Kubileya have to give Her blessing to the new queen in a Full Moon ceremony, like Cyra would have soon? What if Kubileya doesn't like the new queen? Can queen bees be ugly, like Sinope's queen? How do they choose which bee rules next?

This last question gave Leandra pause as she provided her own answer. "Is she marked with a special tattoo or something?"

Penny laughed, shaking her head at the onslaught, trying to answer at least one question in order to end the torrent of words. "Well, if the timing is right, they can *make* a new queen. They will have to feed a young bee just right, at just the right time, and sing the right songs and dance the right dance, just like we do in the Moon Hall."

Sylviu promptly tossed his brush aside and did a quick hop from under the apple branches, grabbing their startled attention before turning his backside to them, bending over, and wiggling his rear in an enthusiastic circle.

"The dance looks like this, if I recall correctly?"

He peered over his shoulder with feigned hurt as both Penny and Leandra let out peals of laughter. Sylviu feigned offense, straightening his leather tunic with a brisk tug of the hem and an audible sniff of wounded pride. Chuckling, Penny assured Leandra the bee dance was much more sophisticated and charming.

"But what about you?" Leandra asked. Brows so pale they were barely visible kissed together on the girl's forehead. "Why don't you have a sword to sting boys with? You're like a girl bee, right? And one day supposed to be Queen."

"Well, your Mama is such a good fighter, and my aunt is such a good Defending Queen, and there are so many capable warriors to protect me, that I don't need a sword. Even the queen bee has fighters who go out and protect the hive. She only leaves the hive when she is a brand new queen, and must find fathers for her babies. But even so," Penny continued, "before I came here to be your Ishassara, I swore a vow to harm none, and welcome all, which is my role as Hearth Queen. That is why brave ha-mazaans like your mother train to defend me, and my mother. That way, we do not need to harm, only heal."

"Oh," Leandra said with far less enthusiasm. Her pink tongue flicked over the honeycomb. "I like watching Mama fight. She's real good."

"One of the best," Penny agreed.

The girl licked the honeycomb again, some of her flyaway blonde curls sticking to the sweet treat. Penny could practically hear her thoughts whirring, though it was likely only the full hives buzzing.

"The queen doesn't even make honey, you said. She sounds kind of useless, except for making babies. Is that all you will do as Hearth Queen? Make babies? Why does the hive even need a queen if all she does is make babies? Can't the other bees do that just as well?"

Penny huffed a laugh, stung in the way only a child's blunt words can pierce one's skin, but another voice answered for her.

"Because every colony needs a leader, else chaos would reign," Antiope said.

Penny looked over her shoulder as her mother approached, her tall white hunting hound at her side. Penny smiled in greeting, but Antiope did not return the gesture as she normally would. Her normally smooth forehead was marred by an almost imperceptible frown, only detectable because it was so rare to see Themiscyra's Hearth Queen appear as anything but perfectly, graciously serene. Despite the wrinkle, her mother remained the epitome of beauty. Antiope's golden hair fell in perfect coils over her bare shoulder, the long folds of her pristine white robe draped elegantly over every curve, as though the fertile and luscious Matar Kubileya Herself had appeared in all Her Glory in Themiscyra's orchard. Penny glanced down ruefully at her own short chiton, once carefully pleated under her wide leather belt, but looking rather rumpled and worse for wear now, next to the ever-glorious beauty of her mother. Leandra stared up at the Hearth Queen with a wider, still sticky "O" as her young eyes took in the radiance of her queen approaching, but even for the young girl, Antiope could barely muster more than a placating, distracted smile. Before she could ask her mother if everything was alright, Antiope said,

"Sylviu, best head to the men's camp. You will return to Galatae early."

Clearly taken aback at being ordered out of the city so abruptly, Sylviu glanced at Penny with a concerned frown, but Antiope did not bother to explain her terse order. She motioned to Penny and Leandra. "Bring the girl to the palace. You will join the children and the attas in the Moon Hall, as my sisters have commanded."

Penny frowned, confused, but Sylviu was the one brave enough to question the queen. "Is there something amiss, Queen Antiope?"

Antiope glanced briefly at Sylviu, then down to the palace below the orchard, the stone golden-red in the midday sun. Penny followed her gaze, but saw only heat shimmering from the walls of the palace into the thick afternoon air, and the sparkle of water as the Terme flowed into the sea. She raised a hand to shade her eyes, then yelped as a bee that had escaped the hive stung her on the tender underside of her wrist. Leandra echoed with her own screech of fear, her short legs carrying her a safe distance from danger, but Antiope motioned the frightened girl back into place with an imperative wave of her hand. More scared of her queen's wrath than any bee, the girl sidled back to Penny's side.

"There are ships approaching," Antiope said. The three of them stared at her expectantly, unfazed by this news. Traders and travelers were frequent to their shores. Penny could not imagine what would warrant such strange behavior from her aunts, or her mother, who generally relished every opportunity to talk trade and treaty with the outside world. She pressed her thumb into the burning sting on her arm, waiting. Sylviu likewise remained where he was, waiting for the real reason to be cast so unceremoniously out of his mother's city when he had only just arrived.

Antiope grimaced, waving a slender hand in a small circle, her gold rings flashing. "My sisters have ordered everyone who is not Savaran—every *woman*, that is," she corrected, glancing back at Sylviu, though she had the grace to appear apologetic, "to wait inside the palace for the arrival of the ships. Lyta has ordered every woman who cannot fight to remain behind the safety of the walls, until we know whether the ships hold friend, or foe. The Savaran is assembling on the beach, despite my protests." Antiope locked eyes with Penny, her face solemn. "If there is a battle on our shores, Daughter, you cannot be anywhere near it."

2

SISTERS

"We can turn them away, Lyta. Just give us the command."

Molpadia hovered near the table, her eyes on Lyta's slender hands as they caressed the edge of the axe blade against whetting stone in a hypnotic rhythm. The zing of metal against rock was as close to a reply as she got, and it did nothing to unclench her jaw, or soften her tongue. Lyta's foot worked the wooden pedal under the table, lending more speed to the wheel's turn, more power to the sharpening.

"Don't be a stubborn fool, Hippolyta," she hissed, and Lyta glanced up at her, a mere flicker of blue eyes at the rarely used name. The one reserved for the Defending Queen, not her wife. Those eyes glanced at the other ha-mazaans milling about the room, collecting their weapons before gathering on the beach, before she returned them to the blade growing thinner, sharper with every pass.

Zing!

"I cannot, Dia."

The stone whirred, the pedal thumped.

"*Why*, Lyta? You *can* veto her in this—"

Footsteps sounded from the Moon Hall, voices carrying into the room before the speakers appeared. Molpadia's frown deepened as her words were cut short.

"This is beyond foolish, sister," Melanippe was saying, her broad-shouldered frame blocking Antiope's entrance to the armory. "We cannot let them venture any further upriver."

Molpadia grunted her agreement and raised her own voice to lend support. "Their ships should already be lighting the sky with fire from our arrows, Antiope. We all know it."

9

Both sisters turned to look at her with matching scowls, and Antiope used the opportunity to shoulder her way past Melanippe. The other ha-mazaans eyed them all and, smelling the pungent, familiar scent of an argument brewing, quickly filtered out of the room. Antiope made her way to the far wall of weapons. Lyta did not pause in her work.

"Ant," Melanippe insisted, following her. Antiope's shoulders hunched, as though her sister's words were blows.

"We welcome all who come to these shores, sister," Antiope said resolutely, studying the options of bows in the bucket. She pulled out one, then pushed it back with a frustrated shove before drawing another. "Just as Matar Kubileya requires of us."

"Even those who would destroy us?" Molpadia said bitingly.

Antiope turned her head to throw a frown at her, and Molpadia was happy to mirror it back.

"You cannot live every moment in fear of men, Dia. And you, Mel, cannot live in fear of visions no one has any proof are real."

Molpadia's face tightened in anger. The Hearth Queen's words had the same effect on Melanippe, as the woman's face darkened further under those blue-black tattoos, her eyes tempests of silver.

"I fear no man," Molpadia said lowly, but Antiope was not listening.

"What's more, *you* do not have authority to make this decision, as Consort," Antiope continued, looking pointedly at her, "nor do you, even as General," she said, sliding her resolute gaze back to Melanippe. "This is *my* purview. Kubileya's hospitality is for all who seek entry through these gates, and Her protection and council is what we offer to those who seek it. That intention is what we assume of all travelers, until such a time it is proven otherwise. And if it is, then the rest is in Lyta's hands. The fact I am even allowing the Savaran to assemble should be enough."

Molpadia huffed a contemptuous laugh, gripping her sword hilt so that she would not be tempted to let her hand fly at the woman's perfect face. Melanippe grunted a sound next to her that was part exasperation, part fury. A sharp *zwing!* rang through the air as the Defending Queen scraped star-iron against flint. Lyta remained decidedly indifferent—*too* indifferent, if Molpadia knew her wife—to the forces swirling about her.

She stepped closer to Lyta again, ready to beseech her to intervene with more than a simple gathering of the Savaran, but Melanippe beat her to it.

"Lyta, speak sense to your sister for once. You know what we say is truth."

"She is your sister, too, Nightmare," Lyta replied evenly, not raising her eyes from her work. "Our Hearth Queen has spoken. I shall fulfill my role if I am called to it, but in matters of who is, or who is not welcome through our gates, only our sister has the authority to say."

A short pause was punctuated by another rush of metal on stone. The hand around Molpadia's sword hilt clenched tighter. She knew what a losing battle this was, to come between these sisters. If Melanippe could not persuade Antiope, and if Lyta was simply going to lie down and let the woman trample their city into the dust for the sake of men's kisses...a knot began to form between her shoulder blades.

"Kubileya curse our mother for a fool when she chose each of your fathers, then, for surely they were both born of asses!" Melanippe's tattooed knuckles were taut as they clenched the axe at her own hip. The General waved her other hand at Lyta. "If your role is not to protect our people from the unwise decisions of a donkey's daughter, then what is it?"

Molpadia peeled her lips back, her eyes bright with warning. "Remember your place, Sister. She is still your Queen," she ground out, but Antiope was shrill in her own fury.

"Cease your tirade, Mel! I have already made the decision."

A long pause, in which all four women's breaths were harsh in the room. Molpadia could taste the hot sulphur of metal cut by stone, bitter on her tongue. The pride of Otrera's daughters grated against each other like the Clashing rocks in the Hellespont, made worse by the whirring of Lyta's whetting stone and the blade against it, and the unbending will of two queens unwilling to submit to the other.

"You *know* this is unwise, Ant," Melanippe repeated eventually, but for all the grim determination in her voice, there was an unfamiliar hint of something else. Something Molpadia thought might be as close as the General had ever come to pleading. The ache moved from between her shoulder blades to her gut, a knot pulling tight from both ends. Her eyes went to Lyta's downturned face. There was nothing there to suggest alarm, or trepidation about what arrived on their shores. Just an aloof calm, despite the terrible visions Melanippe had shared.

Antiope faced the three of them, shoulders slightly crooked though her spine was unbending, her blue eyes implacable, her lips a tight smile over white bone.

"I will not abandon my sacred duties over the fears of dreams and visions, or ideas that men have no place among us," Antiope said, looking at each of them in turn. "The ships, and the men on them, will warm themselves at Kubileya's Flame and be welcomed by Her Breasts, so long as I rule as Hearth Queen. And so long as I, and my daughter, and her daughters after her, tend to the Flame of the Great One, the Hearth shall remain that place of rest and refuge. For *all*."

And with that, their Hearth Queen snatched up a smartly curved bow and a *gorytos* of hawk-fletched arrows and swept from the room, beautiful and regal and naïve as ever. Melanippe sent one last tight-lipped look at Lyta before stalking from the room herself, leaving Molpadia with the sound of blade on stone, and the words of a foolish queen ringing in the air.

"Planning on whittling that axe to dust?" she asked quietly, and the slicing ceased, the whirring tumbling into slower revolutions as the pedal stilled. Lyta shifted on the bench, turning her knees toward Molpadia. She laid the axe on the table with slow, careful hands, then reached those fingers out. Molpadia met them with her own, stepped close between those supple thighs, looking down at the crown of her queen's sunset-ringed head. When Lyta finally raised those blue eyes to hers, the knot in Molpadia's gut tightened painfully.

"There are some things that we cannot run from, Dia," her love said, those blue eyes earnest, beseeching. "And there are some things we must run toward, when the time comes. Just as you ran to me. Just as I will always run to you."

Molpadia was silent for a long time, holding those hands tight in her own, her eyes searching for some kind of promise that her love's certainty was indeed all that was needed for the knot in her gut to unravel, but it only clenched tighter. Lyta smiled, and used Molpadia's hands to pull herself off the bench. She let go, collected her axe, and turned to the door.

"Now, don't screech at me, Little Marmot, but I need you to stay in the Hall with the Ishassaras. No, please don't argue. Not now. If these ships do bring hearts as black as their sails, you are the one who is going to watch over the women and girls, aye?"

Molpadia was already shaking her head. "My place is by your side, Lyta."

Lyta reached the door, turning to smile over her shoulder. "You are already in my heart, Dia. Right where I need you."

3

HERBED WINE

The gravelly gossip of *attas*, grandmothers and elders well past their prime fighting age, or women rendered lame by too many battles, was outdone only by the excited, high-pitched chatter of the young children and Xanharaspas who had not yet earned their place in the city's Savaran. The ha-mazaan cavalry was now assembling full force on the beach outside, leaving the city's most vulnerable hunkered within the protection of the stone walls, passing the time as best they could with delicious food and tall tales and menial tasks which kept hands and mind as busy as possible.

The mosaics painted on the curved walls of the Moon Hall seemed to come alive amidst the noise, until Penny could easily imagine that the wax and pigment ha-mazaans, riding with axes and swords and spears held high, the manes of their mares flying in the wind of their gallop, were indeed descending on the approaching ships, their ululating battle cry echoed in the nervous laughter of eleven-year-old girls and feisty gossip of eighty-year-old grandmothers. She clung to those wisps of imagination as inspiration for the work under her own hands, and tried, even amidst the cacophony that was Themiscyra's entire non-fighting population gathered under a single roof, waiting for danger to descend upon their beach, to give proper care and attention to her craft. So far, the distraction was proving too much.

The last of the evening sun shone through the round window of the Hall, illuminating the tapestry under Penny's swiftly moving fingers. The weaving showed ha-mazaans in full battle gear, some with bare legs, some with tiny threads delicately worked to show their patterned trousers, the finely woven wool dyed with the tree bark or herbs, tubers, or the skins of onions to produce hair of blonde and black and red for each woman or horse. Though the task itself was one of tedium, she had learned to use the work as a time of reflection, and to work into every passing of the loom's shuttle a bit of the reverence for these women she had come to respect, sometimes even fear, in her ten years as their Ishassara.

Ten years since she had left her father's home in Satra. Ten years since she had first come to this place, her mother's home, but which still felt as foreign to Penny as the day she had arrived, nervous of every woman she saw, no matter that she had been whelped to rule here. Ten years since she had sworn a vow to harm none, and welcome all. Six years since she had been confirmed Ishassara on her first moon-blood, and committed to serve Themiscyra as a keeper of the sacred Flame, and as future Hearth Queen. After all that time, she still felt like an outsider, a traveler passing through, a timorous child in a city of fierce matriarchs, and never so much as when the women gathered for a fight, while she watched from the sidelines.

Working on the tapestry did not help that feeling of otherness. Always observing ha-mazaans fighting, but never fighting herself. Weaving and stitching silver and gold threads to show ha-mazaan weapons in action, yet never knowing what it felt like to swing a sword, made her acutely aware, with every pulse of thread over and under, over and under, that she was not ha-mazaan, and never would be.

"Your hands are as skilled at weaving as the Fates', Ishassara," a voice said behind her, and Penny turned to see Areto, round with child, peering over her shoulder at the tapestry.

"Thank you, Areto," Penny said, and her smile came easy for the ha-mazaan. "You are well? And the babe?" Penny nodded toward the woman's swollen stomach.

"Aye, well enough." Areto shrugged, then grimaced, and put a fist to her lower back, knuckling the muscles to ease the tension. "Just a few more days and I could have been where I belong—on our beach with my spear and axe. Except this one," she poked the mound of her stomach, and Penny saw the flesh ripple in response as the babe kicked back, "does not seem eager to make an appearance this side of the Gate. She had better not be one of those lazy creatures who likes to lie about and wait for sunshine before she will do anything useful."

Penny laughed, passing the shuttle through the weft of threads and back again. She shook her head. "I'm sure your daughter will be every bit as eager as you are to join the fight, Areto. I can't imagine a child of your blood ever being lazy. She will probably hit the ground running, and be the ha-mazaan who finally teaches her horse to jump the moon, the way you were riding in the forest yesterday. I nearly ran Tana into the ground trying to keep up."

Areto brayed a laugh that made every ha-mazaan in the Hall go silent for a brief moment and glance in their direction, to make sure a donkey had not entered the inner palace. They went back to their chatter soon enough, seeing it was only Areto.

"Aye, well, Marpe says the girl is still feet first in my belly, so you could be right. As for yesterday's ride, my own mother always said, 'There's no better way to coax a daughter to finally join us on this side of the Gate than a hearty gallop on a fast horse.' Didn't work, though," Areto sighed, then grinned. "And your pony might be small, but she has heart, to even try and keep up with my mare. Just think of how you could ride if your mother let you have a real horse," Areto winked, then brayed another laugh.

Penny returned the smile, and fondly watched the ha-mazaan move belly first through the crush of women toward the table of food against the wall. She had just returned her concentration to the shuttle when another voice interrupted her work.

"Never thought we would be stuck in here with the *kimiz*-churners, did you?"

Penny glanced up, frowning at the insult. Molpadia, Hippolyta's consort, was not speaking to her, though, but to Cyra, Penny's cousin, Ishassara for the Defender's Throne. Cyra glanced fleetingly at Penny, one of those *kimiz*-churners. Then, her grey eyes cold and hard as flint, she turned on her heel and stalked out of the Hall without a word, her black braid swinging with every long stride.

Penny bit her lip as she watched her cousin disappear, wondering if she should go after Cyra and offer some comfort to the person who would one day rule beside her, but she knew there was nothing she could say that would remove the sting of humiliation Cyra must be feeling. Penny, along with everyone else already gathered in the Hall, had witnessed all three sisters, two queens and a General, order Cyra to stand down from the battle due to still being Xanharaspa, even though the ha-mazaan's graduation into Savaran would take place at tomorrow's Trials. Cyra had taken the news of her exclusion with less than gracious acceptance, and Penny could not blame her, but she was sure a *kimiz*-churner was the last person her cousin would wish to speak with about it all.

"You going to make my face more comely than it is in real life?" Molpadia asked, pulling Penny's attention back to her. "You wouldn't want people fainting when they look at all your pretty work, only to come across this."

Molpadia hooked a thumb toward the scar running from chin to forehead, puckering her eyebrow and preventing one of her eyelids from closing completely. Her face had always reminded Penny of her father's leopards. They always seemed to have one eye open watching for danger, or perhaps prey, and Penny smiled warmly up at the ha-mazaan as she remembered Begri's watchful eye above her as she slept.

"I will give your wound all the honor it deserves, Molpadia," Penny said, smiling, and Molpadia snorted in response, before winking down at her and turning on her heel, shouldering her way through the crowd.

Melanippe had ordered several Savaran, Molpadia one of them, to remain inside the palace and protect the Ishassaras and any others who could not wield a weapon or protect themselves. She felt sorry for Molpadia almost as much as she felt embarrassed on behalf of her cousin, but the truth of the matter was that Penny could not understand what all the fuss was about. Other than having black hulls and black sails, as the scouts had reported, there was nothing untoward about ships arriving in Themiscyra, even three at a time. Penny was confident she would soon be at the docks, instructing the offloading of goods, or, if Antiope was feeling magnanimous and especially trusting, in the storeroom recording weights and tallies of grain and oil and tin with her clay and stylus, arguing with traders about the total value being offloaded.

"Penny, your wine."

Caught woolgathering for the second time, Penny jerked her head up to find Marpe, Themiscyra's most senior *atta* and their most highly respected *sivyeti*, holding out a small goblet of wine.

"Thank you, Marpe. I nearly forgot in all the hubbub."

Marpe's wrinkled lips stayed flat and firm despite Penny's smile of thanks. The *sivyeti* rarely smiled, and when she did, it was usually over a wound well-stitched, or finding a recent amputation she had performed remained disease-free.

"Well, don't forget," the old woman said with all the bluntness age afforded. "It won't do to have your headaches returning."

"No," Penny agreed mildly, and drank the wine in three gulps, grimacing at the familiar bitter taste as she handed the empty cup back. She smiled her thanks, but received only a wordless grunt as Marpe turned on her good leg and shuffled back toward the kitchens, her steps firm but halting as her old wound put a hitch in her otherwise purposeful steps.

Licking bitter herbs from her lips, Penny scanned the crowded room, noting every woman in the Hall was occupied, the older ones deep in conversation over *kimiz* or strong wine, the younger ones playing stone games on the floor. Leandra was at their center, demanding they play with her rules instead of ones already established, while the Xanharaspas whispered conspiratorially in every corner, likely imagining every detail of the glorious battle about to commence without them. All of the Savaran ordered to remain inside clustered under the eastern window, but the action was happening on the opposite side of the palace, and there was nothing to see out that window except stables and mountains. Their heads were tipped toward each other in the manner of closely guarded speech, shutting out the rest of the room. Penny was confident they took no notice of her as she stood from her loom and slipped through the crowd, as quickly and quietly as a mouse past the whiskers of a sleeping cat.

4

THE HA-MAZAAN WAY

"You have to listen to me, Mother. Please."

Sylviu took hold of his mother's arms, his grip insistent, but her eyes were full of sorrow when she shook her head. His heart sank further with the weight of fear he had not been able to shake since he had first learned about the approaching ships, a fear that had turned to dread as he saw for himself their black hulls beating against the waves of the Terme.

"Melanippe has already tried this argument with the queens, Syl. I certainly have no hope of convincing them if our Nightmare can't even manage it."

"Then leave the city with me, at least. There is nothing forcing you to stay. Let me take you and Penthesilea to Galatae. With the children." His heart thudded painfully as he thought of all the children roaming Themiscyra's streets. Of Leandra's fiery spark being doused by the dark waves of the ships' arrival. Of Pen, forbidden to lift a sword in her own defense. His mother could protect herself, but Pen...His heart constricted so hard his throat closed up.

"You know I cannot abandon my people, or my city, love." Her tone was full of gentle reproach, and it only made Sylviu more furious. A creak of hinges behind him let him know someone had entered the Tower, but he was too focused on his mother's carefree expression to see if it was Pen. "And Penthesilea would never agree to leave her mother, or the Flame, you know that. It is not right that you should suggest it, either."

Sylviu dropped his hands to his side, stung by his mother's recrimina-tions. Other than Melanippe and Molpadia, Hippolyta's watchdog, there seemed to be no women in this city with any sense to listen. Even his own mother would not hear his warnings, and Sylviu was nearly ready to use his bare hands to tear apart the entire wall they stood under just to vent his frustration with her. With all of them. If only someone would *listen*. The problem was, she was the only one he could tell *why* he was so afraid, but even that was proving ineffective.

"You must remember my vision? About these ships?" He was not supposed to have been inside that Oracle's cave. As a man he was not supposed to have been able to see the things that he had seen, though he had not understood them. He still didn't, but he understood enough to know those black ships brought death. Now, his own sacrilege was working against him, as the visions swimming in his head mocked him with their secrets, and only his mother knew of their warnings. But if she would not heed her own Oracle, then what?

Ossy nodded, her hazel eyes sombre on his face, but then she put a hand to the crown of his head, smoothing the hair that was always out of place there, though Pen had just trimmed it for him when he arrived. "I remember, Syl. You'd do well to remember mine, eh? And like I said, if they bring violence upon us like you saw in those forbidden flames, we will lay waste to every one of them, never fear. Are you suddenly doubting your old mother has it in her? I admit, my bones *have* been creaking in the rain lately."

She smiled, but her teasing fell short of eliciting any humor from him. He swore, and turned his back on her. He could hear the clatter and hum of Savaran gathering on the beach, see the line of archers rounding the entire perimeter, ready to loose their arrows into the sails riding the river's current. He had caught his mother in the courtyard on her way to join them, her armor already in place and her axe already polished to drink men's blood, but so far he was failing at keeping her from going any further, and probably meeting her death. He squinted beyond the shade the Tower gave them, peering north to the docks. The sight of those black sails rocking so close to the city made the hair on the back of his neck stand on end. He tried to shake off the fear, to find some calm, to ground himself the way she had taught him, but it was tearing at his guts. He turned the pain of it into anger, all of it now directed at his mother.

"You're so goddamn stubborn," he ground out, still not able to look at her. "I am telling you, Mother, women are going to die. I have seen it. The least you could do is act like it matters. Like you believe me."

"It isn't that I don't believe what you have seen, Syl, but—"

"But your loyalty to the ha-mazaan Way comes before your loyalty to me."

"Sylviu. That is not what I was going to say."

"You don't need to," he said, a terrible sense of doom pushing him to drive that sharp point home even further. The tension between his shoulder blades became unbearable. He turned back to her, trying one last tactic. "At least let me join you on the beach."

"You should not even be inside the gates with that sword, Sylviu, let alone among our Savaran," his mother said, and her tone was every bit ha-mazaan. She raised one eyebrow the same color as his hair, neither brown nor gold, but something in between. "I may be friends with the queens, but I am not a miracle worker. I believe Antiope herself already ordered you out of the city, and it will not do to break the Laws of Themis and Kubileya. That in itself is what brings destruction. You've already pushed it far enough, don't you think? You should go, now, before you get any more ideas in your head. Leave the defense of this city to us, and take care of yourself."

"I am trying to take care of *you*. Mother, *listen* to me! I—"

"Go, Sylviu! And remember who you are talking to, lest you feel my belt on your backside, full-grown man or not."

His mouth snapped closed before he could shout an oath of utter fury at her stubborn, unshakable ha-mazaan pride.

"Go, then," he finally said through gritted teeth, flinging a fist toward the beach. "Go fight with your precious axe, and I will hide in Galatae until the next time you need pigs for a funeral feast and linen to wrap your dead body in. That is all I'm good for, isn't it?"

He turned and stalked away, his stride so stiff he nearly turned an ankle on the cobblestones.

"Syl!" she called, but he was too furious to respond. He kept walking, his steps taking him toward the Tower door, though he had no conscious thought of where he was going, only that he needed to be away from her before he manhandled her into submission. So goddamn *stubborn*. He paused at the doorway, looking over his shoulder, but his mother's lean frame was already loping over the bridge toward the gathering host, headed for Melanippe on her black mare.

Beyond her tawny head, the black ships hovered on the water like bloated beetles fat from the dung heap, already spilling their guts onto Themiscyra's shore. His stomach twisting further, Sylviu braced a hand against the unlocked door of the Tower, and slipped into the shadows, searching for the only other woman in this city who had ever been able to bring him a moment's peace, even if the location he must find her in was forbidden to him, like so many other things in this damned city.

5

TOWER & FLAME

No one in the Hall noticed when she stepped out of the Moon Hall's wide doors—or, if they did, they made no move to stop her. As soon as she was on the stairs leading to the tower, the door creaking closed behind her, she breathed a sigh of relief, and quickened her footsteps, no longer worried about being silent. She approached the hearth in the centre of the circular vestibule, the Flame's warmth hot and comforting on her cheeks. It danced with exuberance, its tongues licking along logs to then jump into the air and disappear, as though launching into flight. She smiled, then murmured the ritual prayer as she placed another log into the brazier. The small Tower always had a calming effect on her. She didn't know if it was the prayers, or the sensual, heady presence of the Fire itself, or simply the fact that only she and her mother ever ventured here, as they were the only two permitted to tend the Flame, but for Penny, this place was a sanctuary she was grateful for every day. She could center herself, and hear her thoughts, and pretend the Flame could be the companion she needed when the days became too lonely.

The Flame newly fed, Penny moved to the casement facing west, toward the beach. The tower that housed Themiscyra's Flame was a miniature version of the Hall it sat atop, with six columned, open-air windows that afforded a view of the city and the land beyond, in any direction one could desire to see. There was no better view in the palace to see the beach, or the docks, or the river's wide, black waters as they moved north into the Zalapa Sea. It was the one place Penny could retreat when she needed to clear her mind, or simply let her imagination roam without the questions and needs of hundreds of women pressing in on her. As much as she was relieved to escape the crowded, overwhelming noise of the Moon Hall, though, the tableau below stunned Penny, and she braced her hand against the stone column as the scene below made her dizzy with wonder.

The ships had already docked, and broad-shouldered, shirtless, sweat-drenched men walked planks set from rail to rock, disembarking their ships like ants spilling from a rotten log. Despite the fears of both her aunts that they brought violence with them, there was no battle between ha-mazaans and the men who freely roamed the shore, their bronze swords sheathed, some speaking with the heavily armed ha-mazaans, some stretching the strain of hours at the oars from their muscles. Though the spectacle of nearly naked, sun-bronzed men did not go unnoticed by her, they were not what made her mouth gape in wonder.

In her ten years of being a part of this city, Penny had only ever seen small contingents of ha-mazaans gather for real battle. Now, the eastern shore of the Terme swarmed with every available Savaran, their horses snorting and fretting with unmet anticipation, their hooves restless on the gravel of the beach, their riders struggling to bring the usually composed mares into some semblance of control as the beach became more and more crowded with bodies. Ha-mazaan Infantry roamed the banks with spears bristling against the horizon, while archers with their smartly curved bows surrounded the entire host, their short, curved bows slack at their side, but their arrows ready. They outnumbered the men by three to one, at least, outshining the new arrivals in their golden-bronze helmets, their sturdy breastplates made of polished horse hooves, and their weapons gleaming with the sharp, silver tinge of star-iron in the sun's last light. She had never witnessed anything so magnificent as the ha-mazaan army in full array, and the sight caused a peculiar swelling of something unfamiliar beneath Penny's breastbone.

She could not tell if it was pride, or loneliness.

A sudden pounding at the door startled Penny from her ennui. It swung open before she could form a reply.

"Sylviu!"

"Close your mouth, or bees will fly in. Isn't that what your mother always says?"

Sylviu advanced into the room without waiting for an invitation, pausing only long enough to kick the door closed with the heel of his boot before a few quick strides brought him to the casement next to her.

Despite his teasing, Penny struggled to contain her astonishment. It was nothing unordinary to see a man inside the palace walls; any ha-mazaan could bring a guest or a son or father to visit either in the outer village or inside the palace itself. However, a man in the same room as the Sacred Flame was inconceivable. Sacrilege, even. But there was another matter Penny found even more alarming. She pointed at his waist accusingly.

"What is *that*?"

"A sword."

"*Obviously*. But *why*? You cannot be here with that, Syl! You cannot be *here* at all. You flaunt every law that—"

"I am not going to sit by and watch empty-handed while your city—and my mother, you might remember—is savaged by marauders," Sylviu said bluntly, hazel eyes, nearly identical to his mother's, calm yet implacable. "And I am not alone with your Flame, Pen. *You* are here."

Though Penny had her father's lean length, Sylviu had his mother's solid, wiry strength, and probably his unknown father's size, and she realized that sometime in the last year or two, he had grown enough to be able to look down on her, though only by a fraction. She pondered the wisdom of casting him out of the city for a second time on the same day, if only for his own safety, her thoughts spiraling into the consequences Antiope and her sisters would visit upon a sacrilegious lawbreaking man in their midst.

"Besides," Sylviu continued, his tone thoroughly unrepentant, "I know there is at least one person in this city forbidden to fight, and I thought she might feel better knowing someone was looking out for her."

"There are ha-mazaans in the Moon Hall specifically ordered to protect me, Syl," Penny said, though she had to admit his thoughtfulness warmed her heart a little, made her feel less alone. "If any of them—especially Molpadia—found you, you would be returning to Galatae without your hands. *If* they let you return at all. Goddess knows my mother would add you to the Flame herself before she let you out of this room alive." She shook her head. "I don't know if even Ossy could save you. Your mother is just as strict as the rest of them when it comes to Themiscyra's ways."

Sylviu, apparently unconcerned with the consequences of his actions, gripped the edge of the casement as he took in the scene before them, his shoulders hunched tight across his back, but his next words were not about his responsibilities, but hers. "I thought you were supposed to be minding the women and children in the Moon Hall?"

Penny shot him an annoyed glance, which quickly turned rueful. "I was. But these arrivals don't appear to be worth all the fuss, as far as I can see." She waved a hand at the beach, where the mass of people buzzed with conversation that had already turned lively and engaged as the women pulled news of the world from the visitors, and they appeared eager to share it.

"Hmmm," was his only reply.

Penny chewed her lip. It was not right that he should be here, but what harm could he do, really? There was no doubt in her mind that he would use his weapon to protect her rather than harm her, but if any of the other ha-mazaans in the city found him here, in the same room as the Flame, and with that sword…

Sylviu clearly had no intention of backing down, though, and other than ordering him out of the tower, a situation she did not relish, there was not much she could do. She sighed, and he turned his head enough to wink at her before turning his attention back to the beach, scanning the sea of crested helmets and shaggy-haired men mingling with the ha-mazaans.

She had long thought it odd that she had more in common with Ossy's son than Ossy herself—had more in common with the men in Galatae than any of the ha-mazaans in this city, in fact. Like them, she had been taken from her first home when still a child, leaving behind everything familiar to take her place amongst those she belonged with. Like them, she would never join the Savaran in battle. Like them, she was relegated to waiting while the ha-mazaans went on their missions, defended their cities, made their mark.

"This is always the worst part, don't you think?" she asked quietly, her own loneliness quickly overshadowing her desire for her friend's safety. Lawbreaker or not, she was grateful for his company.

"The pageantry?" Sylviu said, though his eyes had fixed on the three ships bobbing in the harbor, and Penny noticed the way his brow creased as he took in the black sails, the bronze shields, the gryffon carved into the prow of the first ship tied to the dock's piling.

"The waiting," Penny said, staring at that gryffon's clawed feet dipping in and out of the water. "I feel like I've spent most of my life waiting. Waiting for my mother to visit me and my father. Waiting for news. Waiting for women to give birth. Waiting for traders to empty their wares. Waiting for harvest season. Waiting to leave my father. Waiting for my father to visit me here, like my mother promised he would. Waiting for war. Waiting for loved ones to return victorious, return wounded. Maybe not return at all."

She paused, her mother's unbound sheath of golden hair shining like a beacon on the docks. Even in anticipation of battle, Antiope took care to be the most beautiful woman on the beach.

"Today, we waited to see who would die, and who would not. Both of us have mothers down there. Both of them could have begun their journey through the Gate today, and yet both of us are forbidden to do anything about any of it, except wait."

The sister-queens stood with two men on the docks, their heads tilted together in conversation. Penny watched her mother's slender white arm glide through the air as she spoke, her long throat tilt back as she uttered a laugh at the bronze-haired, stout man's comment. Though she could not hear her from this distance, she imagined the sound was light and graceful and elegant, easy as a swan's glide in the water. Behind Antiope's golden hair, the beak of the griffon gaped, as though swallowing her mother's golden head with every movement of the waves.

"We are forbidden many things, you and I," Sylviu agreed quietly, and there was a grimness in his tone that made Penny peer at him curiously, but he did not share any further thoughts.

She studied his profile, taking in his straight hair the color of the small mousedeer they often trapped in the forest. The planes of his cheekbones had begun to show a sculptured prominence as the boyish roundness faded away, and from this angle, his eyes shone like new grass, though sometimes they were gold and bronze. He would not be what others might call handsome, but he was kind, and thoughtful, and always seemed to be around when she was most in need of company. He was also the son of one of Themisicyra's senior Savaran, Melanippe's closest friend, and

Cyra's goddess-mother. Penny wondered what her mother might think if she chose such a man as Sylviu to complete her Alsanti. Would she be pleased? Would she disapprove outright that he was not from a prominent bloodline? Worse, would she purse her lips and hum that particular up and down tune that conveyed neither happiness nor displeasure, but something in between, and always far worse?

A noise from the beach drew her attention. A burly, bare-chested man the size of an oak tree stood on the docks with Lyta, the skin of a lion covering his head and back. It was her aunt's laughter she heard, and the man grinned down at her, as though they already shared some great secret together. Next to them, Antiope slipped her hand through the arm of her own companion, beginning to lead him away from the docks, gesturing at the beach, the ha-mazaans scattered along it, the walls, the palace itself, her mouth moving and smiling constantly, so that Penny was sure she was explaining every nuance of their city to the poor man.

"You shouldn't stand here any longer, Syl. Someone will see you."

Even as she said it, stepping back from the casement and tugging at the sleeve of his tunic, Antiope waved in the direction of the Moon Hall, and the tower atop it.

Sylviu slipped sideways behind the column with the quickness of a cat, his face hidden in the shadows, but Penny was sure she saw her mother pause briefly, a small frown on her forehead. Penny raised her hand in a wave, smiling calmly even as her heart thudded with terror in her chest, and her mother raised a slow hand in her direction. The man beside her followed the direction of her gaze, and he, too, paused as his eyes found Penny. Penny smiled politely, unsure if the man could even see her features, but then they were moving on, Antiope steering him along the outer portion of the wall, introducing him to the Savaran women close by.

"You can uncover your ears, now," Sylviu said. "And you shouldn't scratch at that sting,"

She glanced over to find his eyes watching her with that familiar amused glint in the hazel depths. He always seemed to be laughing at her. He pointed his chin at her wrist. "I'm sure Marpe has a balm that will help with the itch."

"I did not have my ears covered," Penny said in clipped tones, and put her hand behind her back where she would not scratch the itchy swelling.

"Well, your shoulders were creeping high enough that you nearly did. Come, let's see to the last of the curing in the storeroom. I left the pigs hanging, but you may want to inspect my work and sign off my return to Galatae with a job well done, so that I may sleep in peace until my next delivery."

"You are leaving? Already?"

Bad enough that she would soon be relegated to the duties of hostess, carrying out the tasks of hospitality to three ships full of men, not to mention tomorrow's feast after the Trials, and Cyra's Ishassara ceremony the day after that. Now she would have to do so without anyone but her mother to talk with. Her only true friend was a man who lived a half day's ride away, and she was more aware of the pathetic reality of that fact than anyone.

"I don't think my absence will be noticed with that many men invading your palace." He nodded down to the beach swarming with men, before turning away from the casement, saying lightly as he headed to the door,

"Perhaps you will even find a dashing young prince to seduce, and have something titillating to tell me the next time I bring supplies. You might even begin your Alsanti."

Penny flushed, irritated he would suggest exactly what she had been thinking about moments before, but with a complete stranger. "I am barely nineteen summers, and my mother is unlikely to pass through the Gate anytime soon. I have several years before I must complete my Alsanti."

He pulled the door open and turned to look at her, his face calm and impassive as always, but there was a curious gravity in his eyes she did not recognize. He did not say anything further on the matter, though.

"I will meet you in the storeroom whenever you are ready, Ishassara."

His steps were hurried on the stone stairs, though she heard a long pause at the bottom of the tower as he wisely made a stealthy exit. Penny absentmindedly prodded the Flame with star-iron poker, blackened from years of use at this hearth. She was left with the uncomfortable feeling that Sylviu had used her title as a very specific reminder of her role, and of his, and, not for the first time since she had come to this city, she wondered if there would ever be a time when she could just be Penny ever again.

"You are leaving? Already?"

Sylviu did not have it in him to meet Pen's eyes, staring instead at the men spilling out of the ships. The tension inside of him was near to breaking, but she was the last person who needed to feel the brunt of his fury, or know how alarmed he was that no one with any sense seemed to care about her protection. Already his short time with her had calmed him, made him feel as though he could get a handle on the thoughts he could not quite organize in his head, made the visions he had seen in that giantess' cauldron less caustic in his mind. Even so, she did not need to know he had no intention of obeying her mother, or his. He had already alarmed her enough just by being near the Flame, and wearing his sword in her presence, but he was not truly sorry for either supposed offense.

"I don't think my absence will be noticed with that many men invading your palace." He nodded down at the beach, realizing part of what he was feeling was frustration that the men had not brought violence the moment their feet touched land, as he had anticipated, and dreaded. It had only proved his mother right, and his own wild imagination wrong, but still, the unease gnawed at him. He turned away from the casement, avoiding her eyes and saying as casually as he could,

"Perhaps you will even find a dashing young prince to seduce, and have something titillating to tell me the next time I bring supplies. You might even begin your Alsanti."

From the corner of his eye, he could see the smooth *kimiz* skin of her throat flush the same color as the roses lining the bottom of the city wall.

"I am barely nineteen summers, and my mother is unlikely to pass through the Gate anytime soon. I have several years before I must complete my Alsanti."

And it will not be with you, Swineherd.

He stifled a grimace at his own unfair thought. Pen had never been anything but kind and gracious to him, a supportive and welcoming and friendly...friend. As she was to everyone. He knew his place. He knew what she was meant for, and it was not the likes of him.

He moved away from her, pulling the door open before turning to look at her.

"I will meet you in the storeroom whenever you are ready, Ishassara."

He finished helping her gut and spit the pigs for their Savaran feast, and carried crocks of olives and bricks of soft and hard cheese from the depths of the storeroom, his heart both eased and tortured by the easy way she laughed and talked with him, but by twilight Sylviu finally told her it was time to obey the order of the queens and return to his home. Penny followed him to the stables, chatting amiably, but then she pressed an extra skin of wine into his hand, and a small waxed cloth bundle of food.

"Honeyed oat cakes, for the road," she said, smiling at him. He smiled back, hoping his face did not betray his guilt, and thanked her. She watched as he mounted the wagon that had come to this place full of pigs for their Savaran feast, and he felt her gaze as the gelding's hooves and the wooden wheels clattered over the bridge. He stared at the men littering the beach, fresh from their baths in the river, their sun-slitted eyes hard on him as he passed through, but he forced himself to pass by without comment. He looked back when he reached the road, and she waved from the Tower, and he waved back as he normally would have, having no trouble making his smile genuine. When she had disappeared from the casement, he snapped the reins against the gelding's back and moved quickly, raising a great plume of dust to make his departure obvious.

As soon as he was over the brow of the mountain visible from the city, though, he pulled the horse to a stop, unhitched the wagon and shoved it to the side of the road, before stuffing the bundle of food into the front of his tunic, and stashing the wine under a log next to the narrow road. He untacked the gelding, and with a resounding smack on its rump, sent it galloping south. If it was hungry, or missing its fellow stablemates, it would be home within a day.

He turned back to the city, grateful the moon had not yet risen and the deepening dusk would hide his passage. He would not be going back home to Galatae until every last one of those men had either boarded their ships and returned where they came from, or finally drowned under the black waters of the Inhospitable Sea.

6

MILK FROM THE MOTHER

"And to you, Matar Kubileya, Who is our Flame, our Provider, our Giver of Life, we dedicate the first sweet drops of precious cream from the teats of Your mares, along with the best of our grain, the seeds of Your bounty, and fat from Your most beautiful lamb. Accept these offerings, and grant us bounty in provision, that we may bless those who rest upon our shores, and in so doing, they may know the gracious care of the Mother."

As her mother recited the familiar ritual, Penny tipped her brimming rhyton, spilling thick, pungently sweet *kimiz* onto the edge of the hearth, where it bubbled and steamed on the hot stone as it was devoured by the Goddess' Flames. Antiope held her arm over the stone cauldron set in the floor, then tipped her closed fist sideways, gently releasing the palmful of emmer seeds onto the same spot, where they popped and cracked in the heat. Lastly, her mother lifted a wooden ladle from the nearby bucket, the end glistening with a dollop of fat sheared from the best lambs, which she released directly into the middle of the flames with a quick flick of her wrist. The fat hissed as it hit the glowing coals, sputtering as it, too, was devoured, the flames barely satiating themselves with the offerings.

The two women stepped back from the heat of the fire, but Penny noticed the way the flames curled inward, smoke rising thick from their center, as though the wood burning underneath was wet and unripe. She said so to Antiope, who pursed her lips, regarding the fire with a judicious eye before turning away to inspect the stack of carefully selected oak, rowan, and ash, the only three woods that could be used to feed the flames.

"Yes, I suppose we must instruct the Xanharaspas to be more careful with their selection after this. Skipping their duties in the kitchens to play with the horses is one thing, but fetching wet wood for our Flame is another. You can tell them so when you meet with them for tomorrow's Savaran feast."

"Me?"

She followed her mother down the narrow, curved stairway that wound down from the tower along the outer wall of the Moon Hall, then out into the night. So many campfires on the beach made the dark shore glitter as though the coals of an enormous kitchen fire had been scattered in haste. Penny tapped the long wooden key hanging from the leather cord around her waist, making sure she had it with her, before jiggling closed the wooden bar of lock that secured the tower. She listened carefully for the distinctive clink of each of the six wooden pins falling into place before turning back to her mother.

"I'm going to be busy now that there are a hundred men to entertain, Pen," Antiope said once the door was secure, "so I think it is only fair that my Ishassara can handle the last preparations for our celebration?" Antiope stopped next to the supplies they had brought out for the traditional welcome of guests. Bags of fermented mare's milk had been brought from the storeroom and piled neatly against the low wall of the courtyard. Antiope lifted one, un-stoppered the waxed leather bag, and tipped fresh *kimiz* into a second rhyton, somehow not spilling a single drop, though her actions were without hesitation.

"There is not a great deal left to do," she went on, "except make sure the Xanharaspas have clean linens for serving, and the pigs you and Sylviu slaughtered are tended on the spit overnight. I think he hung them in the storeroom already, didn't he? So those should be done first thing in the morning, well before sunrise, I would think, so that they are ready in time."

Knowing her mother would have already double and perhaps triple-checked the work of any subordinate, Penny did not bother to reply, nor did her mother pause to listen for an answer.

"I've also requested all of the Hanassas, even the youngest boys, be ready for kitchen duty, as all the ovens will need stoking for the extra bread needed now that we have guests. I am sure you are capable of handling the rest?"

Penny groaned softly, earning a stern look from Antiope as her mother hefted her own rhyton onto her hip, gripping the jug by the curved neck of the mare that served as a handle, its mouth gaping open, ready to deliver milk to their guests.

"Why did so many men need to come now, of all times?"

"It is no use asking why the river flows to the sea, Penthesilea. It just does, and we act accordingly. But just think," Antiope said with sudden eagerness, grasping Penny's arm with a firm hand, her blue eyes intent as she held Penny's copper ones, "What if this is exactly the opportunity we need?"

"Opportunity?"

"Think about it, Pen. You could have your Alsanti completed before next year's harvest! All the worry of planning and traveling to seek out a suitable mate...Kubileya has supplied a whole host of men to choose from! It seems most auspicious, don't you think?"

Penny grimaced, taken aback at the suggestion coming from her mother, and even more so that everyone she knew seemed to be thinking the same thoughts. "My Alsanti? So soon?"

"Yes!" Antiope said, undeterred. "You are of an age, barely younger than when I started. And there are so many to choose from! Handsome, strong, noble men. There are sons of queens amongst them, so I'm told. On what other occasion would you have so many fine specimens to choose from?" Antiope nudged Penny in the ribs, smiling suggestively. "From the ones I have seen, I am sure there are more than a few who know how to please a woman. I'm sure you will have no problem finding one or two who catch your fancy..."

"Mother, if I am now in charge of the Savaran Feast, and with Cyra's Ishassara ceremony on the full moon, I have too much work to do to take a 'fancy' to any of them. How long are they staying?"

Antiope arched a golden brow. "Cyra does not need our help being sworn in as my sister's Ishassara, other than ensuring the Flame is bright and hot. As far as the Feast, I am sure it will not be too much trouble for a few Xanharaspas and even the Hanassas to take some of those errands off your hands. The Achaeans said they are only here for a few days at most, so you will not have time to simper and play about. You must be decisive, and act quickly."

Penny struggled to think of a reply, but Antiope merely clucked her tongue, then chucked her finger under Penny's chin, snapping it closed.

"Don't let the flies in. Go on now. Let's see the skills I have taught my daughter be put to good use, hm?"

Penny looked out over the sea of campfires spread along the beach, where thirsty, sea-weary sailors waited with eager tongues and glittering eyes for the daughter of the queen to serve them fermented mare's milk. The idea that she would pursue any of these men, complete strangers, to conceive a daughter with only days to complete the task left her feeling unsettled, but her mother was undeterred.

"I will remind Toxaris of your exemption from First Blood, if one of them does happen to catch your eye. You never know, love...your own daughter could be with us by summer, if only you put some effort into those lips and hips."

The bubble of her mother's laughter enveloped the night as Antiope turned away, waggling her own hips deliberately, before stepping with a feline grace back into the night, the *kimiz* balanced delicately on one full hip as though it weighed nothing at all. Penny heard more footsteps crunching through the gravel. Toxaris, the ha-mazaan assigned to her this night as personal guard, made her way past Antiope with slow strides to where Penny stood, using the butt of her lance as a walking stick. She smiled at the dark-eyed woman, and her smile was returned, though there was a thoughtful, slightly worried expression on Toxaris' face as the ha-mazaan looked down the path Antiope had recently taken. Penny adjusted the rhyton on her hip, tucked her loose hair behind her ear, and said with quiet resignation,

"Shall we?"

Toxaris eyed her for a moment with those dark eyes before she gestured with her spear in a display of solemn formality. As they approached the first campfire surrounded by men, Penny was surprised to see that Sagitta lounged on the ground among the circle of sailors, her blue eyes sparkling with laughter as the man next to her boasted of his recent exploits at sea. Next to Sagitta, a particularly handsome young man caught her eye, his legs stretched out toward the fire and crossed at the ankle, his bare-chested upper body propped up on an elbow. The light from the flames illuminated the sharp edge of his cheekbones, the strong line of his jaw, the leanly muscled shoulders made strong from months pulling at an oar. He was laughing at a part of the story his fellow shipmate was telling, but his eyes turned to meet Penny's as her footsteps sounded above the talk and crackling fire, and there was a curious heat in her face and a jolt in her belly as the light in his eyes seemed to erupt into a full conflagration at the sight of her. His smile did not fade, but his laughter quieted, and soon the whole circle fell silent.

Suddenly very conscious of the way the folds of the white linen robes clung to her hips and breasts, the way her unbound hair could have used another quick comb before she ventured out tonight, she stepped forward, the golden rhyton curved in the shape of a galloping mare held in front of her, though it strained her arms with its weight. Toxaris hung back in the shadows, the butt of her spear stuck into the ground, her dark eyes watchful.

"Honored guests," Penny said formally, meeting the curious stares of the men with a firm yet aloof gaze, finding security in the training her mother had given her. "As Ishassara of the Hearth Queen, I offer you Milk from the Breast of the Great Mother, that you may know She will nourish and provide for you in all your days, as you keep Her Ways. May you feel Her embrace while you are guests among us."

"I'd like to feel *her* embrace, you get me?" a voice whispered from the other side of the fire, and men chortled with smothered laughter. Penny ignored the crude remark, and stepped forward to complete the ritual.

She extended the horn to the nearest man, pouring the *kimiz* carefully into his mouth, but she could not help but be aware of the first man she had noticed, and how his eyes followed her every move from across the campfire. His attention felt weightier, more direct than the others, his gaze almost tangible on her flesh, like the softest of touches. When she finally made her way around the circle, pouring *kimiz* for each man, repeating the ritual welcome, she finally came to stand next to him. He sat up straight, and his eyes met hers with an unnerving directness. A curling heat trailed through her belly as his slowly traveling storm-green eyes met hers with intimate, unmistakable intensity. After a long moment, in which the heat rushed into Penny's face before spreading down her neck, over her chest, and then coursed through her entire body as a single flame, he raised his face for her to pour the *kimiz* into his mouth.

There was something wholly intimate about it, so that every movement Penny made felt unfamiliar, awkward, ungainly, but she tipped the rhyton, pouring a small stream, holding her breath to be careful and not spill any of the sweet milk. He swallowed the milk without taking his gaze from her face, and she paused a moment longer than necessary before stepping back.

"Drink, and be welcome," Penny said, thankful the words were rote by now after saying them several dozen times already, but there was a huskiness in her throat she did not plan for.

"I am honored to be welcomed by one so beautiful," the man said softly, still gazing up at her. His eyes seemed to devour her lips, and the heat inside Penny's stomach increased to an inferno.

"Aw, keep that froth inside your mouth, Deileon," a voice jeered from behind her. "She isn't going to look twice at the son of a shepherd-king."

"She doesn't need to look at him at all!" a gravelly voice called from the other side of the flames. "Deileon only knows how to fuck 'em from behind anyway, since he's only ever seen our father's sheep go at it. This is the first girl he's ever met, other than our mother and sisters!"

"Shut your mouth, Lykos," the one they called Deileon retorted, as laughter erupted from every man's throat. Deileon looked up at Penny with an apologetic smile. "Pay no mind my brother. He is not the brightest of fellows, and does not know how to speak—or keep silent—when the Queen of Heaven makes an appearance."

The heat inside Penny's stomach turned to roiling tumult, and she could barely tear her eyes away from his face, but Lykos continued to make jokes about everything from his own brother's questionable parentage to his inexperience with women, taking the focus off Penny entirely. She used the moment to steady herself, grateful for the calm, reassuring smile Sagitta gave as that woman's hand gently, very pointedly caressed the handle of her axe laying next to her thigh.

Forcing her shoulders back down from where they had crept toward her ears, and both Antiope and Sylviu's voices echoing in her mind, Penny returned to her task, skin prickling, but unsure whether it was the heat of the fire, the flames in their eyes, or the unsubtle way that Deileon's gaze followed her every movement. She used some of the *kimiz* to refill Sagitta's horn as the ha-mazaan winked at her, before moving on to the man seated at the ha-mazaans right side, and the last one to be served.

"I know why Deileon stares," the man said, also staring. "It's a relief to finally see such a pretty, womanly creature on these shores." He licked *kimiz* from his lips, but somehow the gesture was crude and suggestive, and Penny took a step back, instinctively putting space between them. "Even your hair is different than this one's," he said, jerking his thumb at Sagitta without bothering to look away from Penny. Sagitta raised her eyebrows and drank a long gulp of milk, her eyes shining dangerously.

Penny nodded stiffly, a polite smile in place. She made to turn away when the sailor reached out a hand and caught her wrist in a tight grip, tugging her towards him. Penny's balance shifted as she struggled to keep hold of the rhyton, and she would have stumbled right into his lap, just as he was hoping, had Toxaris not acted, quick and quiet as a panther in the dark. The ha-mazaan lance swung, meeting his wrist with a crack and breaking the man's hold on Penny, while the woman's other hand unceremoniously shoved her backward. Deileon lunged upright to catch her just as she was about to fall. Penny barely had time to process what was happening before the man who had grabbed her was lying prone, clutching a bruised, possibly broken wrist, and both Deileon and Sagitta had their weapons at his throat. The ha-mazaan grinned down at him with bared teeth, her star-iron dagger ready to puncture his vein, though Deileon was not smiling. The other men in the circle howled with laughter.

"You just got your hand slapped by a girl with a stick!" Lykos crowed, and laughter erupted again as the man cringed away from Sagitta's dagger digging into this flesh.

Penny's face burned. She clutched the nearly empty rhyton to her stomach and watched as Sagitta leaned forward to tug the prone man upright by the front of his tunic, while Deileon stepped back to give them room, sheathing his own blade as he looked on. Toxaris, without ever saying a word, stepped back into the shadows, though she sliced her staff through the air with a whistle that was as much a warning as her voice would have been.

"She might be the prettiest girl from here to Wilusa," Sagitta said, "but I would advise you and your men to keep your hands to yourself, unless you are invited to do otherwise."

"I just wanted to talk," the man grumbled, nursing his wrist against his chest.

"Apologize," Deileon demanded.

Brekko glared at Deileon, who glared back. Eventually, the battle of wills ended. With barely a glance at Penny, Brekko mumbled a sullen, "Apologies, lady."

"No harm done, Brekko," Sagitta answered before Penny could speak, but the blade she had not yet sheathed shone with deadly intent as she flipped it easily in one hand, catching it by the handle and then admiring the edge of it in the light of the flames. It did not go unnoticed by anyone watching that she had not needed anything but her small blade to subdue the man, and no one at the campfire doubted the axe at her hip would shear them clean in two if she wanted it to.

"To touch any of our women without their consent is the surest death sentence you could ever receive. Whether she has First Blood or not."

"First Blood?" someone asked. The snap of a log in the fire punctuated the tense silence that followed, as the two men, Brekko and Deileon, stood on either side of Penny, facing the tall, leanly muscled ha-mazaan.

"Moon blood, they call it," another sailor guessed, and there were huffs of uncomfortable laughter.

"Death, we call it," Sagitta corrected, still studying her blade, perhaps looking for nicks in the sharpened edge.

"Death?"

Sagitta smiled at the speaker's thin voice, but there was little humor in her face now. "You should know every ha-mazaan in this city, and our sister cities, is required to complete at least one kill before lying with a man. What's more, those who wish to bind themselves permanently to any partner must prove themselves three times over. Only Penthesilea is exempt from this, as she is the living embodiment of the Great Mother, and has an army of ha-mazaans ready and willing to kill for her, if she so requests it.

"If any seek to touch her without her permission, she will not need to request it."

7

THESEUS

Penny was spared further scrutiny as the men broke into excited murmurs at this revelation, one of them voicing the strong desire to watch a ha-mazaan complete their First Blood ritual on Brekko. Their once more raucous laughter was interrupted by a smooth male voice, the low tones at once intimate and abrasive in Penny's ear.

"Who's this beautiful creature, then?"

Penny turned to find her mother, her aunt Lyta, and Molpadia approaching with two men. She already knew who they were from her mother's descriptions of who she had been speaking with when the ships arrived. Theseus of Athens, from even farther west than her father's home in Satra, and his friend Heracles of Thebes, who was, according to what her mother had been able to tell her so far, on some sort of grand mission for his uncle, and the real reason these sailors crowded Themiscyra's shores.

"This is my daughter, Penthesilea. My Ishassara. What you would call Princess in Attica, if daughters were heir to the seat of Basileus."

Penny noticed the way her mother held Theseus' arm, as though claiming him as her own.

"Penthesilea, this is Basileus Theseus, along with his good friend, the mighty Heracles. Heracles is still being shy about telling us what his mission is, but he is certainly entertaining Lyta with his fabulous stories." Antiope smiled warmly on the man, and Penny murmured an appropriate welcome.

"Penthesilea," her mother said, turning back to her with raised eyebrows. "Theseus has told me his captain has dealings with a certain salt mine on the southern coast of Thrakia," Antiope continued. "Perhaps you can seek the man out while he is our guest, and he will share with you more recent news of your father."

"My father?" Penny said, taken aback, but a flame of longing lit her heart.

"I was surprised, too," Theseus interjected before Penny could ask anything further. His face a nondescript replica of every other man who sat on this beach, with a beardless chin and a mop of straight, wood-colored hair recently washed in the river, barely clean after an entire moon at sea, but there was a gleam in his blue that implied a cunning intelligence. His gaze roamed her face, her shoulders, her unbound hair, much the same way as every man's did when they visited these shores, but there was something about the way he looked at her that made her squirm. Her recent altercation must have made her more sensitive to their gawking than she usually was.

"I didn't think Amazons had fathers," he finished with a sly wink at her, but Molpadia, standing well apart from the group, snorted through her nose and answered before Penny could even think of a reply to such a statement.

"Did you think we sprang from the ground like any shrub? Is that how Achaeans are born, then?"

"Dia."

Penny's aunt frowned down on her partner, Lyta's pale red eyebrows furrowed with disapproval, though Molpadia's sneer did not waver, and the puckered scar over her eyebrow pulled taut.

Theseus merely chuckled, removing his arm from Antiope's grip to step closer to Penny, studying her face more closely in the flickering firelight.

"I only knew your reputation precedes you," he said, replying to Molpadia, still eyeing Penny with a curious, thoughtful intensity she found unnerving. "Your sister-cities in Thebes and Ause only allow daughters born of virgins to live, if what I hear is true. Males are left to die in the hills, since they are a sign the *parthenos* tried to cheat in order to bring forth a child. Do I have that right?"

Penny wasn't sure if the man expected her to be the one to answer, but Molpadia snorted again, and Penny's mother eyed Theseus with an indistinguishable gleam in her own blue eyes, answering before Penny could think of an appropriate reply. "You must have traveled very widely to know of the *parthenos*," she said.

Theseus' smile widened, his face creasing into genuine pleasure as he said formally, "But never to such fine city as what we have seen in Themiscyra. What treasures your city harbors!"

"I hope you find refuge and replenishment of the Great Mother while you rest on our shores, Basileus Theseus," Penny said formally.

"Princess, it is an honor to make the acquaintance of one just as beautiful as her mother, and just as sweet, I can tell."

"Sweet enough that Brekko tried to give her a taste, didn't you, Brekko?" Lykos called out, and the rest laughed again as Brekko hunched his shoulders. Without blinking his eyes, Theseus slid his gaze from Penny's reddening face to the man beyond her shoulder.

"Is this true, Brekko?"

His tone was mild, and yet the group settled immediately into a hushed, tense silence. Brekko squirmed next to Sagitta.

"Just wanted to talk," Brekko mumbled, eyes on his sandaled feet. "I barely even touched her."

Heracles stepped forward, his mouth pulled into a frown under the yawning teeth of the lion. "Your Highness, my most profound apologies if my men have showed anything but the utmost respect," he said. "I assure you they shall be dealt with accordingly."

Penny gestured with a desperate wave of her hand and began to protest that any harm had been done, but the huge man shook his head adamantly, the lion's mane shaking with it. "No, it is unacceptable that the daughter of the most gracious Queen we have ever had the pleasure of meeting be disrespected in such a manner. I promise you this man shall be dealt with. And I promise you, Queen Antiope, and you, Queen Hippolyta, that none of my men shall harm any woman in this city while they are under my command. You have welcomed us as honored guests, and we shall act accordingly."

The awkward tension after his vow was eased when Antiope smiled placatingly, and said, "All is well, I am sure, honorable Heracles. Our ha-maza-ans are more than capable of taking care of themselves, and my daughter is always well-guarded. Now, Penthesilea," her mother said, motioning to her with a summoning hand. "There are other guests to welcome, and the night grows long. Come." She turned her brightest, most gracious smile on the men, and offered a ringed hand to Theseus.

"Basileus Theseus—may I call you King?—I trust my sister will be able to entertain you and your men as my daughter and I complete the rites of hospitality? Whatever amenities we have are yours to enjoy, so please do not hesitate to ask for anything you need."

Penny murmured a standard pleasantry to them all before her mother drew her away once more, Toxaris trailing a few steps behind, the butt of her staff crunching in the gravel as they walked. She looked back to the circle one more time, to find Deileon's eyes following her. He smiled, and raised a hand in silent farewell before letting it fall back to his lap again. The coil of anxiety in Penny's stomach slowly unfurled, and she returned his smile, just a tilt of her lips as her mother had taught her, but it was enough. His face burned like a torch lit from within, and it found a matching fire within Penny.

For all of the banter about beginning her Alsanti here in the city, the suggestion no longer seemed as untenable as it had only hours earlier. She was of age. She had the right, indeed the expectation, to bear a daughter as soon as possible. Why not with this man? Why not, indeed?

8

JEALOUS OF THE SUN

Molpadia watched Lyta's languorous stretch through half-lidded eyes, jealous of the sun itself as its late morning rays caressed every ivory curve and golden hollow she wanted to be touching, and turning that strawberry hair to copper fire.

"Good morning, lazy bones," she said, her voice raspy from sleep, and from an unusually late night drinking wine with the unwanted, but seemingly peaceful guests. The men's presence was a heavy weight in her mind, even though absolutely nothing untoward had come from their ominous arrival other than their stench and raucous laughter, but it pulled her lips into a frown as she remembered the way the one named Heracles had made moon-eyes at Lyta all night. Those thoughts were not welcome to intrude on the hallowed sanctuary that was their chambers, however, and she tried to push them aside.

"Glllll," Lyta replied, turning her head with slow precision and blinking bleary eyes somewhere in her general direction. The Defending Queen was many things, but she was not a morning person.

She had also drunk enough wine and *kimiz* and possibly even mead around the campfires on the beach to down a full-grown ox. Molpadia's tense frown softened into an affectionate smile, and she hauled her lover across the bed with a forceful tug on her firm waist. Her Defending Queen squawked indelicately in protest, and then snuggled her deliciously round bottom against Molpadia's thighs, sighing in contentment.

"You can't go back to sleep, love," Molpadia said softly into Lyta's strawberry blonde hair. "The sun is already above the mountains. We need to be ready for the Trials."

Lyta groaned, squirming her body tighter against Molpadia's. Molpadia tsked her tongue, but did not complain. Other than swinging a sword or hurling a spear, this was her favorite place to be, and no duties of stables or blacksmithing or keeping raucous men in line would ever supersede that.

"I need to dress," she whispered regretfully into Lyta's mussed hair, but even as she did, the scent of it filled her nostrils, and she closed her eyes to inhale. The sigh of resignation that erupted from her beloved's throat was dramatically loud, followed immediately by a groan of regret. Lyta flung one long, leanly muscled arm backwards, smacked Molpadia's bare bottom with a resounding thwack, and lurched into a sitting position. Molpadia did not bother to hide her grin as Lyta groaned again, clutching her head and squinting her beautiful eyes against the piercing light.

"Aye, that is what you get for drinking milk of the Mother *and* wine on the same night."

"Shhh, Dia," Lyta hissed. "Agh! My head feels like someone put a spear through it." Her normally husky voice was deepened further by sleep and drink.

"We are getting too old for such revelry," Molpadia sighed in agreement, sitting up with careful slowness. "Come, let us go to the baths and wash away the cobwebs. The heat will do us good."

Lyta lowered her hands to her lap, the long, slender fingers scarred with multiple white slashes from years of training with axe and sword, but they were only more beautiful for the scars. She turned a wan smile on Molpadia. Even bleary-eyed and sore from too much wine, she was the most beautiful creature Molpadia had ever seen, and her heart squeezed.

"Let's go then, Little Marmot," Lyta said, her tone a clear challenge, trying to get a rise with the nickname.

"You first, my queen," Molpadia offered, secretly relishing the name from those lips, sweeping a hand toward the door.

"You are the one who needs to be dressed for the Trials. And soon, if that blasted, blinding sun is any indication."

"And *you* are the one who needs to deliver Kubileya's Invocation for the opening ceremony, my queen," Molpadia retorted, climbing from their bed.

Lyta scowled, then groaned again.

"Fine. We will go together. But there had better be wine in the baths. A little tail of the horse that kicked me."

Molpadia grinned, and hauled Lyta to her feet. "*Kimiz* and wine and freshly roasted mutton, dripping in butter. Nothing less for my queen."

"Would you stop calling me that?" Lyta said, frowning as she shrugged into a rumpled, thoroughly wine-stained chiton, swaying only slightly.

"I must, my queen," Molpadia replied, tugging the laces of her trousers tight against her waist. She thrust an arm through the leather vest, forgoing the sweaty, smelly tunic that should go underneath in hopes there might be a fresh one in the bath house, and reached for her sword belt, the tension that had been with her for the last day in no way lessened in her gut. "I would not want the men on our beaches to think they can refer to you as anything but what you are."

Lyta snorted indelicately and buckled her own belt under her breasts and around her waist, tugging the heavy, ringed zoster into place.

"These men do not know a queen from a camel."

"Shouldn't you be wearing your real zoster while they are here?" Her frown returned unbidden, and Lyta poked a finger between her brows to push it away.

"No. Pen needs it more than I do. Besides, I have you to protect me, my love."

Molpadia smiled, but her eyes were worried as she watched Lyta finish dressing. Her love turned to the door with a forced determination that fooled no one.

"Come, Dia, we will wash away last night, and maybe after you are done giving these Xanharaspas their last scare before they graduate, you can take a few of our guests to the practice yard and show them how a *real* warrior handles a blade. Perhaps they will not be so proud to show their pathetically dull swords to the world, then."

"Aye," Molpadia said with grim intent as she followed Lyta into the hall. "And Heracles will hopefully think twice before he tries to steal a kiss from you again, else I will use his own dull sword to carve off his bollocks."

Lyta's laugh was like the finest Colchis wine as Molpadia followed her down the stone stairway into the steaming baths. "Perhaps I wanted him to kiss me, Little Marmot. Did you ever think about that?"

Molpadia hoped Lyta was only trying to get a reaction from her, but then she scowled as the tactic proved all too effective. "You aren't serious. Are you?"

Lyta turned wide, falsely innocent doe-eyes on her as they entered the baths, the steam already hot and fragrant with herbs after other ha-mazaans had spent the morning performing their ritual ablutions. Lyta was peeling her tunic over her head as she walked, her lithe body a supple, deadly weapon all on its own. "Why not? If my sister and all the other ha-mazaans can enjoy some fun while they visit, why not us?"

"*Us*?" Molpadia nearly strangled on the word, but Lyta's dimple flashed into view before she dove under the water. Molpadia forced her shoulders to relax, stripping her own clothes off and wading into the shallow end. Lyta came up for air in front of her, rising from the water like a nymph of the hot springs, draping her arms over her shoulders, pressing her body into hers, melting Molpadia's ire with just a simple touch of her hands.

"Don't worry, love," her queen whispered, kissing the scar on Molpadia's brow where it pulled the skin tight, then on her lip, just on the edge, a bare whisper of lips against her suddenly alive skin. "There is only one person I need, and she is right here. She is more than enough for me. No matter how broad his shoulders are, or how tight his ass."

Molpadia snorted even as she kissed Lyta, feeling those lips pull in a grin underneath hers. For a long time, the only sound was the bubbling of the water and Lyta's sighs, until finally, her love pulled away, stretching her arms over her head and arching her back.

"You promised wine and mutton, Little Marmot. How long do I need to wait?"

9

CRUSHED PETALS

"Keep still, Pen, unless you want your lips so big they look like they were stung by bees. Your wrist already looks bad enough."

Penny shifted her bottom on the hard stool, obediently offering puckered lips to her mother's administrations. Antiope patted her fingertip across her upturned lips with quick, confident precision, adding a buttery film of crushed berries and rose petals. Her mother had already outlined both of their eyes with kohl, smudging it into perfect softness and making her own blue eyes even more pronounced. Penny was sure she would never see another woman as beautiful as her mother, and wished for only half of her mother's ethereal, elegant grace.

"Every man will be tripping over his own feet for the chance to be noticed by you," Antiope said, her own lips mimicking the position she had wanted Penny to assume. "After making the rounds last night, I'm convinced you can find at least two to suit your fancy. Such an assortment of strong, virile young men, didn't you think?"

Penny rolled her eyes, but Deileon's face appeared unbidden in her mind's eye, and she flushed under Antiope's fingertips as her mother patted the rouge onto the apples of her cheeks.

"Hm, so one *has* caught your eye, then?"

Antiope straightened, eyes twinkling, and patted the last of the oil on her own lips, rolling them together a few times with a gesture for Penny to do likewise, while she studied her workmanship. Penny allowed herself to be tugged off the stool and positioned in front of her mother's mirror, the length of it reflecting both of them as long white curves of moonlight in the polished silver. She tilted her head to admire her mother's skills. Just a few dabs of roses to her lips and black lining to her amber eyes made her feel like the most beautiful—well, second most beautiful, next to her mother—woman in the world. That was just the confidence she needed if she was going to see Deileon today.

She smoothed her hands over her hips, palms suddenly damp. What would she say if she did see him today? How could she let him know she wished to take a daughter from him? Should she simply ask? Should she sneak a kiss? Maybe he would kiss her first. The idea sent a thrill of anticipation through her belly, and plans of how she could seduce the handsome sailor tumbled together in her mind, but all of her excitement was overshadowed by one looming issue. She pursed her lips at her mother's reflection behind her in the mirror, and said,

"Aunt Lyta and Dia are not going to appreciate you inviting men to the Trials, Mother. I don't even want to *think* about what Aunty Nightmare is going to do when she sees them."

"Your aunts are superstitious old harridans sometimes," Antiope said, waving a dismissive hand. "All of them seem convinced on some level they have come here to make war, but all the men have wanted so far is a bath in the river and sharp knives to shave their chins. Once they see what our women are capable of with horse and sword and axe and spear, my sisters will see we have nothing to worry about. Best case scenario, the Achaeans see how skilled our ha-mazaans are, and see the benefits in partnering with us, rather than making us their enemy. Besides, men are nothing to be feared. Here, let me straighten your robes. Why are they always so fussed? It's as though you sleep in them!"

"I can't think men would come to make war with the ha-mazaans only to stand around on our beach talking and drinking," Penny agreed, as Antiope tugged the pleats of her himation into the perfect folds Penny had never been able to master, even after all these years. "They didn't so much as draw a sword, from what I could see. I still don't understand what all the fuss was about."

"Yes, I did see that you were watching from the Tower, and did not stay in the Moon Hall as instructed, Daughter," Antiope said, bent over Penny's hip. "I also saw Ossy's boy into the Tower with you. You know we will need to purify the Flame now."

Penny flushed guiltily, though Antiope's tone was mild. So Sylviu *had* been seen. She should have known his presence with the Flame would not have gone unnoticed. Her mouth twisted in a rueful smile. She was glad he had managed to leave the city whole and well the evening before.

"And yes," her mother continued, her voice distracted with concentration as her slender fingers tucked fabric under Penny's zoster, "Lyta and Melanippe, and especially Dia, have been too long outside the company of men. They forget we *need* men sometimes, if only to take daughters from their loins. How else are we to secure the Thrones? I know this Basileus has his own thoughts of how the *parthanoi* operate, but really, who believes such drivel in real life? Even a barbarian king should not be so susceptible to such fantastical notions as virgin births." Antiope's perfect mouth puckered as she concentrated on a particularly stubborn fold, and Penny's arms began to ache with the effort of holding them akimbo to allow unrestricted access to her waist. "I know you, at least, know better. And today will be your day to make your move, so best not waste time."

"Hmm," Penny said, still pondering the reaction from her aunts if they knew Antiope's plans. "They will already be unhappy to have men at the Trials. I cannot think it will make the situation better if they learn I am seducing one of them within the gates of the city."

"Psh." Antiope gave one final tug on Penny's robes before standing back to survey the final result. "They do not need to know anything about what you choose to do with your time, or our guests, do they? The only thing my sisters need to worry about is protecting the city, so that you and I can worry about providing more daughters for the Thrones. There, much better. One of these days, you are going to have to fold the robes on your own, Pen. I can't always be twitching and tugging you into place."

Penny inspected the final result in the mirror, but her mother swatted her hands away when she attempted to adjust her zoster.

"It's tight," Penny complained.

"It needs to be, to show off that waist," Antiope said. "You need to leverage what you have, Pen, and what you have is beauty. Look at you!" Her mother's eyes were bright with pride beside Penny's flushed face. "If you plan on seducing anyone, you must use every bit of time to your advantage. That means I will make sure they cross your path at every opportunity, and *you* will give them something worth looking at, hmm? Especially a young man named...Deileon, is it?" A mischievous, knowing gleam in her blue eyes made Penny's cheeks uncomfortably hot. "Mmhmm. Sagitta told me how several of them were quite taken with you. And these robes highlight your hips perfectly, so I'm sure whomever you choose will be thoroughly enchanted. You did a good job with the weave on this linen, I must say."

Caught off guard by the rare compliment, Penny's flush deepened, but she shook her head ruefully. "I don't think any of them are going to notice—or care—about my skills at the loom, Mother. Besides, I would rather pick someone because they are kind, and able to give me a strong, healthy daughter, not just because they think I am beautiful."

Even as she said it, she pictured a certain pair of green eyes and a sculpted jaw, and knew very well she was not being entirely truthful. She very much wanted Deileon, at least, to think she was the most beautiful woman in the city.

"Men are simple, daughter," Antiope said, smoothing her own white robe over her hips and turning to see the back of herself in the mirror. "They feast with their eyes, and we allow them to satiate their hunger, and in return, they froth at the mouth to hand over everything that would cost a lifetime—and a lifetime's fortune—to afford. How do you think I acquired these earrings?"

Penny glanced at the earrings in question, the gold and lapis lazuli beads pulling at the lobes of her mother's ears with their weight, but Antiope was already turning to the door, plucking two long fans from the vase on the table as she went, and handing one of them to Penny.

"We'd best go. Lyta will screech for days if I am late to her Ishassara's Trials, and you, my dear Daughter, have a lot of work to do before we can call this Savaran Feast a success."

10

HEAT

Molpadia strode into the arena next to Toxaris, crested helmet tucked under her armpit, double-bladed axe in hand, the ashen handle worn in a groove from years of curving itself to her fingers. She was sure the sun had never been so hot. There could not have been a worse day to be wrapped in scaled leather and padded linen, feet bound in boots rather than open, breathable sandals, and she knew that as soon as she donned the helmet, sweat would be pouring into her eyes. It was already sticking her tunic to her chest and back, making her neck itch like an Erinyes was trailing its claws down her spine. This Trial would be quick, though, and then she could have her second bath of the day, perhaps in the cold Terme, and be back at the podium before the next Trial had begun.

"Ready?" Toxaris asked beside her, the star-iron spear in her hand glinting brutally above their heads.

Molpadia eyed pale-haired Prothoe and dark-eyed Leya approaching, Leya with her own long spear, and Prothoe with her axe. She nodded, casting a tight grin at her fellow ha-mazaan. "Aye. Let's not make it easy on them."

Toxaris laughed lightly, turning toward the podium and lifting her spear in a salute to the queens. Molpadia did the same, and Lyta's raised fist of salute was all the confidence she needed as she donned her helmet, and turned back to the ha-mazaans. Prothoe and Leya finished their own salute, checked their straps on bracers and helmets, and then pressed their backs into each other, prepared to defend the life of their sister from the enemy, who on this day came in the form of their own training marshals. Lyta's horn burst two quick blasts into the dense air.

Molpadia met Prothoe's icy blue eyes with a fierce grin, and then swung her axe at Leya's neck, lending every bit of strength and speed she had to the blow. From the opposite side, Toxaris slashed her lance through the air at Prothoe's thigh. Both blows were well blocked by the defensive swing of the other partner, but Molpadia was not waiting for another opening. She had already danced to the left, striking at Prothoe's exposed waist with similarly deadly force, and when Leya's spear cracked against the handle of her axe, she gripped it tighter and swung it at that girl's face again, seeing very real fear in the young ha-mazaan's eyes as she did so, but she did not let it contract her force. This was their task. Protect their sister. Defend their partner. Or die, and never be Savaran. She and Lyta had danced this same dance at their own Trials, their backs pressed against each other, their limbs as unified as their hearts had been even then. She grinned, the remembrance of that day and the thrill of this battle rushing through her veins, and swung again.

Prothoe's axe intercepted hers, sending a jolt of pain through Molpadia's shoulder, bringing to life an old injury that gave her more grief these days, but she simply grunted, using the pain to ground her, keep her focused.

"Come on, little hounds!" she taunted, drawing Prothoe away with another furious slash of her axe, the blades locking on each other so that Molpadia could pull the girl off center and force their backs apart. She huffed a harsh grunt when Leya used the butt of her lance to jab her in the ribs, breaking their weapons apart, and the two Xanharaspas came together again, their backs pressed close as Toxaris and Molpadia circled like ravenous wolves looking for a weak spot. Leya twirled the staff, making it whistle an ominous song. Molpadia bared her teeth in a grin and waited for Toxaris to distract Prothoe by hitting Leya, then tried to sink her blade into the pale girl's stomach, but Leya's spear came dangerously close to Molpadia's face, and she leaped back, impressed with the girl's speed. She redoubled her efforts, forcing them to spin and turn and slash, not allowing either of them a chance to attack rather than defend, exulting in the rush of energy that built inside with the effort, until it became effortless, laughing as her axe slashed and tasted blood in Leya's thigh, but only barely, as Prothoe's axe shoved the blade aside before it could do real damage. She was still laughing when Lyta's horn sounded, and all four fighters broke apart.

Chest heaving, Molpadia hefted her axe in a salute to the girls. Toxaris swung her own spear in the air, calling out her praise for their skill, her mouth split wide in a grin between the cheek guards of her helmet. They each grinned back, their first Trial's success bright in their eyes, but their next Trial awaited them in the forest, and both soon loped out of the arena, the hot sun turning the dust from their feet into clouds of ruby under their feet. Molpadia tore off her helmet, sweat dripping, and raised her axe in one last salute to her red-haired queen watching from the dais. She winked at Lyta's holler of pride, and turned toward the river, needing those quenching waters to cool the battle fury and the sun's heat.

"I'm hot. And sticky."

Penny waved the fan of tightly bound feathers her mother had provided, purloined from what must have once been a massive pheasant, to create some movement in the stale air for both herself and Leandra.

"It is very warm today," Penny agreed, fanning air directly into Leandra's upturned face.

They waited in the shade of an enormous sycamore for Sagitta, but in such sweltering heat, even the brief wait seemed interminable. The ha-mazaan had requested Penny bring her daughter to this spot before Cyra's Trial began, though the reason why was still a mystery. After some bribery involving promises of honeyed oat cakes at the evening's Feast, Leandra had finally left her prime spot in the arena's audience, but only when the fight between two newly graduated Savaran had finally ended. That had been only moments ago, but already the sun's heat made it seem like hours had passed.

The girl closed her eyes as Penny fanned, letting the breeze flutter her golden eyelashes, but then she grimaced, her rosebud lips twisting into a familiar pout.

"It's just hotter air," she said accusingly, opening her eyes to glare at Penny.

The girl was not wrong. The heat had already melted the kohl smudged around Penny's eyes, and the rosy balm on her cheeks and lips was now mingled with her own salty sweat, and dirt from the dusty, baked earth underfoot. Penny sighed, returning the fanned air to her own sticky neck, annoyed at the thought Deileon and the other men had not made an appearance in time to witness her at her finest. It would be just her luck to have them show up now, when she looked like one of the women from her father's favorite theatre plays.

"Where's Mama? I'm too hot."

"Your mother will be along soon, I'm sure. Is your sack full of the apples she said you would need?"

"No," Leandra said. Then, as though Penny were the most dense person the girl had ever met, "The *apples* are going to be on the *tree* in the *orchard* when we *get* there."

"Ah," Penny said, and thought it best to say no more. Heat made even the softest of tempers turn irascible, and Leandra was anything but soft. She looked to the arena, hoping to see Sagitta's blonde braids and bright blue eyes, but the edges of the stadium were a sea of people, and it was difficult to tell one ha-mazaan from another at this distance. Swords and axes and spears glinted in the hot sun, fans of peacock and pheasant and stryx waving hot air over hotter skin as those in attendance waited in the brutal midday heat. The intermission entertainment was ending, signaling a new Trial would begin soon. Archers ran into the arena, shooting at smaller and smaller bits of debris tossed into the air, and a few ha-mazaans danced on the backs of their mares as entertainment for the crowd while they waited for Cyra and her fighting partner to begin their Trials. Women from every corner of the city, both warriors and crafters, *matars* and *attas* and the children they cared for, including hanassa who had not reached the age of Separation, ambled about the edges of the fighting arena, and in the center of them all, the raised pavilion where her family watched and judged the most important Trials of the day. As the arena cleared, Hippolyta's ram's horn blew two short blasts, signaling the start of Cyra's Trial. Penny cast her eyes over the milling ha-mazaans impatiently, worried she would miss her cousin's most important day, other than tomorrow's initiation ceremony. But there was no sign of Sagitta.

"Princess!"

Penny's heart jolted. She and Leandra both turned to see several Achaeans making their way past the small knoll to the arena, Theseus at the front of the group, Heracles' distinct lion pelt behind him, and at the edge, moving toward her up the hill with long-legged strides, was Deileon. A different kind of warmth blossomed hot and prickling in Penny's cheeks, before it spread down her chest and into her belly, and she smiled with every bit of her mother's carefully tutored charm as she could manage while her senses began to swim with more than just the midday heat.

11

BEAUTIFUL DAUGHTERS

"Princess Penthesilea, I'm so glad to see you again," Deileon said again as he drew closer. He stopped in front of her, his eyes taking in her face, her hair, her pristine white robe. Eventually, he said, with endearing earnestness, "You are radiant, Princess."

Penny's stomach leaped and thudded like one of the ha-mazaans in their tumbling acts. She could not decide whether looking into his beautiful eyes or at the broad expanse of his shoulders was more distracting, but she did know that the heat she felt in her skin was not going to be quenched by any cool water from the Terme. Nor, she thought, did she want it to be. It was a delicious fire, and she savored the novelty of it.

"Thank you, Deileon," she said, offering her ringed fingers for his kiss. He bowed over her hand, his lips pressing respectfully into the imprint of the golden bee on her forefinger, careful not to touch her skin with his lips, and she was thankful for every ounce of training her mother had given her in matters of stately address, composure, and gentle speech. She prayed to Kubileya they would not abandon her now. A shout from the group below drew her attention, and some of her wits returned when she glimpsed that Theseus had broken away from the group to follow Deileon up the hill, though his own strides were slow and measured up the steep embankment. The rest of the men looked on, shading their eyes against the midday glare, Heracles' fanged headdress giving him shelter from the sun with its thick mane.

"I trust you are enjoying your visit to our shores?" she asked, returning her attention to Deileon.

"Very much," Deileon said earnestly, straightening from her fingers to look down at her with frank appreciation. He did not release her hand,

and it took every bit of Penny's self-control to not focus on the warmth of his fingers, the strength of their calloused grip, the divine pleasure that was her hand inside of his. She wished his lips had slipped just a little bit, so she could feel them on her skin.

"Please, call me Leon," he continued. "Only my father calls me Deileon, and he is very far away from this place, thankfully."

"Leon, then," Penny nodded, mirroring his smile.

"Princess," Leon said, glancing over his shoulder to see Theseus approaching, and lowering his voice for her ears only. "I would have you know that the man who dared to lay his hands on you has been punished, as was fit. He will not be bothering you again."

Penny stared in dismay, her smile slipping, her thoughts still wrapped up in the feel of his skin on hers. "Oh...I did not..." she stumbled over the words, unsure how to address this news. "I hope his punishment was not severe? I do not like to think he suffered for such a small thing."

Leon squeezed her fingers gently, then, to her great disappointment, let her hand go. "Just a few lashes from our captain's whip. Nothing he cannot pull an oar against, but his pride has taken the sting it needed. I consider the punishment too light for such disrespect, but I see you are as kind and as forgiving as you are beautiful, and I can only admire you more for it."

Penny blossomed under his warm stare, but another voice interrupted the moment.

"Ah, it is the lovely Penthesilea hiding in the shadows, I see!"

She forced herself to break eye contact with Leon, fixing a polite smile of welcome as Theseus strolled the last few steps to join them. The man smiled in return, his blue eyes intent on hers.

"Trying to hide, and failing, I should say. Not even full darkness could cover such radiant beauty as yours, Princess. I must say, now that I see you in the full light of day, I know you are indeed your mother's daughter. Only Queen Antiope's flesh and blood could be so lovely!"

Penny's cheeks flushed a deeper red than Chaldesian wine as Theseus' eyes devoured every inch of her appearance. His frank gaze once again took in her robes, the tendrils of hair draping over her bare shoulder, the beads of sweat atop her breasts, the wide leather belt cinching in her waist. She forced herself not to frown with impatience as she wished the man had not needed to interrupt what could have been a perfect opportunity to be alone with Leon.

"Ah, but I forget my manners," Theseus said, sliding his eyes to Penny's companion without blinking, his face still intent. "Who is this lovely Queen of women at your side?"

Penny glanced down at Leandra, whom she had almost forgotten. The girl stood with arms folded across her chest, her mouth a mutinous line.

"This is—"

"I'm Leandra," the girl said, fixing Theseus with a steely glare. "One day, I will be the fiercest ha-mazaan you have ever met. Maybe I will even fight *you* in battle, but maybe not, because you're already old and that would not be fair. My mother is teaching me to fight, you know, and she is better with her axe than anyone else in this city, except maybe Queen Lyta. And maybe Cyra. And my grandmother was Queen Maise, and her husband was King Sagillus, and she's dead, but he still lives somewhere where it snows a lot so I haven't met him yet. Who are *you*?"

Penny bit the inside of her cheek to keep from laughing at the men's astonished faces, but Theseus quickly recovered, his eyes taking on a gleam of amusement.

"I suppose I am the man who will be terrified of you for the rest of my life, young Leandra. Some call me Basileus Theseus, but as you are the granddaughter of a King, I think it is fine that you call me Theseus. I do hope I can see your mother fight today, if she is as magnificent as you say."

"Maybe you will," Leandra said, her tone brimming with doubt. She eyed Theseus' sword at his waist. "Men aren't supposed to have swords, you know."

"Is that so?"

"Yes, that's so," Leandra said, her tone stern and her blue eyes stormy.

"I think the Queens made an exception, seeing as how these men are our guests, and we have welcomed them with Milk from the Breast of the Mother," Penny interjected, before things got out of hand. She was about to tell the guests it would not do to keep her mother waiting any longer, when quickly approaching hoofbeats drew their attention.

Sagitta thundered up the short hill on her golden mare, her crested helmet glittering against her forehead, a wide, toothy grin showing between two bronze horse heads pressed against her cheeks. Behind her thundered Cyra's black mare, with no rider in sight. The ha-mazaan halted her *rhu-tasiya* dangerously close to them, so that both Leon and Theseus instinctively stepped back, but Leandra remained unfazed, her trust in her mother, and her mother's *rhu-tasiya*, thorough and immutable. Cyra's mare laid her ears back in unconcealed fury as she was forced to halt as well, and Penny kept a wary eye on the horse as she greeted Sagitta with a smile. The ha-mazaan peered at the men from under her helmet.

"King Theseus, Deileon," Sagitta nodded in greeting.

The men stared, and Penny could not blame them, as the woman was truly resplendent in her armor, with her sword strapped to the zoster at her waist, and the crest of her helmet towering high above her head.

"Ready, Little Lion?" Sagitta said, unfazed by the attention.

Penny hooked her hands under the girl's shoulders and lifted her up. Sagitta grunted as she hauled her daughter over the mare's withers.

"Ah, I should have guessed such a fierce girl was the—" Theseus began, but Leandra's sudden screech cut off the rest of his words.

"Ow! Your sword is too hot, Mama!"

Sagitta raised an eyebrow at the crown of her daughter's head, though she adjusted the belt around her waist to ensure the hot metal of buckle and sword hilt did not touch the young girl's sensitive skin. She ignored Theseus, and grinned down at Penny.

"Thank you. I would still be coaxing her away from the fighting if you hadn't agreed to help." The ha-mazaan's glance at Theseus and Leon was barely perceptible, but Penny saw the furrow that appeared between her brows as she stared at Penny meaningfully. "Do you wish me to delay until your escort arrives, Ishassara?"

Self-conscious under the curious stares of the two men, Penny realized she had not even thought of having a ha-mazaan present once she had caught sight of Leon. Not wanting to admit she wanted to be alone with at least one of them, she shook her head, smiling up at the woman confidently.

"I'm fine, Sagitta. We will make our way to the pavilion soon, to watch Cyra. Good luck out there," she said, then added, with a nod to Cyra's mare, "Whatever you're up to."

"I'm sure I will need it," Sagitta said, with one last glance at Theseus, then at the group of men still loitering at the bottom of the hill, before reining her *rhu-tasiya* in the direction of the steep mountain trail that led to the orchard. "I and my Little Lion shall give your cousin a Trial worth her sword, never doubt it. I shall see you at the Feast?"

At Penny's nod, the ha-mazaan tugged the black horse and whistled to her mare, and the four of them, three shades of gold and one running shadow, were off at a gallop, scattering the group of men in a frenzy of alarmed shouts, punctuated by Leandra's squeal of delight.

"I have never seen such fine horses," Leon said as they disappeared into the trees.

"Nor such fine girls," Theseus said, then gestured in the direction of the arena with a questioning raise of one brow. To her irritation, Leon withdrew slightly, granting the basileus the position of holding out his arm for Penny. She hesitated for the briefest of moments, but there was little option other than accepting his gesture, and she placed her fingers lightly on his arm as they turned in the direction of the royal pavilion.

"'Tis my dream," Theseus continued, his tone musing as they descended the slope, leaving the shade of the tree and entering full sunlight. At Penny's quizzical glance, he said, "I hope and pray to Athena for a daughter so lovely. She has promised me a special one, you see."

Penny smiled, not having any idea what he was talking about and not interested in learning, despite her duty as hostess to entertain. She glanced at Deileon from under her lashes as they made their way down the hill, but he was also watching Theseus intently, as though waiting for his turn in the conversation. She caught sight of her mother and both of her aunts, as well as Molpadia looking fresh from the baths, making their way toward them, and sighed, knowing her chances at private conversation with the young man of her intentions grew slimmer by the moment. She forced herself to pay attention to Theseus.

"Alas, I must find an equally lovely wife to give me such a prize, and that is proving an even more difficult task than any my friend Heracles has been given! All the best daughters of Attica's demes are being lost every year to the horrors of the Cretan monster, and the maidens left behind are not exactly fit to be the wife of a basileus, if you take my meaning. I am still seeking that special one. The one I have been promised."

Penny was about to ask what he meant, as he clearly wanted her to, when another voice, laced with contempt, spoke.

"You will find no wives in Themiscyra, if that is your intention."

12

SISTER-QUEENS

Molpadia did not miss the way Theseus' smile changed only slightly, sure she saw a glimmer of something quite like satisfaction flash across his bronzed face as his lips twisted in a sly smile.

"Forgive me, Molpadia, but that has not been my impression," he said. "Many of your women have been more than...ah...welcoming to our company, I can assure you."

Molpadia snorted indelicately, stopping directly in front of him with a challenging stance, her knuckles white on the spear she had lifted from a nearby tent as she planted it into the ground very near his sandaled toes. She was aware of Lyta and Antiope halting behind her, and thought she might have felt the sandaled toe of her wife kick her calf in warning, but she ignored it.

"My man," Molpadia's brow raised along with her scarred lip, "it is every ha-mazaan's right to take their pleasure as they choose, so do not take their advances to heart. Especially with thoughts of marriage. Either way, you and your men are not welcome here at the Trials."

"Untrue, fair lady," Theseus replied, his tone lightly mocking as he looked pointedly at her old wound as he called her fair. She let her lip curl at him, unfazed by his contempt. "I was invited here specifically by your queen. I cannot think you would deny a guest his rightful invitation?"

"He speaks truly," Antiope interjected calmly, stepping forward with a smile. "They are here by my invitation."

Molpadia's laugh was disbelieving. "You can't be serious. You wouldn't be so foolish as to break such a tradition for the sake of a man."

"Dia," Lyta said sternly.

"It will only benefit everyone for these guests to see what our ha-mazaans are capable of," Antiope replied easily. "Perhaps an alliance can even be discussed. There is no time like now to come together, don't you think?" Antiope smiled graciously at the entire assembly. Molpadia stood straight, turning to her sister-in-law.

"Are you serious, sister?" When Antiope simply raised her chin, her blue eyes resolute as they met Molpadia's, she sneered and turned back to Theseus, her dark eyes alight with anger.

"Did you know," Molpadia said, leaning her muscular body forward slightly and her voice falling into a conspiratorial tone, though it was loud enough for everyone to hear very clearly, "it is common practice for a Hearth Queen to lay with several men at once, or at least, several in the same week? That way, men do not feel the need to lay claim to our city with their foolish ideas of sons and heirs, because none can ever know who the father might be anyway."

Antiope gasped with indignation, while Theseus looked slightly taken aback, despite his best efforts to appear smug. Molpadia was aware Penthe-silea had been caught up in her jibe, and she regretted the girl's discomfort, but not enough to cease proving her point.

"So even if our own Queen should have her way with you, this does not make you, or any other man she might choose, special. It makes you *convenient*. I daresay she will move on quickly, anyway. There are so many of you to choose from, even if you are all as ugly and useless as a lame aurochs."

Theseus' face darkened and the wolfish light in his eyes turned dark.

"Dia," Hippolyta tried again, more sternly, but Molpadia barely even spared her wife a full glance. That Lyta was supporting this as well...she could feel another row coming on between them, and all because of these stinking, bull-chested brutes.

"I shall see to the preparations for the Savaran tattoos, so that you, my beloved Queens, may remain here with your new interests and not be bothered with such trivial matters as the day's Trials—or our ha-mazaans' futures. Now, if you will excuse me."

"Molpadia!" Antiope bit out warningly, but she was already moving toward the tents where the new Savaran were being tattooed.

"These men are here under guest rite!" Antiope called after her, face pale with anger, and her tone taking on a regal command. Molpadia paused, staring at both queens over her shoulder as Antiope continued. "You will not insult them, or me, without consequence."

"**N**o, no, Queen Antiope," Theseus interrupted, his voice once again smooth, and full of chagrin, "it is me who was in the wrong. I should not have been so uncouth as to mention your women's...free affections. One should not blame a guard dog for biting the heel of one who insults its master."

Penny sucked in her breath as Molpadia turned, every muscle in her body tight with anger and her hand moving down the shaft of her spear with dangerous intent. Lyta murmured a low warning, and for a moment, Penny was sure her aunt's consort would violate guest-right and harm a man under the protection of the Mother's Milk, but soon Molpadia's laugh barked out.

"Ha! I will give you that one, Theseus. I am a guard dog, you are right. But do not forget—*this* bitch may love her mistress, but she is no lap dog, as her face should remind you. She is trained to fight, and to kill. Nothing some lovesick pup says will stop her from defending what is hers."

With a pointed stare at Theseus, then at Heracles, Molpadia stalked away. Antiope was already tutting her apologies to Theseus, who waved a hand in languid unconcern.

"No, no. I can only admire the loyalty of one so ferocious. You are indeed lucky in the company you keep, to be so well protected by such loyal...guards."

Antiope's tight smile relaxed a little, the lines on her forehead smoothing as her brows eased their tension. She waved their party in the direction of the pavilion, saying,

"Please, join us. My niece has already begun her Trials, and will return to the arena shortly to fight for her place in the Savaran. You will want to see her perform, as she is one of the best riders we have. I trust my daughter has been keeping you well entertained so far?"

As her mother moved on with Theseus, her light tinkling laugh floating back to Penny, and Heracles immediately falling into step beside Lyta, Penny found herself escorting Leon to the stairs at the bottom of the podium. She was all too aware of the incredulous stares of the ha-mazaans all around as their eyes fell on the men in their midst, but she simply smiled at them and led Leon up the stairs, apologizing to the rest of the men that there was not enough room in the pavilion for everyone. As soon as they were in the relief of the awning's shade, she offered Leon his choice of *kimiz* or wine. He chose the latter, then grimaced when he realized it was not watered down as he was accustomed to, but he still thanked her politely, and she smiled at him warmly while they took their places behind the others. From below, one of the men called something up the stairs, though she could not make it out. A flicker of irritation crossed Leon's sun-weathered face.

"Ignore them, Princess," he said, his smile apologetic. "They are only jealous that they cannot be so close to you. It is truly an honor, and I wish my companions did not ruin it with their poor manners."

"Our ha-mazaans have already seen to it that they will be more mindful, I think," Penny said, amused, and as he glanced over the railing to see his fellow oarsmen being poked into silence by ha-mazaan spears and swords. "You do not need to call me Princess, though."

Leon turned back to her, his eyebrows flicking upwards. "Are you not the Queen's daughter? Did I mistake your words last night...?"

He was genuinely confused, but her careful tutelage overrode Penny's immediate desire to ease his embarrassment.

Use their weaknesses to your advantage, Antiope's voice chimed in her head.

She shrugged with what she hoped was casual indifference, though her body tingled with awareness with his body so close to hers. Even the hair on her arms stood to attention, as though reaching for him. She wanted to feel the touch of his skin again. For his hands to touch hers. For his thick arms to be around her waist, pulling her close. She shivered at the idea, her easy words belying the increasing tumult inside her belly.

"I am sure it is what you might call it, in your western lands. But here, I am called Ishassara. My cousin, Cyra, is going to be officially declared Ishassara for the Defender's Throne tomorrow, if all goes well today," she added.

"*Ishassara*," Leon repeated, the word an awkward lisp on his tongue. His eyes probed hers with interest. "My sisters will be most intrigued to learn this term. We are far more boring with our titles in Thessaly. My father is *Tagus*, and my mother carries no title other than wife. Nor do my sisters. It will be my older brother, Autolykos, who inherits after my father. I am simply a lowly third son," he finished, his eyes twinkling down at her.

"Never lowly, I can see," Penny replied with what she hoped was perfect ease, and fanned herself with the pheasant feathers, sending tendrils of hair across her bosom for his eyes to follow.

An Ishassari will certainly please my mother as first choice for my Alsanti, she thought, pleased, and then squelched an immediate pang of guilt as Sylviu's hazel eyes came to mind. Her mother was right. Choosing a stranger she would never need to see again would be less complicated.

Leon watched her fan trace lazily through the air for a moment, then looked to the front of the pavilion, where both queens were deep in conversation with Heracles and Theseus. He cleared his throat before saying with careful, tentative words, "If you will forgive my curiosity, Ishassara, why does your city have two queens? Which one has the final say?"

"The final say?"

"Yes. Which one makes the decisions? Enforces the laws? Would it not become very confusing for the common people, with two of them overruling each other all the time?"

Penny tipped her head thoughtfully, and saw the way his eyes followed the movement, followed the line of her neck to where it disappeared inside the collar of her robe. Her confidence surged, and her shyness lessened. For the first time in her life, she understood her mother's meaning of how easy it was to sway a man in her favor. She could bring this man to her chambers this very evening, this very hour, if she chose, and there was a very persuasive, very urgent part of her that was adamant that was exactly the course she should be choosing. She raised a hand to her throat, plucked a loose strand of hair from her bare, sticky skin, and twirled it with slow, deliberate circles. Leon's eyes followed every movement, as a starving cat might stare at a vat of fresh cream. She smiled.

"The roles of sister queens are clearly established. Our Hearth Queen is caretaker of all, provider of all, Mother of all. She is Matar Kubileya's handmaiden. Her Spirit made Flesh. My mother oversees the ha-mazaan's daily lives—the music and song in the Moon Hall, the provision and storage of the city's food, the health and welfare of the children and the *attas*—the grandmothers who no longer wish to join in battle, so instead take care of younger children whose *matars* still fight—" she explained, when her word did not seem to translate into the Achaean language, "the breeding of robust horses and sheep, and dogs to care for them, and, of course, the tending of the sacred Flame, the heart of our city."

Penny gestured to Lyta, still deep in conversation with Heracles. "My aunt Lyta, as Defending Queen, is then free to train new ha-mazaans in the ways of battle, as well as the horses that have been bred for their protection. Her role is to defend the city, the children, the *attas*, the refugees who seek safety here, and most especially, the Hearth Queen. It is the Defending Queen's duty to protect and defend what the Hearth Queen builds and maintains. These are the roles myself and my cousin will fulfill. There is no confusion."

She smiled, and though Leon nodded, his face betrayed a hesitant confusion.

"So...you do not fight with sword and axe, or ride horses with such recklessness, as these ones do?" He gestured to the ha-mazaans entertaining the crowd as they waited for Cyra and her fighting partner to return from the forest for their last Trial. She had been disappointed to miss the first stage of her cousin's fight, but there was a contagious thrill of anticipation in the air as the entire city focused on the return of their future Ishassara.

Penny should have told him about her vow, but something in her wanted him to admire her, or perhaps look at her with that same awe she could see in the men's faces when they looked at the other ha-mazaans. "I will never be called to battle, but I am skilled in the hunt, as any Hearth Queen must provide for the people. I can ride and shoot a bow with the best of them."

"I am sure you are skilled in a great many things, Ishassara," Leon said earnestly, and the flush of heat overtook Penny's body once more.

"So you are to be Hearth Queen when your mother dies?" he continued.

Penny nodded, then slowly smiled. It was a secretive, inviting curve of her lips, and she watched with satisfaction as Leon's eyes followed every movement, before leaning toward him in the most subtle of ways to say softly,

"I will fulfill my right to the Hearth Throne as soon as I bear a daughter," she said. "I just need to find the right father…"

She could not fathom what made her so bold, but it was undeniably thrilling to see the way his eyes sparked, to hear the way his breath caught as he took in the meaning of her words. For a moment, his face was a mask of astonishment, and Penny wondered if she had been too forward, too brash in assuming he would welcome such talk, but after the briefest of glances toward the back of Theseus' head, then at the men below the podium, his eyes met hers with a new intensity, an eager intimacy that left no doubt he was interested.

"Is it true, then, that you and the other…ha-mazaans," he was careful with the word, "are free to choose who you…er…engage with?"

Penny quelled a satisfied smirk, quickly transforming it into a dimpled smile while peeking mischievously at him through her lashes. His eyes were drawn to her cheek like a bee to honey.

"We are free to choose anything and everything we desire. It is why the ha-mazaans choose this life," Penny said, arching one eyebrow and widening her smile a fraction more. His eyes followed it so easily Penny almost felt guilty. "I will admit that right now, I desire…" she broke off the insinuation at exactly the moment his face betrayed an eager, desperate hope, and finished, "to watch my cousin excel at her final Trial. It is beginning!"

The dismay on Leon's face was comical, but also thrilling. Penny felt an internal lightness, an elation of her senses as the full effect of her own feminine power came to the forefront, even as Cyra careened into the arena on her black mare to the cheers of hundreds of ha-mazaans.

"I hope you will join me at tonight's celebration feast?" Penny said, as Cyra deftly turned the horse at full gallop without the aid of bit or bridle. Leon, his attention torn away from the spectacle, gave Penny his full attention, accepting her invitation with gracious eagerness.

Penny smiled, barely noticing as Cyra stood on the mare's cantering back and sped around the arena to the delighted cheers of every onlooking man and woman. She was pleased with this new plan. She would take this man to her bed soon, perhaps even tomorrow, when the moon was ripe and most auspicious for conceiving a daughter. She could begin her Alsanti under the full Sturgeon moon, and by this time next year, she would have a daughter to secure her place on the Hearth Throne. She would make her mother proud.

13

SAVARAN TATTOOS

Glaukia was working on Prothoe's tattoo when Molpadia stalked into the stiflingly hot tent, thin braid still dripping from her cold dip in the crowded river, though she was hot enough with fury to go back again and drown a few of the mouth-breathers who had littered the shoreline looking for a show. Cannabis smoke hung thick in the air to ease the sting of the bone needles, and both the heat and the scent hit Molpadia like a mule's kick where she was already tense from her argument with that rat Theseus.

"Ugh," she spat, eyes adjusting from the blaring sun to the dim interior. Prothoe sat on the low stool, her wrist extended for the mark of the Savaran, and she met Molpadia's eyes with a smile that was both proud and pained. Leya hovered nearby, awaiting her own mark that would show the world she had left her days of being Xanharaspa behind her. Leya smiled as well, though her eyes held a bit of fear in them, likely remembering Molpadia's axeblade seeking her throat.

Glaukia lifted her own scarred brow at Molpadia, their faces nearly mirror images of each other, even down to their battle wounds. Sometimes Molpadia wondered if her older sister had done it on purpose, to keep their sameness intact, though they could not have been more different in every other way.

"What's got you so worked up? Did Prothoe here make a fool of you today, or was it Leya?"

Molpadia ignored her taunting, striding to the near corner to pour water over her hands from a pitcher and basin, though they were likely still clean enough from her quick swim. What could have been a relaxing cool-down had been much quicker than she would have liked, with nearly a hundred men watching her from the beach. One of them had been within spitting distance from her in the river, soothing fresh lash marks along his back. She had paid him no more mind than the rest, but had cut her ablutions short once she had spotted Penthesilea walking alone with a group of men, and so close to the arena. To find out that Antiope had broken every tradition by inviting any of them to witness their Trials was still sticking in her throat almost as much as her memory of the way Lyta's face lit up when that lion-hatted man smiled at her.

Drying her hands with a clean piece of linen, she turned back to the others, motioning for Leya to sit on the second stool. Leya sat, extending her own arm, as Molpadia picked up the bundle of wrapped needles, dipping them in the nearby oxgall and walnut ink mixture. Leya gasped and flinched back when the first needles punctured her fine skin, though she already had eight seasons of moon marks on her arms. Molpadia scowled for her to stop squirming, though guilt made her second poke gentler, as she reminded herself these young women were not the object of her wrath, and neither was her sister.

"It's bad enough that Lyta allows the one with crazy eyes to moon all over her, and laughs at everything he says, but now Antiope thinks she is going to make an alliance with these buffoons," she muttered finally, ducking her head closer to Leya's arm as the ink began to obscure the marks she had already made.

"Oh?" Glaukia said. "For trade?"

"I can't imagine why she would need to break every tradition this city has maintained for a hundred years by bringing men to the Trials, insisting they need to see our ha-mazaans in action, if it were only to procure a better price for olive oil," she said scathingly.

"She invited men to the Trials?" Glaukia repeated, her eyebrows rising, but she went back to her task quickly enough. "Hmm. I suppose it can't hurt."

"It can't?" Molpadia snapped, and Leya flinched again. She grasped the ha-mazaans arm with biting fingers and glared her into stillness before continuing. "I beg you to tell me what good it's going to do."

Glaukia shrugged, wiping blood and ink from Prothoe's nearly complete tattoo and inspecting her work with a considering eye. Her tone was too light, too unassuming when she answered, and Molpadia's frown only deepened.

"I think any opportunity to welcome men and let them see we are not the man-hating, boy-eating killers they have come to think us is a good thing, yes? Some of them are very fine. Daughters, maybe even sons by them, would be a great boon to our population."

Molpadia left off torturing Leya to gape at her sister. "Why is every woman in this place so Goddess damned stupid when it comes to these Achaeans? You want a hundred ha-mazaans to become *matars* at the same time, so that we don't have a functional Savaran left to protect anyone at all? What are you even suggesting?"

Glaukia had the grace to at least flush, though she did not meet her sister's eyes. "I'm suggesting Antiope has the canniest mind I know, and she always has the best intentions for all ha-mazaans, not just the ones who wish to spend their days forgetting men exist at all."

Molpadia huffed a curse and an incredulous laugh in one sound, and returned to her task. Leya's white face let her know she needed to take a gentler hand, and she tried, but it was so Goddess damned frustrating to see every woman turn into a mare in heat as soon as they saw a set of thick thighs and some oar-roughened fingers.

"It's all well and good to lay with them, fuck them so they forget why they came here—though Goddess knows I am still trying to figure that out, too, since Mel's vision seems a wisp in the wind—but at least my own sister should have some better sense than to think we can form any kind of alliance with a swarm of wasps who will always only have their own hive in mind. Our pretty Hearth Queen needs to think with the brains Kubileya gave her, not the sweet honey between her thighs."

14

FEAST

Even with the setbacks of having hundreds of people swarming around her, the daunting, often frustrating task of overseeing the Xanharaspas in their kitchen duties, and the watchful eyes of gossiping attas, Penny found herself smiling uncontrollably as Leon remained at the forefront of her mind. More than once, she caught herself grinning like a fool, but she did not mind. Not even burnt hazelnut and ruined oat cakes could distract her from the thrill of it all. She was going to begin her Alsanti. Maybe even tonight. For sure before the full Sturgeon Moon began its waning.

The Xanharaspa responsible for leaving the nuts and cakes too long in the ovens cast her a sidelong glance of confusion as Penny smiled and dismissed their negligence with an unconcerned wave of her hand, caught up in a daydream of Leon's lips exploring her body, and did not notice when the confused girl scurried away. When she finally took her seat at the raised table, at the opposite end from a triumphant Cyra and Melanippe, Penny still could not hide her grin, but as she scanned the already seated guests while the Hall awaited the arrival of the sister-queens, she did not see Leon among them. When a large group of men entered, escorted by ha-mazaans on all sides, there was only one face she recognized, and her smile faltered at the heat in his gaze. Brekko walked with stiff strides behind the others, his eyes fixed on her face, the animosity there making her stomach clench. She gave no indication she recognized him, though, and moved her eyes over him without pause. Leon was not with them.

At one point, Toxaris came to whisper in her ear the news that Antiope wished for the feasting to begin after the guest-rite had been formally declared in front of the gathered ha-mazaans. Penny thanked the ha-mazaan distractedly, her gaze still focused on the doors, hoping Leon would appear, and she did not even notice when the ha-mazaan left for her own table.

When her mother finally entered beside Theseus, and her aunt Lyta beside Heracles, with Molpadia trailing behind with her customary grim expression darkened further as she glared at the lion pelt covering Heracles' head and shoulders, Penny's smile finally slipped. Everyone had arrived except Leon. Worry that she had made the wrong move, driven the man away with her forward behavior made Penny fret, and she sipped her *kimiz* with nervous impatience, scanning the doorway and the crowd again and again for his face, noticing twice that Brekko had taken a seat with a clear view of her table, but she could not bother to care about his pouting face. She listened with half an ear as her mother performed the formal welcome of the guests, swearing an oath of Mother's Milk for a second time as they exchanged cups of *kimiz* in front of the entire Hall.

Once the platters of food were brought out by Xanharaspas, the olives and cheeses and hazelnuts freshly roasted just moments before being loaded onto the trenchers, and the lamb and mutton still sizzling in their rich oil and spices, but still with no sign of Leon, the bubble of excitement inside Penny's abdomen deflated with slow, agonizing pinpricks of humiliation. She paid no attention to the food, though it had been her own work that had gone into ensuring the offerings would be the best Themiscyra had ever experienced. Her spirits were not buoyed by the exclamations of delight that arose from men and women alike in the crowded Hall as they tasted succulent pig and tender roasted apple, or the rich cheeses cured with salt and smoke. All her attention was focused on how naïve she had been. How utterly foolish. She should have known his imagined attraction to her was too good to be true. Why would someone like Leon ever look twice at her, when there were hundreds of thrilling women in the city to catch his eye?

"Why the long face?" Molpadia said in her ear, and Penny flinched. She had not even noticed the ha-mazaan sit next to her on the bench.

"Just thinking," Penny said, but the way her lips felt weighted with anchor-stones at the corners when she tried to smile was not lost on Molpadia. The ha-mazaan studied her carefully for a long moment, popping one of the too-hot pieces of lamb into her mouth and fighting to chew it without burning her tongue.

"I have a message to deliver. I was surprised to hear the news about you. Is it true?"

Penny's thoughts flew like starlings from a burning tree. "News?"

Molpadia whistled breath through her lips to alleviate the burning before she continued, speaking delicately around the hot meat. "Some rust-haired boy from Thessaly thinks his younger brother might have...hhhhaaaaa, that's hot....might have caught your attention."

Hope flared anew in Penny's breast. She gave an eager gasp as she turned to fully face Molpadia, the reaction causing the ha-mazaan's scarred eyebrow to lift in sardonic amusement.

"Oh, he was not imagining it, then?" She popped a cool olive into her mouth and chewed it much more slowly. "My, my, you do work quickly. Like mother like daughter, I suppose," Molpadia said, her eyes glancing off Antiope and back to Penny. Before Penny could ask what the ha-mazaan meant by that, Molpadia continued. "This boy—his name is something about a wolf? I tried to remember it for you, but all I can think of is wolf, though I can tell you his hair is red as a fox, and he has the spirit of one, too—well, Fox-spirit says his brother was put on guard duty for the ships this evening, and that he begs your forgiveness. Fox-spirit also says he and his brother are joining your mother's hunting party tomorrow, and they hope you are joining them, too. Fox-spirit says his brother is very eager to see you again."

"Oh, *thank* you, Dia!" Penny said, her grin once more irrepressible, but Molpadia did not soften her own mouth. There was a hard light in the woman's eyes as she frowned at Penny.

"Penthesilea, this is not wise, no matter if your mother—"

"I'm sorry to interrupt..."

Molpadia's mouth snapped closed as a young Xanharaspa danced at the edge of her vision, signaling for Penny's attention.

"What is it?" Molpadia said, turning an irritated stare on the girl. The Xanharaspa gulped, eyes wide, but Penny smiled at her encouragingly. She could not have been more than ten summers, not even a woman yet, and this evening's celebration would be the biggest feast the girl had witnessed in her entire life. Penny remembered well the pressure of one's first time serving such an event.

"We are already running low on *kimiz* for the evening. I hoped...the Storeroom is locked, and the Ishassara has the only other key, and Queen Antiope is...preoccupied...so..."

Penny immediately rose to follow the girl out of the Hall, making quick apologies to Molpadia but glad to flee the woman's undoubtedly dire, oft repeated warnings about men. She unlocked the storeroom for the Xanaharaspas, but once free of the noise and chatter, the clank of goblets, the raucous laughter of men and merry ha-mazaans in the Hall, Penny had no desire to return to the feast, especially now that she knew Leon would not be there. Instead, she sought the quiet sanctuary of her chambers, skipping over the stones in the floor as she slipped past the great double doors and up the stairs, her feet echoing the lightness in her heart. She peeked out of the casement toward the ships bobbing placidly in the water. The men who had declined their invitation to feast inside the Hall, or who had been ordered to stay behind and manage the ships, such as Leon, were gathered around a few meagre campfires. She wondered if he was down there, looking up at the palace, thinking of her.

No matter that she would not see him tonight. It was enough that she would see him tomorrow, and probably the next day. Maybe she could even convince Theseus and his odd friend Heracles to stay longer, since they seemed so enamored with their city. Maybe, by this time next week, she would look out at those campfires and think of Leon as the first man she fathered a child by. The first man to help her complete her Alsanti, and forever seal her future here in this city of ha-mazaans, as their Hearth Queen.

"**C**ome to take Lyta's *zoster* by force, he said, and you are just letting them lounge in our Hall with complete impunity," Molpadia hissed, forcing Lyta forward as she leaned behind her back to reach Antiope, uncaring that the subjects of their conversation were seated only a table length away. The men's hands were busy with fresh cheese and olives and hazelnuts, their fingers dripping with juices from roasted lamb and pork, their sanguine smiles begging to be wiped from their faces with the edge of her axe. But getting through to Antiope was like convincing a swan it was an ass, and the woman bared her lips in a smile equally as fierce as Molpadia's scowl.

"Perhaps you missed the part where I welcomed them with milk from Kubileya's own breast, Sister?" Antiope's tones were dulcet. "What would you have me do to punish their talk of war-belts and greedy uncles? Because so far, it's only that—*talk*. You heard Theseus swear his own vow just now, that none of his men will bring harm to the ha-mazaans. If they want a moldy, sweaty *zoster* as a token of their visit, I am sure Lyta has an extra one she can gift them. No one is waging war inside the Moon Hall."

But anyone that knew the unrufflable Hearth Queen could see she was as shaken as the rest of them. Molpadia could not fathom what was keeping both her and Lyta from forcefully ousting the men from the Hall this very instant. She could not decide who to be more incensed with: Antiope, for opening their gates to these swine, or Lyta, for continuing to make cow eyes at that oaf's stories as though they held any truths whatsoever, and were not the imaginings of an insane beast, even though he had just admitted they had intended to make war with their entire host just for the sake of Lyta's belt. Their admission alone should have been enough to rouse Lyta to action, and yet she was chewing her meat in mute, stubborn silence.

"Unless they are required to defend themselves," Mel said from Antiope's far shoulder, her voice low and calm. Molpadia sent a silent look of thanks for the support.

"What?" Antiope said with unrestrained irritation.

"They vowed peace, unless they were required to defend themselves," Mel repeated, staring pointedly at her sister. "A convenient way out of what I could only describe as an afterthought of a vow, especially in a city full of women armed to the teeth, wouldn't you say?"

Antiope's smile tightened as she shifted in her chair. Theseus took that moment to raise a cube of cheese towards their table before popping it into his mouth, nodding his appreciation of the delicious food, and he bared his teeth in a wolfish smile when he caught Molpadia's sneer.

"I would say you have become more like frightened *attas* than a fearless General and Defending Queen's noble consort," Antiope said, still staring straight ahead at the guest's table. "Let *me* take care of the guests in our city, and let Lyta make her deals with Heracles as she will. They have told us their intentions in good faith, and I have no intention of breaking my own sacred bond of the Breast to appease your heightened sense of anxiety, Mel, nor your unmitigated jealousy, Dia. Let it go. Please."

"It is not *jealousy*," Molpadia lied. She remained awkwardly positioned in her sideways lean until Lyta shifted to let her know she wished to end the uncomfortable arrangement. Molpadia straightened slowly, pausing near Lyta's ear to hiss, "I know violence makes you wet, woman, but this is insanity. *Veto* her!"

Lyta turned that chastising expression on her, and Molpadia's pent-up rage unfurled into an inferno so hot she was sure it would scorch the table under her tight fist.

"No need to be vulgar, love," Lyta said evenly. "I find the man and his stories entertaining, no more."

"How much entertainment do you need, wife? Are you really willing to trade our security for some stories of unkillable lions and fools dancing for birds? Are you going to trust they have the honor of a gnat, let alone enough to hold them to their pathetic, ill-timed vows of peace? Think about the women *you swore an oath* to protect."

This time Lyta's eyes clouded with dark anger of their own. She leaned closer to Molpadia's face, her expression fierce. "Don't talk to me about my vows, woman. I am doing everything possible to ensure no blood is shed in my city. Neither men's blood nor ha-mazaan. I have taken care of it. Now either buckle your belt and live with it, or go soak your head in the Terme until you cool down, because I am not going to sit here and listen to you whine just because I enjoy the company of someone who has at least had the courage to get out of his village and see something of the world, maybe even make a name for himself. Mother's tits, maybe I will enjoy a little more than just his conversation, with the way you are acting right now."

The Hall suddenly became too loud, too crowded. Molpadia could barely breathe for the fury Lyta's threat made her feel, but Themiscyra's

Defending Queen had already spent her anger, and she smiled ruefully into Molpadia's livid face.

"I didn't mean that last part, Dia. Come on, you have to admit his stories are fun, no?"

"No."

Molpadia chugged the last of her wine in three long gulps, then shoved away from the table. Lyta frowned up at her, then patted the bench be-seechingly.

"Sit down, Dia. Ant is not going to be persuaded by your scowl."

"She is not going to be persuaded by anything but *you*, Lyta, but you're too busy fawning over that great aurochs of a man to care."

Lyta's eyes clouded with hurt, but then they turned stubborn, and censorious. Molpadia clung to her anger the way a beggar clings to his first meal of the week.

"I will sleep with the horses tonight, in case you want our chambers free for other things," she said, with a pointed look at the ridiculous mane of that lion the man never took off, before plucking an entire rhyton of wine off the table. She turned on her heel and stalked away, wine in hand, the sound of Lyta's command to stay stoking her fury further. Ha-mazaans and men scurried from her path as she bore down on them, shoving the great doors of the Hall more forcefully than necessary, their crack of wood against stone in no way lessening the rage that had built to a seething, frothing tempest inside of her chest. She made her way blindly to the stables, the smell of them an immediate balm to the anger, the snuffle of mares safely in their stalls soothing her chaotic thoughts.

She kicked a mound of hay into submission, and turned to throw herself down on it. A scuffle that was neither hoof nor mouse caught in her ears. She turned, hand on the sword at her hip, cursing herself for a fool that she had left her axe in their chambers. Chambers which were likely soon to be occupied by a bull and a foolish mare in heat.

"It's just me," a familiar voice said.

Molpadia's scowl did not ease. She jerked the sword free, rhyton spilling wine into the hay as she held it carelessly to the side with one hand, and aimed her blade into the speaking shadows.

"You should not be here, Hanassa."

Ossy's son emerged from those shadows, his frown matching hers as he raised an eyebrow at the blade waving in his face.

"Neither should they."

She grunted, but did not lower her weapon. Her eyes fixed on the gleam of bronze at his hip, and her fury doubled.

"You flaunt our Laws, son of Galatae? You think because our shores crawl with vermin that you can be as one with them?"

"I am trying to protect what they have come to destroy," the boy said, his eyes flashing the same color as his forbidden sword in the dim light of the last flickering torch.

Molpadia laughed shortly. "What will a pig-herder do that our Savaran cannot? Antiope and Hippolyta both ordered you out of this city yesterday. I would not tempt my hand, boy. Leave, or I will mete out the Queens' justice here and now."

Sylviu watched her for a long time, until she wondered if he would make her follow through on her threat, though she held no ill will toward Oistrophe's son.

"They should not be here," he said, and something in his quietly stubborn resistance sent a shiver down Molpadia's stiff spine. She waved the end of her sword at him, trying to dispel the tension through the blade.

"Only the Queens and the Goddess Herself know why they are not drowned in flaming ships at the bottom of our river, boy, but that is neither here nor there. If you are not gone from this place when I am finished this jug of wine, I will set the hounds on you and watch them tear your limbs from your body, before I hang what is left of you from the bridge. I do not care if you are Ossy's son, or the King of the Otherworld Himself—to disobey my queen is to die. Now go."

She thought perhaps he might be stupid enough to pull that pathetic sword on her, but he finally turned on stiff legs and shouldered his way into the night. She followed him, taking an awkward gulp of wine from the great jug, using both hands to lift it as she watched him go. His mousy head turned to see if she watched as he made his way over the bridge. She smiled grimly, wine dripping down her chin, and lifted her sword as a promise, and soon he was gone into the night, the nearly full moon lighting his long path home.

When she turned back to the stables, to her chosen bed of musty hay and skittering mice, she took another long draught of strong wine, then another. She did not sheathe her sword, but rested its length next to her, hand resting on the blade as she might have held Lyta's thigh before sleep. She tried not to think about her love following through on taking that man to their bed. Of the idea she might not be enough for one such as her glorious, brave, perfect Defending Queen. She tried not to think of anything at all, but the wine was not strong enough, and she could only try to end the thoughts by drinking more of it, and hoping this nightmare would be over soon, but the moon had long since disappeared behind the distant mountains when the blackness finally claimed her.

15

ZOSTER

Plans of what she would say on the hunt, what she would wear, how she would kiss Leon, or whether he would kiss her first consumed Penny's thoughts and stole her sleep as she lay on the thick, soft mattress she shared with her mother. She was still wide awake when Antiope finally joined her in their chambers, and Penny sat up excitedly, eager to share her plans, but Antiope paced from the window to the small table that held her brushes and jewels, then back to the window again, her eyes on the campfires below.

"Mother, did you hear me?"

Antiope turned from the window, a distracted smile overtaking her features as she murmured an apology. Penny climbed from their shared mattress and repeated her request for a night of privacy in their shared chambers, with far more impatience than the first time.

"Here? Tomorrow night?"

"I thought you wanted me to begin my Alsanti?" Penny said, her enthusiasm snuffed under the wet blanket of her mother's response. Antiope's eyes had a faraway, worried expression, but soon she shook her head, an automatic smile clearing the fog of concern from her face. She put her hands on Penny's shoulders, looking into her eyes with earnest sincerity.

"I do. I do want you to know the wonder of having a daughter, Pen. I want you to know the immense, unbounded love a mother has for her child, as I have for you. I just..." she trailed off, the crease of worry reappearing between her brows. She continued slowly, searching for the words, the orange light of the beeswax candle casting strange shadows across her high cheekbones. "You left the Hall tonight before Theseus made his confession."

"His confession?" Penny's stomach gave a nervous flip.

Antiope did not answer immediately, dropping her hands from Penny's shoulders and moving to the small vanity next to the casement. She sat, and Penny climbed out of bed and moved obediently behind her, taking up the tortoiseshell comb and running it through her mother's beautiful blonde waves. When no more information was forthcoming, however, Penny prodded,

"What was his confession? That he is in love with you already, and hopes to make you his wife? That he wants to be the first King of the ha-mazaans?"

Antiope huffed a small laugh, but it was another long moment before she answered.

"He told us that Heracles had come here intending to wage war with our ha-mazaans. Just as my sisters suspected."

Penny's hand stilled, the brush caught in the fine strands of gold hair about her mother's shoulder blades.

"War? With Themiscyra?"

"Mmm," Antiope said.

"But...why?" Penny asked, dumbfounded.

"For glory, I can only assume."

"Why would they even tell you that? And if that was their intent, why did they not attack as soon as they arrived? Surely they can't think they have a chance against ha-mazaans now that they are completely surrounded? What about guest-rite?" She realized she had begun to sound like Leandra, but there were so many unanswered questions. She shook her head. "It doesn't make any sense."

Antiope also shook her head, her hair swaying under the brush.

"Heracles has come for Lyta's belt, apparently. His Uncle's daughter told him a story that whoever wears the zoster blessed by Otrera has the Mother's authority to rule the ha-mazaans, and the silly girl has demanded to have the belt for herself. Lyta has agreed to give him the one she wears, to keep the peace. But you're right. It doesn't make sense, thinking they could make war on us, and not pay dearly. I never thought..."Again her mother shook her head, her body vibrating with a slight shiver, as a horse feeling a fly might shake it away. "Anyway. They are here now, and they are under the oath of guest-rite, as you say. They will bring no harm to us, and we will bring no harm to them. This is sworn. No man would be foolish enough to risk the wrath of the Goddess by breaking such an oath. I have made sure Lyta and Melanippe—and Molpadia— remember this as well."

Penny resumed brushing her mother's hair, but she had only made one full pass through the thick strands when her original subject for the evening conversation returned to her mind.

"But what about the hunt tomorrow? Leon is supposed to come. I thought it would be a good time to...get to know each other. He wasn't...? No...Leon and the others were not planning on making war with us, surely?"

"I cannot see them all joining a mission to the other side of the world when they knew nothing about its purpose," Antiope said matter-of-fact-ly.

There was another long silence, as each of them thought their own thoughts, until finally, Antiope said,

"This boy, Deileon. Knowing what we know, I think it is best you keep your intentions secret from the other women. The less the ha-mazaans know about you beginning your Alsanti, the better. Especially if you are not leaving the city, as is tradition. So you may bring him to your bed, yes, but I want you to keep your zoster on. Lyta gave you that belt for protection. And of course you must always have one of the ha-mazaans with you. At all times. Do you understand?" Antiope's voice was uncharacteristically stern. "You must be protected, so find one you trust to keep your secret well. Now that we know these men came here with their own intentions, you are not to venture out alone with any of them, even Deileon."

Penny uttered an astonished laugh, her hand going to the thick, finely tooled leather around her waist. She had assumed a ha-mazaan would be with her at all times, even if she brought Deileon into her bed, but now she was expected to keep her clothes on as well?

"I cannot seduce a man fully clothed! It will already be challenge enough to seduce him with a ha-mazaan axe lurking in the shadows. And which woman am I supposed to pick? Once one of them knows, the entire palace is going to know. It is just how this place works. I can't keep my Alsanti a secret forever."

"You can do whatever you need to, and you will," Antiope said firmly, swiveling on the stool to face Penny squarely, her gaze unwavering. Even with her mother seated, Penny felt small and childish under her queen's regal stare. "Secrets are not as hard to keep as you think. Even here. If you wish to begin your Alsanti with this prince from Thessaly, it will be with a guard you trust, and with your belt. Or, it will be with Ossy's boy next week, or with another man from Galatae, or Paphlagonia, or Hatti, or Wilusa in another year, or five years. If you wait for those boys, you may not need the zoster, or even a guard. It is your choice. But, you *will* do as I say, daughter. There is no room for discussion. Now," Antiope said, taking the brush from Penny's hand, her smile adding a gentle ending to words that were hard as stone, and just as immovable, "Your turn. I will braid your hair for the hunt tomorrow, when you can show this Deileon just how fine a rider you are, and just how much of an honor you grant him by taking a daughter from his loins."

16

THE STOREROOM

T he next morning, though it was still well before dawn, Antiope was dressed and heading out the door before Penny had even pulled her riding trousers from the heap of clothes beside their bed. Veti, her mother's hunting hound, lounged on the foot of the bed, barely raising her head to watch her mistress go. Antiope paused at the door, looking over her shoulder, her hair bound in the loose braid she generally only wore when hunting in the fall, or lambing in the spring.

"The two laziest creatures in this city, I'm sure," she said, though she smiled fondly at both dog and daughter. "Pen, would you mind fetching the skin of Chaldesian wine from the Storeroom? I have a mind to discuss trade matters with the Basileus, and he doesn't seem fond of mare's milk. I'm hoping wine is more to his taste. Let's give him our best, to sweeten the deal, hmm? Maybe you can moisten your own lover's lips with a little taste of it, too. Bring Veti when you come."

Penny's agreement was muffled as she pulled her hunting tunic over her head, and by the time she emerged, her mother was gone, headed to the stables to be the first mounted and ready. Penny fiddled with her belt and the straps of her leather sandals and the fit of her plain green tunic, checking and double checking her hair and lips and waist in the polished silver, before finally deciding none of it was ever going to be quite right for a meeting with her potential lover, but it would have to do.

"Heel, Veti."

She made her way quickly through the palace to the main storehouse, encountering only a few early risers on her way, their eyes sleepy after a long night of drinking or entertaining themselves with their guests. The doors of the storehouse towered over her as she approached, the orbs of the Great Mother's breasts centered within each panel glinting copper in the torchlight flickering nearby. One torch was missing, so Penny took the remaining one from its bracket, inspecting the polishing of those copper breasts with a critical eye. The reminders of Kubileya's constant provision for Her daughters spanned as far as Penny could spread her arms, while the great rings of twisted bronze threaded through the nipples were as thick as her wrists. Normally she had to tug on them with the full weight of her body to pull the door open. This morning, though, one of those doors was already ajar, likely left that way by an inattentive Xanharaspa the evening before. Likely the same careless one who had forgotten to replace the torch. She sighed, and reached for the nipple ring. The hinges creaked under the weight of the heavy wood, the sound echoing into the hallway behind her and into the darkness of the deep, cavernous opening ahead as the door swung wide enough to let her slip through.

Veti's ears perked with sudden interest, and her nose twitched in the direction of the cellar stairs, hidden in the dark recesses of the room. A soft clang sounded in the depths of the cavern.

"A very large mouse, hmm?" she said softly, placing a reassuring hand on the hound's sleek shoulder. The hound wagged her tail, tongue lolling, then stilled again as another clang sounded up the stairwell. Veti padded to the top of the stairs, ears perked.

Adding rodent control to her list for the Xanharaspas, Penny lifted the skin of Chaldesian wine from its hook, then whistled Veti to heel, but the hound whined softly, her attention on the dark stairs.

"You will have mighty boars or maybe even a stag to hunt today, Veti. Much nobler game than a poor mouse."

Penny turned away and made her way out the door. She had only just secured the torch in its bracket when Veti barked from inside. Just as Penny was about to repeat her command, a figure rushed from the shadowed doorway, barreling into Penny's shoulder so that she slammed against the stone wall, and knocking the wineskin from her hand.

"Hey!"

But the figure kept running down the shadowed corridor, the long cloak they wore clutched tight around their head, so that Penny never caught a glimpse of their face. Veti skittered out of the room soon after, but

Penny caught the hound's collar, worried the dog would meet mischief if she pursued the intruder. They watched together as the last flap of cloak disappeared into the shadows of the palace corridors. Penny stooped to retrieve the fallen wineskin.

"Princess Penthesilea," a man's voice echoed hollowly in the long corridor.

Veti growled, this time low and menacing, and Penny whirled, the wineskin clutched close. A shadow emerged from the end of the corridor. The Basileus of Athens approached. The light of the torch revealed Theseus dressed in borrowed clothing for the hunt, the leather tunic and boots covering his feet and legs appearing to be part of either Molpadia's or Melanippe's old hunting gear.

"King Theseus," Penny replied warily, placing a calming hand on Veti's raised hackles as she remembered her mother's warnings. She had not thought to need an escort inside the palace, but her mother's warning rang clear in her mind, and Veti was on high alert.

"Should you not be in the stable yard with the others?" she said.

"I'm embarrassed to tell you, Princess," Theseus said without hesitation, moving closer to her before ducking his head in a fine display of abashed contrition, "that I had an escort, yet another divine being, though not half as beautiful as you, I must say. However, I somehow became separated from her, and I am now completely, hopelessly lost. I was trying to find my way to your stables, but I seem to have passed the very same door three times over. This palace is a labyrinth!" he finished, shaking his head ruefully.

"It is grand," Penny agreed slowly. "The stables are just beyond that wall," she motioned, and began walking toward the door which would lead them to the courtyard where the hunting party assembled. Veti placed herself between them, her hackles still high as they walked, her head low to the ground as though she would snake her long neck and chew the man's ankles at any moment. "You must have walked right past the entrance to get to this place," Penny continued, but in her mind, she was trying to recall the mysterious figure she had just encountered. Had it been Theseus? But no, the mystery person had been taller than this man, and not nearly as broad across the shoulders. Still, how the man had made his way inside the palace without an escort was suspicious at best, especially if he had admitted to bringing intentions of violence to this place just the evening before.

"Here, let me carry that for you," Theseus said, taking the flagon of wine from her before she could protest.

"Thank you," she said politely, the response as automatic as it was insincere.

"I see you are dressed like one of them today, Princess. I did not think to see you in anything but your beautiful himation. And yet, even with those strange leg coverings, one could never mistake one of your ethereal beauty for the wild women so abundant in this place." His smile belied the insults to the ha-mazaans, but soon his eyes slid over her breasts to her waist. "That is a fine belt. What animal is it made of?"

"Er—griffon, I would think," Penny answered, her mind scattered by Theseus' quick change of subjects, and uneasy with this turn in particular. Antiope's warning rang louder in her mind, and she quickened her steps.

"Ah, of course," was all Theseus said. Then, "Your mother informed me this palace was built by the Cyclopes according to your grandmother's instructions. Do you know what plants they used to make their acid that cuts the stone? I have yet to find the secret, though I have seen it done. Remarkable, truly!"

The man walked with an easy stride next to her, rambling on in his smooth, unguent tone about the wonder of the palace construction and his amazement at her grandmother's architectural achievements, but apparently, all of his questions were rhetorical, as he never paused to hear any answer Penny might have. She smiled politely and murmured when it seemed appropriate, but her mind was already ahead of them, in the stable yard, where she would soon see Leon. Before they could go through the low archway into the stable yard, however, they were intercepted by Tekmessa, the *zizenti's* shaved head and blue tattoos on her forehead covered in a thin sheen of sweat, though the morning was still cool with fog.

"Ishassara," the priestess said in her soft voice, and both Penny and Theseus halted. "My grandmother requests your assistance with Areto."

"Now?" Penny asked stupidly, casting a glance over her shoulder at the horses and people gathered in the yard. She thought she saw the bright copper of Leon's hair, but it was soon lost in the crush of horses and men trying to mount, while ha-mazaans held the leads of the geldings selected for the day's outing.

"Her pains have been too long now, nearly a full day already," Tekmessa said, though her smile was apologetic. "The babe is breech. Marpe would like you to assist, to learn the technique for a Footling. I have already told Queen Antiope you will not be joining the hunt."

Sighing in defeat as all hopes of spending the day with Leon fled, Penny nodded a rueful acceptance. She had not expected the most difficult part of seducing an Achaean to be the women in her own city, nor her duties as Ishassara, but so it was. She cast one more hopeful look into the yard. Leon was mounted on a slow, elderly gelding most often used as a pack horse, but he was not looking in her direction, and could not see her disappointed face.

"Ah, the mysteries of women's bodies are indeed too much for a man," Theseus interjected, though when Penny looked back to him, he was also looking in Leon's direction. His eyes slid to hers as his slow smile made an appearance. "I will sorely miss your radiance on the hunt, Princess, but I am hopeful you and I can become better acquainted this evening. Perhaps you would like a tour of the ships? I will even have young Deileon escort you, if that is your wish. And you, Priestess, are also welcome."

An uncomfortable fluttering squirmed in her belly. The man looked at her as a wolf looks at a lamb, and it set her teeth on edge. But she only said, "I would be honored, Basileus. May the Goddess bless your hunt today."

Theseus smiled, slow and wide, that wolfish gleam brilliant in his blue eyes. "May She guide me to my heart's fiercest desire, Princess."

And with that odd prayer ringing in her ears, she allowed Tekmessa to lead her away, their steps hurried in the direction of the birthing lodge deep within the central hub of the palace, and all of Penny's plans with the future father of her daughter gone astray.

17

BREECH

"You did say....ahhhhhhhhhrrrggg....you said the girl would...hit...hit the ground...running," Areto panted, forcing her words through clenched teeth as another contraction rippled through her body.

Penny smiled, but concentrated on her fingers wrapped tight around the babe's legs, still deep inside the ha-mazaans body, its impossibly small ankles slippery with blood and slime. She and Tekmessa had spent much of the day inside the copper tub of water with Areto, trying to turn the babe in the womb, while Marpe barked orders and lent her many years of wisdom to the matter at hand, but the unborn infant stubbornly refused all of their administrations. Xanharaspas carried buckets of fresh water in and soiled water out every hour, but Areto had grown tired of the bath, insisting the babe was frightened of water and would not be born in the water. Now, she was on all fours, the dark skin of her naked body drenched with sweat, her hands coiled in the folds of linen spread over the thick straw of the floor in the birthing room, the three women gathered around her nearly as exhausted as she was.

Penny shivered as a breeze from the open windows, cast wide at the ha-mazaan's demand, traced its fingers along her own damp, naked back. Neither Penny nor Tekmessa had paused their tending of Areto to dress once they left the bath, and all three women were naked, sweating, and showing signs of fatigue.

"One more push, Areto," Tekmessa said, her soothing, lullaby voice strained with weariness.

"Aye, the little Footling is ready to run," Marpe said from her squatting position behind Penny's shoulder. "One more push, dear, and we can help with the rest."

94

Areto grunted, then howled. Penny grit her teeth at the animalistic roar, marveling the ha-mazaan could still summon the strength for such a sound, but it worked. The babe slipped further into her hands, both feet entering the world together.

"Yes!" Penny exclaimed, her laughter both frenzied and relieved. She used her shoulder to wipe the sweat from her forehead, not wanting to lose her grip on the babe's tiny legs. "Almost there, Areto. Again!"

Areto pushed again, howled again. The babe's knees showed now, though there was more blood than Penny thought normal.

"Good girl, good girl," Marpe murmured, her voice calm and gentle.

Penny was unsure if the *sivyeti* was praising her, or Areto. The birthing lodge was perhaps the only time the atta let her gentleness show, though no ha-mazaan, nor Penny for that matter, would ever be so naïve as to think the woman's star-iron core was any softer for it. A *siveyti's* role was to sew what was torn, mend what was broken, not coddle the pain endured in the process. But in the Birthing Lodge, Marpe's compassion always showed through, and it was here Penny had first realized the atta was not quite as ill-tempered as she made herself out to be.

Another contraction seized Areto's whole body, her thighs and back muscles rippling with the force of it. Blood pooled over Penny's hands, down the babe's toes, and Marpe clicked her tongue in Penny's right ear.

"No time to laze about now, Areto," the *sivyeti* said, suddenly stern. "Time to get this girl out, you hear me?"

Areto managed a scowl that was at once incredulous and furious as she glared under her armpit at the atta, her braid dragging on the ground as she contorted to see under her shaking arm. "You can go to—"

Her words were cut short by a gasp, and another contraction, and Penny grimaced as the ha-mazaan roared what sounded like a curse at both Marpe and Kubileya alike, but the babe slipped further into the world with the pressure, all the way to the hips.

"It's a girl!" Penny called out.

"No...shit," Areto grunted, but she had to drag heavy breaths to force any more intelligible words out. "You think...I would do all this...work...for a boy?"

Marpe grunted her approval, but Penny's excitement was soon over-shadowed by a new wave of blood that poured over her already red hands.

"Get it out," Marpe hissed in her ear. Penny glanced unsurely at the *sivyeti*. Marpe nodded encouragement, gesturing imperatively for Penny to pull.

"But—"

"Do it," the *sivyeti* demanded, as the blood pooled over Penny's knuck-les.

Alarmed, and with a sick feeling growing in her stomach, Penny turned her attention back to the babe, but her fingers slipped on the girl's mu-cous-covered, bloody skin. Areto's thighs were trembling with exhaustion. Her breath was ragged, and coming in groaning bursts. It was a sight Penny had seen numerous times in the lambing yard, and when the mares foaled every spring. There was too much blood.

"Okay, beautiful, this is it. You have to push, now. Okay? You can do it. All done soon." Tekmessa's soothing voice had taken up a steady rhythm at Areto's head, her hands smoothing over the woman's limp head and shuddering shoulders, both distracting and encouraging the ha-mazaan.

With the next contraction, Penny hooked her fingers as best she could around the babe's chubby thighs, and pulled. Suddenly, Marpe's hands were over hers, pulling harder than Penny would have ever dared, even with a foal or a lamb. Areto screamed, but Marpe did not ease the tension. Even Penny cried out, terrified they would inflict permanent damage to mother and child alike, but then the girl slithered into her hands, and Areto collapsed face down onto the lumpy ground, her sobs of relief and pain muffled in the wet linen and the steady, reassuring tones of the *zizenti's* praises.

Penny gazed down at the new daughter cradled in her hands, but the babe's scrunched, purple face made no sound. The cord, one end still inside Areto's womb, was wrapped around the babe's throat. The lump in Penny's stomach hardened.

"Turn her," Marpe commanded, and once more her hands were on Penny's, guiding her with swift practicality to place one hand on the infant's chest and flip the babe onto her forearm, as though she were a newly leavened log of fresh dough. A knife flashed. Penny marveled at the quickness of Marpe's old hands, gnarled from age and injury, but still nimble enough to fit the blade between neck and cord, and cut the thin, blue piece of flesh without a moment of hesitation. Penny turned the babe upright and crooked her little finger into the babe's mouth, clearing any mucus from her throat, but there were no cries, no coughs for air.

"Massage."

Penny did as the *sivyeti* instructed, pressing her fingertips into the tiny chest, but inside her throat were already hot tears of grief as she thought of all the hope and effort and struggle that had brought this moment to bear, only for this to be the outcome. She could hear Tekmessa chanting softly at Areto's head, singing prayers to Kubileya, and her own lips moved in unison. Areto moaned, turning to see the daughter she had birthed, though blood still seeped from between her thighs. She moaned again, louder, as her eyes took in the tiny, still, soundless form of her baby daughter.

In answer to Areto's moan, a tiny cry came from between Penny's palms. She gasped. The impossibly small face between her fingers screwed into mask of rage, and howled. Penny choked out an astonished laugh, her eyes meeting Marpe's with incredulous surprise as a second, more ferocious, infinitely more angry scream split the air. Marpe smiled with one side of her mouth, and motioned for Penny to place the babe on her mother's chest.

"She has your hair," Marpe said, as Penny moved to Areto's side. "A daughter to run as wild as you in the forest, Areto!" the atta finished proudly.

Penny gently placed the girl on Areto's sticky chest, and the ha-mazaan cradled her daughter with the light of a thousand suns shining in her tired eyes.

"And born on the eve of the full moon, no less," Tekmessa said, smiling. "Your daughter will be a powerful woman one day."

Penny sat back on her heels, marveling at the wonder of birth and life, at how close the girl had come to never joining them this side of the Gate, but at this mention of the full moon, she gasped, and looked up through the round hole in the ceiling of the Birthing Lodge, where the sky showed golden with evening light. She had completely lost track of time.

"I nearly forgot the ceremony," she said, climbing to her feet with weary determination. *And surely Leon will be back from the hunt by now*, she thought with a buzz of excitement adding fresh energy to her weary body, though she did not share the hope aloud. She collected her clothes from where they had been tossed before joining Areto in the bath, and pulled them on hastily, and slinging the belt over her shoulder for the short trip to the bathhouse. She would need to bathe this blood away before she could go in search of Leon, and before the Ishassara ceremony. Though Cyra would likely rejoice to see her cousin covered in blood, meeting the object of her desires covered in the aftermath of birth was not part of her seduction plan.

"I will see you at the ceremony, Ishassara," Tekmessa said, still stroking Areto's hair. The new mother had closed her eyes, and appeared to be peacefully sleeping with the babe on her chest, but Penny frowned, noticing the woman's pallor as the priestess continued. "I may take the Basileus up on his offer to show us the ships. Perhaps I will see you there?"

"Perhaps," Penny said, though she wished for just one hour of alone time with Deileon.

"Go on then," Marpe said, clicking her tongue as she shooed Penny toward the door. "I will bring the newest apprentices in to finish tending mother and child. She has lost more blood than I like, but I am sure she will be fine with prayers and herbs and rest, none of which we need you for. Go on now."

18

HANGOVER

Horses were being tacked and readied for the hunt, but someone seemed to have stuffed those horses inside Molpadia's skull, and now they were kicking their way out. She groaned, flinging an arm over her eyes to shut out even the dim light that reached her pathetic, musty corner.

"You good?"

Molpadia grunted in response to Toxaris' voice, not bothering to lower her arm.

"Don't suppose you want to join the hunt, then?"

Molpadia curled her lip, and Toxaris laughed softly.

"You are probably the only wise one among us. These Achaeans can barely sit a horse, from what I can see. I will leave you to sleep, Dia, but I think our queen was looking for you earlier. She seemed out of sorts. You two fight again?"

"When do we not fight?" Molpadia mumbled from the crook of her elbow, but guilt and anger had begun a new dogfight in her chest as she remembered the evening before, and she had not yet decided which dog would win today. Anger seemed the more reliable beast.

"Right. I mean, you are both rather stubborn. It's almost like you enjoy prickly where others like it smooth, but hey, who am I to say what's what? I haven't even kissed anyone in at least ten years, since I left my village for good, so I'm not one to give advice in a lover's quarrel."

"Toxaris, it isn't that I don't care, but my head…"

"Right," Toxaris said apologetically, "sleep it off, then, and we can practice later in the weapons yard, as Hippolyta wants. Sleep tight."

Molpadia listened to quick footsteps disappearing down the stable aisle, a horse's quick clops following. She sighed, lowering her arm from her face, but it was still too bright. She turned on her side, images of Lyta's censorious blue eyes swimming with her head's movement, and thought she might be sick from drink for the first time in twenty years. She breathed through it, her eyes shut against the light, but she could not shut out Lyta's face, or the vision of her perfect body being touched by that man. She fell asleep to the pounding of her own heart in her head, every thud a dread that she would never be enough for one such as Lyta, and not caring, because she would still give everything she had.

When Molpadia woke again, the afternoon sun was already shining through the western window of the stable, indicating much of the day had already passed. Her mouth was so dry it might well have been laid out in the same sun that dried the straw poking through her tunic. She grimaced, and climbed to her feet with bleary determination. She needed water, and maybe a bath. And probably another cup of wine, just to ease the terrible ache in her skull, where the horses still kicked.

It was agonizingly slow progress to the Moon Hall, where ha-mazaans were haphazardly scattered for their evening meal. It was a much more subdued affair than the previous evening, their conversations hushed and sombre. A few seemed as weary as she was, nodding tired heads over their mugs of *kimiz*, barely giving the rest of the room any notice. Molpadia headed for the barrels of fresh water along the wall. She guzzled a full pitcher of the blessedly cool drink, the taste of it bitter on her fetid tongue, enduring the curious stares of several scurrying Xanharaspas as her gulping spilled wetness over her rumpled tunic, but she merely winked at them before she made her way to the row of wine barrels. Her stomach had settled somewhat, but it would not hurt to have a little tail of the horse that had kicked her, as Lyta would say. Then, she would find Lyta, and she would apologize for being a cranky old mare.

She opened the spigot and filled a cup with sweet red wine, took several long gulps of it, her tongue turning it even more bitter than the water, before topping it up again. She turned to leave, stopping for a moment as the round walls of the Hall kept spinning all on their own.

Too old for such nights anymore, she thought blearily.

When the spinning lessened its pace, she tottered out of the Hall, headed for the bathhouse. There was nothing that a good bath could not fix. Her eyes still spun, and the horses in her head were still furious, so Molpadia nearly tripped over the man walking in the same direction when she emerged into the blinding light.

He mumbled something, an apology perhaps, and stumbled back from her. Molpadia scowled and squinted at the same time. Everything was spinning a little faster now, and she was less certain she could hold down her sick, though she had slept the wine off by now, surely?

"Eh, what are you doing here?" she demanded gruffly, the hand not holding the wine going to her sword hilt. She recognized his face. The one who had been skulking in the river, soothing his inflamed whip marks.

"Just looking for someone," he answered, backing away from her.

Molpadia frowned, then shook her head like a dog. She glared at him, beginning to draw her sword, but already his image had split in two, and the stone walls around them were collapsing, and then she felt her head crack against the ground, the horses finally loose, and all the blinding light no longer hurting her eyes.

19

THE BATHHOUSE

Wﻠith one last murmur of praise to Areto and her daughter, Penny hurried into the heat of a later afternoon sun. She had been inside all day, and the light was bright enough to hurt her eyes, forcing her to squint as she hurried to the nearby bathhouse. When she finally opened the heavy door, waves of steam rolled out, but no ha-mazaans lazed in the deep pools. A small flame flickered in the pit next to the largest pool, heating wet rocks to keep the air in the room hot and steamy. Dropping her belt onto the stone tiles, the dagger and key clanging on the rock, she kicked the door nearly closed with her heel, just enough to let some light in and some thick steam out. She peeled her clothes off, scattering them haphazardly before carefully threading her fingers through the quick braid she had tied to keep her hair out of the way. She ladled another scoop of water over the rocks surrounding the fire, so that they hissed with fresh steam, then dug her fingers into the small basket of herbs nearby, sprinkling them into the burning rocks to release their pungent, skunky vapors. The ha-mazaans used the herbs to ease the tension from their overworked muscles, and they were just what Penny needed to relax her tired body and calm her mind before she tended the flame, and finally, after so many setbacks, met with Leon.

She breathed the vapors in, carefully stepping down the carved stone steps into the deepest part of the pool, and walked forward until the waters closed over her head, relishing the way the heat poured itself over her tired shoulders and swallowed all sound, until she was lost in her own world. She came up gasping for air, barely able to see in the dim light, and felt along the edge of the pool for a pumice to scrub away the day's grime. Finding one that fit nicely in her palm, she used the rough stone against the skin of

102

her arm to swiftly work at the dried sweat and blood now softening in the water's heat, the sight of the blood bringing fresh worry to her mind as she thought of Areto's bleeding, but she was confident Marpe's skills would help the new mother.

A skittering noise floated over the bubbling of the pool. Penny turned her head, but there was only the pop of flames as it ate the last of the wood, the rocks around it venting the last of their steam into the air, the dying fire the only light in the room. Frowning, she turned to face the closed door. She was sure she had left it open enough for fresh air to come in.

"Tekmessa?"

Silence greeted her words, but the intensity of it prickled at the back of her neck. She moved her eyes carefully through the shadows, the paltry flame she had not bothered to stoke doing little to dispel them, instead making them larger and more malleable. Gripping the stone tightly, she moved with dragging steps through the water to the shallow end of the pool, where the air was clearer, though it was farther away from the fire-light. Her flesh pimpled where the colder air touched her wet skin as she left the water.

"I like my women better when they are smooth and clean, and smelling nice. You almost looked like one of *them*, all covered in sweat and blood, and wearing those clothes."

She froze, then turned slowly to see his silhouette outlined against the steam and the flickering shadows. He stood between the pool and the doorway. Between her and freedom. The steam seemed to grow thicker inside her lungs, yet thinner in the room itself as she grew immediately aware of her naked body in a way she had never given nakedness a moment's thought before now.

"Get out," she said, wanting to dive back into the private darkness of the water's secretive depths, but her feet stayed rooted in place.

Brekko laughed lightly.

"Don't worry, Princess," he said, and the shadows in front of the doorway shifted. "I'm only here to talk."

Penny's breath caught, her fist tightening around the rough rock. Her head followed the moving shadows as they drew closer to the fire, closer to her, until his freshly shaven features grew clear in the dim light. She glanced toward his hand when he stopped, the golden shimmer of bronze rings and the distinct shape of the Tower's wooden key dangling from the belt in his fingers. She cursed silently, and moved her eyes back to his shadowed frame, every muscle tense as the hot water continued to thicken the air with steam, making it difficult to breathe.

"Get out, or you will have a hundred ha-mazaan spears in your belly the moment I scream, and shortly after that, your head will swing from the bridge across the Terme."

"You will not be heard, even if you scream. Not here."

He made the statement with such calm bravado that Penny huffed a short laugh of astonishment, but she glanced at the doorway, wondering how loud she *would* need to scream for her voice to carry through thick stone walls and solid oak door.

"Give me that belt, and then *leave.*"

To her surprise, he dropped the belt immediately, the knife and key clanging hollowly on the flagstones between them, but then he took a step toward her. Penny took a step back, but the stone wall was already close behind her. The water was her only way to avoid him, but if she dove into the pool, she would be stuck there, either swimming away from him or hemmed in as he strolled the surrounding ledge, waiting for her to emerge. How long would she need to wait for another ha-mazaan to come? Most were likely at dinner in the Moon Hall at this time of day. She could be alone here for hours. Alone with him. She looked toward the door again, wondering if she could manage to push Brekko into the water and make it through the door, but he saw the direction of her gaze and shook his head, the movement barely visible in the quickly diminishing light. The fire had grown small, the wood almost completely devoured by the flames.

"I'm just here to talk, didn't you hear me? No need to be in such a hurry. Although, there are plenty more who have been eager to...speak with you. I'm sure they can have their turn when I'm done, eh?"

He paused, and shifted his weight forward again. His voice lowered.

"You didn't think I would just forget what you did to me, Princess? That I would hand you over without giving you a chance to make it right?"

A trembling began deep in her belly, moving outward with each sickening thump of her heart. She tried to suck enough air to scream for help, but even her lungs were frozen, her breath only short gasps in and out as icy fingers coiled around the inside of her throat, and squeezed.

"I did nothing to you," she said through tight lips. "And I am already late to meet another, so whatever you think you are doing here, you can forget it. *Get. Out.*"

She bit off the words with teeth that had begun to chatter, as her entire body hummed with danger. Never in her entire life had she wished so badly to be ha-mazaan. But she was not ha-mazaan, and she had not thought to bring one with her to such a simple thing as an afternoon bath.

"You humiliated me in front of my men," Brekko muttered, moving forward another slow step. "Had me whipped ten lashes, for nothing more than touching your whore wrist." He shook his head, an incredulous laugh escaping, but then he shrugged. "And yes, your meeting with Deileon at the ships. Big man himself sent me to bring you. Said to make sure you made the ships, but I figured it was a good time for you and me to clear the air."

"Leon sent you?" she said doubtfully, trying to stall for time but at the same time, not wanting to start an argument with him about what he felt she had or had not done the night of their arrival.

"Not Deileon, Princess. Theseus."

Penny frowned, though her face felt stiff. She tried to distract him with more questions, her eyes shifting to the door and back again. "Why did Theseus send *you*?"

"We're just following orders, Princess. He doesn't care which one of us takes you first. Just that we get the job done. Although, he was adamant that we should save you for him. Thinks he found someone special. He doesn't need to know, though, does he?"

Penny did not have time to wonder at his meaning. Brekko took another step forward. She stepped back, until the stone wall pressed against her back. Brekko reached out, palm up, as though he were inviting her to join him. Penny lunged toward the pool, but he moved faster than she expected. His hand caught in her loose hair, jerking her backward with a vicious tug. She did scream then, more of a howl, and whirled her whole body to lash at his face with the pumice. It caught him in the side of his head, but the force of his tug and her flailing pulled them both off-center. They crashed to the hard stone together, his heavy body landing on top of hers, forcing the scream out of her lungs, and the last of her air with it. He hissed a curse at her, his hand tugging her hair tight against her scalp. He lifted her head by the roots and slammed it down, cracking her head against rock.

Pinpoints of light exploded in her vision as his hand smothered her scream. Pain blossomed, and with it, a dark flower of terror took root deep inside, spurring her into a frenzy of action. She tried to bite his hand, to squirm from under the weight of him, to hit him again with the stone, but he used his elbow to pin her arm, the weight of him crushing the bones of her wrist into the stone floor until she cried out against his hand. He released her hair, and she bucked her body against his, trying to throw him off. She had landed on the thick leather of her belt, and its bronze discs dug painfully into her waist and hip and shoulder blade, cutting her skin as she thrashed underneath Brekko's weight, but she did not stop. Not until she felt cold metal against her throat, and the sharp sting as he pushed the blade hard enough to cut through flesh.

She stopped struggling, her chest heaving with harsh gasps as she struggled to drag air through his thick, crushing fingers against her mouth. Outside, footsteps pounded on the cobblestones, and ha-mazaan voices shouted to each other. Desperate hope flared in her breast. Her heart beat a frenzied tattoo as Brekko tensed on top of her, his eyes on the darkened doorway, his own breathing ragged, but soon the sounds were gone, and the door remained firmly shut. The flame of hope flickered. She dragged another shuddering breath through his smothering fingers.

"Any man strong enough can father an Amazon brat, eh, Princess?" Brekko laughed, his hot, venison-scented breath washing over her face. She thought she might vomit into his hand, but she swallowed it down, worried he would let her choke. His erection pressed into her thigh through the rough linen of his tunic, and he ground his hips into hers, leaving no more doubt in her mind about what he meant by talking.

His left hand left her mouth to grip the wrist he crushed with his elbow, forcing her fingers open with a painful squeeze. The pumice spilled with a clatter onto the floor. He took the knife from her throat to force first one arm above her head, then the other, where he held them both with a grip strong enough to grind her bones together. The blade of the knife returned to kiss her throat, and then glide with utterly gentle pressure across her collarbone and down under her left breast, where he pressed the edge of it into the soft mound, the point of it digging into her skin until she felt hot blood seep down her ribs. Penny stared up into his face and dragged another breath through her chattering teeth. She could not even tell the color of his eyes, the room had grown so dark, but the yellow-white of his teeth were clear as he grinned down at her.

"You will be cut to pieces for this, and then fed to my mother's dogs," she said thickly, but her voice sounded dull and far away, as though she were hearing someone else speak.

"There will be no one left to help you," Brekko said, his voice almost casual, as though they were having an afternoon conversation about the clouds. "Our ships are ready to sail, and your mommy with them. Soon, you will be on them as well. The rest of your women will be asleep. Now lie still, or I will slice your breast from your body and take it home with me as a souvenir."

Penny stared blankly at his dark face, her mind spinning to take in his meaning even as his hand released her wrists, confident that the blade at her breast would be restraint enough. She lay frozen, unable to move as he began to touch her body, his oar-rough palm and thick fingers harsh against her goose-fleshed skin. He squeezed her breasts, her belly, her thighs. He sighed into the side of her neck, his breath tickling her own hair against her cheek. Then his knee was forcing her thighs apart.

The shouts outside grew louder, and running footsteps permeated the thick wood of the door once more. These, too, passed by without stopping. The tiny flare of hope smothered with the sound of Brekko's groan as he entered her. Penny made no sound, only listened for footsteps, for the squeak of hinges, her eyes focused on the low ceiling above them. More footsteps came and went. The door remained shut. For some reason, her mind went to her last moments with Sylviu, his smiling eyes as he helped her spit the last pig for the roast, his hand raised in farewell as she watched him ride away, wishing he would not leave her. She replayed his smile in her mind, holding onto it as one might cling to a raft in a stormy sea, a silent storm inside her own mind.

When he was finished, Brekko lay unmoving, his weight a stone anchor sinking through the dark ocean of her body, his breath hot against the side of her throat. He kissed her neck. More women shouted, their voices a cacophony of noise inside Penny's fogged mind, but even if they came through the door now, it was too late.

They were too late.

Brekko's eyes were closed, his lips pressed to her earlobe. She moved her arm slowly from above her head to her waist, as though it dragged through currents of water. She wondered if the ha-mazaans would indeed hang his head from the bridge. The image of his eyes being pecked out by stryx swung through her mind, and she clung to it, her thoughts following the sway of his severed head like a pendulum.

Brekko opened his eyes and pushed himself up onto his elbows, admiring her breasts in the last flickering of firelight, his face distracted by spent pleasure. He leaned back farther for a better view of her body, his hand following his eyes. She stared into his face for what seemed an eternity, watching his eyes move up her stomach to her breasts and throat. He smiled, almost gently, when their eyes met.

The bronze blade of her knife wasn't long enough to puncture his heart when she stabbed him in the armpit, but it was long enough to make him scream before it hit bone. She wrenched it out as his whole body lunged backward, the knife in his own hand flailing away from her breast, cutting her as it went, but she could still feel the suffocating weight of him when she slashed his throat, the blunt blade dragging against his flesh in a jagged, voice-silencing line. His knife clattered to the stones beside them as he clutched the gaping wound. His eyes bulged as he goggled down at her. The blood from his throat arced with perfect rhythm into the hot pool behind them.

She picked up his own long dagger from the stones, shoved it into his belly, and twisted. She said no words, made no sounds, but inside, she heard only screaming.

He did not yell or cry out. Could not. She held his eyes, still silent, as she used both hands and tore the blade upward, splitting him from groin to throat as she might a pig for the roast. She did not break eye contact, even when he fell forward, crushing her against the hard stones with an even heavier weight than before. She waited for the light in his eyes to go dark, while above them, the fire in the room died completely.

20

THE TOWER

Penny lay frozen in the shrouded dark for what seemed an eternity, the stone under her hips cruel and hard, but she focused on the pain to ground her, keep her inside her body. There was a shrill ringing in her ears, muffled by a dull, pounding ache in her head. Something thick and acrid tickled at her nostrils, burning its way into her lungs. Within the darkness, over the soft susurrus of water, over the sounds of more running footsteps outside and the muffled calls of ha-mazaans yelling orders to each other, there came another sound, strange and foreign. A crisp, leathery crackle, and a whoosh of hot, stale air that smelled of sulfur and rotting flesh as it blasted across Penny's face, pulling her out of her frozen lethargy. She turned her head to cough, but Brekko's body still slumped on top of her, and the weight of it crushed her lungs as much as the heavy smell.

Panic filled her. Every muscle in her body leaped to life, ignited by disgust and fear and the overwhelming need to be away from Brekko's touch. The rock under her bare skin scraped her flesh unforgivingly as she struggled out from under his lifeless body, shoving him away as she untangled her legs from his, his blood helping by making everything slippery. Every part of her that had been cold and frozen moments before began to thrum with a tingling pain, and her lungs burned with the effort of gasping air that had suddenly grown putrid with stink.

A dry sob escaped as she finally freed herself from Brekko's corpse, but then she heard the rustling sound again. She stilled her harsh breathing for a long moment, every part of her attuned to the room around her, her senses probing for another presence, for the threat of another Achaean waiting his turn, as Brekko had promised. She could only hear the water, and her increasingly deafening heartbeat, and the steadily rising clatter of armed ha-mazaans on the move.

The pressure in her head multiplied as she sat up too quickly. She moved a slow hand to the side of her face where Brekko had struck her, to the back of her head where it had struck stone, but even as she felt for split skin or blood, all she could feel were fingers around her wrists, grinding the bones in a painful vise, his hot breath against her cheek, the smothering weight of his body on top of her. She rolled to the side and heaved bile onto the floor, shuddering.

After a few moments of dragging breath through chattering teeth, Penny crawled closer to the edge of the pool, feeling the edge of it with her hands as the rough stone bit painfully into her knees. As soon as she felt the uneven edge, she tipped her body forward into the hot water, like an otter diving deep under the silencing water, the heat of it scorching her cold skin and stilling some of the chattering in her jaw. Briefly, the idea of staying under, swimming deeper, deeper into the black water until everything stayed black, entered her mind. She could open her mouth right now and breathe, and it would all be as nothing, or as one, but she would not need to remember anything. Absurdly, the image of Areto's tiny newborn girl swam into her mind. The way her wrinkled, purple face had been so still when there was no breath in her lungs. The girl had seemed so peaceful. Perhaps it had been cruel to force the babe's breath to come, after all.

The pressure of the water began to feel heavy, but Penny stayed under. Even though her eyes were closed, and the room held no light, Penny saw the hand, reaching toward her, long fingers more bone than flesh curling backward, beckoning. She saw the black eyes, one teardrop of blood staining a bone-white cheek, the whip of snake tail lashing through the water. Great, leathery wings like a bat's spread high and wide above hair that coiled with snakes, their slithering heads arched and tongues flickering on either side of a smiling face, first showing pointed teeth, then a bifurcated tongue of its own. The creature's mouth hissed with the same sound as steam rising from hot rocks, and, though Penny was still submerged in the hot pool, she heard every word clear and sharp as a song of mourning in the Moon Hall.

"Come, then," the being said, its tone at once seething and cajoling. Enmity flowed from its black eyes, and another drop of blood welled where tears might form. "Just open your mouth and breathe. Do my task for me."

Then it laughed, a shrill, shrieking, terrifying sound of pure horror.

Penny jerked her eyes open and kicked off from the bottom of the pool, desperately gulping air as she broke the surface. She looked around wildly in the darkness, but she could not see anything. She was alone with her imagination, and it, too, was turning on her. Bracing her arm to keep her at the side of the pool, Penny scraped her other hand along the floor, feeling for the stone Brekko had forced from her hand. Her fingers found the pockmarked oval, and for a second time she used it to scrub at her skin, but now her movements were frenzied and desperate, her breath coming in shallow, keening gasps. When Brekko's filth was washed away, she did not stop, but kept scraping, until bands of raw welts appeared as the stone scraped flesh under a heavy hand, but she did not notice the pain. Even when she scraped the tender flesh inside her thighs, on the inside of her wrists, on her belly, her ear, she did not use a lighter hand, and did not care that the marks would show for days, perhaps forever. They were better than the feel of *him*.

She finally stumbled out of the water, feeling the floor in the dark for her tunic and trousers, which she donned quickly, heedless of the fact they were damp with the same blood she had just scrubbed away. At any other time, she would have gone out naked from the baths, but now, the thought of another person, even one of the ha-mazaans, looking at her naked body made the bile rise in her throat as she felt his leering gaze on her naked body. She found the edge of her zoster, and tugged the end of it from under Brekko, making the mound of his body turn on the wet stones, hearing his guts spilling onto the floor in the darkness. Her fingers trembled as she fastened the buckle of the heavy leather over her hips, but somehow, the solid weight of it calmed her, like a firm embrace. Lastly, she found the bronze dagger, and shoved it, still bloody, into its sheath.

When she cracked open the bathhouse door, the rush of cool, uncontaminated evening air was a relief to her burning lungs. She looked behind her, to the lumpen heap illuminated by the shaft of light along the floor. Brekko lay with eyes still open, their roundness showing his shock, his neck twisted awkwardly to reveal the gash in his throat. She stared at the sight, transfixed.

She had killed a man. A guest in her home. A guest she herself had welcomed with Milk from the Great Mother. She had not just broken guest-rite, though.

She had broken her vow.

Being in the open, exposed streets of Themiscyra's outer courtyard presented its own immediate problems. The horror of explaining to anyone what had just occurred made her instinctively want to hide, to shelter alone where no one could intrude, and there was only one place in this city she could do that. She moved quickly, keeping close to the palace wall, more for a sense of balance than anything else, but as she neared the Moon Hall and the tower above it, it was clear that the activity she had heard from inside the bathhouse was culminating in the outer courtyard, as what seemed to be half the ha-mazaans in the city were bunched against the open gates leading to the bridge, their spears bristling against the sky, their swords and axes gleaming, their bows strung and ready. Melanippe stalked like a panther along the top of the courtyard wall, her axe in one hand while the other shielded her eyes against the setting sun. The General was looking toward the docks. Toward the ships.

Our ships are ready to sail, and your mommy with them. Soon, you will be on them as well.

Penny ducked into the alcove of the tower's doorway, her heart beating in her throat. More ha-mazaans trotted past, their weapons ready, but they did not notice Penny in the shadows. She could not see what was happening, and, with bruises already blossoming like crushed fruit around her wrists, and welts from her own scrubbing on every visible piece of raw skin, she did not want to make an appearance in the middle of their gathering to ask for clarification.

Suddenly, Theseus' voice rang out, strident and clear.

"Ha-mazaans, hold!"

Penny felt the wave of shock course through the women gathered ahead of her, but she could not see what it was that made them gasp and swear. She fumbled at her belt for the wooden key, her hand unsteady as she wiggled its bent handle into place, the pins in the lock stubbornly resisting the unfamiliar jiggling, but finally she felt them give under the pressure of the key's prongs. She set her shoulder to the wood, and the hinges squealed in protest, drawing the attention of several Savaran. They soon turned their attention back to Melanippe as the General called out to them. Penny took the steps two at a time, reaching the second door to the tower in time to hear Theseus' voice finish speaking, but she could not make out the words. She raced to the casement, then reeled back, gasping in horror.

Theseus held her mother in front of him, one of her arms twisted cruelly behind her back as he walked her forward, away from the dock, closer to the bridge that separated the palace from the beach. In his other hand he held a knife, the blade gleaming sharply against the perfect white column of Antiope's throat. Penny smothered a cry, clutching the stone pillar for support as her knees threatened to buckle.

Along the beach, Achaeans rushed to strap bronze shields to their arms, while others, already prepared for battle, spread along the docks in front of the ships, forming a barricade, or a line of advance, Penny couldn't be sure. The entire Savaran army had gathered, though without their horses, against the gates of the city, their bows drawn and aimed not only at Theseus and her mother, whom the coward was using as a shield, but also toward the first ship in the bay. Against the brilliant sparkle of the water, Penny could make out two people standing on the deck of the first ship. She recognized Lyta's long strawberry braids, her broad shoulders squared against the setting sun as she faced a man covered in the pelt of a lion. They looked like they were arguing, the way Lyta's arms gestured angrily back and forth, though Penny could hear no words. Another movement on the second ship beyond them caught her eye. An Achaean. Red hair, indistinct face, but she knew him by his broad shoulders and the way his head tilted. Deileon. In his arms, a small child, with hair shining golden in the sun, like a dandelion gone to seed.

Out of the corner of her eye, Lyta's axe flashed. Penny did not see which of them drew first, whether it was Heracles or her aunt, but her eyes were fixed on them when Heracles thrust his blade through her aunt's chest, the end of it erupting bloodied and red through the back of her spine.

21

FIRE & RUIN

Penny's scream mingled with every other watching ha-mazaan as Heracles clutched at the strap over Hippolyta's shoulder, his sword sticking through her chest. The air around the palace, around the ships, inside the tower, darkened. It crackled with static, as though a storm full of lightning and swirling darkness had been unleashed the moment Heracles struck the Defending Queen's breast. Penny could feel the charge of it along her own spine, inside her stomach, around her throat.

It was her mother's voice that cut through the shrill, grief-stricken cries of every woman watching.

"Fight, ha-mazaans! *Fight!*"

The ululating shriek of the ha-mazaans' battle cry raised every hair on the back of Penny's neck as they cascaded like a wave over the cobblestone bridge and onto the beach. She watched, stupefied, as women loosed their arrows, their spears, slashed with their swords, hacked with their axes. As they ran, they loosed their arrows at the ship, at the line of Achaeans on the shoreline, even at Theseus, though he still hid behind her mother, dragging her backward toward the ships, though Antiope struggled to get free. She saw one ha-mazaan fall, then another, but the wave poured on, crashing like a tsunami against the rocky shore of Achaeans.

Penny clutched the column of the window as she leaned out to watch the clash, but she did not realize how close she was to the lip of the casement until the dry crackling sound, the same one from the bathhouse, followed by the same voice that had come to her underwater, hissed somewhere behind her.

"These are the dues paid by an oath-breaker."

116

Penny whirled, her hand going to the knife at her belt, but she turned too fast. She flailed to catch her balance as her heel caught the edge of the casement, with a deadly drop to the courtyard looming behind her. She managed to stumble forward, away from the window, but stopped short at the sight before her. The vision she had seen in the pool stood in the tower room with her, on the far side of the Flame, the snakes of its hair writhing like the fire in the stone cauldron. Dark, leathery, sinewed wings were folded tight over a body that showed breasts and hips of a woman, while a gauzy material, darker than a moonless night, pooled on the floor, edged with sable fur. Around her waist, a bulbous black snake coiled, and two more hooked around her elbows to slither down her forearms. They, too, hissed as she extended her white, skeletal arm, and pointed an impossibly sharp finger at Penny's terrified face.

"It is time for you to join the Queen of the ha-mazaans in the Otherworld, Oath-breaker," the creature hissed.

Penny pulled the bronze dagger, the edge of it still smeared with blood from Brekko's throat, and held it in front of her. The blade was barely longer than the palm of her hand, and Penny felt as threatening as a girl holding a flower in the face of a charging boar. The creature unfolded wide, leathery wings, the tips of them hooked with claws, the ends of them reaching across the entire room. She looked around wildly for something more to defend herself with as the Erinyes' malevolent laugh filled the tower.

The star-iron poker used to stir the Flame's embers caught her eye.

Penny lunged.

Her fingers wrapped around the blackened metal, hot from being left too near the flames, but she did not pause. She lashed out with the long, thinly twisted bar of star-iron with a scream of terror lending force to her arm. The Erinyes screamed as well, and the sound of it nearly brought Penny to her knees as her swing sliced through shadow only, making no contact with solid flesh. Still, Penny was sure the creature flinched back when the poker passed through her face, and it gave Penny the surge of hope she needed.

"Begone!" she screamed, and swung the poker again.

The Fire in the center of the tower erupted into enormous, angry flames, driving both the creature and Penny back with the intensity of its heat. She was forced to cover her face, alarmed at the strange intensity of it, the angry crackling as it devoured the already charred wood in the hearth, before it exploded.

Flaming pieces of oak and ash hurtled in every direction, filling the tower with still-burning embers. Penny was flung backward into a column, her head cracking against the stone support. Heat burned her skull, her eyes, her lungs. The last thing she saw was the creature, mouth agape, split tongue flailing between pointed, bloody teeth, snakes writhing, embers from the fire burning their way through the creature's white skin. She heard the creature shriek in pain and fury, before darkness overtook her vision, and she saw and heard no more.

Smoke snaked into her nostrils, coiling itself inside her throat, squeezing her airway closed, coaxing Penny to rise from the depths of ragged dreams trying to tug her further under. She opened her eyes slowly, bright pinpricks of light flashing painfully on the inside of her skull. Despite the heavy, acrid smell of smoke, Penny could see from her position on the floor, with one arm bent underneath her body, her right cheek pressed against the cold, dry wood, the edge of the hearth directly in front of her, that there was no fire.

Themiscyra's Eternal Flame had gone cold.

She jerked fully awake, gasping as her head exploded with throbbing pain. Her fingers were still wrapped tightly around the handle of the star-iron, and she peeled them away with painstaking slowness, reaching with the other hand to the back of her head. Her fingers showed black and shiny in the pale light of the moon when she pulled them away. Gritting her teeth against the ringing in her head, she sat up stiffly, her eyes darting to every place the moonlight touched in the round enclosure, and lingering in those places where the shadows deepened, searching for a woman with wings of a bat and snakes for hair. Images of Brekko's blood arcing into the pool, of his eyes bulging in shock at his own death at the hand of the very person who swore guest rite with him, wedged themselves into the forefront of her mind. Her stomach heaved as the memories returned.

Her next thought was of her aunt's body, the end of the sword protruding from the back of her spine. Heracles reaching for Lyta's zoster, tugging the belt free of her limp body.

Time for you to join the Queen of the ha-mazaans in the Otherworld...

Smoke wafted through the casement once more, thick and suffocating. Gradually, the distant shouts of women calling orders into the night penetrated Penny's fogged mind. She slowly got to her knees, then to her feet, using the column for support. In light of the full moon, the silent waters of the Terme flowed like walnut ink to the sea, with only a few meager fishing vessels secured in the harbor.

The ships were gone.

On the beach, torches bobbed along the shoreline, their carriers rushing from one dark mound to another, sometimes kneeling for a moment, more often moving on to the next dark mound. Penny stared out for a long moment, turning her head slowly to take in the full view, her own ragged breaths accompanied by staccato shouts from inside the palace walls behind the tower. Though she could not see everything, she could see well enough the flames billowing from inside the city walls. She could hear the crackling of wood being devoured by the hungry jaws of flame. The stables were an inferno, the clouds of smoke a tornado of black ash against the stars. Horses careened freely through the city streets, panicked by the flames erupting hot and hungry in every corner of the city.

Everything made of wood was burning.

Penny raced to the door, her bare feet slapping down the steps, then out the heavy wooden door. She did not bother locking it behind her. There was no longer any Flame to protect. In the courtyard, billows of smoke towered into the air, licked on the bottom by flames, lit from above by the moon. Voices called to one another, shouting words Penny could not make out but which rang with an air of urgency she could not ignore. She forced her legs into a stiff trot, feeling every beat of feet against the ground in the pounding of her head, but she focused on the pain to push her on, and to keep other thoughts at bay. She reached the western edge of the wall, where it drew parallel to the river and the docks, and halted.

On the ground nearby, at the base of the wall, a sword shone silver in the moonlight, though its blade was darkened to black with dried blood. A ha-mazaan's brown hand still gripped the pommel. A soft cry escaped Penny's lips as she drew closer. The ha-mazaan wore no helmet, no armor. She wore no clothing at all, as though she had just emerged from the baths. Her black braid bent like a broken stick under her sleeping cheek. Penny stared in horror at that face, the reality of who it was refusing to settle in her mind.

"Areto."

The name came out as a pathetic rasp.

"Areto!" she tried again, stronger this time, but Areto, brand new mother of a brand new babe, remained still.

Penny's stomach heaved, but there was only yellow bile and the acrid taste of fear left inside. Shaking, she bent and touched Areto's body, hoping desperately for signs of life. Signs she was only sleeping. Signs Penny was simply caught in a terrible nightmare, and once she touched something, proved to herself it was all in her imagination, she could awaken back in her soft bed, about to spend a day on the hunt.

As soon as her fingers pressed the ha-mazaan's cold skin, Penny could not pretend it was a dream. Blood had long since stopped pooling under Areto, but the hole in the side of her throat glistened in the moonlight where the blood had not yet dried to black.

"No. No no no no no. Wake up."

Penny's whispered plea went unanswered. She raised her eyes to the beach, beyond Areto's dark hair and once brown skin, now ashen and purple in the moonlight. Ha-mazaans lay scattered along the length of the beach, as far as the dim light would reveal. Shadowed figures moving from body to body, walking the beach in search of injured women. Someone called out, and one of the bodies on the ground stirred, raising their arm into the air as though summoning one of the searchers. Not all dead, then.

The image of Theseus dragging her mother backward across the beach, blade gleaming at her perfect throat, rose unbidden in her mind.

"Mother," she breathed. "Mother!" she called, then louder, urgently, "Antiope!"

Penny lurched forward, not so much running as falling toward the next dark shape on the ground. She knelt by that body, but there was only dark hair and dark eyes, so she stumbled to the next, and the next, finding only horror, finding one dead Achaean, then one who groaned as she moved him, making her spring away from his body as though burned, moving on to find more dead ha-mazaans. Someone grasped her arms, their voice hoarse from shouting and maybe from smoke, as the flames still billowed from the stables on the eastern slope of the pastures, but she only heard her name from lips that were not her mother's and then she was pushing them away, stumbling to the next dark mound of flesh and bone, not knowing whether she wanted to find her mother here or whether she wanted Brekko's impossible, inconceivable words to be true after all.

Our ships are ready to sail, and your mommy with them.

Another woman's anguished cry halted her frenzied progress in the night.

Penny turned, stumbling over the handle of a ha-mazaan spear stranded in the gravel. A moonbeam lit upon a strand of strawberry hair spilled across the boulder of the docks. A woman, broad of shoulder and waist, knelt beside her head, and her wailing pierced through the cold fog into Penny's thudding heart. She moved as though asleep to the shoreline, her legs jelly but her mind repeating the same thought over and over again, *no no no no no*, a mantra that moved her numb feet and brought her to the edge of the docks within moments, where she collapsed to her already bruised knees beside Molpadia.

Hippolyta, Defending Queen and mighty warrior of the ha-mazaans, stared sightless into the night sky, the open wound in her chest blacker than the night itself. When Molpadia howled her grief to the stars, like a wolf caught in a trap, Penny rocked back on her heels, flinching away from the sound.

She watched, stricken, as Molpadia gathered her dead lover, her wife, her closest friend into her arms, cradling her there as she rocked back and forth, her face contorted on the outside by everything Penny knew she should be feeling on the inside. Instead, everything was settling into a numb, frozen wasteland, and all she could do was stare.

Even as she looked on, a haze of unreality slowly settling like gauze over her mind, a shadow appeared behind Molpadia. The writhing form that had appeared to her in the bathhouse, and then again in the tower, solidified in the light of the moon. From its coal-black eyes, the creature wept blood, the red staining the skeletal features of its face and turning pointed, hungrily bared teeth vermillion. Its snake-wrapped arm raised slowly, almost languidly, and the monstrous, terrifying simulacrum of a woman pointed at Penny with a bony hand wrapped in a python.

"You will be mine, Oath-breaker," the monster hissed.

This time, the familiarity of the creature lessened the terror, but brought instead a deep, deep knowing in Penny's cold bones. The moment she thrust her knife into Brekko's sweating flesh, she had brought down a curse not only on herself, but on this entire city, and upon everyone she had once sworn to love as her own daughters. She could no longer deny what she had unleashed. A Night-Born sister, a Hound of the Fates, a mercenary Shadow of the Night sent to do the bidding of the Moirai, to claim their rightful prize—the very soul of anyone who breaks their vow. Only the sacred Flame had saved her back in the Tower; she was sure of it. But now, that Fire had grown cold. No embers burned in the hearth, no seed from which to grow a new Flame.

The creature hissed another laugh into her stricken face, and then it was gone. Molpadia's anguished wails and the desperate calls of dying ha-mazaans, punctuated by the swelling roar of flames eating their way through the palace, were all that was left to fill the expanding night.

22

Burning

Sylviu left Themiscyra at the point of Molpadia's sword, and this time he stayed out, but only because he had to finally admit she was right. His presence was pointless. Unnecessary. Despite what his visions had shown him all those years ago, these Achaeans did nothing but gawk and flex their muscles, and the ha-mazaans loitering with them seemed to be enjoying both. Pen certainly seemed to enjoy it.

He had jimmied that ridiculous wooden lock and broken into the Tower to have a better view of the city and remain out of sight, and had been able to see everything he needed to see. He knew well enough she had been enjoying their company during the Trials, and without the escort of a guard, no less. He had nearly given himself away by yelling for one of the ha-mazaans to at least offer her some sort of protection when armed men wandered their city so freely. He'd been tempted to go out there himself, but he wondered how much of that urge was protectiveness, and how much was jealousy he had no right to feel, and so he stayed silent, hidden, burning nearly as hot as the forbidden Flame at his back, until she had disappeared into the pavilion beside a red-haired sailor fairly dripping his drool down her exposed neck.

Despite his misgivings, the men he watched gave no indication they were anything but wayfarers wandering through, will no ill intentions and no plans to do anything but enjoy Themiscyra's pleasures while they could, so he had gone back to his lair in the stables to fret alone, suppressing his irrational feelings, letting Pen have her happiness, maybe even a successful Alsanti, only to be rousted by Hippolyta's watchdog and sent on his way.

Defeated, confused, unsure why he had been so worked up, heartsick that he had fought with his mother and not apologized, he returned to his stash of wagon and wineskin over the hill, laying in the back of the cart after a few long pulls of wine, hoping to sleep off the frustration. He slept fitfully, dreaming of Pen, and beetles crawling over her beaches, through her hair, over her thighs. The dawn when he awoke was like any other, though, and he rolled from the cart stiff and somber, the last days of high emotion leaving his body as spent as his tired mind.

He began the long trek home to Galatae on foot, not stopping for a proper rest until it was twilight, when a grove of ash and beechwood beckoned for him to make camp. His thoughts were bleary with wine, the skin nearly empty from the long, hot, lonely walk, though he was sure Pen had meant him to savor it over the next moon until his next visit, but he could not help but seek its solace and its quieting, soothing bliss. The thought of her amber eyes made him turn north, toward the low hills where the city nestled, wondering if she were indeed fulfilling his suggestion to begin her Alsanti, as she had every right to. As he wanted her to, of course. The moon glared at him, full and low, but its silver light was not the only thing that lit the night.

A dusky red haze spilled across the horizon.

He could see it well enough, even from a day's walk away.

Themiscyra was in flames.

Sylviu's blood ran cold until it tingled in his face and chest with pinpricks of moving ice. He swore, then started to run toward that false dawn, heart in his throat, then stopped, unsure whether it would be faster to go there on foot, or continue on to Galatae and find his horse. Neither option was good enough. The glow bloomed brighter, smoke obscuring the great constellation of the Winged Protector in the sky. His heart twisted. He turned his back on that ominous sight and began to run the opposite direction.

He needed more than his horse. He needed men with swords, but even as his feet pounded the earthen road and his lungs burned, he knew he would be too late.

23

NO MERCY

Someone, perhaps Toxaris, helped her carry Lyta's body inside, though she tried to do it on her own at first. Numb to everything, Molpadia laid Lyta on their bed, caressed her face, tried to lay down next to her and sleep forever, but someone else pulled her away, would not let her lie down.

"The living still need us," someone said.

The living were too few, though. So many ha-mazaans murdered. So many corpses piling inside the ash-covered courtyard, waiting for their turn to be sent through the Gate along with Lyta, when it should not have been Lyta to lead them.

It should never have been Lyta.

She helped carry both living and dead ha-mazaans inside for the *sivyeti* and *zizentis* to do their work, while the fire ravaged what was left of the inner city, but those flames were beyond their control, now, and the palace itself would not burn. As she worked, she listened to their stories of Heracles' deliberate, brutal murder of their queen for the sake of a war-belt that had not even been around Lyta's waist, though he could never have known that.

Foolish, generous, protective, beloved Lyta.

She listened to their horrified realizations that ha-mazaans were missing, including her own sister. She helped them look for Glaukia on the dark beach, and for Melanippe and Alkippe and Sagitta, and then Sagitta's girl, and she even helped them look for Antiope, dead or alive she did not care, though her mouth tasted of bitter gall when they could not find that woman, just as they had not found the others.

They were still collecting wounded and dead when dawn broke. How the sun could still rise on such a scene was beyond her. The hollow ache inside her chest only expanded with the day's inevitable turning. One of the bodies on the beach moaned as she approached, and it was not the sound a ha-mazaan would make.

"Water..." he said, when he could see her face.

The Achaean had a gouge across his belly like an axe might make, his viscera spilling onto the rocks smelling of star-iron and filth. One hand still holding a dull bronze sword rested a horse's length away from the shortened stump of his arm. He was not going to live, but he was not going to die quickly. Molpadia stared wordlessly as he begged for water again, his lips white in the morning aurora. She waited for the rage that would come, would let her pick up the sword from his severed hand and skewer him through the heart. It did not come. Only a cold, merciless fury. She left him there without a word, and when another ha-mazaan approached to put him out of his misery, she ordered them to stand down, to leave him be or they, too, would suffer as he did.

The next Achaean she found was merely unconscious, and therefore needing an intervention. She dragged him face down over the beach, over the cobblestone bridge, into the courtyard. His head bounced with a crack against the stone stairs as she dragged him through the palace, leaving a trail of new blood down to the cellars, atta and Hanassa and Xanharaspa alike gaping at her limp, bleeding flag of treachery. He would either wake up a prisoner or not wake up at all, she did not care. She added four more to the room before bolting the door with a thick block of hornbeam. She would check on them tomorrow, perhaps, or the day after, when they had taken some time to come up with a good story for her eager ears, and their parched mouths could tell her no more lies in their desperation for relief.

The rest of the men's bodies they dragged outside the city walls, to the farthest end of the beach as the sun shone bright and ludicrous over the carnage. Some still moaned when she hauled them into that pile, but she ignored their sounds. One man they found perfectly disemboweled like a pig for the roast in their own bathhouse, his back striped with fresh lashes. She smiled with grim satisfaction to see the way his eyes bulged from his face, the line across his throat deep enough to show ivory bone. He went into the same heap, and she grunted at the effort to get him on top of the rest, but it could never be high enough for her. There would never be enough of them dead to ease this terrible numbness.

"Fetch the pitch buckets from the stables," she ordered an owl-eyed Hanassa hovering nearby. "And wood from the Tower," she added to a Xanharaspa.

"But it's for the Flame," the girl said.

"There is no Flame," Molpadia answered flatly. The girl turned her face to the dark Tower, the only part of the city with no orange tongues licking the sky, though much of the rest had begun to smolder with smoke, now that the fire had eaten its fill.

No, there was no Flame. Kubileya had turned Her face from them, removed Her protection, and there was only one person in this entire city who could have wrought such a terrible consequence on behalf of her entire people.

One person, and maybe her daughter. All for the sake of men.

$$24$$

SONS OF GALATAE

The sons and husbands of Galatae galloped north at midday, under a sky gone dark with the first rain in months. More than fifty Hanassa rode to Themiscyra's aid, along with twenty-six women who lived in their city permanently now. They saw only upward tendrils of smoke as they crested the hill, the flames long gone cold. The city itself was a wasteland around a palace of blackened stone. No Flame burned in the Tower. It was that minute, damning detail that settled the chill into Sylviu's bones, his breath hardening into a terrible stillness.

It will not do to break the Laws of Themis and Kubileya…That in itself is what brings destruction. You've already pushed it far enough, don't you think?

But just like his mother had not listened to him, Sylviu had ignored her warnings, scoffed at her beliefs. And now, this.

Sentries blocked their way before they even made it close to the bridge, bringing their desperate host to a halt with only their few horses and star-iron weapons laid bare. Sylviu urged his gelding forward to greet them.

"We are here to help!" he called, unsure which ha-mazaan's face hid under that crested helmet. She pointed with her star-iron lance, back in the direction of Galatae.

"You are too late, Hanassa." He did not know her voice, though he thought it might be Koine. Each of her words were their own dark raven poking its sharp beak into his guts. "Take your men home. Ha-mazaans, with us!" she cried, louder, gesturing for the women who rode with them to carry on across the bridge.

"What happened?" he demanded, as ha-mazaans long past the age of fighting as Savaran broke from the ranks of men and thundered past, their horse's hooves burying his voice in a clatter of hooves on stone. He could see by the grim lines of their mouths as they took in the destruction of their city that age would not matter to them now.

The line of sentries held fast against the men, though, the lead ha-mazaan still pointing imperatively with her spear. Sylviu swore, knowing he could not draw his sword or challenge her in any meaningful way without incurring severe punishment. He knew if he tried to force his way past her that is exactly what would happen, but he could see for himself the devastation that had only yesterday been a thriving city, the outer reaches of it now smoldering ashes. He could see the harbor, too.

The black ships were gone.

"Tell us what happened!" he called, desperate. "Is my mother safe? Are the Ishassaras safe?"

The ha-mazaan held her horse tight by the reins, the animal dancing with anxiety in the road, hooves a tattoo of drums in the dust. She lowered her spear, but at him, not to let him pass. Her voice was dark with anger when she answered.

"Men brought treachery and destruction, son of Oistrophe. That is what happened. They have taken your mother, along with our Hearth Queen, our Defending Ishassara, our General, and fifty other ha-mazaans with them on their ships. They sent another sixty through the Gate, including Hippolyta. Penthesilea is the only one left to us of Otrera's blood."

She did not soften her words for the horror on his face.

"Now go home to your pigsty, Hanassa, and let us bury our dead. Men are no longer welcome in this place, especially not while the Flame does not burn. We have already tasted what sacrilege men bring. We do not wish any more of it."

25

AFTERMATH

The next hours were a haze of blood and grief and, more than anything, increasing numbness, as the reality of what had happened, first in the bathhouse, then in the tower, on the shoreline, and finally in the burning palace, permeated every part of Penny's mind and body.

The worst outcome Penny could have imagined had been visited upon her, and upon Themiscyra. The result of her own actions, the punishment for her crime. Not only were there more than sixty dead ha-mazaans littering the beach like so much driftwood, but more than fifty Savaran were missing completely. Kidnapped by the Achaeans, the others claimed.

Both Antiope and Leandra were among the missing.

A dozen ha-mazaans had already searched for the young girl, Toxaris reported, while clutching a gaping wound in her own forearm. Penny remembered her vision of the girl's hair brimmed in sunlight, clutched in Leon's arms aboard the ship. The image burned in Penny's mind until she felt sick with grief and shame, a feeling mirrored back to her in the horrified faces of the ha-mazaans listening as she recounted what she knew. That Sagitta was gone along with her daughter was no comfort. Melanippe and Cyra were also taken, and Sylviu's mother, as well as six of the eight recently graduated Savaran, and enough of the city's most skilled warriors that, coupled with those who lay dead or dying on the beach, meant Themiscyra was practically defenseless now that the majority of its active warriors were gone. Even Tekmessa had been taken, along with the blacksmith's young daughter, Camilla, though Penny could think of only one use the Achaeans would have for a priestess and an apprentice blacksmith. They were both pleasing to the eye, and likely not stolen for their skills in healing or crafting. Her mind shied away from the thought as quickly as it intruded. Any woman who had been within range, who could not fight them off, who had not succumbed to sleep or sword or savagery, was now on their ships, bound for a fate too horrible to imagine, but Penny did not need to use her imagination anymore. She could still smell Brekko on her skin, feel his suffocating weight, hear his grunting. Her heart twisted to think of the other women suffering the same fate, but she kept her thoughts to herself.

There was no opportunity to share what had happened to her, nor what she had done in retaliation. When the reality of the Achaean treachery was fully realized, Penny knew that her own ordeal was the least of anyone's concern, and, with every new piece of terrible information, she was acutely aware they had every right to blame her for the outcome. She had broken her blood-sworn vow, however justified she had been for doing so, and the only consequence, the only outcome, was to be cursed. She was living the truth of that reality every moment of her waking life, while everyone around her suffered along with her, and she did not need to see the Erinyes' Shadow to know it was the truth.

When the sun rose, watery and faint in the eastern sky the morning after the attack, it was more than grief that left many of the ha-mazaans feeling sick. Women retched and trembled with sickness in every corner of the city, smoke rising from the burnt ruins around them, and though Penny wanted to do the same, to empty out the black sludge that slowly spread through her every pore, she knew there was something different about her own sickness to theirs.

"Poisoned," Marpe confirmed to the assembly of wounded, utterly exhausted ha-mazaans gathered in the Moon Hall. "Even the hounds slept, if they were in the Hall for the evening rather than the kennels. I do not think Antiope's hound will awaken at all. They poisoned the water along with the *kimiz*. Maybe even the wine."

"Aye, they poisoned the wine as well," Molpadia said brittlely, her hand on the pommel of her sword at her hip, as though she expected to have to draw it at any moment. Her voice was hoarse from howling her grief at the moon, and from breathing the smoke of the pyre she had lit from men's bodies. "I was asleep before the warning even sounded." She paused, and

Penny saw her throat move as she swallowed, before saying thickly, "I...I was not there to protect her."

A heavy silence followed Molpadia's agonized confession, as every woman in the room grieved not only for their dead Queen, but for the woman who had loved her so fiercely. In the absence of sound, Penny thought back to that morning in the storeroom, and the intruder.

"I think..." she began, her timid voice breaking the silence, and Molpadia's hard black eyes turned to her, quelling the words she was already scared to say, but she knew they needed to be said. "I think Theseus might have had something to do with the poison. He...he was outside the storeroom, the morning of the hunt. And there was an intruder inside, who came out as I was fetching a wineskin. They could have contaminated the drinking supply."

"Only you and your mother have keys to the storehouse."

Molpadia's words were flat, lifeless, but their barb was no less painful. Penny shifted, her eyes falling from that accusing stare to the bloody linen she used to clean the open wound on Toxaris' arm. There was nothing more to say that would not stir more trouble, or raise more questions, so she bit her tongue.

"It doesn't matter which man it was. They were all traitors," Marpe shook her head, her face grim with anger and her creped skin almost translucent in the early morning light streaming through the eastern window.

As exhausted as the *sivyeti* must be, her square hands were steady as she poked a bone needle, threaded with catgut, through the splayed pieces of flesh Penny pinched together on Toxaris' forearm. Penny grimaced a smile at the wounded ha-mazaan in apology for the pain. Though Toxaris' face was pale and a sheen of sweat stood out on her pale brow, she managed a wan smile in return, but soon her black eyes wandered to the bruise along Penny's jaw, then fell to the bruises dotting her wrists, the scrapes made from the pumice now raised red welts along her flesh. Penny kept her eyes on the ha-mazaan's wound, and the flash of Marpe's needle as it threaded through skin to avoid that searching gaze. When that became too gruesome, she cast her eyes over what remained of Themiscyra's women.

The remaining Savaran had scattered themselves throughout the hall, mostly near the doorways, tense and alert should the Watchers signal the return of any more ships. Xanharaspa and Crafters had gathered to lend their aid to the wounded, and *matars* clutched their babes close to their chests while their older children of three or four peered with wide, fearful eyes from behind their robes at the somber gathering. Against the wall, in the arms of a plump, middle-aged woman, Penny spotted dark curls on an impossibly small skull. The babe was cradled in the *matar's* arms, her dark lips suckling a white breast full of milk, but Penny knew it was not her blood mother. She met the woman's eyes, and in them was a sorrow that left no doubt whose daughter it was.

Grief welled inside for Areto, and for her daughter, though she felt the pain as though from the far side of a high, thick wall. Marpe's murmured assurances the woman's hemorrhaging meant her death had been likely in any scenario had been no comfort. The ha-mazaan had spent her last minutes defending the new life she had brought into the world, while Penny had lain unconscious and useless on the floor, the Flame meant to keep them all safe long gone. The girl would never hear her mother's laugh from this side of the womb, and that knowledge more than any other pierced her, bringing the sting of tears to her eyes. She looked away, refusing to let them fall. If she gave in to tears now, everything she held tightly together inside would shatter apart, she was sure.

Three *zizenti* moved through the room, offering the Great Mother's wisdom and comfort to the sick and wounded and heartsick alike. The red robes of the priestesses, so starkly contrasted against the black and dun and white of the rest of those gathered, reminded her so much of blood that Penny could not look at them without picturing first the gash in Brekko's neck as he stared down at her, before her mind skipped like a stone on water to the view of Lyta's chest, black with blood in the moonlight.

Hippolyta's body had been the first they carried inside the palace walls, to prepare her for burial. Later, Penny would assist the *zizentis* in preparing Lyta's body, painting it with ochre and honey and beeswax, before they would lay her in the Great Mother's womb to be reborn. The dead Achaeans had not been treated to the same honors. Molpadia had been swift and relentless in her fury, leaving no room for mercy in this life, or the next. The men's bodies burned in a smoking pyre even now, like so much refuse, the oily ashes blowing towards the Zalapa where they had come from, ensuring they may never return. She could only hope Brekko's body smoked on that pyre, and soon would be ashes blowing in the wind, along with his memory.

The six men who had been found wounded and abandoned on the shore now shivered in the stone cells beneath the palace foundations, awaiting their deaths at the edge of the dullest axe that could be found. Penny wanted to feel some form of empathy for them, some mercy that only she as Ishassara could offer, but her lips remained sealed on their fate, and she knew she would not stay Molpadia's hand when the time came.

"We will have to destroy all of the stored drink, just in case," Marpe was saying, though Penny was not sure what else she had missed as her fogged mind wandered over the assembly. The *sivyeti* tied a knot in the catgut to finish off her stitches, patting Toxaris' shoulder with a cursory tap to let her know they were finished, and the ha-mazaan moved to the next table to offer her stitched arm for bandaging. "We'll fetch water from the eastern spring rather than the inner well, until we can be sure it is set right again."

Marpe paused, turning her tired eyes on Penny.

"And Penthesilea will reignite the Flame, so that Kubileya's spirit watches over us again."

26

ETERNAL FLAME

The Flame. How long had it been cold, now? How long since it had exploded in the face of an angry, vengeful Daughter of Night and Shadow? Penny wasn't sure. Time had become warped, and she could not remember if the sun had risen once, or twice, or not at all since the Flame in the tower, and inside her soul, had gone out.

"Only you and your mother hold keys to the storeroom," Molpadia repeated slowly, some strength returning to her voice. "And that same key opens the passage to the Tower, doesn't it?"

Every woman within hearing distance turned a considering eye on Penny. Their stares were nearly as hard and penetrating as Molpadia's.

"I was with the Flame when it...when it went out," Penny faltered, and it sounded like a confession even to her own ears. They seemed to expect more from her, but she didn't know what to say without revealing everything, and that was something she was not yet ready to do. "It...exploded. I was knocked unconscious. When I woke up, the hearth was cold." She glanced away from Molpadia to the others, then back again, rushing her words to assure their frowning faces. "I will reignite it as soon as the sun shines. I can't right now, with the clouds...I need the sun for the ritual. It will be fine once the sun is strong again."

She finished with what she hoped was reassuring certainty, but Molpadia still stared at her with eyes hard as flint when she said,

"It was you and your mother who welcomed them. Gave them guest-right. You had all sorts of plans with that fox-spirit and his shepherd brother."

"I had little choice in welcoming them," Penny snapped, her skin prickling at the insinuation she would aid such treachery, and also with the guilt of knowing it was entirely her fault, no matter the method. "I did what my mother bade me. What my role demands."

A bubble of hot shame expanded in her throat as Molpadia's scarred lip lifted in a sneer. Penny wanted to scream that she had suffered, too. That her mother had been taken in front of their own eyes. That the ha-mazaans who were sworn to protect her had let one of those men violate her. But to let them know what happened between her and Brekko would mean revealing she had broken her vow, inviting the anger and condemnation of every woman in the Hall, even if they were justified in feeling it.

"You're right, though," she said, with more bitterness than anticipated. "Antiope never should have given them guest-right, if they intended this destruction all along."

Marpe eyed her, pursing her lips as a Xanharaspa poured water from a pitcher over the *sivyeti's* hands, the basin pooling with liquid the color of crushed cherries. "Antiope welcomed those men as guests, as was her duty, child. It was the men who betrayed our sacred hospitality."

Penny turned away, humiliated at being called a child. However much she wished she could be young and free and naïve and not living this nightmare, it felt especially unfair that Marpe would refer to her as one now.

Toxaris took pity on her, though her comment was to the room at large. "The moment Theseus and his lion-pelted friend admitted they had come with thoughts of war to take Hippolyta's belt, they should have been escorted back to their ships and sent on their way, at the very least."

"Their ships should have burned with our flaming arrows as soon as Melanippe told the queens her visions," Molpadia said lowly. She shook her head like a dog, her voice rising. "Yet Antiope let them come anyway. But I will take one part of the blame, at least. I should have bound and executed Heracles the moment he revealed his treachery, hospitality of a Hearth Queen be damned."

There were murmurs of agreement from others in the Hall, but most remained silent. Penny did not look to see who agreed with Molpadia, and who did not.

"The queens had their reasons, and what you suggest would have brought a curse upon all of us, if the sacred hospitality of our city had been breached," Marpe said firmly. Then, misunderstanding the cause of Penny's stricken face, she added softly, "I am sorry for your loss, child. It is more than you should have to bear."

Penny turned her back to the *sivyeti* and faced the eastern window, staring at the blackened ruins of the outer courtyard. Charred posts and the crumbling, still smoldering cinders of the supporting beams were all that remained of the once sprawling outer reaches of the palace, where the fire had consumed everything in its path. The storerooms with the winter supply of grains and dried grasses for the animals burned, and most of the adobe homes within the palace walls had lost their thatch roofs, or their entire contents, to hungry, unmerciful flames. Though the stables were razed completely, the horses had been turned loose by quick-thinking Xanharaspas, and only a few mares or foals needed to be treated for scrapes or burns after their frenzied quest for freedom. Themiscyra's youth cavalry, along with the rest of the palace—or at least those who had not fallen unconscious—had been forced to choose between helping their sisters in the unexpected battle, or joining the bucket brigade in dousing the flames threatening their homes and livelihoods.

And Penny had been the cause of all of it.

Beyond the charred remains of the city, dark clouds gathered in the distant sky, somewhere far over the Zalapa where her mother sailed with Theseus. They mirrored the darkening mood inside of her. Her mother was out there. Fifty-seven women at the mercy of merciless Achaeans, and she, the sole person in the entire city who was forbidden to hoist a sword, as useless to them as nipples on a boar, and the source of all their suffering. If any woman found out how she had broken that vow, a sacrilege that would never be tolerated, she knew her days as their Ishassara would be over. She was no longer so sure she deserved the title, anyway.

She could not tell if it was her exhausted mind conjuring images, or reality, but she was sure the clouds hovered in the shape of an Erinyes, twisting snakes of rain downward into the sea. The sight of the Fury no longer brought panic to the surface, for a shell of numbness had begun to harden around that tight knot of fear implanted deep inside. Everything, even the wrath of the Fury, felt inevitable, irrevocable. The curse for breaking her vow had already found her, had already begun to strip away the life she had once taken for granted, and she knew she would spend the rest of her days, however short they may be, fleeing from its snake-rimmed shadow.

PART TWO

SEPARATION

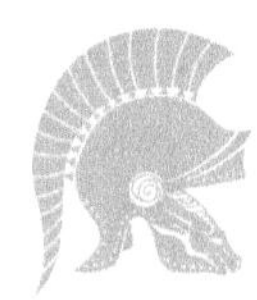

27

DESPERATE

Sylviu tried everything to breach their impenetrable barrier to find Pen and make sure she was truly unharmed, to learn more about his stolen mother and the other ha-mazaans, even going so far as to attempt to swim the Terme upriver from the city. Not even that worked. The current pulled him too close to the city's gates and the sentries, on high alert after the destruction of their city, found him before he could even shake the water from his hair. They escorted him back to the men hunkered in place with a stern warning to either stay there, or go back where he belonged, or burn with the dead Achaeans if he wished. He found himself waiting with the rest of the men for the meager scraps of news one or two ha-mazaans saw fit to toss them every once in a while. His helplessness frothed itself into a seething ocean of rage.

Penthesilea sent him a message, though Sylviu had foolishly hoped she would deliver it herself. He understood why she didn't. He had realized quickly enough she would not want to see him, if their city had indeed been destroyed because the Flame had gone cold due to his own carelessness, though she only knew half of his part in it. She knew enough, though. There was only one person who had been arrogant enough, stupid enough to invite sacrilege in that Tower, and then leave his own mother and friends to suffer the consequences of it. Just like their Kebat had told him, all those years ago, when he had broken that sacred tradition, too. His mother had tried to warn him, and he had not listened. Not even cared.

He spent the hours pacing, and arguing with the other men, and staring at the ruined beams of his mother's city, thinking of his last words to her.

Go fight with your precious axe, and I will hide in Galatae until the next time you need pigs for a funeral feast and linen to wrap your dead body in. That is all I'm good for, isn't it?

What terrible beast in him had made him say such a thing? He tried not to stare at the bay where the Terme emptied into the Zalapa, tried not to think of his mother in the belly of a ship, bound in Achaean chains, his last words to her cutting through her kind, loving heart, but his mind would not give up its obsession. At least he had the hope that she was alive, though he didn't know what to do with that hope. He was as useless now as he had been when she needed him. He tried to concentrate on the fact that Pen was alive, and apparently unharmed. At least there was that.

He was not sure which afternoon it was that the men scrambled for their bronze swords, assembling in quick formation to defend their flank from a new threat, marching the same road they had taken. Sylviu urged his gelding to the front line, sword drawn, but as soon as he saw the crested helmet and the fine, long-legged white horse of the one in the lead, he lowered his sword along with the rest of the men.

"Ho there!" the woman called out.

"Ho, Sinope!" one of the men answered.

The ha-mazaan pulled her horse to a halt, surveying them from the shadows of her helmet. Behind her, their armor glinting in the afternoon sun, a full ha-mazaan contingent crested the hill, their snow-white horses trotting ten abreast in perfect unison, their crested helmets sweeping the sky underneath a bristle of spears.

"You are too late!" Sylviu called, letting his own frustration bleed into the words that had recently prickled his own pride. The woman found him in the line soon enough, her eyes somber as she held his before she looked beyond his shoulder to the ruined city.

"Aye, it seems we are," she agreed, and the steady pound of their army marching inexorably forward made her raise her voice for her next words to be heard.

"Why do you camp outside the gates like desperate dogs, Sons of Galatae?"

"Because they won't let us in!" a man rasped, hurt and anger making his voice raw.

"Because they no longer trust any men, even their kin," another growled, and the woman raised a brow at both. She found Sylviu's face again.

"From what their messengers say, they have good reason. You should go home, Hanassas. Sinope has answered Themiscyra's call. We will send for your aid if we need it."

"Yes, we are Hanassa!" a younger man shouted, urging his horse closer to her, though the ha-mazaan remained unfazed. "Those are our kin, too. Our wives and mothers and daughters. We have a right to protect them."

She smiled, but it was bleak inside the shadows of her helmet. She turned her horse back to the road, and said over her shoulder, "You have a right to your life, man, but remember who gave it to you in the first place, and remember who can take it again. I would listen to your ha-mazaans, and do what they tell you. Go home."

Penny stepped carefully around fleece-covered, bandaged ha-mazaans laid haphazardly on the floor, wiping their blood from her hands as she moved listlessly about the makeshift infirmary that had once been her chambers, ending up in front of Antiope's vanity. She trailed her fingers over the soft goat-hair bristles of the tortoiseshell brush her mother had been using what could have been hours ago or a lifetime ago. Her mind could no longer differentiate the passage of time. Everything was a heavy fog, laden with grief and guilt under a thick layer of protective numbness, under which nightmares writhed.

She lifted the brush, the oval shape of it fitting snugly in the palm of her hand, remembering all the times she had sat right here, on the horse-hair stuffed bench next to the window, as her mother brushed her hair and told her stories of her grandmothers and aunts and cousins, and, most vividly, her own hoped-for legacy. She stared out the high window, the view the same she had seen for more than half a lifetime, almost none of it recognizable to her cluttered mind, save for the shape of the hills. Her eyes were drawn to the farthest horizon in the southeastern corner of the casement, where the river turned sharply to the east, following the valley all the way to the river's source high in the mountains. The mountain itself was not visible, but Penny knew that was where Themiscyra's Oracle dwelled. The same woman who gave every woman in this city, including her mother, their destinies. Their promises from Matar Kubileya for their future as ha-mazaans. Everyone, that is, except Penny, who had been forbidden by Antiope from ever visiting that secret location.

She was about to turn away from the window when movement on the western road caught her eye, a great plume of dust ascending to the sky in a telltale sign of travelers on the road.

"Toxaris!" she called softly, so as not to disturb the women sleeping at her feet. The ha-mazaan soon made her way through the doorway from Hippolyta's old chambers, where more wounded ha-mazaans were sleeping, wiping her bloodied hands on an already dark rag.

Toxaris joined her at the window, quickly spotting the nearest horse and rider.

"Evandre," Toxaris murmured.

"Queen Orithyia's General?" Penny asked, her forehead creasing as she stared at the mass of riders. Behind the solitary rider, the haze of dust along the road dissolved into a single line of horses, ten abreast, until more rows, at least seven deep, crested the far hill one troop at a time.

"Along with her entire army, it would appear, although most all of them are old women now after Themiscyra absorbed most of the younger ones when Queen Sanape died without an Ishassara."

"Why does she come with an army?"

Toxaris' own forehead creased with a thoughtful frown. "Your guess is as good as mine, Ishassara. Perhaps Orithyia wishes to claim the ha-mazaans here as her own, now that..." Toxaris did not finish, but Penny knew well enough what she meant, and turned to her with a shocked face.

"Claim them as her own? She has no right to them at all! My mother will return. And I..."

She could not justify the rest of her thought. It was preposterous to think of claiming these women as hers, even though her mother and aunt were not here to fulfill their roles, even with her cousin Cyra, her future sister-queen, among the missing. Avoiding Toxaris' questioning gaze, Penny trained her eyes on the cavalry of horses and women marching down the western hill towards the palace gates.

"Perhaps Queen Antiope will return," Toxaris said, after a short pause. "Either way, you are still her heir. You are Ishassara, and one day Hearth Queen. You are the one who will need to stand up to ones such as Orithyia when they come. Because more *will* come, even if Orithyia is merely passing by. Themiscyra has the most power and wealth of any ha-mazaan city from Chaldesia to Lydia, so they will be descending on our palace like flies on a rotting hind, seeking their piece of flesh."

Penny fidgeted with the brush in her hand, swiping her fingers this way and that over the soft bristles. She carefully placed it back on the small table and turned away from the window, and away from Toxaris' searching gaze.

"I suppose that means I must be the one to greet our guests, then."

They descended together down the stone steps and out into the inner courtyard, where Sinope's General soon appeared, the rest of the army lagging well behind. Other curious, wary ha-mazaans joined them in the courtyard to watch the tall, lean ha-mazaan swing down from her sweat-lathered horse. The ha-mazaan herself was as old, if not older, than Hippolyta had been, with silver streaks in her short-cropped dark hair, but when she walked toward them, it was with an unhurried, ground-eating swagger that belied her age, and gave testament to a battle-ready vigor.

Penny cast about for a memory of meeting this woman, perhaps at some ceremony or tournament the two cities engaged in on a regular basis, but she could not remember ever being introduced. Still, she pasted on her best smile of greeting and approached the newcomer, feeling self-conscious about performing this role alone, without her mother's lead. The other ha-mazaans gathered around, curious at what news this messenger brought from their queen's cousin.

"It seems we are too late," the woman said without preamble, catching Penny off guard. Whatever she had thought the message might be, she was not prepared for what was said next. "Is it true, then, that Queen Antiope welcomed a hundred men to slaughter your ha-mazaans?"

Penny's tongue froze in stupefied shock. Even Toxaris seemed taken aback, her eyebrows darting upward, and a puzzled frown appearing on her normally placid face. Molpadia's firm voice called out across the courtyard, sparing Penny the need for an immediate reply.

"Evandre. What news?"

"I don't bring news, Dia," the woman said without pause. "I bring an army, to help you defend your city. But I see we are too late."

She punctuated her words with a sweep of her arm to indicate the blackened beams and soot-stained blocks of the outer courtyard, her eyes lingering for a long, thoughtful moment on the still smoldering pile of indistinguishable forms in the far northern quadrant outside the walls. Her twitching nose likely told her it was the bodies of the men she had apparently brought an army here to fight.

"How did you know we needed help defending our city?" Molpadia asked, suspicion dripping from every syllable as her brisk strides brought her face to face with the General. "We fought those bastards two days ago. It takes two full days to ride from Sinope to Themiscyra on a fast horse, and I only sent messengers last night."

"Aye, your messengers met us on the road, and return with us now." Evandre paused before saying, "They told us about Lyta, Dia. I am truly sorry. May she be welcomed into the bosom of the Great Mother, and be reborn swiftly through Her Womb."

After a brief pause, Molpadia replied through stiff lips, "May she be welcomed into the bosom of the Great Mother."

Evandre tilted one corner of her lips upward in a sad smile of commiseration, but Molpadia returned to her earlier question, clearly unwilling to linger on the topic of her wife's death.

"How did you know to bring an army?" Molpadia repeated, more tersely than before, her tone bordering on accusatory.

Evandre considered Molpadia closely, pursing her lips. "We come at Hippolyta's urgent behest." A casual lift of her dark eyebrows was her only challenge to Molpadia's disbelieving stare. "Lyta sent a messenger when the Achaean ships first arrived, bidding Orithyia herself to come here. And not to come alone, if you take my meaning. Unfortunately, Orithyia is still in Paphlagonia—still was when we left, anyway—but I answered the call as best I could without her. We tried to make good time, but it grieves me to know it was not good enough."

"But how—" Penny began, but her interjection only earned her a curious glance from Evandre before she was interrupted again.

"Why did Lyta request *your* army? She told me nothing of it." Molpadia's
body had gone tense, like a caged animal ready to spring.

"Blasted if I know," Evandre shrugged, her thumbs hooked into her thick
belt. "But when one Defending Queen commands another to respond, a
mere General does not question it, eh? Clearly, Hippolyta was not wrong
in her assessment of the situation, though." Another eyebrow went up, and
Molpadia stared back at the General for a long moment before breaking eye
contact with a muttered curse. She turned on her heel and stalked away.

Evandre returned curious eyes back to Penny, her glance flickering just
once over the tight, chevron-striped trousers and linen shift. Penny wondered if she disapproved of a Hearth Queen's daughter being dressed so,
but her old white robes had seemed far too...pristine, too impractical to
be wearing while clearing rubble and scrubbing open wounds. These new
clothes, taken from the back of her mother's wardrobe, somehow made
her feel more like her old self. Specifically, the self that existed before she
had come to this city. Before everything had gone wrong.

"General Evandre," Penny said, her training coming to the forefront
even as the rapids in her mind tumbled over this new information. "As
Ishassara, I welcome you as an honored guest. Your ha-mazaans are not far
behind, I saw, but there is time for refreshment before we speak of...recent
events. Please, join us in the Moon Hall for *kimiz* or wine, or enjoy one of
our bathhouses first, if you wish to be rid of your journey's dust."

The older woman smiled, the warmth of it a surprising light in her stern
and weathered face.

"Such formality!" the ha-mazaan said, and then clapped a hand on Penny's shoulder. "I shall save the baths for later, when this one," she gestured
to Toxaris, who grinned back, "brings me the best Colchis wine in your
cellar, and we can drink to forget our sore joints. Or at least, remember
some of our best adventures. Like that time in Hattusa, when we smuggled
ourselves into the inner palace for a bit of extra revelry, eh, Tox? But first,"
the General said, turning her attention back to Penny, her face falling into
serious lines once more, "my condolences on the loss of your mother and

aunts, Ishassara Penthesilea, and all the women lost. The ha-mazaans of Sinope grieve with you."

"Thank you," Penny replied automatically, before turning to lead Evandre through the entrance gates of the palace and into the Moon Hall. She said, over her shoulder, "Please, just call me Penny."

Evandre hiked her sword belt as they walked. "I cannot do that, Ishassara, and you should not ask it of me. You are your mother's heir. And your mother, as far as I can tell, is…well, she is going to be absent for some time," she finished judiciously. "At the very least, every ha-mazaan should be calling you Ishassara, if not Queen."

Suppressing a grimace at the discomfort of such an idea, Penny led them inside the Moon Hall, then ladled a fresh mug of *kimiz* and handed it to Evandre, who smiled her thanks. After a deep drink, she turned a considering gaze on Penny, while other ha-mazaans took their places at benches and tables nearby.

"From the tale your messenger tells us, and from what I have seen in entering your city, your ha-mazaans need shelter."

Penny nodded. "Our storehouses also burned, including the winter grain for the horses. We haven't enough food left to keep us until the Frost Moon, let alone through the winter, even if we request further tithes from Galatae. They have enough mouths of their own to feed, and some of the women may wish to overwinter there with their husbands or sons, but…" she trailed off, leaving the obvious unspoken, as Evandre was already nodding.

"I speak for my queen, for all of Sinope, when I extend an invitation for all of your women, or at least those who do not want to stay with their men in Galatae, to come to Sinope," Evandre said. "Our city will provide everything you need through the winter rains. You will only last a few more moons before your horses, at the very least, run for the hills to find food. But first, Ishassara," she said, her eyes solemn as they held Penny's, "we shall help you bury your dead."

28

BURIAL

"Molpadia, you cannot shut us out forever. These were our mothers. Our sisters. Our kin."

"Aye. And we will give them every honor they deserve as we send them through the Gate, but we do not need you for that. No men will ever pass through these gates again, do you understand me? You might as well take the younger Hanassas with you when you go. We don't need the brats underfoot eating what's left of our stores."

"What *right* do you have?" Sylviu ground out, his chest burning with a rage he had not thought possible, but it was easier to feel than the guilt underneath it all.

"The right my queen gave me as her consort."

"She was my queen, too. I need to speak with Pen."

"You need nothing, other than the blade of my axe in your throat if you challenge me again, Hanassa. Your mother is no longer here to protect you. Penthesilea needs to look after her city, and reignite the Flame, not stare cow-eyed at boys who do not know their place. That foolishness is what brought us to this end in the first place. She and her whoring mother brought this on us all."

The rage in him turned white, and cold. He took another step closer, his hand on the hilt of his sword, aware the men behind him were equally as livid and distraught at being turned away from the burials of their own families, and equally as frustrated they could do nothing about it without inciting outright violence. Not when this woman barred their way, and every ha-mazaan behind her held their bows and axes ready to cut down the first man who stepped foot on their bridge. The latest message smuggled to them in the night had been news of who still lived and who died, and that the burials were set to begin. It had not been an invitation, but no man who had loved someone in that city was about to leave without honoring their kin.

"You do not have the authority to turn us away," Sylviu said again. One of the men shouted his own obscenity at her, and another cursed at the woman blocking his way, the tensions between them staining everything. Molpadia stared at him without emotion, her scarred face nearly blue in the grey light of the low clouds.

"Authority?" She laughed without sound or humor, her eyes dark and hard as the blackened stone behind her. "This is ha-mazaan territory. The pigsty you live in is ha-mazaan territory. Everything you see and smell and taste belongs to us, including *you*. And I am still Hippolyta's wife, in this life and the next. I am her hand of justice, and I am the one who is taking care of what is left of her city, and her women. That is my authority. My right. Just like killing you would be. Either way, men will not sully my wife's final ritual with their filth. Turn your tails home, my boy, and do not show your face here again."

Molpadia carried Hippolyta's body on her shoulders, leading eight other women who carried the same weight, but not the same burden. They had loved their queen also. Just not as Molpadia had. Not as she still did. Though every other face wept as she cradled Lyta's shrouded shoulder on her own, her tears would no longer come. Tears would not help, anymore. There was no cure for this pain except death, when their spirits could rejoin in the Otherworld, or be reborn again in another life. That was the hope she held onto now.

Penthesilea led the dancers in their drumbeat of mourning behind Hippolyta's shrouded body, and the sound thrummed through Molpadia's hollow chest as a replacement for what had once beat there, strong and sure. She had made the drum herself, marking the sun-bleached, tightly stretched hide on the frame with Hippolyta's own blood, decorating it with whorls and mountains, the spirit of stag and hawk and leopard lending strength to her lover's journey, matching the tattoos Molpadia had inscribed into Lyta's thighs and chest and back when they were barely Savaran, before Lyta had even thought of ever being Defending Queen. But those marks of protection had not been enough. Molpadia's prayers had not been enough. And when Lyta had needed her the most, she had been drowning in her own sick jealousy, letting a man come between her and her only light in this world, before he had snuffed that flame out forever.

Toxaris led Hippolyta's mare close behind Lyta's ochre-stained, honey-drenched body, so that the small mountain became a moving, undulating sea of women approaching the entrance to the tomb, the opening shadowed in the evening sun. Penthesilea ended the chant with an abrupt beat that shocked Molpadia into the present. A hush of expectation fell. They lowered Lyta's body onto the stone table at the mouth of the cave, where all would join the moon in bearing witness to her one last night. She paused for a long moment, then pressed one last kiss to Lyta's honeyed lips through the muslin.

With several hundred ha-mazaans looking on, their faces drawn and weary, Molpadia stepped close to Hippolyta's mare. Toxaris stepped away, and the *zizenti* already stepping forward to complete the ritual paused, seeing the intention in Molpadia's eyes. The palomino's own eyes were as a night sky filled with stars, and in them, Molpadia saw once more her lover's sightless eyes the night of the battle, her bloodied chest, the red-gold rope of her hair twisted under her, marking all the battles she had won but the silken strands now soaked with her own blood, marking the last battle she had never been given a chance to fight.

Molpadia whispered her vow with fierce intention, to the mare and to the one the *rhu-tasiya* was bound to. The others looking on did not need to hear it, though she did not care if they did. She did not care if the whole world heard it, but she could only rasp the words out, low and vicious, the mare's eyes rolling with terror as she smelled Molpadia's spirit burning like a white coal.

"By your blood, wife, and by the blood of your *rhu-tasiya*, I swear on my own soul that your death will not go unpunished. Until our stolen women are returned to us, until destruction has been brought against any who set their hand against the sisters of Themiscyra, against you, I will not rest. I shall seek vengeance against the ones who sought to destroy us, in this life and the next. I will avenge you. And then I will join you. This I swear."

With one swift draw of her arm, she slit the throat of the palomino mare, the blood hot and humid and smelling of star-iron as it spilled past her elbows and pooled at her feet, a proxy for the tears she could not weep. The mare collapsed to her knees with a heavy grunt, ha-mazaan hands guiding where she would fall, *zizenti* voices rising in a song that was as much a wailing as a prayer. As the horse's lifeblood leaked onto the ground, spilling onto Molpadia's shins and feet, she sealed her vow, to Kubileya and the ha-mazaans and the Achaeans alike.

She would take her vengeance against the ones responsible, or she would die trying. Either way, she would enter that Gate soon, to follow Lyta into the very depths of the Otherworld, and she would not be telling her love she had failed her twice.

29

A Leopard's Eye

Penny performed her role in the burial of Hippolyta and the sixty ha-mazaans in a haze of numbness that felt nothing like grief. She was happy to let Molpadia perform the ritual for Lyta, and for a *zizenti* to call the *rhu-tasiyas* of the dead to join their partners at the Gate of the Otherworld, but her own part in the matter was stilted and dry, as though some part of her had been embalmed and buried under the dry dust, shut inside the great stone burial chamber along with her aunt. She could not even bring herself to intervene when she learned from Toxaris that Sylviu and other men, sons and brothers and husbands of the dead, were at the gates demanding to be a part of the funeral rites for their loved ones. As much as she wanted to see Sylviu, to tell him everything, it had also become a terrible fear that he would find out anything about what she had done, and then she would lose the last—the *only*—friend she had ever known. So she let Molpadia, acting in all her authority as Lyta's consort, keep the gates barred, and went about painting the bodies of the dead with beeswax and ochre, until her hands were stained as red as the blood she still saw on them every waking minute.

Areto's body was the first they honored, with her arms laid ready and open to welcome the daughter she would never again hold this side of the Gate. Hippolyta was the last. When it was the Defending Queen's turn, Penny looked on numbly as Molpadia held the star-iron blade against the throat of Lyta's *rhu-tasiya*, the ha-mazaan's lips moving in a repetitive prayer that only her and the horse and her dead lover's honey-filled ears could hear. When the deed was done, and Molpadia's blood-soaked fingers had drawn their marks on Lyta's face and chest, the woman locked her eyes with Penny's, her expression fierce, her scar white against already pale skin. Even in the face of that anger and grief, the outright accusation in the ha-mazaan's eyes, Penny felt nothing, as though her insides were filled with wool and flax, just like Lyta's. She wanted to tell Molpadia she was not wrong to cast blame her way, that she would carry the guilt of their undoing for all of her days, but Dia turned away from her, and a *zizenti* struck a drum to break the silence, the gong resounding in Penny's hollowness, and the others raised their voices in a mourning dirge. She beat her drum with them, leading them away from the graves, but her dancing held neither joy nor grief.

Than night it was Areto's ochre-stained face Penny saw before she drifted off to sleep. The dead mother's dark visage slowly coalesced into a golden eye centered with black, rimmed with long lashes. A leopard's eye. Soft, warm fur of her childhood protector under her hands, the black rings circling copper and gold in a mesmerizing pattern of fur for her fingers to trace, was the first clue Penny had to being in a Dream. The second was the light. She moved in perpetual twilight, the air a periwinkle blue hazed with the last of the day's sun and the first of the evening's fires. She pushed her hands into the thick fur of the leopard, and was rewarded by loud purring, the rumble vibrating through her hands and up her arms, so that it seemed to pulse inside of her heartbeat, and not only in her mind. Penny closed her eyes in the dream, shutting out every other sound, every other vision, to immerse herself fully in the vision that was Begri.

"I have not dreamed of you in so long," Penny murmured, and the purring intensified. She buried her face in the thick, powerful muscles of the huge cat's neck, marveling at the way the very scent of the animal permeated her mind.

"We have waited for you here for a long time, Bella."

Penny jerked her face from the leopard's musky pelt to see the man who spoke. He stood nearby, his form swirled in shadows, as though his legs and feet were part of the oncoming night. He wore the skin of a leopard over his shoulders, the great paws of the cat protruding from the thick leather belt around his waist. Though his face was older, wiser, she knew him even in the shadows of dreams and twilight.

"Father?"

He smiled tenderly at her, and she felt her heart clench.

"Return to your home, Bella. It is time. Find the one who will bring you back to me. Seek out your Seer. She will tell you the Way."

"Father, I—"

Her words were cut short by a deep-throated, vicious whine from Begri. When she glanced at the cat again, the beast's face only inches from hers, the cat's eyes stared with feline intensity beyond Penny's shoulder, and her ruff and whiskers stood to attention, a sign she was ready to pounce. Another low growl of warning rumbled out of Begri's throat, bringing the hair on Penny's own neck to prickling attention.

"Begri—"

She did not finish before the cat lunged. Penny was knocked backward by the enormous weight of the animal, but it was not herself that the cat attacked.

She heard the leathery creak and the furious shriek of the Erinyes mingle with the scream of the leopard. She could not tell if it was the cat's claws or the Fury's talons embedding themselves in the tender flesh of her wrist, tearing at her skin, before their growling roared so loud in her ears that she bolted upright in bed, her breath rasping as loud as the Fury's wings had been.

Even the terror of the dream could not quell the grief of losing contact with her father so abruptly. She had not Dreamed of her father once in the ten years since coming here. She had not Dreamed at all. She had thought of Thrax every day, longed for him, wished for his council and his quiet strength, for his gentle hands, but never had she Dreamed of him, as much as she tried. That he had come to her now, with Begri as his guide, threatened to split a tear in the shroud of numbness Penny had gathered around herself.

Return to your home, Bella. It is time. Find the one who will bring you back to me. Seek out your Seer. She will tell you the Way.

Molpadia's voice echoed over her father's. *Their ships should have burned with our flaming arrows as soon as Melanippe told the Queens her visions...Yet Antiope let them come anyway...*

...Seek out your Seer.

Her father's command echoed in her mind, and she could not disobey. She climbed from the thin mattress of linen and straw on the floor of the room she now shared with a dozen near-death ha-mazaans, and crept to the stairs, then out of the palace. All the way to the roped-in corral that now served as stables, Penny wondered what she was thinking, what trouble she was inviting, but to hear her father's voice again after so long had sparked a new flame inside her chest. She told the ha-mazaan on guard duty she needed air, and the solace of a horse between her thighs, and the woman let her go with no more questions.

Tana's hollow hoofprints on the cobblestone bridge were conspicuously loud in the night as they made their way under a moonless sky, following the river south and then east, towards the Womb of the Mountain. As soon as they were well past the walls of the city, she prodded Tana into a trot, urging her to the fastest the pony's sure hooves could take them on the rocky path up the canyon while dark crowded their way forward. She found the narrow canyon leading to the steep stone steps without issue, leaving Tana to doze at the bottom of the narrow valley, and began her ascent to the narrow cleft in the rock, taking extra care in the darkness so as not to turn an ankle on some hidden stone and tumble back down into the canyon. It would be days before anyone found her if she were to break a leg here, in the middle of the wilderness, after stealing away in secret.

As expected, after hearing so many stories of it from other young ha-mazaans on their first moon-blood adventure, a lioness greeted her at the oval entrance, but the big cat did move to attack or hinder Penny's approach, merely blinking those liquid brown eyes at her and lifting her wide muzzle the sniff the air, as though smelling her intentions. Accustomed to her father's great leopards, Penny felt no fear, and after a respectful moment of waiting, their eyes fixed on one another, the lioness turned and padded away into the inner darkness. Penny followed.

The room the cat led her to was huge and lit only by a small brazier, the flames small and wavering, but it was the walls themselves that seemed to glow from within. Everything inside the room was fashioned of quartz, the stones sharp and flat, like spikes laid overlapping edge to edge to build a curved wall, all the way up to a ceiling covered in discs of polished silver. Penny gazed up at them in awe, turning a full circle to take in the magnificence of the whole cavern, searching as she spun for the person she had come to see, but it was only herself and the lioness, now sitting patiently at the foot of an empty, fur-covered quartz throne at the edge of the room. In the center of the room sat a huge stone cauldron rimmed in bronze, the tapered edge of it nearly as high as her collarbone, and it was toward this that she slowly moved, wondering what could possibly be inside of a cookpot so large. She peered into the depths of it, seeing nothing but shadows, when a voice said behind her,

"You forego your sacred Threshold ritual, only to come here now, without protection of the Mother's blood, and with a Shadow clinging to you like Death clings to a corpse? Should I call it courage, or foolishness, that you would dare such sacrilege?"

Penny spun, stepping away from the empty cauldron with a guilty flush, expecting to see the Erinyes hovering over her, but instead she saw a woman, dark-skinned and imposing, with the amber eyes of a lioness staring at her. The Kebat stood taller than any woman or man Penny had ever seen, towering against the white of the stone walls as though she were a boulder from deep inside the mountain now come to life, moving with slow, ground-eating steps to the center of the room. Long black hair twisted like rivulets of water over her naked, heavy breasts, the ends of the braids knotted with bone beads that clattered together as she moved. Beside her, a second lioness padded silently, the cat's shoulder barely reaching the woman's thigh, though each lioness was easily as tall at the shoulder as Penny's hip. Penny tried not to gape. She had expected another crone like the one her mother had taken her to when she swore her vow, but this was no hag. This was a Daughter of Kubileya. The sight of her magnificent stature gave Penny renewed confidence that surely this was the person who would have the answers she needed, the one whom her father bade her to speak with. But the question she had come prepared to ask did not make its way out of her as doubts held at bay for days suddenly crowded her mind.

Their ships should have burned with our flaming arrows as soon as Mela-nippe told the queens her visions. Yet Antiope let them come anyway.

She stared at that implacable dark face, and asked what she truly needed to know.

"What did you tell my mother on her first moon-blood?"

The Kebat considered her from her great height for several long seconds before saying, without rancor, "I told your mother nothing."

Penny frowned, shifting her weight on her feet as she stared at the dark woman's tattooed features.

"Why do you lie?" Penny demanded. "My mother told me some of the moon-blood prophecy you gave her. You promised her *so many things*. You gave Antiope *and* Hippolyta their promises. You give it to every ha-maza-an! But now Hippolyta is dead! *Both* our sister-queens are gone!" Rage unfurled inside Penny, so that she no longer knew or cared what she was saying as the grief poured out in a torrent of accusations. "Why would you not tell them the Achaeans would destroy everything? Why did you tell my mother our legacy would be so great, so enduring, when it is only destruction, and death, and..." she floundered as thick fingers in her throat choked off the rest. "*Why did you lie to her?*" she finished hoarsely.

The Kebat's expression did not change. Not even a flicker of an eyelid betrayed that the giant woman was affected by this news of tragedy in the valley below.

"I told Themiscyra's Queens no lies. But what prophecies I *did* tell them are theirs alone, child, and not for you to know. Tell me, why do you really come here?"

Penny stared at her, the anger coiling inside of her a new, terrible feeling she had never known before, but more pleasant than either fear or grief, or even the cold numbness that had kept her safe since being in that bathhouse. Her lip curled.

"I came here to find out whether you were a fraud. To know if that's why my mother never let me meet you."

Two weeks ago, she would have abhorred such rudeness, such disregard for the esteem of her elders. Something about the arrival of the Achaeans, and the aftermath of their fateful visit, the recurring memory of Brekko's fingers squeezing the bones of her wrist until she thought they might be pulverized completely, but only that memory, over and over again, until her mind went dark for the rest of it, her aunt's bloodied chest and sightless eyes, the sound of Molpadia howling at the star-strewn sky, the image of all the dead and wounded ha-mazaans, the charred ruins of the city, the absence of her mother, and worse, the growing suspicions of Antiope in the downfall of their sisters, had loosed a recklessness in Penny that could not be contained. Her normally meek and reserved self seemed to have fled along with her mother. She bared her teeth and seethed at the giant as she waited for an answer.

But the Kebat only stared at her, expectant, and Penny forged on.

"I came here to see if you could tell me why? *Why!* Why we didn't know before we welcomed them, if you have such clarity, such insight. Why we couldn't stop them. Why he..." she shook her head, unable to say it out loud. Her next words were more desperate. "I came to find out how to get my mother back."

"Antiope will never return to Themiscyra as Hearth Queen, if that is what you have come to find out."

Penny stared, uncomprehending. Her anger began to deflate, and a terrifying hollowness began to fill its space, but the Kebat went on before Penny could think of what to say to that terrible, terrible revelation.

"Your mother is long gone through the Gate, child. But her destiny should not be what brings you here, so many years after your first moon-blood."

The hollow feeling expanded. Every fiber in Penny's body twisted slowly from hot to cold. Her face went numb as all the blood drained to her toes, and her chest squeezed with a pain she had never felt before. Something prickled on her skin, on her face. She thought it might be tears, to go along with the breaths now barely gasping out of her lungs, but she was too cold, too dazed to know for sure.

"You are a liar."

"Who speaks lies, but the one who seeks to dishonor Kubileya Herself?" The censure in the Oracle's voice was clear. "Kubileya has blessed you, and you dare question Her Kebat?"

Her words were a slap in the face, even though they were calm, a mere chiding, but they quieted Penny's smothered crying more quickly than any words of comfort might have. She felt Brekko's hands on her wrists, his weight on top of her, crushing the air from her lungs.

"Blessed me?" she rasped. "*Blessed*?"

"Yes. Matar Kubileya blesses you, child. As She blesses all of Her Daughters."

Penny huffed a laugh, too stunned to argue or question, but the anger was returning, clearing away the tears, refueling her courage. She held onto that feeling as the giant woman moved, walking past her to the edge of the room, turning to face her again as she sat with weary slowness on the furs of the crystal throne.

"Kubileya's wisdom is great, child. Never doubt that. She has seen your suffering. She has blessed you with everything you need to reach the destiny you desire. But if you do not tell me what that truly is, I cannot give you the answers you seek."

Penny did not hesitate this time.

"I want my mother back. I want life to be as it was. I want this terrible mess undone. I want..." *I want to have never gone into that bathhouse.*

"Ah."

The oracle's smile was full of grief, as though she heard what was unsaid, and it twisted Penny's guts.

"I cannot give you what you ask. No one can. I cannot bring your mother back once she is beyond the Gate. It is too long, now. But your fate still awaits you, as does the true desire of your heart, if you would only seek it out."

Penny stared, dazed, and her next words came unbidden through stiff lips. "She *left* me. She's gone, and...and I want to know if she knew all along. I want to know if that is why she forbade me from coming here on my first moon-blood. Because she knew she was going to abandon me, and never come back, just like you say. Why did she even bring me here? I don't belong here without her. I am not one of *them*."

Until she said the words, Penny did not realize how the truth of them burned like hot coals under her breastbone. She thought her grief expanded moment by moment because of Brekko, because of Lyta, because of the countless dead and missing ha-mazaans, because of Leandra. And it *was* because of those things, but the core of it came down to one very simple fact: her mother had taken her from everything she knew and loved when they left her father's lands in Satra, separated her from everything and everyone she had belonged to, and now Antiope had abandoned her, left her alone in a place she didn't fit in, to a people she would never be part of, and there was no one left in a city of warriors who would ever love her the way her mother had.

30

DAUGHTER OF THEMISCYRA

"You are not alone, child." The Oracle's interruption of her thoughts was gentle, and all too knowing.

Penny held her chin high under that considering stare, wishing everyone did not see her as a child when that was something she would never be again, but the Kebat kept speaking, not giving her a chance to argue.

"The threads of Antiope's fate weave just as they were foretold, though she tangled them with her own weaving. It is your own fate you must worry about."

"And what is that? To bear daughters for the Thrones of a ruined city? I cannot even provide food and shelter to the women left in my care. In another month I won't even be able to feed the goats! *Everything* is gone. Why should I bring more daughters into a city that is destroyed? Into a world ruined by men's savagery?"

Why should I ever let a man touch me again, just to birth his child for a ruined cause?

The Kebat turned her lips up at the edges, the blue marks of her tattoos curling inwards along her cheeks. "You have more strength in you than you know. However, your fate is not woven by me, and it is not for me to tell you the whole of it if you cannot tell me what you truly want. I can only tell you that a daughter of Themiscyra needs you."

"A daughter?"

"A child. It is she whom you must recover, before all is lost for the future of the ha-mazaans. Matar Kubileya spreads the seeds of her people far and wide, that they may flourish in new lands, and bear the fruit of new futures, but the child is key to that hope."

"Leandra?" Penny clung to the thought of Sagitta's daughter, the rest of the Kebat's words gibberish. "Are you talking about Leandra? She lives?"

The Kebat stared with those lioness eyes, inclining her head. "Seek out the child that grows where the black ships sailed, and return her to her people. You must take the girl from the one who would destroy the ha-mazaans, and their future. This is the destiny I can tell you, Bellatrix of the ha-mazaans, but only you can make it your fate."

"I think you mistake me for someone else, Oracle. I am not even a true ha-mazaan. And you are wrong to call me Bellatrix. That is only my father's name to tease me."

The woman's tattooed chin lifted, then tilted, her golden eyes roving over Penny's linen leggings, the tight leather vest stolen from her mother's closet, too tight across her shoulders, the rumpled tunic underneath, and finally, to the leather belt she wore around her waist, the bronze dagger sheathed at the hip, the keys to the Flameless Tower and burned storehouse hanging useless from its rings.

"You are as much ha-mazaan as any woman who seeks shelter within the walls of your city. You will fight until your last breath for what is right, for justice, for victory, even if you know all hope is lost. That is what I see in your heart. That is the ha-mazaan Way. Rest assured you shall find your destiny. Seek your father, who walks with you in Spirit. He will tell you the truth of who you are. Seek the woman who will guide you to him, and teach you the way back to yourself, and to your ha-mazaan spirit. Then, seek the girl in the West, where the black ships sail. If you do this, the Keepers of the Flame will send Kubileya's light unto the far edges of the earth. This I can tell you."

"The truth of who I am? What are you talking about?"

"Anything more I say to you will only be clouded by your own doubt. I can only tell you that you must return here with the child, or hope is lost to you."

"How? *How* am I supposed to do that? She is on the other side of the world, in the hands of men who destroyed everything."

"You have an army of women more than capable of helping you succeed wherever you may lead them."

Penny huffed an incredulous laugh. "I have never even held a sword. I am Ishassara to the Hearth Queen—I will raise daughters, not armies. I cannot lead an army when I have sworn a vow to never harm another."

"You have already broken that vow, have you not?"

The Kebat stared with those feline eyes, and Penny felt them prodding the truth inside her very soul until she squirmed with the shame of it.

"I cannot undo what has already been done, and neither can you," the Kebat said eventually, her tone gentle. "But if you wish to free yourself of a vow foolishly uttered, and of the spirits haunting your every thought, you must absolve yourself of the oath you swore, and free your soul from the consequences you have wrought."

"How?"

Hope flared in Penny's heart. Perhaps she did not have to suffer the curse, after all. But then she remembered the beach littered with dead women, Areto's sightless eyes, Lyta's blank stare, the beams of the great stables charred to ash, Molpadia's cold anger, and the hope fizzled out. It was already too late. She had already suffered the consequences. Others had suffered far worse. Still, she could not help but wonder what the Oracle meant.

"Who can absolve me of my vow?"

"Whomever you swore your promise to can release you from it. This has always been so. It will be they who can tell you the rest of your destiny, also. The rest of your past. By then, you may even be ready to hear it."

Penny's thoughts swirled, taking her back to a midnight road full of exhaustion and trepidation, and the same lines from her mother's lips repeating over and over in her head. The old blind woman tucked away in a cave many times smaller than this one, her fingers constantly weaving, insisting Penny should not say what she had come to say. Warning her of the consequences. A terrible dread came over her.

"Yes," the oracle nodded as though she could see inside Penny's mind. Perhaps she could. "Undo what should not have been. Find the ones who will guide you to find yourself. Find the girl, and you will find hope for your future. Now go, Bellatrix. And the next time I see you, I shall call you Queen, and you will believe me when I tell you who you really are."

Sylviu returned to Galatae with the others when Sinope's army departed, riding at the edges of their unified ranks in a dull haze of grief that slowly congealed itself into a thick, dark anger. He was not sure who he was more angry with: himself, or Molpadia and her supporters, or the treacherous Achaeans, but all of it swirled together until it was one massive clot of sick inside his chest. He had to go after those ships. He had to at least try and find his mother. He thought of the things she had dared share with him, her own visions of a future she had seen in a stone cauldron high in a cave. Visions of men and women together, living in harmony. Visions he had always hoped would supersede his own, and erase from his knowledge any other future that might exist.

When he laughed, the bitter sound made one of Sinope's ha-mazaans toss him a disapproving scowl, but he paid her no attention. The fact that part of his own terrible visions had already come to pass, and therefore the rest might as well, brought him no comfort. He would find the ones who had brought destruction, and he would find his mother.

His own future, good or bad, would have to wait.

31

DEAD

"Dead," Penny repeated.

She could not bear the stark horror, the disbelief, the grief in the faces staring back at her, so she looked instead out the window, at the clouds hanging low and sodden above the river, their drifting mist shedding the tears she was no longer capable of crying. Everything within her was dried up, hardened like dried venison, thick and sinewy and just as dead.

"But..." Marpe began, her voice conveying the shock everyone in the Hall was feeling, before she shook her head and demanded, "Tell us again, child, what the Oracle said. Every word as you can remember it."

Penny sighed, looking away from the weeping sky to stare blindly at her hands. She picked at the skin around her nails, roughened and split from days of soaking them in lye and hot water, though she had not visited the baths for a proper wash since the night of the attack. She had thought carefully all the way back down the mountain what she would tell the rest of the ha-mazaans, and while she had erred on the side of caution, she told as much truth as she could. Marpe had been suspicious of something from the very first, however, and Penny tried not to squirm under the old woman's stare as she recounted her carefully rehearsed words for a second time.

"That my mother has long gone through the gate. That a daughter of Themiscyra—Leandra, obviously—still lives and must be recovered, else all is lost for the future of the ha-mazaans here in our city. That Matar Kubileya is spreading the ha-mazaans far and wide so they may flourish in new lands. That I must...that I must be the one who brings Leandra back. That the Flame will not be re-ignited until the girl is home again."

She finished the much-abridged version before it became too complicated, or worse, exposed too much of the truth she did not wish to share with them.

That I must travel back to my father's lands, my childhood home, my real home, and absolve myself of my vow. That if I do not, the curse I have unleashed will destroy us all. That if I fail, this Shadow that lingers even now in the corner of our Moon Hall will devour me, and then you, and then everyone else I have ever loved...

Marpe's eyes narrowed, and even from the corner of her vision, Penny saw the way the *sivyeti* peered at her with a curious expression on her wrinkled face.

"Your mother has long gone through the gate..." the *sivyeti* repeated, mumbling the words. Then, louder and more insistently, "What about the rest of the women? There are more than fifty others stolen. She said nothing about them?"

"Just that my mother is dead and a daughter of Themiscyra, a girl, lives on. She did not clarify about the rest."

"And you must be the one who retrieves Leandra?"

As soon as Penny nodded confirmation, still avoiding eye contact, Marpe shook her head, suddenly brisk.

"No."

Penny looked up, unsure if the woman was contesting Penny's truthfulness, or the idea that she would be the one to bring the girl back, but Marpe carried on without waiting for a response, turning her back on Penny entirely.

"Orithyia is the only ha-mazaan left with any authority to lead the ha-mazaans to attack. Besides, the Ishassara should not leave the city while the Hearth Queen is gone," Marpe said dismissively. "There must be one of you to tend—" The atta broke off as she remembered there was no Flame to keep alight.

"My mother is—"

"Dead, yes," Marpe interrupted bluntly, turning back to Penny. "I heard what the Kebat told you. All the more reason for you to stay here where you belong."

"Alone?" Penny asked incredulously, and when Marpe frowned, confused, she waved her hands at the curved walls enclosing them. "This is all that is left, Marpe, and in another moon, the ha-mazaans will go to Sinope, just as we have arranged. Do you really expect me to stay behind and tend a cold hearth, while the rest of you winter together?" Penny uttered a brittle laugh, the sound harsh even to her own ears. "Even if I do not seek out Leandra, who we *know* is alive and captive, at least you will grant me the dignity of living the winter as the one of you, and not some hermit alone in the ashes!"

Even Penny was astonished at her outburst, but Marpe's response was instantaneous, her tone unrelenting.

"But you are not one of *us*, are you?"

Penny stepped back as though struck when the older woman laid the truth so bare, but the *sivyeti* did not stop.

"You are Ishassara to the Hearth Queen, Keeper of Matar Kubileya's Eternal Flame. And if it is somehow true that Queen Antiope no longer lives, that means you have one year to complete your Alsanti. We cannot risk the only remaining blood of Otrera running into a den of wolves for the sake of one small girl."

They stared at each other, Penny's face stinging with horror at the thought of following through with what she had had every intention of doing just a fortnight ago.

"She is barely more than a child," a voice said, and Penny dragged her gaze away to find Evandre, of all people, pushing her way to the front of the watching crowd, her face pulled into a disapproving frown.

"She is a woman six years already," Marpe retorted, staring Sinope's General down, her posture intimidating even from her short stature. "Either way, she is Themiscyra's woman, not Sinope's. No need for Orithyia and her ilk to be sticking their noses in our business."

"Oh?" Evandre replied evenly, cocking her hip and crossing her arms. "I think it became our business the moment we agreed to take in several hundred ha-mazaans for the winter. We are one people, atta Marpe, not some collection of men's villages constantly at war with one another."

"Themiscyra is Themiscyra, and Sinope is..." Marpe trailed off, raking her eyes over the taller ha-mazaan contemptuously, making Evandre stiffen, "not where Penthesilea belongs, at least not long term," Marpe finished. "You reinforce my point, though, General. Sinope's Hearth Queen is long dead, and your Flame spent. Even Chaldesia and Lykastia rely on Themiscyra to keep the Flame burning. If Antiope is lost to us, it is Penthesilea who bears the burden of continuing on Kubileya's Light."

A long, uncomfortable silence met these sobering words. Ha-mazaans throughout the hall shuffled and murmured lowly to one another. Molpadia's voice, stunted and quiet, filtered through the chatter among the ha-mazaans.

"The girl is right. Even if Antiope is dead, the Oracle didn't say the rest of our ha-mazaans were. We still need to go after them. Penthesilea can go to Hattusa or Wilusa and fuck every prince she sees for all we care, but we need to bring our women home." The crowd parted for her to pass as she made her way with slow, deliberate steps, but she was not looking at Penny. "All of their *rhu-tasiyas* still live, except for Melanippe's," Molpadia continued, and at this reminder, many ha-mazaans responded with murmurs of excited agreement. "Even Antiope's *rhu-tasiya* still lives."

"A *rhu-tasiya* can live many moons after its ha-mazaan's death before its spirit is called to the Otherworld," Toxaris reminded her. "Especially if there is no *zizenti* to complete the rites for the dead. The Oracle does not lie. If she said our Hearth Queen is dead, then Antiope is held in the bosom of Matar Kubileya now."

After a brief silence in which everyone considered these words, Marpe said, "You're right, the Oracle does not lie, but she obscures the truth whenever she desires. We should not base our actions on the mewlings of that hermit. Besides that, Penthesilea disobeyed her mother's wishes by going to see the Oracle at all." The atta turned her fierce scowl on Penny, wagging a wrinkled finger to emphasize her words. "It was not your place to go behind our backs and seek knowledge that wasn't for you."

"It is every ha-mazaan's right to meet with the Kebat," Evandre put in sternly.

"What does it matter?" Molpadia demanded. "We need to seek vengeance upon every man who set foot on these shores, and take back our women. Anything else is cowardice, and leaves us open to further attacks." She looked around blearily, her throat moving as she swallowed. "I *will* kill

Heracles. I promised Lyta I would, with the blood of her own *rhu-tasiya* to seal my vow, and I am no oath-breaker wishing to bring a curse on my soul."

Penny winced, but another ha-mazaan said, "Aye," and there was a chorus of agreement from the crowd, though not as many as Penny would have liked.

"It is not our Way to leave our homes and wage war on other kingdoms, or seek vengeance on those who wronged us. We would forever be at war," Toxaris said.

"It *is* our Way to protect the daughters of Kubileya," Molpadia answered without hesitation. "It *is* our way to defend our women, to keep them free. How do we do that without going after them?" Her cold eyes turned on Penny, and her lip lifted. "Or would you have us wither away in Sinope, while the daughter of the one who destroyed us all flaunts herself at every passerby? Perhaps we are meant to escort her to every palace in the land searching for the perfect Ishassari to father her brat, while they mock us for our failures, our cowardice? Whether she succeeds or fails at her Alsanti, it will be too late for the women who were sacrificed, only for her and her mother's insatiable need for a man between their thighs."

Audible gasps from the crowd did nothing to quell Penny's surge of anger, or the hot shame that quickly followed. To her surprise, however, it was Marpe who came to her defense, turning her formidable frown on Molpadia.

"We know your heart is heavy for the one you loved, Molpadia, but it is no cause to insult Hippolyta's sister, or her niece, who *is* your future Hearth Queen. You may have once had the Defending Queen's authority as her consort, but now you only have what we grant you. Remember that."

Molpadia made no reply. When no other ha-mazaan came forward to either support or reproach her, she turned on her heel, edging her way back through the crowd to the table she had left. Penny watched the woman drop heavily onto the bench and take a long swig of wine from the cup she had left there. She could not feel anything but sorrow for the ha-mazaan, even after such an insult to both herself and her mother. There was enough pain in this room to last a lifetime. Everyone had lost someone they loved.

The idea of losing more women to war, to senseless vengeance, made the bile rise in Penny's throat, and pushing it from beneath was the terrible thought that every one of these women now expected her to fulfill her Alsanti before the next Sturgeon Moon. To lay with a man, and bear his child, and then do it again with another if she had a son instead of a daughter.

The thought sent a shiver through her, an unfamiliar disgust she had never before experienced at the thought of her future or her duties as the Hearth Queen's Ishassara, and she crossed her arms against the chill.

This is my vow, and may my death be swift and merciless, may a curse descend upon me and my blood, should I ever break it...

Even if she could bring herself to complete her Alsanti before the next Sturgeon moon, she could not do it under the shadow of a curse, dooming her daughter to some terrible fate possibly worse than Penny's own. She needed to do as the oracle had said. She would find her father, and undo her vow, and then, only then, would she think about her future as Themiscyra's Hearth Queen.

32

SINOPE

It was a strange procession that wound its way westward, traveling away from what remained of Themiscyra and moving towards an uncertain future. Only a handful of older women had chosen to move south and remain in Galatae with the men; the majority had chosen to move to Sinope, until the spring, when they could return and rebuild in earnest. More than two hundred women rode their mares, and at least half their number led geldings behind them, those horses' backs heaped with what was left in provisions and supplies. A few were laden with sloshing bags of fresh mare's milk, churning itself into precious *kimiz* with every step, replacing what had been poisoned by the Achaeans. The backs of some were draped with bundles of wool and linen, still smelling of smoke, and yet they were all that was left to make new tunics for the winter rains. Crafters had constructed rudimentary wagons from freshly hewn timber, to replace those lost alongside the stables, and these they loaded crocks of butter and olives and fresh honey, and everything else that would sustain them over winter. They filled one wagon with Silpa's anvil and hammers, and another with the most precious of all the treasures within Themiscyra—the pieces of stars that had been gifted to the ha-mazaans by the Great Mother herself. These sources of star-iron wrested from the talons of a griffin by Melanippe before the birth of Penny's cousin Cyra were the precious, well-guarded secret of ha-mazaan weapons' superiority, and the greatest asset their army had in battles against inferior bronze. From these, Silpa would spend the winter forging new weapons to replace those taken by the Achaeans, replenishing their weaponry, along with their sense of safety.

Penny wore her hunting bow across her chest as they rode out, as well as the new dagger Silpa had fashioned for her from star-iron, the first Penny had ever claimed as her own. The blacksmith had not questioned Penny's request for a new one, and Penny was grateful to the woman for her discretion. Though she knew she was the least proficient of any ha-mazaan if it came to defending their caravan from marauders, she wished she could have strapped a heavy axe or sword to her hip instead, but she could not flaunt her broken vow and risk the ha-mazaans' censure by strapping an axe or sword to her waist.

The journey was a blur of checking provisions, comforting the younger children who did not understand their plight, wrangling the wandering foals and sheep out of the hills and back onto the road, all while attempting to decipher the oracle's cryptic message. She ran the Kebat's words over and over in her mind, like spinning wool onto a spindle, trying to make the skeins whirl neatly together, but the only nubby thread she could cling to was that her mother was dead, and that Penny must end this curse she had unleashed in order to bring Leandra home. Much of the Kebat's message she shied away from, tucking it in the same place in her mind she tucked anything to do with her time in the bathhouse, or that moonlit night on the beach where so many ha-mazaans lay dead and dying, or the long, dark hours afterward, when the Erinyes unleashed its vengeance.

Though it normally would have taken two days to reach the sister-city, their slow caravan of sheep and crude wagons and unruly foals meant their progress was slower than normal, so it was the third morning on the road with the sun climbing higher somewhere behind an overcast, heavy sky that Toxaris inelegantly shoveled a fistful of dried venison into her mouth as breakfast, chewing loudly in between comments about the struggle of Penny's horse to keep up with the rest of the caravan with her short legs.

"We'll be the last stragglers through Sinope's gate, the way she moves," Toxaris said, gesturing at Tana with a stick of venison.

"I think she is doing very well, considering her age," Penny said defensively, suppressing a gag as the pungent smell of the meat wafted into her nostrils. The ha-mazaan tipped her chin at Penny questioningly, holding out the last of the partially consumed jerky.

"Hungry?"

Avoiding looking directly at the chewed mass, Penny shook her head with an adamant shudder of revulsion at the smell, grateful that the ha-mazaan's generosity was short-lived and the rest of the meat, along with its overwhelming odor, quickly disappeared. When their caravan of horses, goats, sheep, and weary ha-mazaans finally crested the hill overlooking Sinope, though, Toxaris shifted on the back of her fine mare, the horse's ears flickering in readiness for a new command other than plodding beside Penny's elderly pony.

"Do you think this is going to work? Our two cities mingling all winter long?"

Penny frowned, sliding a glance at the older woman. "I don't see why not. We are all women. All ha-mazaan." *Except me.*

"Not everyone sees eye to eye on what that means, though," Toxaris said.

Penny frowned, her eyes sliding back toward Sinope's squat walls. She had not given much thought to whether she and the rest of Themiscyra would actually be welcomed with open arms, or if Evandre's invitation had been given only as lip service to the bond shared by cousins, but her worries were alleviated as they approached the gates. Evandre, who had returned to Sinope more than a month prior to ensure the city was prepared for an influx of refugees, rode out to greet them on the back of her fine white mare, accompanied by several more ha-mazaans. The general cantered forward from their party to speak with Toxaris and Molpadia after saluting Penny in her brisk way, the three of them speaking in low tones at the front of the train as they meandered down the last of the hill towards the city. Sinope itself was a squat stone palace on the edge of a rocky cliff, the waves of the Zalapa crashing against the rocks below. The last time Penny had been here she had been visiting with her mother, finalizing trade deals with several kings in Bythinia and beyond, but Orithyia had been away on one of her many forays to the south, from which she always returned wealthier, and in possession of more horses than when she had left. She wondered what the city's Defending Queen would think of so many women descending on her small fortress, depleting their stores and invading their privacy and causing inevitable squabbles for months on end. Penny's musings were cut short when Evandre finally broke away from her huddle of ha-mazaans and rode toward her.

"Ishassara Penthesilea," Evandre said formally. "I'm afraid Queen Orithyia is not yet returned from her sojourn with King Pylameneus. I will stand in her place and offer the same welcome you gave to me, and to my women." The woman smiled kindly. "May you and your people find shelter here, and may your hearts heal as we drink together under the light of the moon. Welcome, Ishassara. I hope you feel comfortable to call this place home, for as long as you need to."

"Themiscyra is forever in your debt, sister," Penny replied, but her own smile was forced, her face tight, and her stomach once more roiling with twin feelings of trepidation, and now guilt.

33

SYLVIU

As much as Penny appreciated the offer of hospitality from Sinope, and in fact relied on it for the safety of the women who were now technically her responsibility, she neither ate their food nor slept in the bed provided, so as not to dishonor herself as guest. When it was time for the evening meal, she found the *matar* who cared for Areto's babe, asking to see the child and then avoiding the woman's curious eyes as she pressed a kiss onto the crown of the girl's golden forehead, breathing in the sweet scent that was her perfect skin, nearly coughing when it turned to cloying sulfuric ash in her lungs. She said no words, made no promises, knowing how worthless her own words had become, no matter how fiercely they burned in her heart. She left *matar* and babe, the ha-mazaan's questions unanswered, their grief for Areto a silent understanding between them.

For the second time in as many months, she stole away in the night. Tana was reluctant to leave her warm shelter, but there was enough wind forcing itself off the cold sea and into the southern lands that every noise her hooves made was well-hidden by a shrieking, autumnal gale. Still, Penny felt her heart in her throat with every creak of the stable doors, every hoofbeat against the cobblestones as they rode away from the citadel and into the frigid night.

Once she had made it to the eastern rise of the road, she looked back, toward the edge of the cliff and the stone outcropping where Sinope sat, squat and plain. Doubt clawed at her as the wind's fingers combed ruthlessly at her tightly bound, unfamiliar braids. She was abandoning the people she had been born to care for, born to lead and nurture and provide a safe haven for, and yet she knew she would be the cause of their ultimate destruction if she stayed. She also knew that if they ever found out it was her own dishonor that had brought violence and death upon them all, they would never welcome her back. If she did not cleanse this stain from her soul, it would spread decay amongst their entire people. She needed to set things right before she could ever be among them. With that knowledge in her mind, Penny reined Tana away from Sinope, along the open road to the south, towards Galatae.

She made it to the wooden palisades of the men's city by noon the next day, although she was not sure who was more exhausted, her or Tana. The road south was one she had traveled many times with her mother to and from the home of the Hanassas, collecting tributes and taxes of grain and pigs at the turning of the seasons. Still, she had never traveled it alone, in the dark hours of the night, and every hoofbeat seemed to echo back to Penny's ears with the drumbeat of wings and, strangely, the smell of freshly pulled flax stalks resting in the shallow waters of the swamp, decaying its outer core in preparation to be combed and spun into linen. The smell was so distinct, so familiar, that Penny almost drew comfort from it, though she quickly came to realize it would turn to rot in her nostrils, sulfuric and hot, and the Erinyes would whisper its threats through the wind.

Though she saw no wolves or other predators, it was still a relief to spot the tall spikes of wood marking the city at the edge of a wide plain, where men tended the fields of grain and herds of pigs that sustained the ha-mazaan cities through the winter. The scouts had spotted her well before she arrived at their gates, but there was no formal greeting party to meet her as those gates swung wide. Penny ruefully remembered her clothing, and her braided hair, and realized they did not recognize her as the queen's daughter. She was simply another ha-mazaan. Unsure whether to be grateful or dismayed at what felt like an abrupt loss of identity, she halted Tana outside the gates, and called to the nearest guard to fetch Sylviu. The man peered at her curiously, itching at his nose with a thick finger, but he did not argue. His face disappeared from the battlements. No others paid her any mind, as ha-mazaans came and went from their city regularly, but Penny felt conspicuous nonetheless. Her legs were weak with fatigue when she slid from Tana's back under the shadow of the high timber walls, and she used the short horse's shoulder as support, leaning her forehead against the mare's warm neck as she breathed the scents of horse sweat and dust from the road, along with the distinct odor of pigs from inside the city walls. Bile rose in the back of her throat, and she breathed deeply, willing the nausea to subside, but it only made matters worse as her nostrils filled with more smells of stink mingled with roasting fat and sickly-sweet mead from the nearby gatehouse, and behind it all, the cloying scent of brimstone.

"You don't look very good."

Penny snapped to attention and whirled to face Sylviu, who stalked silently as a cat across the rutted road, until he was little more than an arm's length away from her. His eyes raked her from heel to forehead, his gaze lingering an extra moment on the long braid hanging over her shoulder, the end of it tucked into the wide leather of her belt. She frowned.

"It's a pleasure to see you, too," she snapped, then flushed when he raised an eyebrow, his eyes resting on her face, which she was sure was pale with fatigue from her journey, if not the last two moons of unending nightmare. His own was etched with lines of grief and weariness, as though he had not slept for weeks.

"I would have seen you sooner, if not for your rules."

"They are not my rules," Penny retorted automatically, but her heart was not in the words. She felt her throat tightening with everything she wanted to say, so settled on what she could. "I sent you a message, after you tried to enter the city." She shifted her feet as his unrelenting gaze seemed to penetrate through all the layers she had carefully been building for the past three fortnights. He nodded once, lips pressed together.

"I got your message."

When he offered no more, Penny shifted her feet again. "I'm sorry, Sylviu. About your mother. There is still hope for her, though. She may still live."

"Aye," he nodded, "and I will find her, if she still lives. If she doesn't, I will kill the one responsible. You have my word on that." His tone was harsh with grief, his eyes steady on hers but full of a sorrow she understood well, and also something else. She almost thought it was guilt. He paused, shifting his own weight from one foot to another as he studied her face. "And I am sorry as well, Pen. For..." he swallowed, and his eyes fell from hers. "For your mother, also," he finished, so quiet she could barely hear it.

She nodded, not trusting herself to speak, but then his eyes moved past her shoulder to her horse, and his eyebrows met as he saw the sweaty chest and tired, drooping head of the mare. He glanced around, then turned his frown directly on her.

"You didn't come all the way from Themiscyra alone, did you?"

Penny raised her chin, a part of her warmed by his concern, and another part exhausted by everyone's attempts to coddle her. "No," she said. "I came here from Sinope, where the others will be staying there for the winter."

Sylviu snorted. "How foolish of me. I should know there are only wolves and bears and men on the road from Themiscyra, and not from Sinope."

"I'm fine, Syl."

"Oh yes, I can see that you are perfectly normal." Again his eyes flicked over her body, and this time they lingered on the knife at her belt, his sharp gaze noting the shine of star-iron rather than bronze, before they returned to her face. The air between them suddenly felt charged the way the sky crackles before a bolt of lightning, and she could not break her eyes away from his. He took a step closer to her, until she could have easily reached out to touch him without even stretching her elbow straight—until she feared he might reach out and touch her. Her breath caught and lurched in her lungs like a rabbit in a snare.

Would she welcome his touch? Could she? Part of her craved it, but she was not sure if that was simply a yearning for comfort and familiarity, or if it was desire. She feared much of her longing stemmed from the simple need to imprint new touch over the last she had experienced, but she doubted anything could cover the mark Brekko had made on her soul, even if the bruises had long faded. Sylviu made no move to touch her, though. He simply watched her, noting the emotions that flowed as swiftly as a river water over her face, and he let them pass without comment. She smelled the clean musk of him over the other scents wafting from the city and breathed it in, wondering at the sorrow welling within that mingled with a confusing relief as she realized he would not cross the unspoken boundary that lay between them, as wide and deep as a chasm between two lonely mountains. Another smell was there, as well, behind the musk and roasting meat and the sweat of her travel. It smelled of swamp, and sulfur, and it reminded her of why she could never welcome his touch in the first place, if she cared at all for his safety, or his future.

"What do you mean, 'where the others will be staying for the winter?'"

The intensity of his question caught Penny off guard, pulling her out of her spiraling thoughts and releasing the trapped air from her lungs in a tired sigh.

"I came to say goodbye, Syl. I didn't want you to worry."

"What are you talking about?"

Penny's stubborn resolve returned in the face of his disapproval, but she also cursed herself silently for thinking this had been a good idea. It was true, she had not wanted him to worry, and since he was the closest she had to a friend, she had thought it the right thing to do to tell him she was leaving. Now that she was here, however, she could see the error in her thinking.

"I am leaving. For Satra. To my father's lands. I...I am not sure when I will see you again."

Sylviu's frown deepened, but there was a new light in his eyes as he studied her face with increased attention. "Pen, talk to me. What is going on?"

"Nothing, Syl. I just—this is something I have to do. There is someone in my father's lands I must see."

"Your father lives halfway across the world!"

"Not quite," she said wryly, shrugging with what she hoped was nonchalance, though she was filled with her own trepidation at the daunting distance between her and her childhood home. "I have made the journey before, when I was much younger."

Sylviu snorted. "Yes, with your mother, who has perfect aim with her arrows even when she's wearing a blindfold. Pen, if this is about your Alsanti, you know I will—"

"*No.*"

The word was too rushed, too adamant, and it earned another intense searching of Sylviu's hazel eyes on hers. She did not want him to say what she knew he was going to say. She did not want to tell him why she could not think of that right now.

"It has nothing to do with my Alsanti. I don't...I don't even know if I will complete that."

Sylviu shook his head firmly. "You are Ishassara. You would forfeit your right to the throne, Pen." When she simply stared at him, he shook his head again, his eyes gone dark with worry. "I need you to tell me what is going on."

"I am, Syl, if you would listen! I came to say goodbye, and—"

"Have those she-cats you live with been using their claws on you?" he spoke over her as though she had not answered. There was a fiery edge to his tone she had not heard before. "Has that guard dog of Hippolyta's done something to drive you away? Did something happen with those men—"

"*No*—"

She had never lied to him before, but he couldn't even hear her in his rush of words.

"What is it? What would make you come here, alone—which is one of the most foolish things you have done in the ten years I have known you—only to tell me you are planning on riding *this* half-dead nag," he waved an angry hand at Tana, "to the other side of the world. That drug the Achaeans gave you must have addled your brain if you think I am going to let you do *any* of that."

"You do not *let* me do anything, Sylviu son of Ossy," Penny hissed, her spine stiffening.

"Oh, come off your high horse, *please*," he said, as close to raising his voice to a level she had never heard him use. "This is *me* you're talking to, remember? I know what you can and cannot do. What you're sworn not to do. You need the protection of swords and able fighters to make a journey of that distance, through all the clans of the north and west. Surely there are Savaran who will take you where you need to go?" He stopped, and eyed her with increasing horror, his hand smacking against his thigh. "You did not tell them you were going, did you? Pen, this is madness!"

"The matter of where I go, or how I go there, is not open for discussion, especially with a man from Galatae!" She knew the words were cruel and unfair as soon as they left her mouth, and pressed her lips together to stop their flow even as hurt flamed in his face. She sighed through her nose, forcing a soothing gentleness she did not feel into her words. "I came to say goodbye, so that you would not worry, but I see that was a mistake. I'm sorry."

She turned back to Tana, taking up the reins. His hand gripped her upper arm with tight fingers and spun her back, pulling her toward him. Penny did not pause. Did not think. She shoved him with every ounce of strength she had, and he stumbled back, losing his grip on her arm, but she didn't stop there. The dagger was in her hand and pressed into the thin wool of his tunic before she could reason whether it was necessary, or even something she wanted to do. She reacted with a speed she had not known she possessed, and it was only when she saw the astonishment on his face, followed quickly by a cloud of anger, and something that looked too much like betrayal when his eyes looked at the blade against his ribs, directly over his heart, that she understood her reaction had nothing to do with him, and everything to do with Brekko. By then, it was already too late.

Penny lowered the knife much more slowly than she had drawn it, but Sylviu stepped back further, his expression shuttered, his gaze now unreadable as he stared at her.

"Sylviu," Penny began, desperation staining his name that should have been an apology, but then she stopped. What more could she say? She had no desire to tell him the gruesome details, to explain why her instinct was to defend herself rather than welcome his touch. He would never hurt her, and she would never hurt him. Would she? She stared at the star-iron blade, then tucked it into its sheath with shaking fingers, uncertain if that was truth, or simply what she wanted to believe. He was staring at her with a shuttered expression she had never seen before.

"I was going to offer to go with you, as protection, but I can see you are more ha-mazaan than you claim to be, after all."

She did not know if it was the accusation or the disappointment in his tone that hurt more. Her face flushed with the heat of guilt, and shame.

"Sylviu, I—"

"I wish you a safe journey, Ishassara Penthesilea."

And with those words, he turned on his heel and left, slipping through the gate as silently as he had appeared, leaving only a lingering whiff of sulfur and a deep, cold ache inside Penny's tight chest.

34

OCEANS APART

Sylviu's stomach dropped when the guard told him a ha-mazaan waited outside the gates, refusing to come inside. Had they finally brought word of his mother, and the others? Were they come to tell him all was lost, and bring this crushing weight to a brutal, terrible conclusion? He could not bear to hope for anything more, as hope was the most painful barb in his already tormented mind.

But when he passed under the wooden tower he saw Pen, her golden head bowed against the neck of her old pony, bent low as though she had been carrying the weight of the entire world on her shoulders. He took in the pallor of her skin, the gauntness of her cheeks and throat, the way her arms hung limp, and his own worries fled.

"You don't look very good."

He meant it to convey concern, but her eyes were full of reproach when they met his, and he cursed himself silently for a fool. He wanted to pull her to him and hug her tight, tell her he had missed her presence and her laugh and her smiles, that had never seen anyone so beautiful, even if her kind eyes were now full of a terrible sorrow that ate at his heart.

"It's a pleasure to see you, too," she said, and he heard the caustic edge to her tone clearly enough. He raised an eyebrow, waiting for her to finally lash out at him, blame him as she must. He thought about confessing everything—how easy it had been to sneak into that oracle's cave all those years ago and receive a message that had altered his future, for better or worse. How easy it had been to jiggle the pins of that stupid lock on the Tower. How easy it had been for Molpadia to walk him over that bridge and away from protecting those he should have protected. How useless he would have been to them all anyway, even if he had stayed. How his failures were eating him alive every waking minute. Instead, he simply assured her of the only truth he had the courage to share.

"I would have seen you sooner, if not for your rules."

"They are not my rules. I sent you a message, after you tried to enter the city."

"I got your message."

"I'm sorry, Sylviu. About your mother. There is still hope for her, though."

"Aye," he nodded, trying to convey with his eyes all the things he could not say, all the promises he could not make, for fear of failing her again. "And I will find her, if she still lives." *And the others, too.* "If she doesn't, I will kill the one responsible. You have my word on that."

Even if it was himself who needed to atone, his own life he would need to offer, he would do what it took. He shifted his feet, the weight of everything he knew he should be saying heavy on his chest.

"And I am sorry as well, Pen. For..." he swallowed through a dry throat, looking away from her as his guilt clung hard to his ribcage. *Sorry for my sacrilege that doomed you all.* "For your mother, also." He barely managed to keep the truth inside, knowing it would only cause her more pain, knowing she would hate him if she found out how he deceived her.

He looked over her shoulder as she nodded stiffly, finally registering the state of her horse, and the fact it stood alone under the shadow of the palisades. His worry was a sharp stab that quickly eroded the guilt.

"You didn't come all the way from Themiscyra alone, did you?"

"No," Pen said, an unfamiliar, almost mutinous light to her eyes. "I came here from Sinope, where the others will be staying there for the winter."

Sylviu snorted. "How foolish of me. I should know there are only wolves and bears and men on the road from Themiscyra, and not from Sinope."

"I'm fine, Syl."

"Oh yes, I can see that you are perfectly normal." He looked pointedly at her gaunt face, her haunted eyes, the star-iron dagger he had never, not once in ten years, seen her feel the need to carry. He knew it was only for show, a symbol for men to take pause at, even if they did not know she couldn't use it on them. He was glad she had it, but his gut somehow twisted even tighter. He wanted to ask what had happened, why she suddenly seemed so...he couldn't put his finger on it, but she was different. Harder. More distant. He didn't like the thought of her alone, when she was supposed to be protected, especially with such a foolish vow hanging over her head. She was watching him with those hind's eyes, searching his face for something he could not fathom, her wide lips parted as though about to speak.

He took a step closer to her, pulled toward her as the ocean is pulled by the moon. He wanted to pull her into his arms, to tell her he was not worthy to offer his services but if she was leaving to complete her Alsanti, he would take her wherever she needed to go, help her find the most worthy, handsome Ishassari she deserved to father her daughter. As soon as he moved closer, though, he saw something in her eyes he had never seen before.

Fear. Of him.

He heard her breath catch, and a dark shadow moved across her face. His own grief expanded until it was an actual pain somewhere behind his heart. Perhaps ones such as Molpadia had whispered their poison in her ears, or perhaps it had simply been...everything, but he wrestled between anger and understanding at the very obvious fact she did not trust him. She had every right not to, but it still stung. He kept his arms at his sides, fingers twitching with longing. Her earlier words filtered slowly through the sorrow that terrible truth unfurled.

"What do you mean, 'where the others will be staying for the winter?'"

She stared up at him, eyes sad, but resolute.

"I came to say goodbye, Syl. I didn't want you to worry."

Cold dread began to worry its way into his mind along with the sorrow. He peered at her. "What are you talking about?"

"I am leaving. For Satra. To my father's lands. I...I am not sure when I will see you again."

He had expected her to say she was leaving to complete her Alsanti, but Satra? There was something more in her face he couldn't decipher. A desperation in her voice he needed to wooderstand. To fix. "Pen, talk to me. What is going on?"

"Nothing, Syl. I just—this is something I have to do. There is someone in my father's lands I must see."

"Your father lives halfway across the world!" He frowned at her, sure she was playing games, but she merely shrugged.

"Not quite. I have made the journey before, when I was much younger."

Sylviu forced down a surge of sudden panic, making a sound of pure disbelief. She did not appear to be playing with him. "Yes, with your mother, who has perfect aim with her arrows even when she's wearing a blindfold. Pen, if this is about your Alsanti, you know I will—"

"*No.*"

Sylviu bit back the rest, hearing her refusal loud and clear. He wondered if she thought he was offering to help her complete her Alsanti and be the father for her child, and nearly laughed out loud. He knew that could never be. She didn't need to say it. Still, the rejection stung, whichever way she meant it.

"It has nothing to do with my Alsanti. I don't...I don't even know if I will complete that."

Taken aback, Sylviu shook his head harder, trying to find some balance in the emotions shifting under him like sand. "You are Ishassara. You would forfeit your right to the throne, Pen." But she only stared at him, and he had never seen her eyes look so lost. The cold dread began to overtake him. Something was very, very wrong.

"I need you to tell me what is going on."

He was vaguely aware she started to say something, but Molpadia and the other angry ha-mazaans gnashing their teeth at him rose in his mind, their vicious tongues lashing at him and the other hanassas until they left the shadow of Themiscyra's blackened walls.

"Have those she-cats you live with been using their claws on you? Has that guard dog of Hippolyta's done something to drive you away? Did something happen with those men? What? What would make you come here, alone—which is one of the most foolish things you have done in the ten years I have known you—only to tell me you are planning on riding *this* half-dead nag to the other side of the world." She had tried to answer, but he was too worked up to listen. Fear was running away with his tongue, but couldn't control it, or his next words. "That drug the Achaeans gave you must have addled your brain if you think I am going to let you do *any* of that."

"You do not *let* me do anything, Sylviu son of Ossy," Pen hissed through tight lips, and she sounded every bit her mother's daughter, regal and furious and condescending in one.

"Oh, come off your high horse, *please*," he said, stung more than he cared to admit. "This is *me* you're talking to, remember? I know what you can and cannot do. What you're sworn not to do. You need the protection of swords and able fighters to make a journey of that distance, through all the clans of the north and west. Surely there are Savaran who will take you where you need to go?" He stopped as the realization struck home. There was only one way the other ha-mazaans would have let her travel all this way unprotected. "You did not tell them you were going, did you? Pen, this is madness!"

"The matter of where I go, or how I go there, is not open for discussion, especially with a man from Galatae!"

She might as well have used her new dagger on him, the way those words sliced into the very same wound that had been festering since he and the others had been shunned from those city gates, and in truth, for many years before that. Since his own mother had brought him to this place and left him behind, the divide between ha-mazaan and Hanassa an irrevocable, humiliating reality he had never recovered from. He stared at Pen, unable to quell the surge of hurt, followed quickly by anger, but he knew the latter was mostly at himself. He had brought this on himself. He needed to remember that.

She murmured, "I came to say goodbye, so that you would not worry, but I see that was a mistake. I'm sorry."

She turned away from him, shutting him out, but he couldn't let her go like this. She was his best friend, and she needed his help. He caught her arm without thinking, meaning to beg her to let him be the sword she could not carry, let him try to make up for what he had already failed at so miserably, and protect her like he was meant to. One second he was about to speak, and the next her hands were shoving him, hard, her whole body lending its weight to her push so that he stumbled back in the dirt. Her eyes were wild, almost feral, her teeth bared in a rage he had never witnessed on her peaceful face, stunning him into a shocked silence. He felt something sharp in his ribs. When he looked down, the star-iron dagger was in her hand, pressed into the linen of his tunic above his pounding heart.

Disbelief, grief, confusion, anger, shame…so much shame…all of it roiled within him. He stepped back carefully, watching those unfamiliar eyes follow his every movement, feeling something in him break off that he had not even known was holding on by only a thread.

"Sylviu," Pen said, her voice low, maybe a warning, but she said nothing else.

He swallowed, searching her face but finding little there of the one who had once been his closest friend. The wildness was gone, and in its place, a bleak, distant anger. She was lost to him almost as surely as his mother, the waves of mistrust and betrayal separating them, carrying them further and further apart as surely as the black waters of the Inhospitable Sea had carried away his mother. Out of all the emotions in that dark ocean, anger was the only one that brought any sense of safety, of familiarity, and he clung to it as a man clings to a rope on the edge of a long-adrift raft.

"I was going to offer to go with you, as protection, but I can see you are more ha-mazaan than you claim to be, after all."

He had not meant it to sound like an accusation, but the truth of his own feelings was too heavy to contain, and he saw his words land like bruises on her pale skin. He needed to let her go, before he caused any more pain.

"Sylviu, I—"

"I wish you a safe journey, Ishassara Penthesilea."

And with that, he left her standing outside his city's gates, before he did or said anything else he would regret, when he already had enough of that to drown him in that heavy ocean between them.

PART THREE

STRANGERS

35

ALONE

The road west from Galatae was unfamiliar and seemingly unending, but Penny knew it would eventually lead to the waters of the Hellespont, where she would seek passage for herself and Tana on a ferryman's raft. That was at least another week's journey, and now that the extra provisions she had planned to take from Galatae were not an option after her falling out with Sylviu, it would only be a few days before her own stores were depleted. She had brought hard bread, cheese, and a flagon of wine, as well as a sack of grain as large as she could fit in the leather satchel, but those were not going to be enough for the long road ahead, especially in the cold rain that had begun to fall, soaking through her heavy wool cloak and turning the ground to sodden mud.

The first day after leaving Galatae, she broke two arrows trying to take down a boar, though luckily it chose to fling itself into the forest rather than turn those deadly tusks on her in revenge. Unwilling to sacrifice more arrows, or her own life without backup of fellow ha-mazaan spears a normal hunt would have provided, she finally settled for snaring a scrawny, barely edible rabbit for her evening dinner. The smell of flesh roasting over her small fire, protected from the rain by only a few sparse fir branches overhead, did nothing for her appetite, and she had to force herself to swallow even a few bites. When she had forced enough down her gullet to stave off the cramps of hunger, she resigned herself to sleep on the cold, damp ground, her sodden cloak and Tana's blanket her only covering from the increasingly heavy rains as the boughs of the trees waved their arms above her like human specters sweeping away the scent of burning sulfur the fire seemed to give off. She barely slept. Her dreams were full of grasping hands, cold stone pressing into her back, the growl of leopards, and Sylviu's beautiful eyes turned cold and angry, and then turning away from her completely.

Penny awoke bleary-eyed and fuzzy-tongued to a drizzling grey dawn, feeling as though she had eaten the fur of the rabbit instead of the flesh. Her head pounded with the relentless beat of a mourning drum, pain lancing inside her skull with every movement, every blink, every thought. With every sip of cool creek water, she wished for it to be Marpe's herbed wine. She would even welcome the *sivyeti's* censure for missing her medicine for so many days, but the water would need to suffice. Even that crisp drink proved too much for her stomach, though, and she heaved her evening's meal onto the muddy bank as soon as she stood up. She lay on the bank for a while in the rain, feeling every pulse of her heart in her head. She just wanted to sleep, and wake again when the pain was gone. But she could not sleep when she needed to be traveling. Eventually, every muscle screaming with the effort, she sipped more water from her cupped hands, forcing it to stay down by sheer stubborn determination. She considered the need to eat, but even the silvery trout swimming beneath the water could not tempt her to force more food into her seething stomach. It was Tana she needed to worry about feeding. The rain was falling steadily now, bringing with it the icy touch of winter, but the scorching, dry summer had left little in the way of foraging for Tana, and the lack of proper food would soon begin to show on the poor mare if Penny did not find proper fodder for the horse. When they set off for another long day of travel, she did not push their speed as fast as she would have liked, assuring herself it was right to spare the old, steadfast mare any more hardship than necessary, when in reality her body could not have handled a faster pace.

For the first time since she had formulated this plan in her mind, Penny began to feel the doubts creep in. Every step they took closer to her father's lands also led them farther away from the safety and loyalty of the women who were her sacred calling, her birthright. Now her memories of her last moments with Sylviu and her own body's betrayal after only a few hours of hardship only served to make the hardships of traveling through unfamiliar territory all the more terrifying. Penny had never felt more alone in her life, as she moved between the two separate identities she constantly carried within. Thrax's daughter, and Antiope's Ishassara. Who she once had been, and who she might never be. There was one thing that kept her moving forward, through rain and sleet and heavy winds, away from the life she had been born for and back to the one she had left forever.

She desperately wanted to see her father.

She missed the way his skin smelled of campfire smoke and sweat after training in the hot sun. She missed how he would pick her up, big hands around her ribs, and swing her high in a circle against the blue sky, until Penny's voice would grow hoarse shrieking with unadulterated joy. How she would squish her hands into his thick red beard and smush his face together until he laughed, too. Most of all, she missed the stories he would tell as she huddled close to his broad chest and twirled the laces of his jerkin around her fingers, the fire crackling merrily in the background. Stories of griffins far to the east. Stories of men who were supposedly half horse, vicious and virile, who thought nothing of killing humans and could run for three days without tiring, but had still the greatest knowledge for healing of any beast known. Stories of women who lived high in mountain caves, with eyes as milky and blind as a cup of sheep's milk, but who were just as dangerous, just as deadly, as any warrior on a battlefield. Stories of vengeful Furies who punished oath-breakers. She especially missed his terrific leopards, their spotted coats soft and almost hot to the touch, the way their stomachs kept her back warm when she slept amongst them, which was often, and how their rumbling growls thrilled her as much as they terrified her. How he trained them to hunt bear and deer and stryxes, while the dogs were set to guard the goats and cattle, and how they all adored him. Almost as much as she had. Still did, though it had been nearly ten years with nothing but bags of salt from his mines to appease her heartsickness.

But now, she was following his call to her, returning to him as he had asked in that Dream, as the Oracle had instructed. Once she was with her father again, everything would be made better. He would help her undo this terrible thing she had done. She was sure of it.

These hopeful memories of her father drew her onward, but unaccustomed as she was to the daily hardships of journeying without the luxury of pack horse or others to share the burden of watching for wolves and bears and lions, she began to tire. The third morning she awoke less refreshed than the night before, and less hungry for the fresh fish she caught with the makeshift spear she had fashioned from one of the broken arrows. The headache never faltered, and in fact increased in intensity until she grew sick with the pain, sometimes needing to lean over Tana's sodden neck and vomit only water and bile onto the forest floor, but still, she pressed on. The fourth day found her vomiting the berries she had listlessly forced herself to eat, her headache nearly blinding her with its agony, so that even sleep did not improve it. When she dismounted from Tana on the evening of the fifth day, she stumbled when her feet touched the ground, her head pulsing with an ache all the way through her skull, her mind's eye replaying when Brekko had slammed it into the stone floor of the bathhouse.

That memory alone was enough to make her stomach heave, but she steadied herself, and breathed through the pain. Her legs were weary after an entire day in the saddle, though she had done the same ride many times before when hunting in the mountains, and that was much more difficult than sitting a horse on a flat road. This time, though, she could barely summon the energy to pull dried grass from the soil and rub Tana down with it before fetching enough fresh fodder to sustain the horse for the night. Still, she needed to fetch dry wood for a fire, so she dropped the last of the grass for the hobbled mare, straightened with a grimace, and retrieved her unstrung bow and quiver from the pile of tack at the base of the nearby sheltering tree. Bending the bow with a grunt of effort that made her shoulder ache, she hooked the string over the end, then ducked her aching head through and adjusted it across her chest, leaving her hands free to collect any dry wood or edible plants she might find in her foraging. With a last pat on Tana's shoulder, Penny melted into the dense forest of ash and beech still dripping with wet from the day's rains.

The presence of the forest was an immediate balm to her tired, agitated mind. Only the sound of her own boots against the loam and the chatter of one frantic squirrel interrupted the silence. She walked for a while without worrying about what she had come to collect, the movement easing the cramps from her legs as she tried to work some heat into joints stiff from cold. When the makeshift camp was well behind her, she paused to breathe the familiar scent of decaying leaves, sodden earth, bark, and lichen. She felt a moment of elusive peace, and breathed deeply once again.

The peace was gone as quickly as it had come. Something about the wet forest triggered her memory, as Brekko's voice sounded inside her head. Instead of the soft mist of the forest, hot steam filled her lungs, and the suffocating pressure of Brekko fell on top of her. She tore the bow over her head to relieve the pressure on her chest, inside her head, but it was no help. A hissing began in her ears, and the metallic smell of blood filled her nostrils. Scales whispering against themselves and scratching over stone filled her ears, and the soft laughter of the Erinyes echoed in her mind, or perhaps in the forest nearby. Her vision narrowed, turning black at the edges, and she fell to her knees, retching, but her stomach was long empty. For several moments the darkness overwhelmed her, her breath dragging in and out in agonized gasps.

A creak of branches above made her lurch to her feet in alarm, and she drew an arrow to nock it. Her head spun, a dizzying twirl of eye and mind against the undulating landscape, making the tree trunks sway alarmingly.

"These are King Pylameneus' lands you trespass on."

A man's voice, deep and unhurried, but still a stranger, still a threat while she could not even see straight, and immediately Brekko's face swam before her own as her lungs tightened with painful intensity. She felt as though she was once more scrubbing her tainted flesh underwater, wishing for the water to fill her lungs so she need never surface, but he had decided to join her for one last leering look, one last taunt. She knew how foolish that was, because she had killed Brekko herself, but the fear was as real as that day. She drew her bowstring taut, though there was nothing to aim at but shadows and leaves and dripping lichen.

"These are Matar Kubileya's lands," she said finally, once she could trust her voice, scanning the trees as she tried to steady her breathing.

"You're wrong about that. King Pylameneus claims everything you see."

"No man owns a tree, or a stream, or the dirt that lies between them. Not even a king."

"Is that so?"

Though the impression of Brekko faded, she had no face to match the voice to. The man remained in the shadows, camouflaged better than Penny would have thought possible considering how close his voice sounded. She raised her arrow a notch, sure his voice came from somewhere in the branches of the towering beech at the side of the path. She drew a breath to command he show himself when he said,

"Who is Matar Kubileya?"

"What?"

"I said," the voice drawled with patronizing slowness, and also from much higher in the branches than she had originally suspected, "*who* is Matar Kubileya? Your mum? Grandmum?"

Penny's head spun. "Don't be a fool. Show yourself."

The distinct sound of someone jumping from branch to branch, then from branch to ground reached her humming ears, and every muscle in her body tensed. There was more rustling, and Penny struggled to maintain the bowstring taut and not loose her arrow into the forest, when a man stepped from the densely shadowed thicket of alder in front of her. He was a young man, maybe one or two summers her senior, certainly not older than twenty, with a head of unruly black curls and a face of dark stubble that had not been tidied by the edge of a blade for several days. He was taller than her, rather gangly looking, like a new colt whose body had not yet grown into its arms or legs. What skin showed beyond his rather rumpled tunic was free of tattoos, like any child of six, and his eyes, almost as dark as his hair, were lit with a curious, entirely unafraid twinkle, though her arrow was aimed squarely at his chest. His wide, slightly crooked smile was swift, catching her off guard. She swallowed, raising her chin, adjusting her arrow to sit directly in the center of his heart.

I shall harm none, and welcome all.

Her own sing-song voice echoed mockingly in her mind, but she had already broken her vow once. She had no intention of letting him come anywhere near her, vow or not, crooked, somewhat foolish smile or not. He was a stranger, and she was alone. Her fear turned hard and cold in her belly, where a familiar trembling had begun. The ache in her shoulder was magnified with the effort of holding the bowstring taut. Her head still felt underwater, and she shook it, trying to silence the sudden high-pitched ringing in her ears, edged by the flap of leathery wings, but the movement only served to make her eyesight warble, so that she was looking through a dark tunnel.

The man shook his head, tsking his tongue, and said, "I'm not the one trespassing and babbling names. How am I the fool right now?" He took a step toward her.

She did not mean to loose her arrow so soon. She would not have needed to if he had stayed where he was, but the moment he moved forward, the ringing in her head intensified to a shriek and she felt her fingers straighten, allowing the arrow to fly. Her darkening eyesight made it difficult to find his center as she would a deer, and her trembling made the arrow fly wide. She breathed heavily, fumbling for a second arrow with stiff, slow fingers as the stranger peered first into the forest after the stray arrow, then with concern at her face.

"At least the king's deer are safe, if that's the best aim you have."

"They are not 'the king's deer'," she heard herself say, as though in a deep, echoing cavern.

"Ah yes," he said smoothly, unperturbed as her arrow once again aimed somewhere in the direction of his heart. At least, she hoped it did, since he seemed to have split in two, his image doubled in her wavering vision. One of those images contained the shadow of a snake-wreathed face, the eyes wide and the mouth agape in a show of pointed teeth. Penny's stomach heaved.

"This Matar Kubileya..." he continued, then paused, and both of his heads, with four dark eyes, peered at her strangely. "Are you alright?" he asked, but his voice now sounded far away on the other end of that tunnel. He took another step forward, but superimposed over his body was the image of a woman wrapped in snakes, her split tongue slipping between her teeth as she smiled, while blood dripped from the corner of her eye. It, *they*, took another step, and a hand coiled inside the body of a python reached toward her.

"Stay away," Penny said through cold lips.

"You don't look well..."

The man's voice trailed into a fog of noise, and though she could see his lips were still moving, his brow was creased in a frown, the image of the Erinyes was there atop them. The olive skin of his face and his great dark eyes moved through the shade of the Fury and came toward her, and she thought she heard the bugling of a horse's war cry and the stampeding of hooves, and her second arrow flew harmlessly, uselessly wide beyond one of his left shoulders, before the tunnel closed in, and all was blackness.

36

HARPALION

Penny awoke to the sound of blunt teeth tearing grass directly beside her temple, and a fire snapping with hot sap. The heat of it was close enough to pinch her flesh. She opened her eyes slowly, wincing at the light. A rush of memory flooded in, and she started fully awake, confusing the pressure of heavy blankets on her chest for another body pressing her down. She flung them away from her and sat up, instantly woozy, looking around wildly to find exactly what she feared she might see.

A young man with olive skin and unruly black curls sat on the ground next to a merrily crackling fire, though the sun blazed overhead, his black eyes watching her like a curious satyr even as a white-toothed grin split his face.

"She lives!"

Penny scrambled for her knife.

Her fingers fumbled at her bare waist for several seconds before her mind understood the dagger and the belt it hung on were gone. Frenzied with panic, she looked around wildly, finding her bow leaning against a tree, still strung. Her quiver and arrows lay next to it. She scrambled to her feet and moved backward, eyes on the man the entire time, meaning to grab her bow and put some distance between them at the same time. The moment she stood straight, though, the dizziness overwhelmed her, and she swayed dangerously to the side. If not for Tana's warm shoulder suddenly beneath her outstretched hand, she would surely have tumbled into the fire. Her breaths came in harsh gasps for several seconds as the blackness at the edges of her vision faded back into painfully bright sunlight.

The man had not moved from his seat at the base of a young oak, but his expression showed a wary concern as her eyesight cleared.

"I did not think sleeping with that heavy belt looked very comfortable. It didn't seem to help your breathing, so I removed it. Sorry. It's in your pack."

Penny stared at him, dragging another breath in through her nose, and letting it out slowly through tight lips. They stared at each other over the fire, but when Tana moved the support of her shoulder away from Penny, she took a step backward, bending carefully at the knees to pick up her bow, so as not to set off the nausea, but also keep him in her vision at all times. Slowly, her arms as weak and spindly as the arrow she carefully nocked and aimed, she dragged one more tight breath into her lungs, and said,

"Who are you? And what do you want?"

The bow creaked with its familiar protest as she drew the arrow back, but even that effort made her arm tremble. Sweat stood atop her brow, and along her lip. She felt feverish and frozen all at the same time, and her headache as fierce as ever, but the last thing she was going to do was let this satyr know that. The satyr in question sighed, and she was quite sure he rolled his eyes, an action no person other than Sylviu had ever dared in her presence since she arrived in Themiscyra.

"Not the bow again, I beg you. It took me ages to find your stray arrows last night." He shook his curls at her, his expression mournfully reproving.

"What are you doing here?"

"Well, I was looking for a particular horse, but it seems you found him before I did. Or perhaps he found you. I'm not certain anymore."

Penny scowled, fearing his pointing finger was simply a ruse to distract her focus, but she allowed herself a quick, furtive glance in the direction he indicated. There was nothing there. Her eyes snapped back to him immediately, but he had not moved. He smiled, his eyebrows lifting.

"A fine and furious stallion, very well-trained, I am told, though he still wouldn't let me tie a lead, and has disappeared into the trees again. Maybe you could help with that? He seemed very attached to you, running out of the forest and trampling everything in sight, except for your body, and then only allowing me near you once I had promised to be gentle. Quite the night, I assure you. But now he is gone again, and my father is going to tan my hide *before* he flays it from my body, just as promised."

"What are you talking about?" Penny demanded. "You still haven't told me who you are."

He sighed, and got to his feet with gangly, coltish movements, ignoring the creak of her bowstring.

"My name is Harpalion, fair lady. But," he wagged the finger in the air warningly, as though to cease words she was not speaking, "my friends don't call me that. They call me…" he turned with dizzying speed on the toes of one foot, stooping to pick something up from the base of the tree he sat beneath. Penny held her breath, wondering if she should shoot him while his back was turned, but when he straightened and turned back to face her, it was not a weapon he held.

"Harp."

He seemed very pleased with this introduction. Penny stared dumbly at him and the instrument he held for several moments, at his white, foolish grin and his dark hands as they caressed the finely carved wood of the small instrument, before he tickled his fingers across the strings to create a waterfall of sound. He wiggled bushy eyebrows at her.

"And you are…?"

"Bellatrix."

She did not know what made her answer him at all, let alone use the name only her father and the Oracle had ever called her, but she thought it best to keep her real identity a secret.

"Ah, Beautiful Warrior. A fine name for a pretty girl with a bow, even if she cannot shoot it."

Penny loosed the arrow into the ground at his feet, a bare finger's breadth from the thin leather covering his toes. This time when she drew a replacement from the quiver at her heels, her fingers were not clumsy, or slow. Even through the headache, she could feel some strength returning, and with it, her confidence.

Harpalion strummed a hand across the strings in a sound that somehow conveyed both surprise and humor together, then swept both arms outwards, one still clutching the instrument, and bowed from the waist.

"I stand corrected. It is indeed a *very* fitting name," he said, and when he straightened, the grin he flashed was definitely not mocking. "A true Bellatrix you are, and I am at your mercy. Aha! I see your awakening has summoned the stallion back into our presence once more. I suppose I must thank you for that."

Penny glanced in the direction he indicated, and saw the shining edge of a golden flank at the edge of the forest, but she caught a movement out of the corner of her eye. Harpalion moved as though to step past the fire and come toward her, the hand that did not hold the instrument outstretched.

"Don't," Penny warned. She was ashamed of the fearful plea even as it left her lips, but it halted his movement forward. His smile slipped, and he eyed her consideringly for a long moment, tucking the harp close to his ribs. Absently, he withdrew his reaching hand and stroked his fingers down the strings, eliciting a soft, soothing chord that held a hint of a question in it.

"I will not," he said finally, his eyes somber as they held hers, his meaning evident even in the succinct, quiet delivery. Slowly, with one more strum of the strings, he folded his long legs underneath his body, and returned to sitting cross-legged on the ground, all the while holding her gaze.

"So, this Matar Kubileya you were jabbering about last night," he said without preamble, appearing entirely unconcerned about the arrow still threatening his heart. "Who are they?"

Penny stared at him, but he merely squinted up at her, the rising sun directly behind her obscuring his vision, and strummed another soft, questioning chord on the strings. She felt the tension in her shoulders loosen, and her pull on the bowstring eased. She pursed her lips, answering him despite her wary uncertainty with acerbic questions of her own.

"The Great Mother? The One you walk upon? Live within? The one from whom all are born and reborn?"

He shivered dramatically, eyebrows raised. "Brrr! Intriguing. I wish I could tell my mother of this Kubileya. She would likely have much to say about how I was not born from her loins after all. Especially considering that is what nearly killed her."

Penny narrowed her eyes at his grin. His teeth shone white against his dark skin as he strummed a triumphant chord.

"I think you refer to Cybele, yes? The one my mother and uncle Rhys call Bendis. I have not heard this name you use for her. *Kubileya*," he said, with a flourish of his hand that began at his chest and ended with his fingers outstretched in the air before him, as though waiting for a golden chalice full of wine to be handed over. Then, he repeated the entire process, this time emphasizing a different part of the Great Mother's name.

"Kubil*eya*!" He paused dramatically for a long moment, eyes fixed in rapturous attention on the tips of his fingers, as though he was trying to conjure the Great Mother from the sky rather than the earth below him. Penny frowned down at him, the bow slack at her side now. Was he soft in the head? His eyes shifted slightly in her direction, twinkling even brighter behind his summoning hand. He resumed a sane person's posture once more, plucking the strings absently with two fingers, the tune both playful and curiously familiar, though Penny could not place it.

"Tell me, Bellatrix, mighty huntress, what brings you here alone, save for your adorable pony, to trespass on my father's lands?"

"Your father's lands?"

"Yes, yes, Kubileya's lands and all that," he flapped a long-fingered hand with easy grace, "but actually, in reality, my father's lands. I regret to admit that my father is King Pylameneus, yes. He is particular about who is and who isn't welcome this close to the city, you know. If it had been anyone other than me you stumbled upon, you would not have wanted to miss with your first arrow."

Hope flared in Penny's breast. Pylamaneus...

There was still at least one ha-mazaan she had not sought support from. One ha-mazaan who had the authority to command the Savaran, and who would surely have reason to avenge the terrible crimes committed against her kin in Themiscyra. One person who would be able to grant her the help she needed in retrieving Leandra from Attica. A new plan began to take form in her mind, a plan that seemed far wiser, far more strategic than making it all the way to Satra on her own, with only Tana as a companion.

Seek the woman who will guide you to him, and teach you the way back to yourself, and to your ha-mazaan spirit.

Penny tried to keep the desperate excitement from her voice when she asked,

"Does your father have any guests right now?"

He peered up at her, strumming a chord that sounded...suspicious. She eyed his fingers quizzically.

"Maybe," he said finally. "My father often hosts war councils and hunting parties and the like. Too often, if you ask me."

Penny bit her lip, considering her best options. Finally, she settled on the most brazen one. If Orithyia was with her nephew, the King of Paphlagonia, she needed to find the ha-mazaan queen as soon as possible.

"I have come to see him," she said boldly. "He should be expecting me."

"I doubt that," Harpalion replied with dampening bluntness. "My father doesn't allow many women into his presence. Something about his mother, you see. She used to be...well, if you know my father as you say, then you know who my grandmother was."

"Queen Sanape," Penny said, and was rewarded by a discordant strum.

"Hmm," Harp said, peering at her closely with those dark eyes. "In any case, I was planning on taking you to Ganghra, anyway, so that my mother can work her magic on you. She's a Healer, you see, and you seemed to need, er," he flapped those long fingers at her, "healing. Even though I am not supposed to go back there until...well...that is another matter. I would have taken you last night, but I was not sure if I should move you that far."

Penny was glad he had not, but she asked warily, "How far?"

"Only a day's walk. Less, if I had a horse."

The look he gave her, then her horse, then her again, was clear enough.

"There is a horse right there," Penny said, waving her hand in the direction of the golden horse at the edge of the woods, though it had moved no closer during their conversation, instead lurking in the distant trees as though not wanting to be seen.

"That," Harp said, "is not a horse. That is a beast, whom no one in their right mind would ride. Which is exactly why my father sent me on this impossible, and very likely deadly, mission. But *you* have a horse."

"She is not big enough for two."

Harpalion sighed dramatically, making Penny's lips twitch, despite her wariness.

"I suppose you should be the one to ride, then, since you are the one going about fainting in the woods..." he punctuated the sentence with a mournful strum.

"I was not—" she began indignantly, but another discordant strum interrupted her protest.

"You were, though, and in the most inconvenient of places. I will have you know I put my back out to bring you all this way, and once I found you had a horse hanging about, which would have been extremely useful, I was very perturbed." The next strum sounded petulant, but the glint in his eyes let her know he was teasing, and she relaxed her stiffening spine.

"Er...sorry. And thank you," she said awkwardly, feeling she should acknowledge the effort he had made to help her, but thoroughly uncomfortable with the realization that he must have carried her all this way, and she had been completely vulnerable the entire time. She shivered.

"I was just cold and...and in shock a bit, I think. A lot has happened recently."

"Hmm," he said again, with a strum as punctuation, but it was a gentle sound, and he said nothing else.

She eyed him warily, but he was already ignoring her, rustling around in a small leather rucksack beside his hip.

"Well, if you are sure you will not topple from the back of that horse—which is tiny enough that the fall surely would not harm even my nearly-dead grandfather," he said bluntly, "then we should be off, so that you can have your meeting with my father, and I can witness his displeasure at someone else besides me."

He rose to kick dirt over the fire and stomp it until it was thoroughly extinguished. Then he tucked the harp under his armpit, scooped the leather sack from the base of the tree to slung it with a carefree toss over his shoulder, and gestured a slender hand toward her.

"After you, fairest of lady warriors. I hope you like bawdy songs, because that is what I plan on singing."

37

GANGHRA

Harp kept his word, singing many bawdy songs, some which made Penny's ears burn and her cheeks flame, but most of the journey he spent telling stories punctuated by dramatic flourishes of music. Traveling with anyone, especially a man, after so many days alone was an adjustment, but Penny quickly grew to appreciate her eccentric, expressive companion and his grandiose style of communication. With every dramatic story he told, and every strum of his strings, her feeling of unease at being alone with him dissipated, though it did not disappear entirely. She could reason in her thoughts well enough that not every man would turn on her as Brekko had, but this test of that conviction felt too soon, and too inescapable.

Despite her wariness, Penny learned far more about him than she would have thought possible in such a short time. The man could chat the ear off a magpie. She learned he was twenty summers, that he was the only son of King Pylameneus and Queen Truti, and a great disappointment to his father, who had only ever wanted to sire a mighty warrior, and had instead been granted a milksop musician, according to Harpalion's telling of it. Apparently, his sisters were no better as fighters, despite their illustrious ha-mazaan lineage. He told her they had all been married to chieftains in the southern lands surrounding Wilusa long ago. She quickly learned he would strum his harp to emphasize any point in a conversation, no matter who was making it, and she saw how he sneezed when Tana got too close to his face. Even so, he had an easy, undemanding manner that set the horse at ease and immediately raised Penny's respect for him. The stallion he claimed to be seeking was following some distance behind. Once or twice, she caught a glimpse of gold through the trees, though the horse remained

204

obscured by trees and shadows, a golden specter flitting in and out of existence. At least it was not the Erinyes, and for that she was grateful.

By the time they skirted the edge of the rugged mountain, and the low wooden walls of the city's buildings came into view, Penny felt as though she had been the one to walk the whole day. She was exhausted, her stomach in knots, her mind fogged by both pain and the incessant noise of man and harp. Yet she was also...comforted. Listening to Harp prattle on about everything from composing his latest ballad to how his father threatened to disinherit him on a daily basis somehow lessened the weight of everything terrible that had happened since slipping into the thick dark fog of that bathhouse, and everything that came after. There was something about him that was so unthreatening, so easy, that Penny felt lulled into a sense of comfortable companionship.

She was almost disappointed when he pursed his lips into a frown and ceased talking about anything at all the moment the sentries were within earshot. His entire demeanor changed as soon as they passed under the lifeless pennant flags posted at the low stone wall marking the perimeter of the village. His spine straightened, his easy smile twisted as though he tasted something sour, and his stride stiffened. Men dressing carcasses of enormous elk hanging from scaffolding inside the gates eyed the two of them with either suspicion or open curiosity, but once they recognized Harpalion, they gave Penny only one more glance before going about their business.

"That's where you're headed," he indicated the building as they drew near, and then he stopped walking altogether, seemingly reluctant to go closer. Penny's fingers clutched at Tana's mane in sudden apprehension.

"Are you not going to introduce me to your father?" she asked. Harp looked up at her with a wry smile that was noticeably dampened compared to when they had been alone in the forest.

"I thought he was expecting you?"

Amusement in his tone softened the accusation, but Penny shifted uncomfortably on Tana's back.

"I have business with his guest."

"Your queen is the one expecting you, then?"

"She is not my queen."

Harp eyed her sideways in that knowing way, his fingers twitching as though to strum a chord, but the harp was safely tucked away in his bag. He began walking once more, though his steps were noticeably reluctant. He nodded.

"She does seem a bit of a harridan. I can understand why you might have needed to renounce your loyalty."

Penny smiled, shaking her head.

"I am not from Sinope. She isn't my queen."

"Oh? Surely one with such a fine zoster and such a fierce bow is no swineherd's daughter."

He had spent so much time talking on the walk that she had been able to avoid divulging anything too personal, but now he stared at her, and the bow slung across her chest, with pointed expectation.

"Themiscyra."

Again, that sideways look, and his dark eyes seemed to see more than just Penny's face.

"Bellatrix of the Themiscyran ha-mazaans. I am honored to still be alive, fair huntress."

Emboldened by their easy camaraderie, Penny arched an eyebrow down at him, though his head came almost to her shoulders next to Tana's short legs, and tried to mimic her mother's most haughty expression.

"As you should be."

He grinned, and Penny smiled back. For the first time in a long, long while, she felt as though she had made a friend.

Harp led them to the stables first, a low-ceilinged building with stalls facing outward into an open courtyard, the small openings half the size of those in Themiscyra, but Tana would not mind, as she was only half the size of most horses. She did not pay Penny any further attention once Harp heaved freshly dried grass into her feeding bucket and sealed her in with the rope across the doorway. Then he sealed the golden palomino in the nearby space, the stallion submitting meekly enough to being roped in, and earning an irritated mutter from the young man for his troubles. Harp put the sack he had been carrying next to her bow and quiver in a small cubbyhole outside of the stall, then, after a moment's hesitation, he tucked his beloved harp next to them, careful that the strings of catgut were not in danger of being tangled by the arrows.

He led her through a maze of buildings, past people going about their daily business, most of whom paid them no mind, until they were somewhere in the center of the settlement, in front of a long, low-roofed building with an enormous, rough-planked wooden door. Harp waved at her to go ahead into the dark interior, and when he closed it behind them, the torches flickering in their sconces. The dark passageway gave Penny pause for a moment, and she eyed Harp warily, waiting for him to lead the way, noticing all of the good humor had fled from his eyes, his mouth set in a grim line as he moved past her. She wondered, not for the first time since stumbling upon him in the forest, what he had been doing in the middle of nowhere, with only his harp and a small sack of food and his absurd excuse of tracking down a rogue horse.

A heavy door loomed ahead, with two sentries posted on either side. They eyed both Penny and Harp with far more suspicion than she expected for a king's son, making no move to open the door as they approached. The sounds of men enjoying drink and food echoed through the heavy timber doors. Harp turned to Penny, tugging his long tunic to center and adjusting his belt, his fingers twitching the air convulsively now that his harp was stuffed into a shadowy crevice.

"Ready, Bellatrix of Themiscyra?"

Penny nodded, and Harp signaled for one of the guards to open the door. It swung wide on well-oiled hinges, revealing a hall longer than it was wide, with torches flaming around the perimeter lending a smoky, oily haze to the windowless room. Penny squinted eyes that suddenly burned, and followed Harp inside, doing her best to ignore the inspection the guards afforded her braided hair, her trousers, the tattoos on her fingers, before giving Harp what she could only consider an insolently suggestive eyebrow raise and a grin. It was not as though they had not seen tattoos before. She knew Orithyia was here, and the ha-mazaan Queen would likely be covered in them, both for protection, and as a sign of her status.

The clamor in the hall lessened as men—and only men, as far as Penny could tell—turned to watch their entrance with curious, not quite hostile, but definitely not friendly stares. One man sat at the far end of the table, his wide shoulders hunched over his plate, his dark head bowed close to the table as he shoveled food into his mouth with his fingers. Judging by the young boys on either side of him, one holding a clay pitcher of wine and the other fairly dancing on his toes in anticipation of an order, Penny presumed him to be King Pylameneus.

"Father," Harp announced, his rich timbre heightened nearly to a squeak. The man looked up, a deep frown indicating their presence had been noticed, before the man went back to eating. Harp continued. "I would like to introduce you to the fairest guest the Eneti have ever welcomed. I present to you the glorious Bellatrix of Themiscyra."

Harpalion's elaborate wave was thoroughly muted compared to the first time Penny had seen it, but his eyes twinkled with a secretive smile as he waved her forward. All eyes were on her now.

"That was quick work, boy," the king said, barely looking up from his food. "I didn't think you would have it in you."

Penny frowned, sending a confused glance at Harp, but he kept his eyes fixed on his father. The king took another bite from the leg of bird dripping grease onto his plate, then asked before swallowing, "What brings you into my lands, girl?"

"I seek counsel with Queen Orithyia," Penny said, as confidently as she could manage.

"Come to tell her that her washing is done?" A man seated to the left of King Pylameneus said, and there were a few low chuckles from the men on either side of them. The rest ignored her altogether, some who had their backs to her not even bothering to look in her direction.

Penny grit her teeth. "I bring news that her cousins are dead, and her kinswomen kidnapped. Themiscyra is destroyed."

38

ORITHYIA

Even Harp snapped to attention at this. Every pair of eyes in the room focused on Penny, this time with far more interest. A few glanced over their shoulders with considering stares, their eyes moving from her scuffed boots to her striped trousers marking her as ha-mazaan, to her mother's once-white tunic, now so full of holes it could be used to sift pebbles from gravel, and finally to the thick leather zoster around her waist.

The King's frown reappeared, and he lowered the leg of the bird back to his plate.

"What's this?" he demanded, his tone disbelieving.

"All of my cousins?"

The voice was deep, slightly rough, as though they had inhaled the smoke of too many campfires, but it was not a man's timbre. Penny looked at the back of that head more closely, at the cropped gray hair, the edges of it rough and haphazardly trimmed as though someone had used a blunt sword on a windy day. Their shoulders were covered in scaled armor, even at the dinner table, but their frame was not quite as wide as the man to the right, and a thick belt of studded leather, a twin to Penny's own, circled their waist, from which hung a short sword that looked suspiciously like star-iron. They did not turn toward Penny, but remained focused on whatever food was on their plate.

"Hippolyta is murdered," Penny said, with the quiet dignity of grief. "Melanippe is dead as well, and both of their *rhu-tasiyas* with them in the Otherworld. More than sixty others were buried with our Defending Queen. And..." she swallowed, her lips wanting to say "my mother" but her own grief stopping the words before they betrayed her identity, "Queen

Antiope was taken, along with more than fifty of our best Savaran. We have reason to believe she has also been...been killed."

"Taken? Killed? By whom?"

Again her voice was cool, but now there was a tone of disbelief that set Penny's teeth on edge.

"Achaeans. Theseus, a Basileus of Attica, and Heracles of Thebes. They brought nearly a hundred of their men from Mycenae and beyond."

"Is that so?" Again, the voice was cool, unhurried. "And how was it that only a hundred men attacked and conquered a city filled with the best archers and Savaran among our people? Were they as drunk as my sister?"

Penny flushed, but lifted her chin. "Poison, Queen Orithyia." The woman still had not turned to acknowledge her presence, leaving Penny to tell her news to her shaggy grey head. "The men were welcomed with guest-rite before anyone knew they intended war over Hippolyta's zoster. They drugged our well and our wine, and even our *kimiz*. The ha-mazaans tried to stop them from...from leaving with our Queens, but our army was overcome by the poison. Our stables and our storehouses were also burned. The Flame has gone cold in our city's hearth. Those who could travel have sought shelter and protection in your own city, Queen Orithyia. Themiscyra could not sustain us through the winter."

The silence after this was drawn out and heavy, as every listener absorbed the information. King Pylameneus stared at Penny with solemn, considering eyes, and some of his men looked between her and Orithyia, waiting for a response. She could feel Harp's warmth at her side, his eyes on her face, but she did not look at him. Finally, Sinope's Defending Queen twisted in her chair with a creak of leather, slinging an arm over the high back of it to face Penny.

Her face was older than expected, the skin scarred from battle and weathered from sun, giving her a swarthy, sea-faring look. Her eyes were the same blue as Penny's mother's, bright as bluebells, but far less friendly. Where Antiope's eyes had been bright with curiosity, Orithyia's were piercingly sharp, hard as agate, and once they settled on Penny, looking her over with a stare that quite obviously found her wanting, she felt as though she were being sliced and skewered by the sword that hung from the ha-mazaan's waist.

"So why are you here, Bellatrix of Themiscyra?"

Her tone was dry with suspicion. This was not the welcoming attitude Penny had hoped for. She shifted her weight from one foot to another, considering her next words carefully.

"To ask for your help."

"It seems I have already provided that, hey?" The old woman cocked her head just slightly to the side, like a bright-eyed bird listening for the squirm of a worm. Her eyes sparkled with some emotion Penny could not read. "Especially if Themiscyra's greedy ha-mazaans have already invaded my city and begun to drain my stores?"

"The help of your sword," Penny clarified stiffly.

Orithyia raised an eyebrow the same color and sharpness as star-iron. "It seems too late for that, don't you think, girl?"

Penny's flush deepened, and she clenched her hands behind her back. She glanced meaningfully at the men at the table, all of them eyeing her with varying amounts of curiosity and suspicion.

"I would request a private audience with you, Queen Orithyia."

Orithyia made a scoffing sound. "Let me guess. You want me to lead what is left of my women into a war against all of Mycenae—after marching them and their horses halfway across the world, and fighting who knows how many battles along the way—because my cousin was foolish enough to welcome these men into her palace, and probably her bed?"

Orithyia's tone was no longer mocking. It was scathing. Penny opened her mouth to reply before her courage failed completely, but the old woman was not done.

"You want me to put my ha-mazaans in danger because you miss your pretty Hearth Queen, and a few good riders? So that you can feel like you've finally made a mark against some man no one has ever heard of, in some city that will one day be ashes under the sand?" Orithyia shook her head side to side, like a bull about to charge. "No. No," she repeated, with another shake. "Sacrificing even one good woman for the sake of vengeance is futile. I will not lead my women on such a worthless, childish fantasy."

The Kebat's words flooded into Penny's mind, the memory moving her lips as though in a dream, without her conscious effort. "I will lead them."

Penny knew better than anyone that she was not even fit to lead the drummers in a Moon Hall dance, let alone a ha-mazaan army to war, and that this was not why she had come here. But once the words tumbled out, dancing naked in the open air, she could not take them back, and she could not quell the rising feeling of purpose as she said them.

"You!"

The queen's shock was visible, and it overshadowed her contempt for a moment, before she barked a loud, donkey-bray of a laugh that made Penny's heart ache in memory of Areto.

"*You!*" she said again, slapping her thigh. A few of the men at the table laughed with her. The old queen had a black gap where one of her front teeth should have been, the hole gaping as she tipped her head back to let loose another guffaw.

The sudden scrape of Orithyia's chair legs against the timber floor made Penny flinch, but she held her ground as Sinope's Defending Queen, a much shorter woman than she had assumed, stalked toward her, one hand on the pommel of the sword at her hip. Penny remained as still as she could manage, trying to breathe normally and will the fiery heat to recede from her cheeks as Orithyia slowly, deliberately stepped in a wide circle around her, looking her up and down with an air of extreme skepticism, like one might examine an unsound mare being bartered for too much gold.

"You, a girl whose perfect skin and straight nose shows me she has never been in more than a scuffle over kitchen scraps. Whose hands have clearly never felt the blisters of sword or axe," Orithyia pinched Penny's tunic sleeve between her fingers and lifted her stiff arm into the air, wiggling it so that her offensively soft hand was made obvious to all those looking on, before dropping it again and continuing her slow circle. "*You*, a mere child, thinks *she* will lead *my* women, *any* women, any *ha-mazaan*, across seas and mountains, through the heart of enemy lands, into battle against an army of men who have already proved themselves too great for Melanippe, the mightiest warrior of all ha-mazaans? Men who bested the all of the finest Savaran my cousins ever trained? You will lead them? *You?*"

By now Orithyia had moved in a full circle around Penny, and she did not know whether her stomach heaved from pure anxiety, or fear, or the smell of old garlic and licorice root on the queen's breath. It washed over her already hot face as Orithyia punctuated her scorn with another contemptuous laugh, the sound echoed soon after from several throats at the table. Penny's eyes fell under the queen's haughty stare, and she fixed her gaze on the dusty tips of her boots, wondering why she had been so reckless, so foolish, so stupid to say such a thing to such a woman. She did not even *want* to lead the ha-mazaans to war. She wanted to find her father, and rid herself of this curse, but the moment she had listened to the Queen's talk of leading the army west, some strange desire had overtaken her better judgment. She knew now that it was a desire for vengeance, just as Orithyia had accused her of. Penny's silence did nothing to help her cause, but her tongue had become thick with shame. It was Harp who finally came to Penny's rescue, though it seemed an impossible task.

"She is as good with an arrow as any of your ha-mazaans," he said from behind Penny, and there was a mulish tone to his words that surprised her. Orithyia took a step back and, with an exaggerated inclination of her head, examined Penny from head to toe once more.

"A bow and arrow, you say? How novel! And is that your strategy for this battle, then, Bellatrix of Themiscyra? You are going to lead the ha-mazaans into a siege and launch arrows at their walls, poking the stones until the noise of it drives the men crazy and they finally give you what you want? Hey? Is that your plan?"

Penny was still looking at her toes, teeth grinding so that she was sure the whole room could hear it, but at this she scowled at the old woman. In for a pinch, in for a dollop, she thought, raising her chin.

"We will fight them with whatever weapon we need to if it means we at least tried. Don't you think we owe that much to the women they took? Even if we fail, at least we will not have been old attas sitting at home, mouthing our gums and drinking with men."

She met Orithyia's eyes squarely, mutinously. Orithyia returned the look with a sudden brilliance to her eyes that Penny could not like.

"Excellent," the queen said, her tone switching so quickly from mocking to thrilled that Penny was disconcerted, and for a moment, thought the queen had relented and was agreeing to summon her army. Orithyia twisted smartly on her heel, marched back to the king's side, picked up the wooden mug from her empty place at the table, and downed its contents in a few loud glugs. Everyone watched her in silence, until she thudded the cup back to the wooden table with a sigh of satisfaction, wiped the back of her arm across her glistening mouth, and turned to face Penny once more.

"Tell you what, girl. If you can keep a sword in your hand for longer than five breaths in a fight against me, a 'gummy old atta', I will let you lead my army through the Gates of the Otherworld to fight the Shadow itself, hear? I will even leave my own sword here, to keep my spot at the table."

She was already unbuckling the thick leather belt strapping her sword to her hip, and she held it above the seat of her chair, as though about to drop it, when her eyes snapped back to Penny with a considering look. She drew the sword from its loop and dropped just the belt.

"Better yet," she said, stalking forward, "you can use it."

Penny barely had time to flinch as Orithyia thumped the length of the sword into her chest, and then continued walking. Instinctively she clutched the heavy weapon against her body, lest it drop and shear her toes from her feet. Penny fumbled for words, to plead for the queen to cease this nonsense, but Orithyia was already approaching the doorway they had just entered, back when Penny's heart had been so hopeful, so naïve.

"Coming?" Orithtyia said over her shoulder, her tone still light, and then she disappeared through the doorway the guards held open for her. They did not shut it behind her, but held each door with an air of expectation that Penny would follow. She stood rooted to the spot, awkwardly clutching the heavy, unfamiliar star-iron, feeling the tense, expectant energy of the room shifting around her. Her eyes met Harp's.

"Perhaps a plan may have been wise," he shrugged, his voice barely over a whisper. "Still, my father watching Orithyia kill you will certainly be the distraction *I* need to stay alive a few more hours."

Penny forced the stiff corner of her mouth to move in response, but it was nothing close to a smile.

39

Girl Against Queen

When Penny emerged into the courtyard, the sky overhead had grown dark with ominous clouds. Orithyia was already twirling a long staff in the air, the tip of it making a harsh whistling sound as she brought it from high above her head to stop with perfect precision a hair's width above the trampled ground. Penny's legs were stiff, her steps awkward as she approached the queen. She glanced nervously over her shoulder to Harp as he jostled for a position at the front of the group forming a ring around the small courtyard. He smiled at Penny encouragingly, and wiggled his eyebrows up and down.

"Ha!" Orithyia barked, startling Penny, but her focus snapped to Orithyia as intended. Still, she wasn't ready for the staff smacking into her knuckles. The borrowed sword immediately dropped from Penny's fingers into the mud as she squawked in pain, clutching her hand to her chest.

"Pick it up," Orithyia prodded, her tone irritated. The burning pain blossoming in Penny's knuckles quelled some of the terror in her chest, and an anger began to seep through her fogged head, burning away some of the humiliation. She bent and scooped the sword from the mud as the first drops of rain tickled the back of her neck, dribbling down her tunic. When she stood straight again, Orithyia was circling like a leopard prowling its prey, and Penny clutched the hard pommel of the sword against the palm of her hand until it bit her flesh, bending her knees slightly in anticipation of Orithyia's lunge. She pushed the vision of the men's eager faces from her mind, though their numbers had already grown from what had followed them outside from the hall. If she was to be humiliated in front of these bloodthirsty onlookers, it would not be because she was a coward. She hefted the sword, the weight of it painfully straining in the muscles of her forearm, watched for her best opportunity as the queen circled. When she saw an opening, she swung with all her might at Orithyia's staff.

The queen blocked the blade with casual ease, knocking it from Penny's hand with a flip so quick she did not even know how it happened. A few of the men laughed, delighted, and Penny grit her teeth harder, plucking the sword out of the mud for a second time as the rain began to pelt in earnest. She bent her knees into a crouch again, feeling her thighs protest as she held the pose for too long, and when she thought she saw the opening she needed, she lunged. Orithyia barely moved, only swayed to the side, and Penny's blade went wide. She was already off balance when the queen lashed out. The sword flew from Penny's grip with a clang of wood on metal. Deep voices groaned and laughed at the same time from all around as Penny fumbled for the sword's handle in the mud, bringing the blade up in desperate frustration, but Orithyia was already swinging.

This time the blade landed in the mud at King Pylaemenes' feet. Orithyia stepped back, lowered her weapon, and grinned, the gaping hole where there should have been a tooth flashing into view.

"I do not know who your *matar* is, girl, but she failed in raising a worthy ha-mazaan. Even my newest Xanharaspa could wield a sword better than that." Orthyia's chilled blue eyes swept over Penny before her lips curled in a slight sneer. "Worse, you reek of fear. You will never lead a group of children out of the kitchens, let alone front an army. You are no ha-mazaan. Take yourself back to Themiscyra and learn the way of the Crafters. Weaving thatch and linen is probably all those hands are good for, and it sounds like your ruined city needs some new roofs."

The men had grown silent as Penny trembled with shame and humiliation. Orithyia turned away, thrusting her staff into the hands of the closest man, and strolled back toward the open door of the hall. Slowly, the men followed, disappointed that their entertainment had been cut short by severely uneven odds, but even through the mortification of it all, there was a desperation inside her chest. She thought of her mother, and the terrible fear on Antiope's face that day on the beach. She thought of Hippolyta's bloody chest, her sightless eyes staring into the night sky. She thought of Areto, who had picked up a sword to defend the child she would never hear laugh, never teach to ride a galloping horse across the open fields and trails of their devastated city. She thought of all the ha-mazaans taken captive inside the dark bellies of those ships, probably even now being sold as slaves or concubines to Athenian men and women, if they had not already lost their lives to waves or weapons. She thought of Leandra, and her golden lion's mane of hair, and the way Theseus had looked at her.

"Then you lead the army! Unless you're too old, or a coward!" Penny called after her.

Orithyia paused, looking over her shoulder. One star-iron brow raised, and again, the blue eyes and the familiar gesture reminded her so strongly of her mother that it made Penny wonder what her great-grandmother Marpesia had been like, to pass such strong traits on to her granddaughters. The queen tilted the corner of her lips into a rueful smile, and shook her head.

"I am too old, you're right. My days of being hungry for battle and thirsty for the blood of men are over, girl. These old bones have no wish to ride to the edge of the world and back again, especially for the sake of vengeance. It is not our Way. Besides," she turned and continued walking, "anyone foolish enough to pit their army against men clever or strong enough to kill Hippolyta and Melanippe, and to kidnap my wily cousin, will not be returning home. You seek a different fool for your task, but it will not be this one."

The queen disappeared inside the lodge, and Penny was thankful for the obscuring rain as she fought to maintain composure. One of the men passing by ruined her attempt when he cuffed her gently on the shoulder and said,

"Don't fuss, girl. That woman is tough as dried aurochs' balls, and even more full of piss. But she's right, nonetheless. Don't waste your time pushing guts back into a fatal wound." His hand lingered on her shoulder for a moment before he said, his tone entirely different, "However, if you're looking for a man to breed you and replace the daughters lost to Themiscyra, you know where to find me..."

"Fuck off, Gorm," Harp said from behind her, his voice more grim than she had heard from him before.

With a pronounced leer and a wink that may have been an attempt at humor, the man shouldered his way through the rain, leaving Penny to fume at his back, her skin crawling where his hand had touched her.

"You probably should have declined her offer to fight," Harp said. "Considering how bad you are with a sword and all. Here."

He offered said sword to her, the blade dripping with sludge, and as she accepted it with thoroughly bruised fingers she channeled some of her dejection, pain, and frustration into a steely, ungrateful glare. He threw his hands up in mock horror.

"No, please don't stab me! It would take too long to die, the way you use that sword like a shovel."

Penny's look turned mutinous, but he merely laughed that peculiar, light-hearted laugh.

"Come," Harp said, steering her back towards the hall. "Let us get some warm food, and some dry clothes, and we will drink wine—did you know my father's wine is the best in a thousand leagues? Even better than that juice from Colchis—and we will discuss how you seem to enjoy making very unwise decisions. Maybe that's why I like you."

40

MEN'S MUSIC

Ganghra's hall was a fraction of the size of Themiscyra's, yet somehow, twice as noisy when filled with the Eneti men and their rough way of speaking. However, Penny found the cacophony a welcome cover for the argument Harp insisted they have in the center of everything, with his own father just an arm's span to his right, and Orithyia's scowl not far beyond.

"I'm telling you, Bella, that you are not going to get past the borderlands without meeting an untimely—and likely painful—demise. You can't—"

"And I'm telling *you*, Harpalion, that I have no other choice. So if you won't help me, I will do it alone. Just like I was alone before you basically kidnapped me."

He growled something under his breath before hissing, "How are you going to get there alone?"

He drew his wildly gesturing arms back into some semblance of decorum after his father sent them both a quelling look. Orithyia barely glanced at them. They had not spoken since re-entering the hall, but there had been a moment of mute understanding as Penny had returned the queen's newly polished sword and she had accepted it silently, sheathing it in the belt that had already found its way back to her trim waist. There was nothing to say. Penny knew enough about her by now to realize begging would have the opposite effect that was intended. No, she would need to proceed without help from Sinope's queen, just as she had originally intended, but Harpalion, though barely more than an acquaintance, had taken exception to the idea.

"I don't think *this*," Penny locked eyes with him and waved a brisk circle with her hand to indicate the whole room, "is the right place to discuss the *how* of it, Harp. Or any of it, really. Why don't you tell me why you were sneaking away from your father's hall with that noisemaker of yours? Do you really expect me to believe it was for a lost horse? Your father hasn't said one unnecessary word to you since you arrived."

Harp bristled.

"Noisemaker."

He choked out the word as though it were a curse, and glared down his hooked nose at her.

"I'll have you know," he continued scathingly, "that *noisemaker* belonged to my grandfather, the finest harp player from here to Wilusa, second only to *me*. Men *pay* me to write songs about them. To sing about their exploits in both battle and bedchamber, to strum a melody to their lady loves so they can finally have the kiss they've always longed for, to remind their sons and grandsons—and daughters and granddaughters—of how things really are in the world. That *noisemaker* can spin your desires into something real, something tangible, so that you can taste it on your tongue when you hear the music play. That *noisemaker* can change your life—even *save* your life. Do not roll your eyes at me!"

"You play a piece of wood and some catgut, Harp. And yes, I'm sure they are beautiful songs, very lively, but they are a *man's* songs. Any bag of wind can sing. Anyone with fingers can strum a harp. However, it is only women's voices that reach Kubileya. This is known. Even my father would tell you a man has no power in song, and he is a priest."

Harp appeared to be swallowing his own tongue. Penny leaned her chin on her fist, eyes wide with feigned innocence as he apparently grappled with the truth. She was not prepared for the heat in his scowl, though, or the sound of his chair sliding backward as he lurched to his feet and stalked away from the table, then out of the door. Stunned for a moment, she did not immediately call after him, and by the time she realized he was actually offended, that she should apologize to a friend she had only just made, he was well away from her, and out the door.

The feeling of being suddenly bereft was impossible to deny, especially as she looked around the room at all the faces of strangers, all of the men sitting alone, or some even with their wives, who looked at her with a glint she recognized well now that she knew what it signified. She repressed a shiver of discomfort, realizing Harp's presence had been more of a buffer to that feeling than she had realized. Her eyes fell on Orithyia. The queen watched her, that strange fire in her blue eyes, so like Antiope's, but an expression of contempt on her weathered face. Orithyia tore a bite of hard bread with her remaining teeth, chewing it aggressively while holding Penny's gaze.

Penny squirmed. Then, she frowned and stared right back, straightening her shoulders, determined not to let the woman intimidate her.

"Eh," the queen said, waving the stump of bread to emphasize the grunt. "Who did you say your mother was again?"

"I didn't."

"Come then, don't be shy. Shouldn't be many ha-mazaans in Themis-cyra I don't know. Who's it, then, eh?"

Penny fumbled in her mind for a woman the queen would not know. "Harmonoe."

"Who?"

"My mother is a...a weaver. A Crafter."

"Ah, so you are a Crafter, then?" Orithyia's satisfaction with this idea was salt in Penny's open wound of humiliation. Her jaw stiffened.

"I am one of atta Marpe's apprentices, in the Infirmary. I apprenticed as *sivyeti*. Not graduated yet, though. I just helped her with the birth of a Footling two moons ago, before..."

"Ah, a stitcher, then?" Orithyia's bird-eyes watched every twitch of Penny's nervous face. "Come in handy after battle, *sivyeti* hands. Much better use for them than *in* a battle. As you already showed us."

Penny flushed as Orithyia's gap-toothed, humorless grin appeared, and there was something challenging in the way the queen held her gaze, something taunting. It was the sudden, discordant strum of a harp that broke their stare. Both women turned to see Harp in the center of the room, his instrument hugged close to his chest.

"I told you I would burn that blighted thing if you dared waste your time on another note before you did your duty by my kingdom, boy."

King Pylameneus' voice lashed the room like a whip, and though Penny could see the blood drain from Harp's cheeks, his lips also pressed together in a determined line. Still, it was her eyes that he held, not his father's, as he strummed another discordant sound into the room. Penny shifted on her bench, her eyes darting from the young man's hurt face to King Pylameneus' apoplectic one.

"The horse is returned, Father, just as you demanded, and Bellatrix is here as well. And thus, so am I." Another strum, this time slightly mocking.

Penny glanced between them in confusion, and the king looked as though he were about to say more, but Harp's fingers tickled over the strings, bringing forth a new sound entirely, and the Hall fell into a hushed, expectant silence. The first notes of an actual song floated over the crowd, lulling them at first with a gentle melody, but then gripping every listener with an impossible harmony no six strings should be able to make. It was when Harp finally sang, his voice tenured and pure, that the hair on Penny's neck stood on end, and her arms rose in gooseflesh at the sound of it. She could not tell if it was the words he spoke in a language she did not recognize, though she spoke several, that made her head swim, or the music itself, coaxed as smoothly from the instrument as one might drip honey from a hive, or if it was his eyes, dark and intent, and never wavering from Penny's face. She was light-headed when the last sound faded. Joy and sorrow swirled inside her chest beside bittersweet longing. Above and below it, anger, sadness, pain. Love. Fear.

She pushed this last one away, allowing the bittersweet strangeness of all the others mingled together to overpower it, as Harp politely acknowledged the praises of everyone in the room, even the gruff one from Queen Orithyia, before he cast one more pointed glance at Penny, and once more left the room. The well of emotions still roiled inside of her as she watched him go, but a new feeling emerged once Harp was gone. A feeling she had experienced only a few days prior, watching Sylviu disappear back inside the gate of his city, his anger evident in the set of his shoulders and the cold formality with which he used her title, and not her name. She barely knew Harp, had in fact known him less than a full day, and yet she could not deny the sense of loss pulling at her gut like a stone when he did not return.

Two potential allies driven away by her thoughtless actions, her sharp words. She felt the chasm widening between her and everyone else, a dark ravine filled with the secrets she could never reveal, the lies she could no longer pretend were not purposeful, and the guilt she could no longer escape as those terrible things separated her from everyone she might care for.

The blessing of having used an alias and thus of being an afterthought to everyone in the entire village was that no one noticed when Penny finally crept away. The guards at the doors let her pass without comment, and as she made her way through the maze of narrow corridors and back outside, she breathed a sigh of relief. She sweet-talked a young, naïve serving girl at the kitchens into giving her some hard cheese and day-old bread before making her way back through the haphazardly placed maze of outbuildings, in what she hoped was the direction of the stables. Tana nickered a soft greeting that led her forward, the pony's shaggy forelock bursting haphazardly over the top rope. She scratched the small horse under the chin, peering into the darkness to find the hook Harp had looped the horse's bridle over. The horse in the nearby stall stomped its hooves and blew a long, whiffling snort. A huge head, twice as long as Tana's stubby nose, reached over the ropes, neck arched and ears pricked toward her in a curious, hopeful greeting.

"I have no apples for you," Penny whispered apologetically, but something about the way the horse bobbed its neck beckoned her, and she left Tana's side, approaching the stallion warily.

The horse kept its ears pricked forward, but Penny halted a respectful distance from those potentially vicious teeth, uncertain whether the stallion was indeed friendly, or merely appeared so to lure unsuspecting victims into its path, as Harp had claimed. The tall animal merely watched her with shining black eyes, reflecting the stars even in the shadowed darkness under the stable roof. She could make out the pale gold hair and white mane and tail, the fine arch of the neck, the strong slope of shoulder meeting broad chest, and the long, long legs of a horse meant to run. Cautiously, she stretched out the back of her hand to the horse's nose, letting him sniff her fingers, and when he showed no sign of fear or aggression, she used the back of her fingers to gently stroke the bridge of his nose. The horse pushed its golden head into her hand insistently, and Penny smiled, obeying the command for a more thorough scratch. A sigh of pleasure wheezed out of the huge horse as Penny's nails caught the itch under the chin in just the right place, making her smile widen. A dangerous thought began to take shape. She eyed the horse consideringly. Then, she glanced over at the shaggy outline of Tana's forelock barely peaking over the top of the stable door. A pang of guilt coursed through her. She had nearly a month of hard riding to reach her father's lands. Tana had been her companion since she had arrived in Themiscyra ten years ago, but, though sturdy and faithful, she was barely more than a pony, and her legs were neither swift, nor made for fording rivers and carrying a rider long distance. Penny looked back at the stallion blissfully enjoying his scratches. As much as it pained her to leave her faithful companion behind, she knew what her decision had to be.

She moved back to Tana's stall, took hold of Tana's nose with both of her hands, and pressed a hard kiss into her muzzle.

"I'm sorry, girl. I wouldn't leave you if it wasn't important. But you're going to be well taken care of. I promise. Harp will look after you. He seems kind. And when everything is done and settled, I will come back for you, and we will go back to Themiscyra, and you can eat all the fallen apples in the orchard that you want. I will even save you some pieces of honeycomb. Deal?"

Tana snuffled her lips against Penny's chest, and she took the gesture for agreement even if it was a blatant search for aforementioned apples. Swiftly, so as not to lose conviction, Penny unhooked a bridle from the wall, then slipped in next to the tall palomino and slung the reins over the horse's neck. He accepted the bridle without hesitation, indicating some training, at least, but Penny was still a bundle of nerves as she led the horse out of its stall and down the narrow corridor between the buildings. She was nearly into the open crossroad of the next lane when a voice said behind her, curt and cool,

"I could swear the horse you rode here on had legs half as high as the one you're leaving with."

She whirled, her free hand clutching at her dagger as her heart surged into her throat. She hissed a breath out as Harp's tall shadow emerged from the dark, her fear replaced with a surge of relief that he had come to see her off, but just as quickly that relief was overshadowed by the anxious doubt that he had perhaps come to raise the alarm, instead. Especially now that she was quite obviously stealing someone's horse.

"I suppose I should tell you," he continued politely, "the western road washed out in recent rains, so best go north and follow the coast. Unless you were planning on thrashing around through the forest again. Oh, and that is Queen Orithyia's new stallion you are stealing. She's barely had him a month. My father recently disowned me for losing him, and if he goes missing again he will likely behead me. Are you sure you want that?"

Penny had just begun to relax her tense shoulders, the knot in her stomach untwisting with relief that he was not intent on stopping her, but this unexpected bit of information made the anxiety return tenfold.

"Er..." was all she could think to reply, eyeing the stallion as the full weight of her intentions took shape. Was she truly bold enough, or indeed, *foolish* enough, to take the Queen of Sinope's own horse? It was highly unlikely it was her *rhu-tasiya*, since Harp indicated the horse was newly come to the queen, but to steal a ha-mazaan's horse was close to sacrilege. However, having a horse trained in the ha-mazaan's ways would only serve her better on such a journey. Beyond Orithyia's wrath, there was little reason not to take the horse, despite Harp's insinuations about his father's intentions. She set her chin.

"I need the fastest horse, and this one is it."

When there was no argument from Harp, she said, less confrontationally, "Thank you, Harp. For all your help. And I'm sorry for hurting your feelings."

"You did not hurt my feelings," Harp said with stiff formality, his shadowy form moving closer in the darkness. "You insulted my entire existence." He ended with a forceful sniff that let Penny know she was definitely not forgiven.

She smiled. "You will make sure Tana is taken care of until I can return?"

The whites of his eyes showed briefly in the darkness of his face, and she suspected he was rolling his eyes again.

"No concern for my head, I see. My father knows horses better than anyone except my uncle Rhesus, even if he does prefer his mules. Your pony will be taken care of better than a new babe by its own mother, I assure you."

"Thank you," Penny said again, and there was a long silence, with only the restless shuffling of the stallion's hooves on the packed dirt. "I should go."

Harp sidled around the stallion warily, then moved quickly toward the town gates, pausing for a moment to scout ahead before gesturing them to follow. Silently, they made their way down the narrow lane to the edge of the village. Once outside the low stone wall, away from any ears that might be listening, Harp turned to Penny, but she rushed to speak before he could.

"Please tell your father I stole the horse, so that he does not behead you."

"Hmm. How little you know my father."

She smiled into the dark, and an awkward silence bloomed wider between them. Finally, Harp said,

"Are you sure you want to do this?"

Penny nodded, though she wasn't sure he could see it. "I have to."

"But you don't have to go alone. Surely—"

"I am running out of time, Harp. Orithyia was my last hope of convincing the ha-mazaans to my cause, but I can't delay any longer. There is something I must do, before it is too late for..." she swallowed thickly, "for everything. My father is my only hope, now."

"I just don't like the thought of you traveling halfway across the world alone. You need protection."

Penny thought of the long road ahead, the days and nights alone on the road, meeting who knew what dangers, especially the two-legged kind, but she forced the lump of fear down with a loud swallow, and said,

"Kubileya will protect me."

Harp grunted. Unsure of what else to say, Penny turned to the stallion, who waited patiently at her shoulder.

"Here, I will help you—" Harp began, but before he could finish, Penny leaped and swung herself up, settling herself behind the stallion's withers. She gathered up the reins and grinned down at Harp's unconcealed surprise in the starlight, reaching her other hand down to him. He reached back, and she squeezed his hand.

"Be safe, Bellatrix of Themiscyra."

For a moment, Penny felt guilty for not telling him her true identity, but it was safer this way. For both of them. She realized she did feel safe with Harp. He reminded her, in his own way, of Sylviu. Both were gentle, and kind, and showed their true selves to her. Neither looked at her in that way that some men did, like she was a rabbit, and they a wolf. And neither deserved a woman plagued by the consequences of her own choices, or for their lives to be torn apart by a curse she had not yet found a way out of.

With a last squeeze of her hand on his, Penny clicked her tongue and sat tall and the stallion, most definitely trained in the ha-mazaan ways, moved forward at a brisk walk. She had just nudged the horse into a long-legged, smooth trot, when the curiously mournful chord of a slowly strummed harp drifted down the road behind her.

$$41$$

STYMIED

Penny had not been gone from Galatae's gates more than a few hours before Sylviu came to his senses. What had he been thinking, to send her away like that? He thought about going after her, forcing her to accept his help, but he could not stomach the thought of her scorning him again. He would need someone else to do the job for him, and there was only one place to find them.

Despite his reluctance to put himself in front of Molpadia's hounds again, Sylviu rode to Sinope that afternoon, arriving well after night had fallen. To his surprise, his request for an audience was not met with rejection, and the sentries escorted him with quick efficiency into their Hall, making him leave his sword with a guard. Ha-mazaans were scattered throughout the place, crowding every table in the room that was half as big and nowhere near as grand as Themiscyra's Moon Hall.

"What is it, Hanassa?"

The same woman who had led an army past him and the other men at Themiscyra's gates met him now, her face weathered by time and battle, her eyes firm on his, but a familiar voice interrupted before he could answer.

"It's Ossy's boy, Ev. Sylviu, what are you doing here?" Toxaris asked, her dark eyes worried as she came to stand next to the other woman. Sylviu eyed them both, but he addressed Toxaris, trying to keep the worry from his voice and failing miserably.

"It's Pen," he began, but a woman's cold voice interrupted him, dragging a scowl across his face as his eyes found hers in the slowly gathering crowd.

"Aye, your darling has finally gone to swell her belly with a daughter. What of it?" Molpadia's voice was harsh in his ears, her dark eyes flakes of obsidian.

Sylviu shook his head. "She is not completing her Alsanti, if that is what you think."

"She has to, boy. Are you here to whine that it isn't with you?"

"Dia, enough," Toxaris chided, waving her hand to quell the other woman's retort. "Sylviu, what do you mean?"

Sylviu kept his gaze level. "I mean she came to Galatae to say goodbye, and to tell me she is not going to complete her Alsanti." Even Molpadia's brows lifted at this news, and Sylviu wondered if he should have kept that bit to himself, but he needed them to understand how very wrong he knew everything was.

"She told me she is going to Satra. To her father's lands. She is going alone, and one of you, several of you, need to find her and go with her. She can't be out there alone when her vow will not even let her protect herself."

Penny set a brisk pace for the first while as she headed away from the Eneti village and moved north, toward the coastal road, as Harp had advised. The stallion moved with graceful ease, his gait smooth and untiring, but as soon as they were well away from the settlement, she slowed his movement to a more sustainable walk, patting his neck appreciatively. Never had she sat such a beautiful, smooth animal. She could see why Orithyia had chosen him for her own.

"I shall name you Lappeyo," she murmured at one point. "What do you think of that? Peyo for short?" The stallion rewarded these words with a swift twitch of his left ear. She smiled. "Peyo it is, then."

The name meant "glowing," as embers do in a fire, and just as the horse did, as though lit from within. He seemed to glow even in the moonless night. She stroked the fine muscles of his neck, and rode on, pleased with her reckless, hasty decision to steal the animal. He was definitely a boon to her travel plans, which included following the road throughout the night, and then camp down during the day, until they reached the Hellespont ferry crossing. Her plan seemed to be perfect, until the first fingers of dawn were reaching into the swiftly scuttling clouds in the eastern sky, and Penny began to feel the ever-present knot in her stomach tightening to a painful intensity. The pain had an unfamiliar sharpness to it now, a clawing that seemed to start in her spine and work its way all the way around her hips and then up into her shoulder. A shooting pain made Penny gasp with surprise and curl inward to relieve the pressure, making the stallion twitch his ears and slow his walk. Unwilling to lose what precious darkness they had left, she breathed deeply through her nose, and urged the stallion back into a trot, eager to make it within sight of the northern coastline before daybreak. The next cramp was even worse, and though she made no sound, the stallion halted completely, sensing the tension in her body. This time when the pain passed, though Penny clicked her tongue and squeezed her thighs and nudged the horse with her legs, the stallion stood stubbornly still, his ears trained backward, his head arched in firm resistance to her hand on the bridle.

When the next pain struck, Penny doubled over, swallowing a cry as she buried her face in the stallion's mane. She lay there for several moments, panting, the horse remaining perfectly still, and when the pain finally eased, Penny realized she would have to halt her progress earlier than expected. She turned Peyo into the forest at the side of the narrow road, thankful he did not resist her direction this time, and they made their way with slow, careful steps through the trees, until the growing light revealed a small, well-hidden patch of soft autumn grass surrounded by trees shedding their leaves.

Penny stifled a cry between her teeth as another cramp seized her, and she leaned against Peyo's withers, her face buried in the wiry warmth of his mane, feeling it ground her with its heady smell. There was a faint whiff of sulfur to it that made her back tingle, but then a wave of pain rolled through her stomach, up her chest. Briefly, Penny was aware of the stallion's watchful black eye trained on her, his left ear following every movement. Somewhere nearby, the dry, rasping laughter that ended in a hiss seeped into her consciousness, and she thought Peyo might have heard it, too, the way he pinned his ears back, but then, before she could sit straight and look for the source of the sound, the blackness overtook her.

When Penny awoke, forcing her eyes to open against the painful intensity of the light, the air had brightened to a star-iron sky heavy with clouds. Foggily, she turned her head to see Peyo standing over her, his bridle still on, the reins trailing under his nose, and his hip cocked in a posture of sleep. She remembered the smell of his neck, and the sound of a Fury's malicious laughter before everything went dark. She must have fallen from his back when the Erinyes appeared. There was no smell of swamp, no hissing of snakes in her ears, though. Penny could have almost believed everything was fine, if not for the disgusting scent of roasting venison invading her nostrils, and, even worse, the annoyingly spritely tunes of a harp being plucked with obnoxious volume somewhere close by.

Blearily, her body only weakly obeying, she forced her eyes wide open and turned her head, only to gasp in dismay as she was met with a stranger's face peering down at her, their flossy mound of grey hair a perfect halo against the similarly colored sky. The woman's wide dark eyes and curly hair identified her immediately as Harp's mother, even if Penny had never set eyes on the woman.

"Bellatrix," the woman said, laying a hand along Penny's brow. "How are you feeling?"

Confused for a moment at the name, before she remembered this is what she had told them, Penny tried to sit up, but the woman's hand pressed her back down with firm insistence, and Penny found she did not have the strength to argue. To her horror, Orithyia's frowning blue eyes appeared over the stranger's head, glaring down at her with undisguised anger. The music Harp played changed slightly, to more of a lilting tune,

"I should have known you would do something foolish, girl, since you set that precedent the moment I met you," Orithyia muttered with biting scorn. "To your credit, though, I didn't expect you to be able to steal my horse. Almost impressive. Good thing he seems to have taken a liking to you, maybe even a *shining*, shall we say? Otherwise, we might not have found you in time. And good thing, too, that Harpalion was smart enough to follow you in the first place."

The realization that she had been found so easily, her plans stymied yet again, along with the stench of roasting venison wafting closer, was the last straw for Penny's nauseous stomach. She used what strength she had to roll on her side and vomit, barely turning her head in time to avoid soiling the unfamiliar woman's robes. She had not eaten since the previous day, so there was only bile, and soon she was left shaking and spent, one woman regarding her with sympathetic concern, the other with steely disgust. The harp strummed a plaintive chord that threaded through the air with a lingering ring of distress.

"Hmmm," Orithyia said, and met the other woman's eyes with a sharply raised eyebrow.

"I will need to check her," the stranger said, and Penny turned an irritated frown on them both, but she did not have the strength to resist.

"Here, take some wine," the woman continued, speaking gently, offering her a drink from a gourd at her hip. Penny obediently sipped, if only to wet her lips, but she could not swallow more than a mouthful before the nausea threatened to overwhelm her again. She shook her head weakly, and the woman sat back on her heels, glancing at Orithyia. The queen stood straight, belying her own short stature to tower over them both with haughty disdain.

"Harpalion tells us this is not the first time you have collapsed?" Orithyia demanded.

The accusation in her tone would have made Penny squirm had she not felt so weak. She nodded once, her head rustling leaves on the ground. She was covered with her own rough cloak, and someone had placed her on top of what smelled like a well-used horse blanket, but she still felt cold all the way to her bones. Penny looked away from the queen's eyes, so like her mother's, yet set in a face so entirely different, and waited for the queen to begin her lecture.

"I see," was all Orithyia grunted, before gesturing to the woman still kneeling. "This is Truti, Pylameneus' wife, and Harpalion's mother. She is learned in the ways of our *zizentis* and *sivyetis*. She is going to examine you."

Penny tried to smile at the woman, but a sharp pain in her abdomen, then her shoulder, quickly turned it into a grimace. Truti leaned forward, worry creasing her brow as she watched where Penny clutched at her stomach.

"Your stomach hurts? Here?"

Penny nodded, but then motioned to her shoulder as another shooting pain made her grit her teeth. A flush of shame overtook her as she realized without a doubt that this was the curse unleashing its devastation on her body. She looked around wildly for signs of the Erinyes, but there was only grey sky, and Peyo's golden legs, and Harp's dark curls bent over his instrument. He must have felt her gaze, as his dark eyes flashed to hers for a brief moment, full of worry and some unfathomable emotion, but then his mother was speaking again.

"And your shoulder?" Truti asked doubtfully.

Penny nodded, wary, but the woman's wide eyes were kind and her fingers gentle as pulled the cloak back and pressed them into the joint of Penny's left shoulder, and then down the arm, pushing against Penny's wrists and throat and even the side of her breasts, making Penny wince at the tenderness there, but when she moved on to Penny's abdomen, the swift, sharp pain made her gasp involuntarily. Truti's brow creased, and she palpated more carefully along Penny's stomach, then lower, then sat back on her heels, regarding her in somber curiosity.

"How long have you felt nauseous?" Truti asked.

Penny avoided Orithyia's suddenly penetrating eyes, keeping her attention solely on Harpalion's mother. "A few days. Maybe half a fortnight," she hedged.

"And your last moon-blood?"

Orithyia crossed her arms, her face a thundercloud of disapproval before Penny even answered. She kept her face carefully composed, though the shame doubled inside of her, and the cold turned to a frigid dread that began to penetrate into her very marrow.

She whispered hoarsely, "Two weeks before the Sturgeon Moon."

It was Orithyia who finally broke the silence, in which Penny thought the whole forest must be listening for what was said next.

"You're pregnant."

It was an accusation, not a question. Penny's lungs would not hold air. She stared up at her mother's cousin, her thoughts fading into a numb panic, the cold in her bones turning to ice.

"Goddess' tits, girl, don't turn into a scared guinea hen whenever I speak!" Orithyia's stern face did nothing to relieve the pressure in Penny's chest.

Truti frowned up at Orithyia, then stood, but whatever she was about to say was cut off by a sharp wave of Orithyia's hand, though the queen was still staring down at Penny, her sharp eyebrows moving upward toward the clouds. Slowly, the ha-mazaan knelt into a crouch at her side, and this time when she spoke her eyes were fever-bright, and her voice was deceptively soft, but every syllable held a pulse of dangerous intent.

"And how is it that a mere girl of Themiscyra, not yet blooded with her first kill—and I will eat my sword if I'm wrong about that—is pregnant with a man's seed?"

Penny was forced to summon every ounce of courage to continue meeting those angry eyes staring down at her, but the queen was not waiting for an answer.

"You break ha-mazaan Law, and yet have the temerity to lecture *me* on not taking our women to war, and to their certain deaths?"

"I break no Laws," Penny retorted, then flushed guiltily, knowing she had broken the ultimate Law—that of a blood-sworn vow. Her intention to scowl back at the ha-mazaan was thwarted by the pain in her stomach, and she was forced to simply grit her teeth until the cramping eased. Orithyia regarded her with that curious light for a long moment, then nodded, as though her suspicions were confirmed.

"So, a Themiscyran ha-mazaan is with child, yet she seeks to convince me to wage war, then runs away, stealing my horse to do so, without any thought that those she is destined to serve might want her safe inside her city in order to complete her Alsanti, like the good and dutiful Ishassara she is meant to be? What do you have to say to that, Penthesilea?"

42

CONFESSION

Penny gaped up, only vaguely aware of the discordant strum of Harp's music as his fingers stuttered into silence at the Queen's accusing words.

"Aye, I know who you are, you foolish twit. Did you really think I would not recognize Antiope's Ishassara? Even if she did keep you hidden every time I was passing through, your very speech betrays my cousin's manipulative influence." Orithyia twitched an angry hand through the air, her lips a flat line. She waved the same hand in the vague direction of Penny's stomach. "You are the only one in your city exempt from First Blood or the age of enlistment for *matar*, and likely the only one stupid enough to follow your mother's wishes to be heavy with a man's child before you even learn to lift a sword." Orithyia folded her arms across her flat chest, nodding. "Aye, your identity is easy enough to guess, Penthesilea, but make no mistake, I like you no better now than I did when you were a simple, stupid girl pretending to be a warrior. I wonder, though, how long did you think you could hide such a thing as being heavy with babe? Why did you not tell us? Unless you're acting shy, of course, but for an Ishassara who is trying to inherit the Hearth throne, I would think you would be less timorous when it comes to talk of whelping babes, hey?"

Penny opened and closed her mouth, like a carp on the end of Orithyia's fishing line. The queen tsked her tongue impatiently. The ha-mazaan's fierce blue eyes quelled any denial that Penny might have tried to formulate. Finally, as both women stared at her with expectant expressions, she answered quietly,

"I didn't know."

235

"A Hearth Queen's Ishassara did not know she was with child? You expect me to believe that?" Orithyia's stare pinned her to the ground.

She had not known. Not fully. She had suspected, as she had spent enough time with the *matars* to know the signs of sickness, of loss of appetite, of dizziness. They had been building for days, but she had been too afraid to admit the truth to herself. She could have mixed the herbs to treat the sickness, even, but there was one main difference between her sickness, and every other woman who found herself queasy at the scent of venison. Women who enlisted with the *matars* welcomed such inconveniences, for they were sure signs they would soon whelp a child, just as they had chosen to do. But Penny had not chosen this. Had not wanted this. Not yet. And then, there was the matter of her curse.

Penny shivered, and Truti moved to her left side to kneel again, putting her hand on Penny's shoulder.

"She is correct, then, Ishassara?"

The crackling fire was loud as Penny finally nodded, but the pain in her shoulder increased, and she grimaced, closing her eyes, letting a black wave of nothingness overtake her. For a long time, she drifted in and out of consciousness, the pain tugging her awake, the sound of the harp sending her back into a haze of sleep. She even thought she saw her father's leopard once, behind the blackness of her eyelids, but when she opened them, it was only the woolly vision of Truti kneeling to feel her brow. Orithyia was now standing with arms folded, overseeing Truti's administrations. A frown tugged at her weathered face when Penny finally focused her gaze, consciousness and pain returning at the same time.

"Is the father an Achaean?" Orithyia asked quietly.

There was a drawn-out silence, the flames snapping loudly, before Penny nodded.

"Yes."

"Did you choose him?"

A longer pause, while the entire clearing seemed to strain to hear her answer. Penny wondered why Harp was no longer playing. She breathed deeply in the fraught silence, trying to find some balance inside of her tumbling, numb mind, trying to find the right words. Finally, she shook her head once, unable to speak. Orithyia nodded, as though she had already known the answer. Truti frowned in concern into Penny's pale face, meeting her eyes squarely.

"I am so sorry, Ishassara. That is not something any woman should endure."

The kindness in her eyes made Penny's throat close completely, but the woman continued, taking Penny's cold, clammy hand in hers. "I do not know if you will carry this child for a full ten moons, though. Your symptoms tell me the babe may not grow within the womb itself, and you must already be two moons along." Her large eyes were sorrowful as she searched Penny's face. "If that is the case, we must give you herbs to stop its growth, or it will continue to grow where it shouldn't, and you will surely die."

Penny made a sound like an animal might make when it finds itself snared in a trap.

The panic that had lurked at the edges of her mind for days, perhaps weeks, twisted out of control, and her thoughts grew black and elongated with horror. In the space of a few moments, she had confirmed not only one of her long-time dreams for her future—to carry a child under her heart and fulfill her role as Ishassara, and future Hearth Queen—but also one of her worst nightmares—that she carried a child borne of violence and rape, and not by choice. And now, this woman was telling her that this choice, too, would be taken away from her, whether she wanted to make it or not? She stared at Truti in mute helplessness, while more voices drifted to her ears, the words broken and disjointed like her mind. She thought she heard the low rumble of Evandre, Orithyia's General. The answering voice was calm and measured, with a lilt at the end of the words from where her mother's speech still influenced her. Toxaris.

How had Toxaris come to be here?

Penny tried to lift her head, to see if the voices were real, or if she were hallucinating, but she didn't have the strength. They sounded far away, on the other side of a thick curtain of fog.

"She should drink your herbs and be rid of it anyway," Orithyia was saying, her blunt words no harsher or softer than normal. "If this was not her choosing, it is only a kindness. Besides, the babe would be the child of a raping, murdering Achaean."

Truti stood to face the queen, her hands settling on her hips, but it was Toxaris who responded, her tone sharp, her voice moving closer.

"It is my Ishassara's choice to whelp the babe or not." She appeared in the corner of Penny's vision, and then Evandre's tall frame as well, so that all four women were towering above her. "And if she does bare the babe, it would have nothing to do with the father, anyway. A Hearth Queen's child has no father. You do not know what Kubileya plans for it. My Ishassara does not need pressure from the likes of you, Orithyia."

"The likes of me?" Orithyia's voice was flat with disdain. "Do you mean a woman who has suffered the same indignity? Do not speak of what you do not know, Toxaris. I speak what is best for the girl."

Evandre frowned at both of them. "She will have plenty more opportunities to choose other fathers for other daughters, as you say, Orithyia. But you must both remember, the choice is the girl's, whether or not she is meant to bear Themiscyra's daughters, and whether or not it was her choice to lie with him."

"She could die if she does not end it now," Truti put in. "However, the snake melon is not gentle. It is not the same as the drink to simply be rid of a babe. There is a chance she would not be able to bear another child, if I give her the drink to stop this one."

"But...she is Ishassara to our Hearth Queen," Toxaris said, her voice hushed with shock. "It is her duty—her *destiny*—to bear daughters for the Thrones. There must be another way."

Truti shrugged. Orithyia scowled. Another silence swelled, the tension a tangible, metallic bitterness hovering in the air between them all before Evandre asked quietly, "And how will we know, one way or another, if the babe grows inside of her womb, or outside?"

Truti shrugged again, glancing down at Penny's stricken face.

"The signs tell me it is likely the babe is not properly placed, but there is no way to be sure, other than waiting." She turned back to the General. "However, if I am right, the longer we wait, the more likelihood that your Ishassara will surely die. She has maybe a day, maybe two, but three at most, before it is too late."

Another silence, eventually broken by the softest notes of a harp, barely audible, the tune at once a sorrowful melody and a soothing lullaby. Penny's throat closed with tears of anger, of frustration, of fear, as the others stared at each other above her prone body. The unfairness of it all was staggering. First the bathhouse, then her mother, now this? She hadn't even properly wrapped her head around the idea of being with a babe, let alone *his*, and now she was being forced to choose whether to keep it or not. She was expected, without knowing with any certainty if it was truly necessary, to end it all, and possibly her own future as Hearth Queen. All in one deceptively small, completely life-changing choice. Or possibly die from not choosing at all.

This is what comes of breaking your solemn vow, she thought.

This is what atonement looks like.

She thought of Leandra, and any of the stolen women who might still be alive, far away in Theseus' lands, possibly subjected to the horrors she herself had endured in the bathhouse, but day after day, without end. If she did not make the right choice, or even if she made no choice at all, those ha-mazaans would continue to suffer, and it would not matter what her supposed destiny was meant to be. If there was one choice she could make that ended another's suffering, despite what it cost herself, she knew she had to make it.

"You are right," she interrupted the women whispering above her, and four sets of eyes jerked to her face looking up from the ground. "It will be my choice, and only mine. I need to speak with Orithyia. Alone."

43

HA-MAZAAN

Evandre immediately moved away to tend to the fire, and Truti nodded politely, saying, "I will search for the snake-melon plant, Ishassara. It will be best to be prepared, just in case. Son, I will need your help."

Toxaris lingered, her expression uncertain, but Penny met her eyes calmly, and said with a calm authority she did not feel,

"I need the queen's ear alone, Toxaris."

The ha-mazaan capitulated with a slow nod. "I will help the Healer."

Then it was just her and the queen, who did not bother to relax her wide-legged, crossed-arm stance, towering above Penny on the ground, glowering. Penny grimaced up at her, and said quietly, "I don't care to shout this to the world."

Orithyia grunted, but finally descended in a slow crouch next to Penny's shoulder, grumbling louder as she folded her legs under her to sit with a heavy thump.

"My bones feel as old as the mountains on rainy days like this." When she was settled on the dead leaves, she turned expectant blue eyes on Penny.

"I have broken my vow."

It was much easier to stare straight up at the grey sky above than the woman's too-bright magpie eyes.

"What vow is that, child?" Orithyia's voice was calm.

"The vow I swore when I was eight, to the Oracle. I sealed a vow with blood and honey to harm none," Penny said quietly, watching a dark cloud rip apart high overhead as though a great hand tore it in two. Perhaps the same hand that was now tearing at her heart. She swallowed past the lump in her throat. "But I killed the one who attacked me." She paused, before glancing sideways at the queen and adding, "I am not sorry for that

240

part. But it remains true that my vow to harm none has been broken, and this…" she waved a weak hand over her body, but they both knew she meant something much bigger, "this is the outcome."

Orithyia nodded slowly, her eyes observing Penny with that curious light that was becoming quite familiar. "And why would a ha-mazaan swear such a vow?"

Penny's brows furrowed at Orithyia's ignorance. She was at a loss for words for a moment, before reciting exactly what Antiope herself had told her numerous times.

"Because I would be Hearth Queen and I should have no need to sully myself with another's death when I would…should have a…" the lump grew bigger as reality penetrated itself sharply into the conversation, and suddenly Penny had to avoid the queen's piercing gaze again as she finished, her voice growing faint with grief. "Should have a Defending Queen and a city of ha-mazaans to protect me."

"Again, my cousin's words ring heavy from your lips," Orithyia said eventually, her tone dry, but still calm. She stared down at Penny, the fingers of her left hand tap-tap-tapping against her knee. "So you broke this vow, that I am guessing your mother made you swear—do I have that right, girl? Ah yes. I presumed so—but you broke it anyway, seeking justice for an attack on your person, for the defilement of your sacred body. If that's the case, you're giving me reason to finally have some respect for you, hey?"

Penny eyed her askance. "I…just told you I broke a sacred vow made to Matar Kubileya. An oath sworn in front of an oracle, breakable on pain of death—forfeiting the Womb of the Great Mother if I do not keep it. Dooming myself and my offspring to a lifetime of curses— and *this* is what makes you respect me?"

Orithyia's blue eyes were alight with cold fire. "Your mother made you into a sorry excuse for a ha-mazaan, girl, and anyone who meets you knows it. But it would seem you have some backbone after all. You did what you needed to do, despite the limitations she put on you. The fact that you know you acted with righteousness and strength, regardless of a promise you were manipulated into making, means you might just have what it takes to be ha-mazaan after all."

Penny bristled. "My mother did not manipulate me into anything! She—"

"She made you swear a promise when you were a child," Orithyia interrupted. "A promise you had no context for, after living apart from your sisterhood for your entire childhood. I have it right, don't I? My cousin was gone for those eight years, while Otrera made excuses that her daughter was seeking out gloriously mighty foreigners to sire her many children. And yet, Antiope returned with you, and *only* you, when you were nearly a bleeding woman, and she had already ensured you would never be one of your own kind. She kept you from your sisterhood, and then she made you swear an oath that you would *never be a part of that sisterhood*. Do you not see, girl?"

Penny wished Orithyia would stop calling her girl. Another wave of nausea hit her, another piercing pain that shook her whole body, and she breathed deeply, waiting for it to pass.

"*I* was the one who didn't want to live in Themiscyra. My father loved my mother—loved *me*. He wanted us to stay with him. And I *would* have stayed with him, if she had let me. It was my home!" This confession felt even more raw than the first one, but it was true. "But I know what honor is, as much as any ha-mazaan. I was whelped to be Themiscyra's Hearth Queen, to bear more daughters for the Thrones, to keep the Flame alight. To be a Mother to all. These are my destiny. I swore the oath because it was what I was born to do."

"And how do you know that?" Orithyia asked, returning to her calm, calculating stillness, though her fingers tapped on her knee every few heartbeats.

"Because..." Penny trailed off in frustration as she realized she had fallen right into the queen's trap. Orithyia's eyes were bright with anger, her mouth a flat line.

"Aye, girl. You know because your mother told you. And I am telling you there may be something different in your future than what you blindly, *foolishly*, I will add, swore an oath to. In fact, there must be a different path, as you have already set yourself on it by breaking that very vow."

Penny stared up at Orithyia mutely, unable to form a proper argument or counter the queen's logic. Another burst of pain squeezed at her.

"It is a wicked thing to break a vow," Penny said quietly, looking away as the pain intensified. "My mother's death, the dead Flame, the dead ha-mazaans...this pain...this doomed child...it is all my punishment for being an oath-breaker. It does not matter what my mother did, or didn't, do. The Achaean who attacked me doesn't matter. It is what *I* have done that matters now. And what I must do. What the Kebat has said must happen for my curse to be broken. But maybe...maybe it is too late."

When Orithyia's hand unexpectedly settled on Penny's shoulder she started, meeting the ha-mazaan's softened gaze in surprise.

"I am sorry this has been your path, Penthesilea. No woman should endure such a thing."

Immediately, Penny's chin trembled and hot tears overflowed. She was used to the Defending Queen's gruffness, her unyielding expectations of strength and stoicism, and this sudden display of compassion was over-whelming.

"You did right by defending yourself, by claiming justice for a wrong committed against you. This is nothing to be ashamed of. It is what makes us ha-mazaan, to know such strength is in us, and to act accordingly. To protect what is ours. It is why we have First Blood rites, and it is why our ha-mazaans must serve in the Savaran before they may enlist as *matar*. Even my sister completed these rites, though her duty was to the Hearth Throne. I think your mother somehow convinced you, and her sisters, that these things were unnecessary for a Hearth Queen, hmm?" She continued before Penny, thoroughly overwhelmed with confusion, even had a chance to nod. "But you are also right that a vow, once spoken, is immutable. Now, tell me what you mean when you say the Kebat has given you a way to break this curse."

Penny swallowed, trying to control her breathing. "She has said I must seek out the one who heard my vow, and either be absolved by her or face the consequences."

"And who heard your vow?"

"I—I don't know who she was. My mother took me there before we traveled to Themiscyra. It was...in a cave, in my father's lands," she supplied lamely. "She was weaving, though. I remember that. Lots of skeins, all such different colors. I had never seen anything like it."

Orithyia sucked in a sharp breath of surprise. It was the first sign the woman had ever given that her feathers could be ruffled, and it did nothing to calm Penny's nerves.

"Well...damn," the queen breathed softly, and then fixed Penny with gimlet eye. "I am assuming she is the one you were wanting to get to when you asked for my help traveling west? And the one you were running off to when you stole my horse?"

Penny nodded. "Her, and my father."

Orithyia's face was as grave as she had ever seen it, but the woman's usual harshness was not present.

"So what do I do?" Penny asked, her voice thick.

"What do you want to do?"

Penny blinked, then grimaced as her stomach and then her shoulder turned to a fiery mass of pain. When it eased, she considered the queen's question, while the ha-mazaan watched her with a concerned frown.

What *did* she want? Did she even know? It was not as though she had ever been given the luxury of such a choice. From the moment she could understand speech, both her mother and father regaled her with tales of what her future held. She, Penthesilea, had been born to serve the ha-mazaans in Themiscyra as Hearth Queen. She had never known anything different. Never considered another path. Both of her parents had instilled in her the necessary values and lessons such a path would require. They had both prepared her to be Mother. Now, for the first time in her short life, Penny wondered whether bringing new daughters into this world was the most responsible thing she could do. As much as she longed for a daughter, many daughters, the idea of bringing an innocent babe into a world that now seemed cruel, cold, unflinching in the face of one begging for mercy, only to see her suffer the inevitable pain and agony life would bring, seemed entirely unfair to an innocent child. And yet, if she did not bear daughters, she would be abandoning her very reason for existence, her primary duty as Hearth Queen. She would be abandoning every reason her mother ever had to be proud of her, and, most of all, every excuse she had ever clung to in order to be part of the ha-mazaans at all.

Orithyia raised her eyebrows at the silence.

"Do you want the child, if you can carry it?" Orithyia asked, seemingly reading her mind.

Penny's gaze was pulled back to the shifting sky, as though the answer could be found in the roiling storm gathering itself into a thick blanket of wet threatening to drench them at any moment. She didn't know what she wanted. She didn't know how to make the right choice, or if there even was one. Could she save her life now, only to give up everything she had been born for? Could she face her own death if she didn't make that choice? What if she lived, and the babe, too? Could she raise a daughter born of violence? Could she look upon the face of an Achaean son, knowing the blood of his father flowed in his veins?

"I don't know," Penny said hoarsely after a long silence, while the opposing choices tore her apart inside just like those clouds. "I thought..." she shook her head against the ground, staring at the sky, but it was no longer clouds she was seeing. "I don't really know what I thought, but not that I was actually pregnant. Certainly not that I would have to make such a choice. Everything happened so fast, and so many ha-mazaans had much worse happen to them. Lyta...the ones who were taken...there were more important things to think about." She turned her head to look at the queen. "I actually even planned to seduce one of those Achaeans, and begin my Alsanti early, but..." Orithyia raised her eyebrows, but did not interrupt, even as Penny paused to choose her words. "But now, after everything...I don't feel ready. I know being a *matar* is my duty, but...now I know I still have so much to learn. And..." Penny swallowed, not able to meet Orithyia's eyes, "...what if I only see *him* when it's born?" She dragged in a shaking breath, her voice thinning even more as she continued. "But what if...what if I choose to take the drink, and can never fulfill my role as Hearth Queen? What if I never see my own face in any daughter, or even a son? How can I choose that? How can I choose at all?"

Orithyia sighed, stretching one leg out and drawing the other knee up to rest her arm on it. "If Truti is right, my girl, this will not be a choice you even get to make unless you want to die, and I doubt that. Let me tell you something, though." She looked down at Penny with a somber expression. "To bring children into this world is a sacred act, duty as Hearth Queen or not. My sister never wanted children, hey? But she fulfilled her role, as our mother and your great-grandmother intended—and she was miserable doing it. Aye, you heard me. Miserable as a bear with no pelt for the winter, let me tell you. Seeking out men she could not even stomach in order to sire new daughters, but as the Fates would have it, bearing only son after son. Until the fourth man finally gave her a daughter. That girl barely saw twenty summers before she split her head open on a rock, leaving my sister with no legacy. No daughters to take the throne. I think it is why Sanape turned to drink, hey? She sought to escape the life that had been chosen for her, but her sense of duty to our Way was too strong to let her truly break free, even when she thought she had failed."

The queen shook her head, her eyes taking on a faraway look, as Penny lay stupefied. A Hearth Queen who had not wanted children? Who wanted to break free of a Way that was sacred, that provided the best course to freedom for all of them? Penny had so many questions, but did not want to interrupt as Orithyia continued.

"Evandre is right, though. Whether or not Truti is correct in her diagnosis, it must always be your choice. That is what we fight for, and why we live as we do. It is what makes us ha-mazaan. No one will hold you to a fate that is not your heart's desire, not if I have anything to say about it. Especially not this. But from what I know of you, I am assuming you will not make your decision without consideration of the role you have accepted, and the vow you have made as Ishassara."

Penny nodded, swallowing around the thickness still in her throat.

"I will also say, so that you may have all the facts before you decide, that I have made up my mind. Changed it, in fact." Those magpie eyes were shining as Orithyia tipped her head to study Penny's questioning face. "I will take you to Satra, and help you find this woman you swore your vow to, but only under one condition."

"What's that?" Penny asked warily, even as hope surged inside of her.

"That I train you, vow or not."

"Train me?"

Orithyia tilted her head in a nod.

"To what? I—"

Another wave of pain radiated up from Penny's abdomen and into her shoulder. She hissed softly, shifting on the blanket, panting. Orithyia waited for her to settle again before saying,

"To be ha-mazaan. To be a woman every man will fear to tread upon. That is the true destiny you were born into, no matter what your mother says."

44

ACCUSATIONS

Penny's eyelids had been stitched closed. Someone, or perhaps something, maybe a horse, was lying on top of her, crushing her with its weight and making every muscle and bone hurt. She groaned softly, and when she finally managed to pry her eyelids apart, saw she was no longer in the damp forest under the open sky, but in a soft, albeit lumpy bed, in a mostly dark room lit only by a small fire burning in a nearby hearth, and timber walls all around. There was no crushing horse, but heavy blankets of sheepskin and, when she twitched her hands against it, what felt like a wolf pelt covered her from chin to toe. Between the firelight and where she lay, a figure lounged on a low chair, their cropped silver hair gleaming in the firelight. Orithyia's chin rested against her chest as she snored softly, her neck cranked at an uncomfortable angle to achieve the position.

"Where—" the word came out as a whispered rasp, so Penny licked her lips with a dry tongue and tried again. "Where are we?"

Orithyia awoke immediately, lurching to her feet and moving to Penny's side with swift urgency, her blue eyes searching every feature of Penny's face before she pursed her lips.

"We are back in my nephew's home. How are you feeling?"

"I need to pee."

Wordlessly, the queen stooped and lifted a plain clay pot from the floor, raising her eyebrows at Penny, who stared at it in dismay.

"Don't be so shy, girl. We've been helping you use this for days."

"I've been asleep for days?" Penny struggled up in alarm, shivering as the furs and sheepskins fell away from her.

Her memories were foggy, but she remembered the bitter taste of the drink Truti gave to her, though it had been another day and night before someone had found the snake-melon growing in a protected grove that saw more sunlight and less frost that everywhere else in the valley. She also remembered the pain. She remembered the worried faces of the other women hovered above her, their probing eyes fading in and out between episodes of blackness. She remembered the smiling eyes of a satyr as he lifted her from the ground and carried her somewhere. Maybe here. She remembered his music lulling her mind further into a fog. Strangely, what she remembered most vividly was the face of her father, his kind, honey-colored eyes so like hers smiling down at her, as though he stood next to this very bed, and his voice clear as a bell as it joined in song with Harpalion's. She even remembered Begri's low purr. How strange that her father once again met her in a Dream, when she had not been able to See him for ten years now. And Begri, too. As though they suddenly remembered she existed.

She focused again on the queen as the ha-mazaan tsked her tongue softly, her blue eyes watching Penny's face closely.

"You lost much blood, and were fevering quite badly. We did not want to move you, but Truti thought it best you be in a warm place out of the rain. Is the pain still with you?"

Penny shook her head. "I feel as though an entire herd of horses trampled me, but the pain from...before...is gone. So...it's done, then? It's over?"

They both knew what she meant. Orithyia's finger's fidgeted with the rings on her zoster. "I think the matter is done now, yes. As for your future as Hearth Queen...only Matar Kubileya knows that, girl."

This time, Orithyia's use of "girl" brought Penny some comfort, a curious sense of belonging, rather than shame. She nodded, though there was a hollowness in her chest that was as unexpected as it was painful. What was done was done, and there was no turning back. The fact she had had little choice on the matter did not lessen the grief. It was very possible everything she had prepared for, everything she thought she had been born to do, was gone from her future forever. It was also possible she had chosen to let go of a life that might have lived to have a great future, if she had given it the chance. Now, she would never know.

"I need water," she mumbled. Her throat and her lips were parched, and the chamber pot Orithyia still held was very much in need. The queen nodded.

"I will ask the servants to fetch you some broth. You have not eaten in days. Your clothes are there, if you want them, but you should rest longer."

The queen simultaneously plunked the empty chamber pot to the floor and gestured to a folded pile at the foot of the chair before she turned toward the doorway, where she paused, her hand on the latch to pull it open. "You had all of us worried, child. Even Harpalion. The boy seems to have taken a shine to you. His father will be overjoyed to hear it, even if you are not." She smiled at Penny's confusion, revealing the gap in her teeth. Then, she was gone.

Penny climbed out of bed with agonizing slowness, made use of the chamber pot, though it pained her to do so, before dragging her tunic over her head. By the time she pulled on her trousers, her legs felt weak and unsteady, so that she tottered on her feet like a newborn lamb, and there was a stitch in her side like she had run for hours. Thankfully, her clothing was much drier than it had been when she had been in the forest, but she still felt chilled. She had just moved away from warming her hands at the fire and was resting her tired legs at the edge of the soft bed when Orithyia returned, followed by Toxaris and Truti. She started to stand, but Orithyia gave a sharp movement of her hand that was clearly an order to stay put.

"Ishassara, how do you feel?" Toxaris asked, her dark eyes moving over Penny's face in concern.

"Tired," she said truthfully. Truti approached with silent, swift steps across the small room and placed the back of her hand against Penny's brow, frowning in concentration. Before Penny could react, she had already stepped away again, nodding to Orithyia. The queen nodded back, pleased, then folded her arms, her feet spread wide apart in her customary stance as Truti excused herself, assuring them she would check back on Penny later.

"I have told Evandre and Toxaris of our plan, Penthesilea, and Toxaris has some things to say about it that I think you should hear," Orithyia said as soon as the door closed behind Truti.

Penny looked from the queen to the ha-mazaan, wondering warily how much the woman knew.

"I told her the whole truth."

Again, it was as though the queen could see the thoughts inside her mind. Was her face really so transparent?

"No use hiding it from the ones who can help you," Orithyia said, moving to sit in the chair she had been sleeping in.

Toxaris still viewed Penny through narrowed, concerned eyes. Penny wondered if the ha-mazaan judged her for the choice she had made. The very practical, impossible, terrible choice. She waited as the woman twitched her fingers against each other, her teeth worrying slightly at the corner of her mouth. Finally, Toxaris said,

"Ishassara, I owe you an apology. Every ha-mazaan in the city owes you an apology."

When her eyes met Penny's they were dark with shame, and suddenly the ha-mazaan dropped to her knees at the edge of the bed. Toxaris clutched Penny's thigh with both hands, just above the knee, and stared up at her, the shame still bright.

"I am so, *so* sorry, Ishassara Penthesilea. You should never have needed to break your vow. You should never have been left to fend for yourself. We—*I*—accept the responsibility, and the weight of your consequences, as my own. I swear to you that I will do everything in my power to make this right. I hope you never have reason to doubt again that I, and those who serve you, will be there for you when you need us."

Face contorting, Penny held out her hand, and Toxaris grasped her by the wrist. They held each other's arms that way, wrist to wrist, a silent pact between sisters, for many heartbeats as they both struggled to contain their emotions.

"Thank you, Toxaris," Penny said, when she could. "It wasn't your fault, though. I hope you know I would never blame you, or any of the ha-mazaans. It was my own lack of...well, of everything ha-mazaan that let him hurt me."

Toxaris bowed her head, her fingers squeezing Penny's wrists, before she stood again, her dark eyes still shadowed. "Ishassara..."

"What is it?" Penny asked, looking from ha-mazaan to queen and back again. Toxaris took a deep breath.

"Ishassara, if it is your wish to continue on this path, to train as one of us..." she paused, shifting her weight on her feet. "There are other ha-mazaans in Themiscyra who will not allow this. Please, hear me out before you say anything," she said in a rush, heading off the argument building on Penny's lips. "I am not speaking of myself. I will support you in whatever path you choose. But there are some who have sworn to uphold your mother's wishes, who have made their own vows, and I think they will not be as easily convinced to let you abandon your oath."

Penny shifted on the bed, the wooden slats under the mattress creaking. She looked at Orithyia. "If I am absolved of my vow, I do not see why they would be held to theirs."

Toxaris was shaking her head. "You know I am speaking the truth, Ishassara. If you go back to Sinope or to Themiscyra as ha-mazaan, those who have sworn to your mother will not allow you to abandon the Hearth Queen's vows. Even if...even if you can still bear a daughter, and you can complete your Alsanti, they will not forget the pledge your mother bade them keep. They are foresworn to serve Antiope, and to keep her secrets. Everyone who swore their allegiance to your mother is bound by the same expectations, and they will suffer the consequences of breaking that oath. I cannot see how you can convince them otherwise, whether it is to help retrieve our women and avenge your mother, or not."

"What secrets? Who are these women? Are you speaking of Marpe?"

A small grimace twisted Toxaris' mouth. She paused for a long while, her glance beseeching Orithyia's silent face. Orithyia finally gave the slightest inclination of her head. Irritated with their games, Penny said,

"Will you stop coddling me and treating me like a child? What is going on?"

"Ishassara, Marpe is the one who insisted we find you, after you ran away."

"I didn't run away, Toxaris, I was—"

"Perhaps my words were not chosen wisely," Toxaris interrupted quickly. "When we found you were gone, Marpe was beside herself with worry. She kept saying we needed to find you before it was too late. That you needed to have your medicine. Her old bones did not allow for her to ride south or west when more search parties set out, so she...she tasked me with giving you the herbs if I found you."

Toxaris fished under her belt for a small packet of linen, their pungent smell immediately familiar. It had been more days than she could remember since she had drunk the herbs for her headaches. She had had headaches, yes, and the dizziness, but they had eventually dissipated, and once her pregnancy had been confirmed, she had assumed they were all a part of the same symptoms. Penny shook her head ruefully, feeling guilty for making the *sivyeti* fret on her behalf.

"She should not have been so worried, but she is an atta. It is her duty to worry." Penny smiled at the ha-mazaan reassuringly, thinking fondly of Marpe's hovering, and her constant fussing over Penny, thankful the woman had always taken such care of her.

"You never did have headaches, Ishassara Penthesilea."

Penny looked at Toxaris, and shook her head slowly.

"I think I should be the one to say if I've ever had headaches or not, and I can assure you, Toxaris, I have had very *bad* headaches. Hence the medicine Marpe made for me. I've needed to drink it most of my life. Since I came to Themiscyra, in fact. If I don't, if I forget to drink the herbs for a few days, the headaches are always quite terrible, and the sickness sets in, and it doesn't go away until I have the wine again. I even thought that was...what was wrong with me."

Both of the women listened to her explanation without interruption, but when Penny finished, they stared at her with varying degrees of hopefulness, as though she had more to say. She raised her hands palm up in exasperated confusion, until Orithyia finally said,

"Marpe was drugging you, poisoning you since the moment you came to Themiscyra, girl. With your mother's permission—nay, under Antiope's orders, I don't doubt."

"I don't know about that—" Toxaris said, but Penny said overtop of her,

"Drugging me? *Poisoning* me?"

She laughed.

Toxaris and Orithyia did not laugh. They stared at her intently, waiting. Penny sobered, looked between them with growing incredulity.

"What are you saying? That my mother was trying to poison me my entire life, and Marpe was helping her? That they intentionally gave me a drink that helped my headaches so that—so that what? Because if I did take the herbs, there was nothing wrong. No headaches. No side-effects. You couldn't exactly call that an effective poison, could you? What would be the point?"

Penny studied Toxaris' face just as intently as the woman studied hers. Orithyia watched them from her chair, her fingers over her mouth, her eyes bright with hidden thoughts.

"I don't know about your mother's part in all this, Ishassara. That is Orithyia's line of thinking. But the drink was not for headaches. If you did not have it regularly, it would *cause* headaches."

Penny felt anger stir in her belly, a beast uncoiling from slumber, stretching its limbs and clutching from below at the back of her throat. What they were trying to convince her of was madness. Perhaps, in their own strange way, they were only trying to assure her that her course was the right one, that she should not feel guilt or regret about abandoning her role in search of a new one. Maybe they were attempting to tell her that she should not grieve her mother? Whatever game they were playing, Penny had had enough.

"My mother would have no reason to poison me, nor would Marpe. Marpe is our best *sivyeti*. The woman who attends the birth of every new ha-mazaan. She is our eldest atta. You are speaking treasonously."

Penny said this last with harsh finality, directly at the ha-mazaan who had only moments before sworn her loyalty, but the anger was growing hot in her belly. Toxaris paled, but she was Savaran, and no coward. With one last quick glance at the queen, she said quietly,

"It was not poison, you are right. It was a drug, like I said."

"Where is your proof?" Penny shot back. The white-hot rage was growing stronger, but under it was an even worse feeling, a seed of fear, wriggling its way through the anger, trying to surface from the soil of doubt that was growing more fertile with every day, every insinuation made by her own mind, by the Kebat, by Molpadia, and now by these two.

"My proof is these herbs," Toxaris said, pinching the packet between thumb and forefinger in front of Penny's face. "Marpe told me what plants to search for if I ran out of these dried ones," Toxaris said. "She thought I would not know what they were for, and she was right. But Truti knew. I happened to find some when we were searching for the snake-melon, Ishassara. I brought several plants back with me, thinking it would be good to have fresh stock, but Truti was horrified that I would think to feed them to you. She threw them in the fire, and said I must be mistaken. She insisted they were not for...for what I was told they were for."

Penny laughed, and it sounded wild to her own ears. "Toxaris, are you really going to trust some woman who is not even ha-mazaan, who is not a trained *sivyeti*, over our most senior atta?" Immediately, she flushed with guilt for the unfair words, knowing Harp's mother was the one who had ultimately saved her life, but this was beyond acceptable. She shook her head. "I have forgotten to take my medicine a hundred times before, and there's never anything worse than the return of my headaches, which the herbs *help*. It doesn't mean anything."

45

CASTAWAYS

An uncomfortable silence filled the room. Penny's rumbling stomach finally broke the taut stillness, but it was quickly overpowered by a brief tapping at the door.

Evandre entered, closing the door discreetly behind her, and gave Penny a swift smile and a nod of greeting. "Ishassara Penthesilea, you are looking much better. There's even a touch of pink in your cheeks. I'm glad to see it."

"Thank you," Penny murmured, knowing that pink was the visible sign of all the anger still roiling in her veins.

Evandre turned to Orithyia, who remained seated, her fingers steepled in front of her face in a pose of thoughtful contemplation.

"Orithyia, Ainippe has returned. She seeks an audience."

"Bring her."

Evandre hesitated, and Penny was not blind to the way the woman's eyes twitched so as *not* to look in her direction. Orithyia grimaced, and fluttered her hands.

"The girl is going to find out sooner rather than later, Ev. I'm not going to play more of my cousin's mind games with her. Bring Ainippe in."

Evandre bowed her head and slipped out of the room.

The three of them waited in stiff silence, Penny with an increasingly expanding gnawing in her stomach as it begged for food she had not had in days, while footsteps echoed on creaking floorboards outside the room. Evandre did not knock this time, but ushered in an unfamiliar ha-mazaan, the woman's face flushed and dewy with sweat, her chin and forehead covered in smudges of dirt as though she had recently wiped a muddy hand over her face. She gripped the pommel of the sword around her waist in a familiar Savaran stance.

"Ishassara Penthesilea, this is Ainippe. She joined our search party from Sinope, when we set out to look for you," Evandre said.

Ainippe smiled, showing a wide gap between her two front teeth, and her eyes were kind when they smiled down at her.

"And I sent her away as soon as Harp led us to you in the forest, to tell your ha-mazaans you were safe with me," Orithyia put in.

"I am happy we found you in time, Ishassara Penthesilea," Ainippe said, and Penny returned her kind smile.

"I did not expect you to return so fast, Ainippe. You must have ridden like the wind." Orithyia eyed the ha-mazaan's unkempt clothing and mud-splattered skin.

"I rode as fast as I could, Orithyia. I thought you would be most interested in the news."

"Well?"

"The rumors seem to hold truth. The castaway's story has been corroborated by several fishermen along the coast. In the weeks after the attack on Themiscyra, many of them pulled bodies from the sea in their nets, all of them dead. Two more were found on land, alive, wandering farther west, possibly attempting to walk home. Molpadia has already done her work on them, though for now they live. They all tell the same story as the first castaway."

"Castaway?" Penny asked, thoroughly confused. Orithyia flitted those blue eyes her way.

"Might as well give her the full story, Ainippe. She's got a stubborn streak that tells me she won't believe you, but we'll give her the facts, nonetheless."

"Well, his story *is* quite unbelievable, so I don't blame her," Ainippe said, her lips quirking as she glanced at Penny.

Penny breathed deeply through her nose, then out again, her feeling of light-headedness returning. "I'm sure everything you have to say will be just as enlightening as my previous conversation. But for the love of the Goddess, could I please get some food?"

Toxaris fetched her a bowl of warm, thick broth, and a thick slice of dark bread with warm butter that smelled distinctly of old billy goats, and unfortunately tasted the same, but Penny was too hungry to care. She devoured the simple meal with more speed than care, while the others conferred in hushed voices outside her door. They were speaking of an Achaean castaway, she was sure of it.

Her mind flashed with Leon's toothy smile, his eyes staring intently into hers as they shared stories in the shade of the pavilion. Immediately her face flushed with humiliation at her own naivety about his intentions. About the intentions of every man who had set foot on their shores. She shook her head with an angry twitch, and drained the last of the broth from the bowl, but a niggling worry wormed into her head as she listened to the ha-mazaans murmurs outside the door. What if the castaway was Leon? Was Molpadia torturing him for information? She shook her head again, angry and irritated at herself. What difference would it make? Every one of those men was complicit in what had happened to her, and to her city.

The squeak of the floorboards interrupted her thoughts as Orithyia returned, Evandre and Ainippe following close behind, and finally Toxaris, who shut the door with a soft thunk behind them. Evandre was chewing something, and held out her hand to Penny, who accepted the offering automatically. It was a plum, shriveled and old. She took a tentative bite, and was surprised at its sweetness. She smiled her thanks at the General.

"Well, best get on with it, Ainippe, so we can deal with the girl's denials and get on with things."

Penny tried not to glare at Orythia as Ainippe immediately obeyed the queen's clipped command.

"You were gone from the city before we found the man, Ishassara," Ainippe began. "A castaway from the Achaean ships. He gave us news of your ha-mazaans. Specifically, your mother."

"My mother?" Suddenly, Penny was all ears, the piece of plum in her mouth all but forgotten.

"Aye. The man says he was on the beach dousing his cooking fire when he saw Antiope and Theseus arguing, and then he saw the ha-mazaan army advancing. According to him, your women attacked first. He insists there was not supposed to be a battle, after they had already pledged peace. But something went wrong. Something with Theseus, and your mother, as well as Hippolyta and the other man. Hekeles? Helekas?"

"Heracles," Penny said, and the ha-mazaan nodded.

"So something went wrong, and their plans were foiled. He definitely admits there were plans—he isn't too bright, so he can't really tell us those plans in detail, but he also says those plans changed when Theseus met you, Ishassara."

"When he met me?"

"So the man says. Solois is his name. Did you know him?"

Penny shook her head.

"He claims Theseus gave orders—in secret, apparently, so even Heracles and those loyal to him didn't know—that you and your mother were to be at the ships that night, and all the other women were to be drugged. He was going to take both of you, and maybe some others, but…"

Ainippe paused, and Penny swallowed. But she had been waylaid by the very man sent to collect her, and then she had been waging a battle of her own, tackling the Fury she had unleashed.

The ships prepare to leave, and your mommy with them. You will be there too…

"So the ships sailed without you, but they *did* have your mother. And that's where the man's story takes an interesting turn."

"Said he tried to steal a kiss from the Queen," Evandre said around a mouthful of plum, interjecting this news as though she couldn't wait for Ainippe to reach that part, "and ended up taking a long cold bath for his efforts. Thrown overboard by this Theseus himself. Wish I could have seen it!"

Penny had just popped the remaining piece of plum into her mouth, and now she swallowed it nearly whole, coughing until tears welled. Toxaris came forward to pound her back until she waved her hand.

"Steal a kiss? From my mother?" Penny wheezed.

"Like I said, not too bright," Ainippe continued, the gap between her front teeth flashing into view with her grin. "Apparently, though, your mother encouraged him. Spent the better part of that first night seducing him—his words, not mine—offering him whatever he wanted in exchange for freeing her from her bindings. So he tested her with a kiss, which *he* says was both passionate and real," Ainippe shrugged at Penny's grimace of disbelief, "but they were caught by Theseus. Solois was tossed into the waves for daring to touch Theseus' prize."

"His prize?"

"Aye," Ainippe said. "According to his account, the men had all been promised a prize for joining the mission, as long as Heracles was successful in gaining Hippolyta's zoster. And apparently, Theseus had no hesitation claiming Antiope as his own as soon as they landed on your beach, but at some point, according to Solois, Theseus and your mother came to an agreement. Apparently, one of the other Achaeans who was found wandering says that agreement came to an end somewhere on the Inhospitable Sea, when some of the captured ha-mazaans commandeered one of the three ships. He says men were killed, and one of the ships lost in a storm. No one knows what happened afterward."

Penny sat for a moment, trying to digest all of it, but one question trumped all the others. "What kind of agreement did my mother have with Theseus?"

Orithyia answered, her voice grim. "Theseus planned to make Antiope his wife, girl. According to the men, she agreed. They say she was on her way to be Queen of Athens."

NEGOTIATION TACTICS

Penny sat behind the trestle table of Ganghra's crude wooden-walled Hall, drowning her loud thoughts in the louder cacophony of men and the murmurs of women and the first children she had seen since coming here. Harp's music was helping calm her frazzled mind, but only a little, as the tunes he played from his corner were too jaunty for her current mood. The ha-mazaans sat on the other side of Orithyia, absorbed in their own conversation, pausing every so often to down food or drink. Penny listened with half an ear, the questions they had raised growing bigger with every passing hour.

One of the young serving girls, her face a mixture of fear and awe, approached their table with a rhyton of wine, and Penny extended her cup automatically, seeking the solace of the sweet drink's haze. Orithyia covered the rim of her own cup with her palm and a curt shake of her head. At any other time, Penny's ingrained sense of hospitality might have prompted her to ask if the queen was not feeling well, or if she did not prefer wine, but at the moment, she was feeling anything but sociable. The girl moved on with slow steps, her wide eyes devouring every detail of the five women at the table. For someone who lived in the city of a Hearth Queen's son, she seemed entirely enraptured by the ha-mazaans, as though they were fabled figures from her childhood stories come to life.

Her attention wandering again, pulled by Harp's spritely tune, she did not hear Orithyia's question until the queen barked it in her ear a second time.

"Do you agree, Penthesilea? Or shall I have Harpalion sing you the plan so that you actually pay attention?"

"Plan?"

"Goddess' sake, girl. You're as wool-headed as an unsheared ewe. The plan to send women to Attica, and report back to us on what they find. Have you been listening at all?"

Penny forced her attention to focus on the queen. "Not really," she said bluntly. "You seem to have no problem making plans and pulling strings and coming to conclusions without my interference."

Orithyia grunted, her sharp eyes searching Penny's wan face, but she did not berate her as expected. Instead, she only said, "I am proposing to send some of my women, and some of yours, to infiltrate this home of the infamous Basileus Theseus. As spies. Perhaps they will find something unexpected, eh? Something your Oracle did not mention when she told you of your mother's death. We need to know this girl you seek is where the Kebat said she is. They will bring us news of what they find, but it will take several fortnights for them to travel there and return, if my estimations are correct. Once we have more information, we can make better decisions about what will be done about your city, and your stolen ha-mazaans. No war is won without proper strategy, and proper strategy requires proper information."

Penny sipped her wine, mulling this over. Finally, she said, "We don't want war, do we?"

Orithyia sighed. "The Antiope I remember was as quick as a viper, and just as cunning, and yet here sits her daughter, as slow as an ox with two legs pulling a cart of bricks uphill. If my spies bring back news that your ha-mazaans are indeed slaves for an Achaean dog, we will be marching our armies west to take them back, and I cannot see any outcome *but* war. Isn't that what you wanted?"

Penny's head was spinning, although she didn't know if it was from too much wine, or this unexpected news that Orithyia was willing to help her in her mission to bring Leandra and the others home.

"Who will go as spies?"

"I will go, Ishassara."

Toxaris smiled at Penny's worried frown. "Someone must, and I am sworn to you now, so you know you can trust me. I hope you know that, anyway. I know there are a few others we can trust. Koine and—"

Penny was sure she saw the name Areto forming on the ha-mazaan's tongue, the words halting abruptly as dark memories intruded. The look they exchanged was full of shared grief.

"I will go also," Ainippe said. "There are several others I can think of who wish to see the Undying Lands for themselves."

"Remember that you will go by ship, Ainippe," Orithyia warned. "Horses will be a very limited part of your journey. We can't afford to waste time."

Ainippe's face fell, but she nodded acceptance even as she muttered, "I hate ships. But yes, it will save time."

"Meanwhile, Penthesilea, you and I will travel to this childhood home of yours, to find your father, and this woman you swore your vow to. The spies will meet us there, and we will strategize more then. But first, I was hoping you could use what I have yet to see any evidence of, but which your woman here," Orithyia pointed to Toxaris, "assures me you have learned well from your mother."

"What's that?" Penny asked warily.

"Negotiation tactics."

Loathe to invite further insults, she asked warily, "Negotiation for what?"

Orithyia cut her hand through the air to indicate the length of the hall. "Men."

Penny tipped her head, considering the queen's words. "You wish to join our armies with men if we march on Attica?"

Orithyia gave a curt nod. "Eventually, perhaps. But right now, we cannot risk your Themiscyran ha-mazaans knowing you have broken your vow, which means I am not going back to Sinope to round up an escort to travel with us, and I don't relish traveling across the world just the two of us. We need a show of numbers for that kind of travel. These men are the best answer we have."

She said nothing further, but Penny nodded slowly, but frowned, eyeing the queen. "Will Pylameneus not respond better to such a request from you, his own aunt, and a Queen besides?"

Orithyia snorted indelicately. "The man barely tolerates me. Tolerates my ha-mazaans even less. You will notice no women born here in the village carry swords or axes, though he cannot deny us our rightful place. His disdain for our way of life bleeds into every decision he makes, but he needs us, and he knows it. What *we* need is as many men as he can spare, and perhaps a few of his horses. We may have no better lasso to loop around his neck than a girl with your pretty face, and, hopefully, your mother's skill at prettily convincing speech. I can't think my nephew will be immune to your type of charm if you use it right."

Penny looked at the king seated at the head table, his dour face already heavy with drink. She squirmed and her stomach heaved at the thought of drawing his attention purposefully, as the queen suggested. "You want me to *seduce* him into allegiance?"

Orithyia shrugged with casual ease, waving a half-eaten bird wing in the air dismissively. "He is a simple man, and not a very smart one, but his blood runs hot. I have the feeling my cousin taught you all her tricks, and you certainly have the looks for it. It will be the fastest way to get him to agree to our terms, I think. But if you do not wish to do it, I will understand."

Penny was not completely sure she did understand. Only months ago, the idea of using her charms to gain the compliance of a man had seemed inevitable, natural, but now it brought a bitter taste to her mouth. Still, they needed numbers, and she had been tutored enough in the delicacies of negotiation that she knew the queen was probably correct in her assessment of the king, and of his weaknesses.

"I will try," she said finally, and Orithyia nodded in satisfaction.

"Go on, then."

"Now?"

"What better time?"

Penny bit her lip. She thought she might have more time to prepare a strategy, come up with something pretty to say, but Orithyia's eyes were unwavering. Penny sighed. Then, she straightened her spine, and her tunic. Her hands went to her braids, hesitant at first, but knowing it would be to her benefit, her fingers made quick work of separating the strands, and she smoothed the loosened waves over her shoulder to fall in a cascade of honey to her waist. She relaxed her features into a calm, sweet smile, and prepared to channel her mother's best tone of diplomacy, then stood, scooping her goblet of wine in her hand.

"King Pylameneus," she called, and Harp's fingers quieted on the strings, bringing the Hall to an expectant hush. Penny smiled at him gratefully, and though he returned her smile, his dark eyes were worried as they slid over her loosened hair, then rested on her face again, but she turned her own gaze to his father.

"I wish to thank you and your wife for the hospitality you have gifted me in my time of need. As the Ishassara to a Hearth Queen of Themiscyra, I am honored by the care your wife has shown me in the arts of Healing. I am forever in her debt, and therefore yours." She smiled at Truti, and the woman smiled back with hesitant shyness.

Pylameneus eyed her consideringly, appearing surprised at her address. "You are a kinswoman, and welcome anytime under this roof," he replied, and though the words were said by rote, she heard sincerity in them. "I have not yet offered my condolences on the losses you have endured. Your mother and the rest. The destruction of your city." He did not mention anything else, and Penny was grateful her own, more personal loss had been kept between the women, and Harp.

Penny inclined her head. "Thank you, my lord. Themiscyra is indeed in dire need of help. I hope we can count on all who have benefitted from our city's wealth and protection, and all of our city's blood kin, to aid us now that we find ourselves in an hour of need."

Pylameneus paused, but honor dictated his response, as Penny had counted on. "Aye, Themiscyra can count on Ganghra in whatever matter is most pressing. Supplies for rebuilding, I would guess. We have plenty of lumber. I might even be able to grant a few of my good mules. Get the work done in half the time."

Penny mirrored the King's smile, but with less pomp, and more sorrow. "Again, you have my sincere thanks as Ishassara, and the thanks of all the residents of my city, King Pylameneus. There is a need more pressing than lumber and mules at the moment, though."

"Oh?" His tone was wary, his expression guarded. Penny brushed her hair from her neck, and cocked her hip, turning her smile somewhat pouty.

His eyes followed every move, though his wife sat close to his elbow. Penny tamped down the surge of guilt, and steeled herself for what was needed.

"There is much to yet learn of what the future will bring our devastated women, my lord, but there are those who were taken that deserve our help. We must bring them home if we can, but we cannot do it alone."

"Bring them home?"

"Yes, my lord. You would not have us abandon our kin to a life of slavery and death? We would never consider such a fate for anyone in a city under our protection. Nor would Sinope, I am sure. Not without reason."

She heard Orithyia's sharp breath beside her, and Evandre's laugh quickly concealed as a cough before she lifted her mug to her lips and gulped her wine. Pylameneus had lost his wariness, and regarded her with outright animosity for being cornered in such a way, but his tone was theatrically woeful when he said,

"Do you mean to tell me my aunt has agreed to send her women to be slaughtered overseas, just for the sake of a few girls?"

Penny dared a quick glance at Orithyia, who shoved a wedge of bread into the juices on her plate with unnecessary force, but did not seek to answer for herself. Penny returned her gaze to the king.

"Themiscyra and Sinope will prepare to march on Athens depending on what news our emissaries bring us. We are hopeful that our allies in both north and south will join us in seeking justice, if that is what it comes to."

"Justice. Yes, of course. But what can my small army provide that your own ha-mazaans do not already have?"

Penny detected an undercurrent of something more than what showed in the king's woeful expression. She had the feeling of wandering through a darkened hallway rife with danger, where at any moment she could stumble into an unforeseen trap, and she hesitated, collecting her thoughts.

Honesty in matters of trade and negotiation is often the swiftest and most sure way of garnering cooperation, her mother's voice echoed in her head.

"Men," she finally answered.

The king's eyebrows lifted, and a new spark lit his eyes.

"A daughter of Themiscyra admits that women alone are not enough to contend with other kingdoms in matters of war?"

Though Orithyia snorted loudly and shook her head over her plate, she still did not say anything. Penny smiled demurely.

"One must fight fire with fire, my lord. In this case, fire is numbers." Her smile sharpened. "While our ha-mazaans are, you will surely agree, better trained, better conditioned, better organized, and better disciplined than any other army in the land, we no longer have the numbers to dissuade unnecessary attacks against our forces on the march between here and Attica, nor to sustain a siege there, if a siege is required. And while we have the courage to face the city of Athens with the numbers of Themiscyra and Sinope alone, we would rather succeed in our mission, and success requires numbers. For the sake of my mother's memory, and the lives of all the women who were taken, I am sure you can see the wisdom in the plan. But we cannot simply create more ha-mazaans out of thin air, so we must add men to our armies. Hopefully, your men."

"You are very confident in your women's abilities, considering you yourself are not a trained warrior, from what I understand." Again, a light in the king's eyes belied the slow words, the carefully placed smile of platitude.

"The prowess of the ha-mazaans speaks for itself, I think, King Pylameneus," she said, not taking the bait. "You are known here in Paphlagonia, and beyond, for the greatness of your horses, for the white mares you breed and the mules which you use to plow your fields and move your timber. I do not need to be a horse to acknowledge the power and majesty of one, the reliance every state has on their strength and endurance. It is the same for the abilities of our ha-mazaans."

Pylameneus took a long drink, and then chewed a piece of pheasant with slow deliberation, somehow managing to look even more melancholy. It was his wife who stared at Penny with a look of entreaty, as though pleading with her to not further the conversation, or perhaps not wander further into the king's trap, but Penny was now curious as to what game he was playing. It was not long before she had her answer.

"Does it seem fair to you, Ishassara Penthesilea, if the ha-mazaans are so righteous, so skilled, that they would seek the help of the very men they cast out of their cities? If numbers are all you need, are the taxes we are required to pay your queens not enough to purchase mercenaries? Are the endless tributes of grain and pigs and cattle not enough to trade beyond the Pontis, if mere numbers are what you require? Is it truly necessary to ask the abandoned sons and brothers of your perfect women to lend their lives as a solution to a problem that is not, when all is said and done, their concern?"

The hall's silence deepened into an uncomfortable hush, as though all the air had become trapped in the lungs of everyone listening. She could feel Orithyia's eyes burning into her, and Harp's uneasy frown was clear in her line of vision, but she kept her eyes locked on Pylameneus. Penny was no stranger to resentment, especially of a child to their mother, and it seeped from the king's bones as nauseous vapor from a bog. Now that she had glimpsed something of the man's true heart, she suspected the reason Orithyia had asked her to be the one to make this request would never succeed. She would not appeal to the man's sense of kinship, or tug at his heartstrings as a fellow child of a Hearth Queen, nor seduce him with her wiles, as Orithyia had intended. The man held animosity not only for his mother's preference for wine over her relationships, but her preference for her culture, her values, her ha-mazaan way of life, over her attachment to her son. Penny understood his pain more than she had anticipated, but she did not hesitate to leverage that understanding for her own use.

"It is fitting that we call upon the honor of all who have kin within the ha-mazaan cities, and all our allies, just as they have previously called upon us, yes," she said, her voice taking on a hard edge that had previously been missing. "But any man—or woman—who must be convinced of the wrongdoing of those who defiled the sacred hospitality of the Great Mother is not our ally, and we will not be theirs. You, Pylameneus, were made king not because of your own merit, but because of who your mother was. A ha-mazaan Queen. Do not forget it. The tributes you pay are merely your assurance that your own kingdom will not be destroyed and the lands your men occupy will not be taken, either by enemy forces, or back into the care of Kubileya's daughters. For we take lives as surely as we grant them, and any who would seek to stand in our way shall not know our mercy."

Even Penny was surprised by the righteous anger roiling in her chest, pushing the words out with quiet ferocity. The ha-mazaans at her table stared at her, but she continued, determined for the sake of her mother's memory. For the lost ha-mazaans. For Leandra.

"It is not only for our own need that we ask for your men to aid us, King Pylameneus. It is for the sake of your sons, and your son's sons, though the unwanted daughters of your people will continue to be welcome in our cities. If any choose to ignore Themiscyra's call, it is on their own heads. But know, if you do fail to honor your blood-ties to us, the tributes you pay now shall only increase, and the ease with which you live in our lands shall be no longer. What we lack in numbers, we more than make up for in courage, though that cannot be said for all. Even a ha-mazaan Queen's son."

She thought it might have been Orithyia who laughed, though her ears were ringing with the blood pumping in her veins. Pylameneus' face burned with fury.

"You have no authority to threaten such things, girl," the king growled, unease threading his voice with new tension. "I would rather sell my kingdom for a flagon of wine to the Hatti, or hand it over to the goats in Wilusa than lead my men into such a useless, utterly preposterous war for a few girls."

"I will lead them."

Harp stepped forward, his instrument tucked under his arm, his face grave as his dark eyes met Penny's shocked ones.

"If Themiscyra calls, I will answer, as a lord of Eneti. Our men, *my* men, will answer with me." He turned stiffly to face his father, who wore his own shocked mask, though fury was close behind.

"I will lead them to war, just as my king has always demanded. Haven't you, Father?"

PART FOUR

THRAKIA

$$47$$

FAREWELLS

Penny settled the heavy bronze helmet over her braids, pulling the cheek guards forward over the sides of her face as the padding prickled its horse-hair filling into the top of her head. She had never felt so much like an imposter as she did when dressing as a ha-mazaan every morning, but Orithyia insisted Penny become accustomed to helmet and greaves along with a sword and spear in case of an attack, even if there were fifty of Harp's men, and Orithyia herself, surrounding her for protection as they journeyed west. Every morning the prickle against her scalp transformed into a stab of shame, knowing she was neither qualified nor permitted to call herself ha-mazaan, but even so, she was glad for one thing: with her face covered by the helmet, with her hair tucked into braids and her tunic and trousers covered in stiff leather armor, Penny could move about hidden from the world, anonymous in a sea of soldiers and other ha-mazaans. She could disappear, and not think twice about her oft-mentioned beauty, or how presentable she was as the Hearth Queen's daughter. She could be free, even though she felt this new identity fit as poorly on her as a leopard skin over an elephant.

Penny emerged from the tent she shared with Orithyia, the stink of Lygos' nearby harbor and its fishing boats pungent even through the steady drizzle of rain. She fumbled with the buckle to attach the sword to her belt, having little success in keeping it from tangling in the folds of her cloak. So far, she had only found the weapon to be a tripping hazard, but the queen insisted she not only wear it, but practice with it every morning, even though Penny was already more than sufficient with a bow and spear. As both she and Harp were horribly incompetent with sword and axe, both of them were forced to participate in a daily schedule of weapons training, though so far they were relegated to hacking at straw men and stumps, or, if none of those were available, to flail at the air with their blades like hallucinating fools. She was already late for their morning drills, but when she finally turned her frustrated scowl from her scabbard's buckle to seek out Harp, she realized their small contingent was no longer alone.

A dozen people moved about in the morning downpour, tending to the last preparations for travel as they waited for the approaching ferry from Lygos' western bank. Six of those were ha-mazaans hailing a ship to Attica, where they would infiltrate Theseus' city in search of the lost ha-mazaans. Several Eneti men who had volunteered for the same mission, brothers of the Sinopean ha-mazaans. They had been recruited by their sisters with the express need of male spies, and had happily agreed to an adventure to the other side of the world. One was Harp, whose pledge of solidarity she would forever be grateful for, and whose friendship she had come to treasure. But it was the person Harp was speaking with that made her steps falter, and her breath squeeze to a stop in suddenly tight lungs.

Her steps halted at the sight of the familiar stubbled jaw, the square, slightly lopsided shoulders as he hunched in the rain, his right hand gripping the handle of the short bronze sword at his hip, his feet braced wide apart in a stance both relaxed and challenging as he stood facing Harp's slender, rigid frame. They were arguing about something, teeth bared and hissing lowly at each other, though she couldn't hear the words. Then those familiar hazel eyes found her, and his words stopped as the blood rushed to her head, her cheeks flushing hot as his eyes took in the tall crest of her helmet, then flicked to the sword at her waist.

"Sylviu!" she managed with a tongue grown thick and heavy, removing the helmet as much out of embarrassment as the desire to greet him unfettered by the prickling of it, and started moving forward again. She was aware of Harp's disapproving scowl, but her eyes were fixed on Sylviu's stern face.

She had other words she wanted to say, a whole chorus of them crowding her tongue, but they were barred from exit by the fearful expectation they would be scorned. *I'm sorry. I would never hurt you. I didn't mean it like that. How are you? I've missed you. I have something to tell you. So many somethings. It's all my fault. Even your missing mother. My fault.*

As Sylviu's eyes held hers, though, they were filled with a strange light that she couldn't identify. Perhaps it was the same accusation she had seen last time, only now there was a distance that had only grown into something more substantial, more layered. More impenetrable. More...final.

"Ishassara," Sylviu replied, and in that one word, Penny knew she had not been forgiven.

Her steps slowed, and she resisted grasping the hilt of her sword for comfort, a nervous reflex brought on by weeks of Orithyia's relentless tutelage. She tucked the helmet under her arm, trying to hide it even as his eyes wandered over her ha-mazaan garb with unconcealed distaste. She stopped when she was within arm's length of both men, her tongue twisting on what else she could say, especially now that she could see the way his nostrils flared and his lips pinched, the way they did when he was truly angry. Harp's dark eyes glanced between them, a new expression on his face that Penny could not quite decipher, though the scowl was still there. She braced herself, lifting her chin and staring Sylviu in the eye, determined not to show how much his censure stung.

She wondered what he knew about her. If he knew about the attack, the doomed pregnancy. The broken oath. If he knew, and blamed her for the aftermath. He had every right to, but the fear that he might resent her for his own pain cut like a knife in her gut. All those stifled secrets and that sharp twist of guilt made her next words harsher than she intended.

"What are you doing here?"

Sylviu inclined his chin to match hers. "I am going to find my mother. And your ha-mazaans." He paused a moment, his bronze and green eyes flitting over Harp, then over the weapon at her hip once more, before he said, "I promised I would, didn't I? I still know how to keep my vows."

Penny kept her gaze steady, but breath rasped through a suddenly tight throat when his eyes slid away from hers, as though he could not stand the sight of her. Maybe he did know everything. Why else would he say such a thing if he did not already know she had broken her oath? She could feel the grief in him, the anger—no, the rage, but it seemed too deep for it to be only about her. She knew he grieved for his mother, for his friends, for Cyra and Eri, and all the ones who had been taken from him. Of course he was angry. He had a right to be, and she must accept that part of his anger must be directed at her as well. She shifted her feet, and summoned her mother's training to the fore, keeping her face as impassive as she could while humiliation and hurt roiled inside her chest.

Harp cleared his throat, his fingers twitching against his thigh as though they strummed six strings, and he opened his mouth to speak, but Sylviu continued, his tone sharper now.

"What are *you* doing here? You are not planning to come with us to Attica, surely?"

Penny's face tingled hot, then cold. "Not right now," she evaded.

"Bella and I may proceed to Attica, if you and the others bring good news," Harp interjected, and Penny noticed he shifted his body toward her.

"Bella?"

Sylviu did not look at Harp when he asked the question. Penny willed every muscle to stillness in order to keep from squirming under his increasingly accusing stare. Harp answered before she could explain.

"Bella, yes. But you are correct in calling her Ishassara. She is your future Hearth Queen, after all," Harp's tone was haughty, unfamiliar. Sylviu broke eye contact with Penny to stare at the other man, the silence now heavy with unspoken challenge. His gaze was icy, but there was a sardonic twist to his mouth that Penny could not like.

"Potentially my Hearth Queen, if she completes her Alsanti," was all he said, and his eyes slid back to hers, a knowing glint adding force to the twist of his lips.

Penny clutched the helmet so tight against her ribs it hurt.

"Aye, well, she will have her choice of queen's sons to complete her Alsanti with over the next few months, so do not worry yourself," Harp said, his voice grown cold, and Penny finally tore her eyes from Sylviu to stare at Harp, her brows lowering. She had not expected Harp to push that agenda on her, to so blatantly posture himself as a contender.

"My Alsanti is nobody's business but my own," she snapped, and both of them looked back to her, their expressions unreadable. Penny managed to smooth her own face into impassive calm, determined not to part ways with Sylviu the same way as last time, but knowing there was no hope in repairing what had been broken between them, especially here and now.

She said formally, as she would have before the Flame in Themiscyra, "Sylviu, may Kubileya be ever watchful over you, and keep you safe on your journey. I hope and pray you find what you are looking for."

He paused a long moment, glancing once at Harp, his eyes inscrutable before they returned to hold hers, before he inclined his head a fraction. "I hope the same for you, Ishassara."

He strode away, his steps long but something about his stride jolting and uneven, as though he were trying not to hurry away from them. From her. Penny swallowed the thick lump choking her throat as she watched the back of him go, his mousy hair gone dark from the rain, his shoulders hunched from the wet, or maybe from the same terrible weight that was now crushing her from within.

"Do not worry about a pig-herder's words, Bella," Harp said quietly.

Penny turned the full force of her scowl on him despite the gentleness in his tone, the agony of loss fueling a hot anger in her chest. The rain hissed in her ears like snakes, and the mud smelled of swamp, and all of it choked her further.

"Do not *ever* presume to speak for me," she said, finding it difficult to breathe when her chest was squeezing so tightly.

Harp looked stunned, then immediately contrite, but Penny did not let his contrition stem her anger. "And do not *ever* speak of Sylviu like that again. He has *every* right to be angry with me. But *no* man has the right to decide *anything* about my Alsanti, or *me*."

"Bella, I'm sorry! I only wanted to—"

Harp's frantic apology was interrupted by a shout from Evandre. They looked to see the ha-mazaans gathering on the docks, where the ferry that would take them across the small strip of water straight to the village of Lygos was finally arriving. With the smell of swamp making her senses swim and a last glance of irritation at a stricken Harp only serving to make Penny feel even worse, she turned on her heel and stalked away, her abrupt departure briefly marred by her sword and cloak catching her leg and nearly tripping her face first into the mud.

As Penny threaded through the gathering group of ha-mazaans readying to depart, she brought her cloak up over her hair, shielding her already wet head from the rain, and approached Toxaris. She stepped forward to squeeze the ha-mazaan's arm, careful of the recently healed wound there from her battle against the Achaeans, though Marpe's skilled stitching had by now healed into a puckered pink scar. Toxaris smiled gently, her dark eyes nearly disappearing under the mounds of her cheeks.

"Farewell, Ishassara. I hope you find what you seek in your father's lands."

Penny smiled back, some of her anger dissipating, though there was a burn of hurt and shame underneath it that she knew would have no balm to heal it.

"Safe journey, Toxaris. And if...if you do find Leandra, please let her know we—I—have not forgotten her. That we will come for her, and her mother. Give her my love. And maybe some honey. Remember how much she loves sweets."

Toxaris' smile turned bittersweet, and the ha-mazaan's fingers squeezed her arm. "No need to thank me, Ishassara. I go in service to you, and to my sisters who are stolen. Leandra will not be forgotten by anyone." Toxaris glanced over her shoulder briefly, gauging how much time she had, then met Penny's eyes with grim determination. "Ishassara, I know you do not wish to hear it, but you will remember what I told you, and be wary? It is no longer wise to trust everyone you once knew."

Penny's smile twisted, but she nodded, not wishing to argue with the ha-mazaan when farewells were being said. She glanced at the others preparing to leave. Koine shoved an extra bundle of dried meat into her pack as she scowled through the rain, clearly disgruntled at the unfavorable weather for the launch of what promised to be a lengthy, arduous journey. Sylviu stood at the edge of the dock, a large leather satchel secured to his back, and another in his arms, his posture betraying his impatience to board. He did not turn to see her, but stared resolutely at the flat-bottomed ferry and its red-faced men hauling against the chain, pulling their way across the waters to shore. Penny swallowed, wondering if Toxaris included Sylviu in her warning. Toxaris drew a breath as though to speak again, but then Evandre was there, clapping the shorter ha-mazaan on the shoulder with brisk camaraderie.

"Got your buckles strapped tight, Tox? We'd better get to Lygos before this rain drowns our waiting ship to the bottom of the sea before we're even on it." The General raised her face to the sky, her short hair directing steady rivulets of rainwater down the back of her neck and under the thick leather collar of her armor. "Goddess' tits, why could we not have had some of this last summer, when we needed it, instead of all of it at once right now? Bah!"

She shook herself like a dog, spraying water across both of them, then grinned apologetically. "Apologies, Ishassara. I hope the weather is better for your own journey, though I likely hope in vain. Especially this deep into autumn. I am sure Orithyia will run you into mud as well as she would into dry dust, though, never worry. Remember, she might be a dragon, but she only eats the weak."

Evandre grinned tightly, and Penny smiled wanly in return. Evandre clapped her on the shoulder once, hard enough to leave a bruise, Penny was sure. "We will meet again in a few moons, Ishassara Penthesilea. Hopefully with good news."

Penny nodded. "Hopefully. Be well, Evandre, and Goddess' speed to your ship."

"Aye, we'll need it," Evandre said wryly, squinting through the rain at Ainippe, who paced to and fro at the edge of the docks, her eyes on the ferry being tethered to the shore. "Only the Goddess' perfect speed will do. If we go too swiftly, Ainippe will likely seizure from alarm. If we go too slowly, she will surely die of vomiting. Either way, it's going to be a rough couple of weeks without the divine body of a horse between my thighs, and only these idiots to keep me company."

48

COMBAT TRAINING

"Not like that, foolish girl! Your arm will break. Do it like this."

Penny's face burned as Orithyia, old enough to be her grandmother, easily plucked the sword from her stiff fingers and demonstrated a move with an elegant flourish of hands and delicate, quick footsteps as light as a dancer. The blade swished past her hot cheek with alarming speed, arced in a flash of wet rain behind Orithyia's head, and then returned like a bolt of lightning, the point aimed at Penny's heart. The queen's blurred arms and legs instantly contorted into a perfectly still pose that resembled a crane poised to spear its beak into water.

They had been on the road for just over a month, now, and it had not taken Penny long to realize the queen was made of solid star-iron. Her spiked hair was not the only part of her that showed it, either. The woman was unfazed by the elements, by physical exertion, by long days on the back of a horse, or by longer nights on the hard ground. Harp, forbidden to return to his own kingdom unless, in his father's words, he had finally proved himself a man, was the only other person besides Penny unaccustomed to the hardships of the road, but the ha-mazaan made no allowances for their softness. She even pushed the fifty men who followed Harp, until they grumbled at their lot in life, to find themselves thrust into the care of the king's milksop son and a ha-mazaan queen they had spent a lifetime learning how to resent.

Despite her own struggle, there was one thing Penny had in common with all of those men, including Harp. They all agreed Orithyia was a tyrant.

"Do you see?" Orithyia demanded, then relaxed her stance, flipping the sword with a deft flick of her wrist to grip it by the blade and offer it back to Penny pommel-first.

"No," Penny grumbled, accepting the sword with churlish resignation. "I cannot make my arm bend the way yours does."

"Your elbow bends, girl. It is your mind that is too stiff."

Penny flattened her lips into a tight line of frustration, but she did not say more for a very real fear of retribution at the end of Orithyia's stick.

Orithyia used her toe to flip her staff from the slick stones and into her hand, then swung it with a whistle at Penny's face. Penny barely brought her blade up in time to keep it from connecting with her throat. She parried another swing, and a jab, but on the queen's third attempt, her sword clanged to the cobblestones. Even though there was not a full circle of men watching this time, the outcome was just as humiliating. Penny threw her hands in the air and wrenched the helmet off her head, wiping rain from her face with a frustrated hiss, but Orithyia was relentless.

"Again."

"I can't—"

Orithyia swung, forcing Penny to jerk backward. The thin, bone-breaking shaft of wood hissed past her mouth, forcing her so far back that her heel slipped on the wet rock. Her backside met hard stone with a thud that jarred her teeth. Her helmet skittered away from her hand with a hollow clang, but the expectation that the old woman would relent at her prone position was naïve, and Penny yowled when the wood connected with her shin. Orithyia was aiming for the other leg when Penny scrambled backward, fingers desperately fumbling for her sword on the ground. She hefted it overhead just in time for her arm to vibrate all the way to the shoulder with the shock of their weapons connecting, and the length of her sword dipped wildly under the force of Orithyia's swing. Still, the queen did not relent. Orithyia swung again.

"Enough!" Penny cried.

Sinope's Defending Queen did not hear it. The staff connected with Penny's shoulder this time, and she yelped in pain and more than a little fear, scuttling back on the hard ground. She took a third blow, above her elbow, and thought her arm might be broken. Orithyia was not going to stop. Maybe she was going to kill her, Penny thought, scrabbling frantically on the gravel, but there was no escaping that staff's vicious landings. Orithyia was going to beat her to death with a stick for stealing her horse, for letting her cousins be killed, for increasing Pylameneus' animosity even while forcing his support, for dragging her into a journey with no end in sight and subjecting all of them to the torture of the road, and endless days of fatigue. Perhaps simply for irritating her.

Another crack of wood against her thick leather vest, though not thick enough that ribs could not be broken, and Penny screamed in frustrated agony. Her blood surged, and her senses sharpened. The pain in her leg and arm receded as she rolled out from another vicious blow, and lunged to her feet. This time, Penny did not give Orithyia time to swing her staff. She thrashed at Orithyia's throat, then thrust her blade at the queen's chest, carelessly, desperately, without regard for the fact that this woman was not actually her enemy.

Even in her angry, fearful defensiveness, Penny was no match for the seasoned ha-mazaan, who had seen more battles than Penny had seen years, and who had the scars to prove it. Her staff blocked Penny's blade before it was anywhere near to piercing flesh, but even as she swatted her sword aside, Orithyia stepped back, lowered her weapon, and grinned.

"That's more like it," she said, a gaping hole where there should have been a tooth flashing into view.

Penny panted. Rain pelted her face, and Orithyia's, though the ha-mazaan didn't seem to notice. The pain she had thought receding flooded back with increased intensity, and it took everything Penny had to not drop her sword, clutch her battered limbs, and whimper.

"Now, what changed?" Orithyia asked with perfunctory terseness, her mouth settling back into its compressed line, not quite a frown, but always conveying a sense of slight dissatisfaction.

"What do you mean, 'What changed?'"

"You finally used that sword like you meant it, girl. So what changed, here?" She rapped the end of the staff smartly on the top of Penny's head, not hard enough to hurt, but she winced anyway, more out of fear than pain. "Inside your head, something changed while you were floundering on your back, hey? What was it?"

Penny's chest heaved, and she squirmed against the tight leather vest, trying to hide how she was forced to favor one leg, how the fingers on her left hand twitched as they grew increasingly numb.

"You wouldn't stop. I thought you were going to kill me, or at least break my bones. I just...I reacted."

Orithyia raised her black eyebrows. Her eyes were slightly mocking, but there was an unfamiliar light in them as well. Laughter, perhaps?

"I would indeed have cracked your bones if you had not defended yourself," she said, entirely uncontrite. "Do you think a man will not kill you if you only mewl that you've had enough? That he will let up, give you a breather, show you mercy because you are too timid, too tired to go on once your fingers are sore and your muscles shake? That he will give you time to primp and tidy your hair before he kills you, so that you can be buried in your grave looking your best?"

Penny flushed hotly under that iron stare. The light she had thought to be laughter flamed hot as Orithyia stepped closer. It took every ounce of courage, or perhaps stubbornness Penny could muster not to cower from that flinty gaze.

"When you fight against men, there is no room for weakness, Penthesilea. There is no time for tiredness, or fear, or begging for a reprieve. It is not only that they will most likely be physically stronger than you. They will look for any chance to bring you to your knees, and they will take it, without mercy. They will smell your fear, and they will exploit it. You must rid yourself of that fear, girl. But to do that, you must first banish that stench of doubt that lingers over you like stink over a swamp."

For a tense moment, Penny wondered if the queen could actually smell the presence of the Erinyes the way Penny could. She had not yet admitted to anyone, but especially not to the queen, that the Fury haunted her. The Erinyes appeared at the most random of moments, usually when Penny felt the most vulnerable, but in truth she knew it was always there, breathing its sulfuric laugh into her ears, taunting her, waiting for its moment. So far, she had been able to deal with the creature on her own, to hide its malevolent stink, but if its presence was now making itself known to the ha-mazaan, Penny feared her last secret would be the end of everything. Penny feared Orithyia would abandon her to her fate if she revealed such a monster dogged her every step, as no sane person would continue to align themselves with anyone so cursed.

She must have made a sound, because Orithyia stepped back, but only slightly. She raised her eyebrows, and Penny refocused on the queen's words.

"*That*, my dear girl, is what changed. You no longer doubted I would hurt you, *truly* hurt you, and you no longer doubted you needed to protect yourself. Just like you never doubted in that bathhouse. It is a start. But when you face a man in battle, in negotiation, even in bed, you will need to be far beyond the thought of protecting yourself. On the battlefield at least, the only thought can be destroying your enemy, before he destroys you." Orithyia paused for a long moment, holding Penny's eyes, before she finished. "I am not here to train you at sword and staff, child. I am training you to believe in yourself."

For a few breaths, the sound of Penny's harsh breathing and the now gently pattering rain drowned out many of the sounds of their temporary camp, but some noises floated through the trees. She heard the jingle of harnesses as men prepared horses for another day of travel, and their chatter as they finished their morning meal. It had been the same routine the full span of one moon to the next, since they had made their own crossing into Lygos, and set out on the northwestern road to Satra. Each morning, well before dawn, Orithyia forced Penny and Harp out of their bedrolls and into the often windy, always chilly elements, drilling them in every aspect of weapons training. Of battle against the enemy. Of war. After the ha-mazaan had thoroughly humiliated her pupils, she would send each of them on some athletic task. For Harp, it generally involved horses, for as gifted as he was with animals, he still sneezed every time he was around them, and the queen seemed to think that the more exposure he had, the less severe his reaction would be. So far, unfortunately for poor Harp, her plan had yielded no results. For Penny, the athletic task generally consisted of climbing the nearest hillock three times over, or descending the steepest, murkiest gully possible to fetch the queen a suitable rock to sharpen her blade against. Every day produced the same result—exhaustion, failure, and an extreme desire to be warm in her home, wherever that was, sur-rounded by everything familiar and safe, and not exposed to the relentless, merciless knowledge that the task she had set for herself—to learn the ways of the ha-mazaans, to rid herself of this curse, and ultimately, to rescue Leandra and the others from the clutches of men—was an impossible one.

Even so, Penny sensed there had been some change in herself since leaving Paphlagonia. Her arms felt stronger, her reflexes faster, and her focus sharper when there were blades edging past her face and throat. Not fast enough to be any match for a real warrior, but Penny was encouraged, nonetheless. She couldn't deny the queen's training was effective. Not all of the changes seemed to be physical, either. There was a new sharpness to her thoughts, a focus that had not been there in Themiscyra, even before...everything. Now, with every strained muscle, with every breathless, agonizing journey up the nearest mountain and back, in rain and sometimes snow, Penny felt a new confidence in realizing she was in control of her own body, her own mind, and especially her own thoughts. Orithyia's tactics were working, though Penny had certainly not believed in her first week of training that she could ever feel encouragement from failing at the same things day in and day out. Still, she barely smothered a groan of protest when Orithyia abandoned her lecture and shielded her eyes from the rain to peer through the mist at a nearby shale slope, the top of it nearly completely obscured by mist.

"Bring me the white rock at the eastern tip of the cliff. I will have your breakfast ready if you return before the last fire is out; otherwise, your horse will have it as reward. Again."

Penny's stomach rumbled in response. Peyo had already eaten her dinner of gruel and dates the evening before, when she had failed to complete that mission in the time Orithyia deemed worthy, leaving Penny to spend the night hungry and cold in her bedroll, resenting the very horse she had grown to adore. She peered through the mist to see the stone Orithyia wanted, a small white boulder that would only be tossed aside as soon as Penny brought it back. It was high enough up the steep embankment that Penny's heart sank, and her stomach rumbled again in anticipation of remaining empty for another several hours.

"I'll even lighten your load and carry your sword back to camp. Hand it over." Orithyia held her hand out for the weapon. With a resigned sigh, Penny obeyed.

"Get on, then."

Her bottom smarting from Orithyia's ungentle tap of encouragement with the end of her staff, a gesture as close to affection as the queen might ever show, Penny turned to face the mountain, sighed again, and began her ascent.

49

Snake-Rimmed Shadow

By the time she had scaled the mountainside, the climb both difficult and dangerous due to the loose rock that slipped under her feet, pulling her down three steps for every one step upward, the rain had ceased. Now, she could barely see through the fog that had pulled itself down, thick and heavy as a newly sheered fleece. She dragged air into burning lungs, sitting on a small, unstable jut of rock to allow her shaking thighs a moment's rest, her hand braced on the white boulder beside her hip. It was roughly the size of her own head, and she would now need to carry it back down the mountain when all of her strength had been depleted by the morning's exhaustive training. In the camp far below, prickles of fire glowed through the fog, though they began to wink out one by one, doused in preparation for striking camp. Three fires remained. Her stomach rumbled, insistent.

There was still time.

She considered the path she had taken to get up the mountain. Dark marks in the shale showed her zig-zagged trail from one small, stubborn sapling to another, as she had used their spindly spines as handholds to pull herself up the steep slope. She could take the same way down, and follow the course she already knew to be safe.

Or, she could eat breakfast.

She hefted the boulder in trembling arms and viewed the slope again with a measuring eye. The queen wanted the boulder delivered as proof of ascent, but she had not specified *how* it should be delivered. Another campfire winked out below, and Penny could almost hear the hiss of steam. The men likely doused the flames with their own urine, as they were in the habit of doing every morning.

285

With a mighty grunt and heave, she launched the rock out and away from her body, watching with satisfaction as it arced into the air, then hit the side of the mountain with a crash of stone on stone. It bounced, then bounced again, loosing an avalanche of shale behind it, until it finally rolled to a stop very close to the small, flat-rocked clearing where she had spent the morning fighting with Orithyia. With a smug grin of satisfaction, Penny followed the rock straight down.

She was not quite halfway down the mountain, the sound of sliding rock a steady hiss and clatter in her ears, that Penny heard the familiar laughter. Familiar because it clung to the edges of her consciousness as she slept or woke, worked or rested, haunting her every move. Soon after, the smell of a burning swamp infiltrated her senses, choking her lungs with its stench. She swung her head around wildly, searching for that snake-rimmed shadow she knew would be nearby, but she was moving too fast down too steep a slope. Her momentum carried her forward, and she could not slow the speed of her sliding, could only brace her knees and follow the flow of loosened gravel, then hop to the side and adjust again, sometimes skipping impossibly, dangerously long leaps forward, nearly tumbling head first down the steepest part. She did fall, near the bottom, hands and forearms taking the brunt of the impact, only her bracers saving her skin from being peeled off the bone.

Instantly the shadow was upon her. She could feel the suffocating weight of it, squeezing the air from her lungs, the dry crackle of the beast's wings unfolding, then folding around her, shutting out even the grey light of the morning, the dry, scaled slithering of a snake coiling over her chest, smothering her further. Black spots crowded the edges of her vision and a faint moan escape her tight chest as she thrashed helplessly under the weight of the crushing shadow. Cold laughter echoed inside her skull, and those skeletal arms squeezed harder, the stench gagged her, the hissing drowned out even her own muffled cries. Fuelled by a desperate panic, Penny reached for her sword, then remembered Orithyia had taken it. There was only the small star-iron dagger Silpa had made. She wrenched it free from her belt, and sucked what air she had left to scream at the creature, but the moment the blade was free, the Erinyes was gone, leaving in its wake an absence of sound and smell that was nearly as ominous as its sudden arrival.

Penny scrambled to her feet and bolted, not pausing to look for the Fury, nor wait for it to return. She nearly forgot the white boulder until she stumbled over it. She grabbed with desperate fingers, the weight of it even heavier now, but she clutched it against her ribs and raced for the safety of the camp, the ground at least level and steady under her feet now that the shale was behind her. Peyo greeted her with an enthusiastic, slightly accusatory whinny when she emerged from the trees into the camp. She whistled back to him as she ran, and he waved his white mane like a flag.

Harp raised a hand from the far side of the encampment, where he was busy packing supplies into the wagons, and Penny smiled in return, unable to return the gesture with her hands full of rock, but between the comforting presence of both the stallion and Harp, her tension began to ease and her breathing steadied. The Erinyes had retreated. There was no immediate threat. She practiced the breathing technique Orithyia had been teaching her, calming herself further, and returned Harp's smile with a short nod.

Harp sent a grimace of commiseration before going back to his own task. Penny swallowed a familiar pang of guilt for dragging him into this, though it had been his own foolish decision to wager his entire inheritance on a nearly impossible mission. Still, it was her mission, not his. Despite his reckless choice, she was grateful for his gentle presence, for the sound of his music and song each night around the campfire, and for his friendship. She had grown to trust him, even after their brief, awkward altercation at Lygos. Harp did not seem to hold resentment about it, though, and she found herself relying on his steady presence, his good-humored comradery that carried them through the strange circumstances they found themselves in. She only hoped that he would remain safe, and that the bitterness between father and son, king and heir, would not be forever worsened by Harp's association with her. She had also reconciled with herself that some of the comfort she found in his friendship was the balm it had become for the loss of Sylviu's support. The rupture of that relationship haunted her almost as much as the Erinyes, but the damage was done, and it was too late to change anything now. The best she could do was hold on tightly to the friends she still had, and not do anything that might bring them harm, or drive them away, as she had inevitably driven Sylviu away.

50

DREAMER

Orithyia sat on a log in front of the only fire still burning. She barely glanced up when Penny thudded the boulder at her feet then dropped, utterly exhausted, onto the log next to her, breathing still hoarse and muscles aching. The ha-mazaan ladled thin oats, lumpy with pieces of date, into a wooden bowl, then handed it to Penny without a word. Penny extended a shaking hand, gratefully accepting the offering, and the silent accolade of completing a mission as tasked. Orithyia said nothing, merely went back to eating her own meal, but Penny knew she had satisfied the queen's requirements. If Orithyia knew there had been some extra effort involved, such as a tussle with a malevolent creature bent on vengeance, she might even be proud of her protégé, Penny mused, but then she dismissed the idea as wishful fantasy. She did not think Orithyia had ever been proud of another person in her entire life. Meeting the woman's expectations was difficult enough. There was no hope of exceeding them.

Penny spooned gruel into her mouth, savoring every hard-earned bite. She briefly considered sharing about her encounter with the Erinyes, but what would she say? That a creature of the Otherworld haunted her day and night, appearing without warning? That Penny knew it was the manifestation of her curse, and she waited in dread for the creature to not only attack her, but to strike out at someone else? That she lived in fear of being responsible for even more collateral damage than she already was? What could Orithyia do to help her, anyway? She was no priestess, no *zizenti* with the power to influence the Otherworld. No. The burden was hers to carry, and hers alone, and she refused to embroil anyone else in trouble any further than they already were. There was nothing to be said, and unless the queen had seen her thrashing about on the side of the mountain, she did not need to explain herself. So they sat on a fallen log and ate in companionable silence, satiating the hunger only physical exertion can bring.

A muffled snort at her elbow startled Penny from her musings. Peyo, his feet still hobbled so that he did not seek his own adventures in the wilderness overnight, as he was wont to do, had managed to shuffle his feet until he was within arm's length of Penny's hands.

"It is good you found your *rhu-tasiya*, girl," Orithyia said, eyeing the horse that had once been intended to carry the queen into battle with a gimlet eye. "The ha-mazaans who might oppose your training as a warrior will have a difficult time arguing it is against the will of the Mother, with him as your guardian."

"I suppose, though I am sure they will find other reasons to doubt. It is less lonely having a *rhu-tasiya*, though," Penny admitted. "He is even with me in my dreams, now, though he is not fond of the leopards there."

"What now?" Orithyia's sharp, curious gaze focused on Penny. "Leopards?"

Penny shrugged uncomfortably, berating herself for the slip. She had not told the queen of her dreams just like she had not told her of the Erinyes, for fear of too many questions that she would not know how to answer, but she finally said,

"My father has leopards. I dream of them, sometimes. Or one of them. My father used to tell me that his leopards were the equivalent of my mother's *rhu-tasiya*."

She ate the last of the gruel, save one dollop and a piece of date, and offered the wooden bowl to Peyo. He licked it with a long, thick tongue, his eyes drooping in satisfaction.

"Did he, now?" Orithyia eyed her with curiosity. "And do they use the same marks, your father's people? To bind their spirits to their leopards?"

Penny shook her head again, her hand covering the newly poked tattoo on her thigh, the traditional mark the ha-mazaans used to bind themselves to their spirit's guardian. Peyo had been made her *rhu-tasiya* before their journey, after the queen insisted the horse was no longer any good to her, and had already chosen for himself. "Sired by Boreas himself, and just as fickle as that North Wind," Orithyia had grumbled, and then insisted on tattooing Penny's mark herself, making the bond with the horse permanent, even beyond the Gate to the Otherworld. She had never felt more like one of them, one of the ha-mazaans, than when Orithyia had sat back to admire her handiwork, her fingers smeared in blood and ox bile and ink, and proclaimed it the best tattoo she had ever done. Penny had marveled at Peyo's likeness, though the ink was blue-black and the horse was golden, but the fire was there, the power, the fierce beauty.

She had never thought of the similarities between the tattoos of her father's people, and those of the ha-mazaans, before now. She considered the queen's question for some time before saying, "Their marks are more a sign of status in the tribe, but for the Bessi, they are hereditary. There are different tattoos for the Bessi, the royal priests and priestesses, than the rest of the Satrae, and for every part of the tribe there are marks that are given to bind one to their service in this life, and to Sabazios when they are reborn."

"Sabazios?"

The stallion licked globs of gruel off his lips as Penny stood to wipe out the bowl, and then clean Orithyia's as well. When she was finished, she moved the braid behind her right ear and turned her head for Orithyia to see the swirling three-circle mark there, the blue lines no doubt gone blurry with age.

"Sabazios, the Twice Born God," Penny said. When Orithyia's expression remained blank, Penny continued. "In my homeland, they consider the Mother too holy to speak with directly, so they worship Her son, Sabazios. He who sacrifices Himself to Himself every year, as a representation of the Mother's blood, then re-Fathers himself into being, so that the World may be reborn also."

"Hmph," Orithyia grunted doubtfully, her fingers tapping on her own thigh, but squinted at the mark behind Penny's ear. "And what does that mark mean, then?"

"It marks me a Dreamer of the Bessi, like my father."

"A dreamer? Do we not all dream?"

"Yes," Penny nodded, but the queen's eyes were intent, now, and she knew half-truths would not satisfy her. "But for the Bessi, Dreaming is more like...like being awake elsewhere."

Orithyia scratched hard at an itch on her thigh.

"Explain."

As it was not a request, Penny tried to find the words to explain what she had known since she could use language, but which no one had ever used words to explain to her, not even her father. She had come into this world knowing how to Dream, meeting her father in that place, and it was there she had learned what could not be spoken of in words. It was that place she had struggled to return to when her mother had brought her to Themiscyra, with all the stress of being in a new land, a new culture, a new society of women with their own expectations she never seemed to be able to meet, but she pushed the uncomfortable thought away, and focused on explaining the matter to Orithyia.

"When a Dreamer sleeps, their Spirit walks the Otherworld," Penny said finally. "I mean, it is not exactly the Otherworld. It is more like the place between here and the Otherworld."

"There is no place between here and the Otherworld," Orithyia said immediately.

Penny thought for a moment. "Perhaps you could think of it as a wall between here and the Otherworld, and a Dreamer walks the top of it, Seeing into both places at once. Seeing both Light and Shadow."

Orithyia shoved a stick into the lingering coals of the fire, stirring up embers and sparks, her frown still firmly in place.

"A wall makes sense, I suppose," she said slowly. "They say there is a Gate, after all. Must have something to connect it to."

"Exactly!" Penny said, encouraged by even a slight give in Orithyia's iron resistance. "And in some places that wall might be tall and thick, almost impossible to scale or see beyond, and in some places it may be thin, crumbling, or low enough it can be easily scaled, so that if one climbed to the top they could see far into the distance of both places at once."

Orithyia nodded slowly, considering this. "And one can climb this wall in their dreams?"

"It is the best way I can think of to explain it, but yes. A Dreamer has access to those places where the wall is easily climbed, or is crumbling, and what they See and do in those places is then echoed in the waking world. They can meet other Dreamers there. The most powerful of Dreamers can meet anyone there. It is here the *rhu-tasiyas* walk, also, while their spirits protect their people. They can be Guides, leading the Dreamer to the places between the worlds where the wall is thinnest, or easiest to scale. My father relies on his leopards as Guides in Dreaming. Now that I have Peyo, he will guide me there as well."

"I see," Orithyia murmured, though her fingers twitched as though she wished for a weapon in them, and Penny knew the queen's mind was spinning like a maple seed falling from the sky, whirring faster than Penny could keep up with.

"And you dream of this place between the worlds a lot, lately? Of your father's leopards?"

Penny looked to the last embers in their fire, but it was her father's golden eyes she saw, and Begri's low rumble in her mind.

"Not of that place, necessarily. I am unpracticed in Seeing beyond the wall without my father's guidance. I...I have not Dreamed since I left Satra, really."

"Oh?" Orithyia's magpie eyes were bright with that inner fire Penny was coming to recognize meant the queen was already ten steps ahead of anyone else. "But you have dreamed in this other place lately?" Her tone caught Penny off guard, and for some reason she felt like she had stumbled into a trap nearly as dangerous as the wings of an Erinyes.

"Well, yes—"

"And how often were you dreaming *before* you ran away, before you stopped drinking the herbed wine?"

"I was not running away—"

"Spare me the semantics, girl! Did you or did you not have these dreams before you left Sinope?"

Penny thought for a moment, recalling her father's plea to seek out the oracle. She raised her chin, defiant.

"I did, actually. I dreamed just after the men destroyed the city. Before I went to the Oracle. My father was there, with his leopard, and he is the one who told me to go to her."

"And you drank the wine that day? And all the days previous?"

Penny stared at the ha-mazaan, her mind skipping back in time.

"Well, no...not all the days. Areto's birthing was complicated, and I never thought to take my medicine. There wasn't time. And then...the bathhouse...and then we were tending the wounded...burying the dead..."

Orithyia nodded as though it was all the proof she needed.

Penny shivered, unable to formulate a convincing denial of what the ha-mazaan insinuated. Doubt's once soft green shoots firmly rooted inside her stomach and expanded into a sturdy sapling, its woody trunk and sharp branches thickening into her lungs with every shallow breath. She had not been able to enter her dreams since she had come to Themiscyra, it was true, but she had always thought it a manifestation of change, of uncertainty, of abandoning one way of life and everything she had ever known for a completely foreign city, and all the expectations that came with caring for its daughters. She had thought the loss of contact with her father had meant her own ability to Dream was simply not strong enough, not well trained enough. She had been only eight summers, after all. Not even a woman yet. Not every child of a Bessi had the ability to Dream. She simply assumed she had grown out of the sensitivity, and away from her father's teachings, as so many new expectations crowded out her childhood flights of fancy.

Her headaches *had* coincided with coming to Themiscyra, however. Had in fact been the very cessation of Dreaming, and the onset of her indescribable loneliness amongst an entire culture of women she felt she could never truly be a part of, while she grieved the loss of everything she had once so thoroughly, so naively taken for granted.

To think that Marpe, the woman who had taken her under her wing, taught her the arts of Healing, of bringing new life into the world, of mending wounds, of stitching life's ragged tears back together, had been drugging her all that time, simply to restrict her from that sleeping realm of Dreams, was ridiculous. Even more ludicrous, the idea that her mother was behind the scheme. What possible reason could Antiope have for keeping her from Dreaming? It made no sense.

"If you can truly See things happening in this in-between place, it would be a dangerous thing for someone who did not want their workings made known," Orithyia said, following the trail of Penny's thoughts with all the skills of an expert hunter. "For someone with something, or *many* somethings, to hide, what you describe sounds like the ultimate threat to secrecy. Would you not agree?"

"My mother had nothing to hide. She kept no secrets."

"You had better work on convincing yourself before you try and convince me, girl. Every woman has secrets. Antiope was the Queen of Secrets. *Every* Hearth Queen is. And until you can come to accept that your mother may not be the perfect manifestation of your Goddess on earth, as apparently everyone has convinced you she is, and until you can admit she has flaws that are not only very human, but possibly very dangerous, you will never be able to see the truth."

That night, exhausted in body and mind, the crackle of flames nearby her bedroll and the stars a swirl of bees seeking the hive of the moon filling her mind with an insistent buzzing, Penny closed her eyes, and thought of her father. She focused every bit of energy she could still muster on recalling Thrax's features, his scent, his smile, the deep timbre of his voice. When she finally slipped into sleep, all those memories coalesced into one, until she could feel his presence beside her, his spirit walking with her. The details were so real she thought she might reach out and touch the roughly spun green wool of his tunic, run her fingers over the cool silver of the engraved broaches holding his cloak in place, stroke the fine, bristling copper hair of his beard as she had done so often as a child.

"Father," Penny said, and all the longing of her lonesome life lived in that one word.

"Bella," Thrax answered, and all the love she could ever hope for was in his voice.

"I don't know what to believe anymore. Who to believe."

Penny glanced at her feet as she confessed this. They stood on the precipice of a mountain, and her feet were dangerously close to the cliff edge. She pressed back against the hard rock of the cliff face, shuffling closer to Thrax, until she could smell the musk of his skin. His eyes, the eyes he had given her, gazed at her with all the love she once remembered feeling from him, but that had somehow grown so distant.

"Believe in yourself. Isn't that the most important thing?"

She shook her head. "I'm the one that ruined everything. It all fell apart because of me. They're all dead because of me. And now, my mother...I don't...I can't."

Penny began to weep, and her father watched the tears fall with sorrowful calm. Then, he reached out a hand, his thumb wiping one of the tears away. She could feel the callous on his fingertip, the skin roughened from years of work and weapons. She wept harder. Something soft and warm appeared under her hand. She glanced down to find Begri padding close to the cliff edge, unconcerned by the sheer drop next to her paws, the animal's great square head pushing insistently at Penny's palm, seeking a scratch under the chin, but there was something in the cat's eyes that looked like a warning, or a command, or both. Suddenly, they were no longer standing on a cliff. They were on a narrow dirt trail in the middle of a pine forest, the stars and moon shining above them humming with a life of their own. The Waterbearer knelt at the edge of the indigo sky, pouring out her stream of stars, the river of them flowing white and milky across the firmament, while the Overseer, half man and half horse, stood proud at the zenith of it all.

Peyo emerged from the trees at the edge of that path, his neck arched and glowing like a sword flaming with the heat of the forge, his golden coat luminescent in the twilight of the Dream. The moment seemed more real than many waking ones in the past several months, and she breathed deeply, the night air cooling the heat of shame that had begun to burn in her flesh in the waking world.

"Your Guides watch over you," her father's voice washed over her with gentle strength. "I watch over you. Your mother watches over you. There is no journey more important than the one back to your true self, Daughter. That is where I shall be waiting for you."

51

SWORDPLAY

"Hah!" Penny exclaimed, her laugh triumphant as the tip of her extended sword pressed into Harp's exposed neck.

Harp shoved her and the blade away from him with a sharp kick of his heel into her lower stomach. Penny flailed backward with a grunt, nearly losing her grip on the hilt and her feet slipping on the slick, fresh dusting of snow on the ground. Her grunt turned to a snarl of frustration as she recovered, and used both hands to swing the sword at his leather-covered ribs. Harp's own blade, made of bronze and not star-iron like hers, for Orithyia was adamant that, ally or not, he was still a man, blocked her blow. Penny swung again, and again. Each time, Harp managed to block her blade, but Penny was gaining ground now, forcing him back one step at a time, keeping him in a defensive stance rather than allowing him to switch to attack. She thought she saw alarm in his eyes once, but he blocked her again, and she kept pushing him.

She relished the thrill of energy zinging through her body, especially unencumbered by shield and helmet like she normally was. *This* is what it felt like to be ha-mazaan. This is what it felt like to have power. It was a heady thing, and she fed on it, savored every new skill the last months had taught her, every lesson that translated from mind to hand and feet, even as she drove Harp back and back and back, their feet turning the pristine snow to ugly mud as the morning sun began to warm the earth.

Harp grunted a curse as she effortlessly parried his desperate lunge. She saw an opening to his exposed leg as he feinted against her left side. If she lunged, she could actually wound him, and that thought alone gave her pause. She hesitated just long enough that he danced away from her reach entirely, grinning.

"Stop!"

Orithyia's shout brought them both to a panting halt, and they turned to face their taskmaster with equal amounts of wary expectation. Orithyia stalked closer, walking forward as though tilting into the wind, though the day was calm, her arms crossed over her chest as they always were when she observed from the sidelines, ever critical.

"Harp, fetch General Mursilis. Now."

Harp turned instantly and trotted toward the troops, his obedience unquestioning. Penny removed her helmet, wiping sweat from her brow and trying to catch her breath in the reprieve, knowing it would not last long, but she glanced at Orithyia questioningly.

"You had an opening," the ha-mazaan said shortly. Accusingly.

Penny inhaled a cold breath into her burning lungs. She glanced after Harp, who had found the General, and was pointing in their direction. "I didn't want to *actually* hurt him."

"Exactly," Orithyia spat, her tone filled with disgust. "I don't know if it's your ridiculous attachment to that oath, or your fuzzy-headed feelings for the boy, but your practice days with my nephew are over. Time to learn that you cannot pussyfoot around when a man has a sword in his hand."

"But—"

"Those are the mountains of your father's lands, aye?" Orithyia cut her off, waving a hand to the north. Penny followed the direction of her hand, taking in the familiar crown of peaks along the horizon, the hills raised like the nipples of the many-breasted Mother ready to suckle the frigid sky. Penny nodded, wary, and Orithyia continued. "Then we had best test your skills now, before we are beset by his armies, and you are so worried about scratching someone with that sword that you forget what it's for."

Penny's confused frown turned to a contemptuous laugh. "My father will not set his armies on us."

From the corner of her eye, she saw Harp returning with his General, and the man did not look pleased to be summoned away from his morning gruel, especially for a ha-mazaan queen's unknown demands.

"Oh?" Orithyia asked. "You can guarantee we will not be met with an army of mercenaries that we do not have the numbers to dissuade?

Everything I have heard of your father tells me he is less than welcoming of strangers traipsing this close to his mines."

Penny rolled her shoulders under her perpetually damp cloak to ease some of the tension there. Though the snow had ceased before dawn, the morning was cold. Small pellets of ice were beginning to form on the whiskers of the horses being readied for the day's journey, and their breath puffed clouds of white into the air. Somehow, Orithyia was immune to the cold as much as she was to the rain, but Penny knew by now the ha-mazaan always had something more important on her mind than the weather: strategic maneuvers, their next camp location, keeping their small army safe from attack. She shrugged at Orithyia's suggestion that her father would be one of those they would need to defend against, her eyes still warily watching Mursilis' approach.

"He will have scouts out, I am sure, but once they know my identity, there will be no problems."

"Your father will definitely welcome you, then?"

Penny eyed the ha-mazaan uncertainly. "Why would he not?"

"Fathers don't often regard their daughters with much care or concern in this world, girl," Orithyia said bluntly. "It is one thing for your mother to take away a meager daughter with nothing to offer him. Other than marriage contracts with rival tribes, perhaps, and a few sons to spread his blood outward, but in this land, a girl child offers nothing but trouble. I can see how he may have been pleased to see you gone, especially if it was to become queen of your own lands one day. Something a father might think favorably upon, when he thinks of his daughter at all. But returning with an army of men, and asking for his help...?" Orithyia shook her head. "That is an entirely different story."

Penny thought of her recent dream, the way her father had smelled, the love in his eyes when he assured her he was watching over her. The touch of his hand on her face. She had to believe his love was real, or there was nothing else for her to rely on. She scowled at Orithyia as the General halted close by, waiting for the reason for his summons. Harp stood by awkwardly waiting for his next command.

"My father is a man of honor," Penny said. "I have no doubt he will welcome any of his children home with open arms, especially his daughter." Penny paused, chewing her lip, then admitted, "My half-brothers, however, are another matter."

Even as her tongue slipped out the word home, she felt the truth of it. She had not felt at home since the moment her mother had led her away from Satra. Now that she was returning to her homeland, would it feel like home? She was not the same person she had been when she left. Would her father notice these changes in her? Would he see the young woman he had always been so proud of, or would he see a scared little girl, an easy target, a foolish and naïve girl who got herself into an impossible situation and now had no way out but through, while dragging hundreds of innocent people, including Orithyia, through that mire with her? And what if the woman was right? What if her father had wanted to be rid of her? If his relief at her departure was why he had not visited her all these years?

"Half-brothers?" Orithyia's impatient question interrupted her worried spiraling.

"My father's sons. Especially Glinn. He's likely a chief in his own lands by now."

"And is it you this Glinn will not welcome, or this army that follows behind you?" Orithyia swept her hand to indicate the men beginning to douse their fires.

Penny hesitated, drawing her cloak closer to her chest, the other hand gripping the sword handle as though it were an anchor holding her in place. She had not thought about her younger brothers in years, but she remembered the way Glinn had once kicked her hard enough in the shins to bruise her for a week, all because she had been the one her father chose as his hunting partner that day.

"Both," she finally admitted. "Out of all of my father's children, Glinn is the one I would assume will be the least happy to see me again."

Orithyia frowned. "All his children? How many children does Thrax have?"

"I don't know," Penny said, and when Orithyia's eyebrows floated upward, she shrugged and said, "He has likely had more since I left. He...has several wives, you see."

Orithyia's eyebrows climbed higher somehow, making her forehead a washboard of astonishment, but it was General Mursilis who said, his tone clouded with either disbelief or awe, "Several wives?"

Penny shrugged one shoulder and tapped her sword against her calf, irritated at the man's tone, and worried at his reason for being summoned to intervene in her swordplay.

"It is how the tribes stay peaceful, and ensures everyone is provided for. Resources are shared, and alliances sworn and kept. It is a good way to keep peace. My father is only king of his own tribe, you see, though he is priest of many tribes, for the Bessi priests and priestesses who can Dream are more rare, and hold more power than kings, but there are thousands more tribes through the mountains and valleys, and therefore a thousand more kings. Once, he told me it was his dream to unite them all under one banner, but I cannot see that ever happening. I also don't think he could manage that many wives."

Orithyia made a contemptuous "Psh" sound, but then, the brisk tone of commander returning, she faced General Mursilis.

"These two will no longer practice together. You will practice with Penthesilea every morning, and with Harpalion in the evenings instead, since they are no longer of any use to each other."

Harp gawked, his dark eyes widening in alarm as they met Penny's resigned ones. Mursilis bristled at being commanded in such a way, and by a ha-mazaan no less, but Orithyia had no time for his, or anyone's, resistance.

"Stand down, man. You want the boy to live as much as I do, and I would rather this girl not lose her limbs the first skirmish we encounter because she feels timid about hurting people. We've been lucky so far, but if she is wrong about the greeting we will receive, we will need every sword we have. You are up to dancing against the wind a few minutes every day, surely? That's about what it will be. These two fight like kittens still, so I cannot think it will be too much for you, but if it is, by all means, I will ask Hakli to practice with them instead."

Mursilis stiffened, his skin mottling with fury under his thick beard. Penny was sure that he would have struck the queen down then and there if he was not a man of honor, and well-tenured in the conflicts of military life.

"As you say, Queen," the man said finally, but Penny was not prepared for what happened next.

The man drew his sword and slashed at Penny without warning. Searing pain exploded along the side of her face, the General's blade cutting into her exposed jaw before she could even lift her sword. Vaguely, she heard Harp shout in alarm, and even Orithyia reared back in surprise, but the man was swinging again, and she barely brought her sword up in time to deflect the blow from catching her in the throat. Her arm immediately went numb from the force of the impact even as the burning in her cheek intensified, and she could feel hot rivulets of blood stealing down the neck of her tunic.

Mursilis withdrew, circled, and struck again. Penny dodged, knowing she could not match the General for strength or skill, but her cloak tangled in her legs. She cursed, and heard the word echoed back from Harp, who was hissing something very loudly to Orithyia. Mursilis lunged again, and Penny dodged again, but he anticipated which direction she would move and his blade was there, the flat of it smacking soundly into the back of her skull. She went down hard in a tangle of cloak and sword, her head ringing like a bell. Mursilis stepped on the edge of her cloak, making it gouge into her throat and choke her, and also trap her. She heard him laugh. It was mocking, and behind it, the Erinyes laughed with him.

Penny writhed on the ground, her hands ripping at the pin securing the cloak as the burly man lifted his bronze blade overhead. Harp shouted something, his voice desperate, but in the corner of her vision, Penny saw Orithyia hit his sword arm with her staff, then push the panicking man back, her magpie eyes fixed on the unfair fight as though it was the most entertaining thing she had witnessed in three moons. Most likely it was, because Penny was about to die.

Mursilis swung. Penny rolled. The pin released and her cloak came free from her shoulders as his sword embedded into the ground where her throat had just been. She leaped to her feet, sword ready, teeth bared. The General was not as slow as his large, aging body suggested, however. He feinted twice, and on the third lunge, Penny could not sidestep his blade, or the weight of the man behind it. He took her back to the ground with the force of his own body, knocking the blade from her icy fingers. Her breath punched out into a cloud of ice in the air, but she could not bring it back in again, no matter how hard she tried. Mursilis grunted with the impact, then rolled, struggling to gain his footing, but Penny was no longer in the cold foothills of the mountains, fighting for her life in the snow and mud.

She was in the bathhouse, and Brekko had thrown her to the rock floor, and the steam was suffocating her lungs. She could feel his hot breath in her mouth, the pinch of his fingers on her flesh, his weight between her legs. When she heard him laughing, and when the Erinyes laughed again, she did not hesitate.

The star-iron dagger was in her hand, and then it was in flesh.

The jolt of it staggered her back to cold reality. Mursilis bellowed, the dagger protruding from the meat of his thigh, and then Orithyia was between them, and Harp was helping her to her feet, his mouth moving with words she could not understand, and his hands coming away from her jaw were covered in blood, but she was alive, and Brekko was not, and she knew for a fact that any man she faced may be stronger than her, may be a better fighter, may even take her with him to the Otherworld, but she would not go there without a fight.

52

ATHENS

Athens, Greece, Dark Moon, 1206 BC

The priestesses' call commencing the sunset ritual rang out through Athens' city square, slithering over the ground in the wake of Sylviu's steps as he hugged to banks of the narrow river flowing into the southwest harbor. He walked easier with the woman's shrill call and the echoing horns reverberating in his ears, knowing most of the townspeople would soon be gathering at the far edge of the towering precipice the city was built around, as though the mountain was their shrine. Their attention would soon be wholly devoted to the charlatan who claimed to be able to raise the dead with his medicines, leaving him free to find what he was seeking.

It had only taken a few days for Sylviu to find the pulse of the town that Basileus Theseus called home. It had only taken a day to become familiar with the habits and needs of the people inside of it, including their religious fervor. They were obsessed with peculiar rituals involving the sun and herbs and snakes and shiny black rocks that seemed to be nothing more than star-iron, all of it making little sense to him or the other spies, but their habitual and perfectly timed distractions afforded the perfect opportunity to move around undetected. While the Athenians lit candles to blind and deaf nymphs and moaned prayers and played with snakes in caves, Sylviu rifled through their homes, their storage facilities at the docks, their temples, their latrines, their whorehouses, though the last brought the bile to his throat and he had to force himself not to think about actually finding any of the ha-mazaans in such a place. Especially Leandra. As it was, he'd found nothing.

He would leave no stone unturned, though, and he knew the other spies were also doing what they could, despite the limited movement the women had here in this foreign place. He tried not to let the unease of potential failure dampen his resolve, but they were no closer to finding any signs of their missing women than the day their own ship had slid into the harbor next to the damning sight of that familiar, gryffon-prowed black ship. The very sight of it had triggered a near-feral rage inside Sylviu's breast, but even more dangerous, more painful, was the feeling of hope that had surged there. Hope he would soon see his mother again, and hug her tightly to him, and whisper his apology for saying such terrible things to her that last time. For committing acts of sacrilege that had brought this fate upon them all. Hope he could swing Leandra into the air and hear her screech of laughter, her lion's mane of hair shining in the sun as she giggled at him. Hope he could return to Pen and gift her with more than just the news that he had succeeded in keeping this promise, at least. But the longer that hope of finding them went unmet, the more painful the feeling in his chest became, and he wished the rage was all that he could feel.

Now, after nearly a week haunting every dark corner of this place, there was only one spot he had not managed to search. The Cecropis was a geographical oddity. The limestone outcropping sat on top of the soil as though it had been pushed out from under the earth by the thumb of an underground giant, a raised scar on an already tumultuous skin of earth, the nearly vertical cliff walls on all sides towering above the deme below offering only a glimpse of the thick hedge surrounding the entire perimeter of the plateau at the top. From the bottom of the cliffs, only that hedge was visible, its thick and spiney bracken completely obscuring what lay behind it. Viewed from the distant hills to the north, however, the marble palace squatting behind that hedge was impossible to hide. But looking from afar was not enough. He needed inside, and there was only one entrance.

A long, sloping pathway arced from the base of limestone walls up the steep path to the top of the Cecropis, and that path was heavily guarded by a multitude of soldiers no spy or even local citizen was going to get past without an invitation. There would be no slipping past them, no furtive night-time forays up that slope, either alone or with the other spies, but that did not mean he had given up. Not if there was any chance his mother or Leandra were up there, suffering only the Goddess knew what kind of fate.

Sylviu ducked into the shadows of an olive tree as voices approached from behind, tucking himself against the thin trunk until the pair of women had safely passed. They were busy chatting and giggling, wicker baskets of laundry balanced against their hips as they wound their way through the reeds toward the narrow river. They took no notice when he slipped behind them on silent feet, making his way onto the footpath they had come from and moving in the opposite direction of their chatter, soon lost from their sight. He pulled the cloak lower over his head, though the weather here was too warm for such clothing, and craned his neck until that tall hedge at the pinnacle of the Cecropis snagged his eyes. Behind it were walls of smooth white stone, plain and unadorned, and filled with every secret he was looking for, he was sure of it.

The place pulled at Sylviu the way only one other place had. The day he had entered the Kebat's cave uninvited, unwelcome, breaking every Law forbidding men from being in that place, Laws his own mother had raised him to believe were sacrosanct and unbreakable, had been the day his life had changed forever. He was still not sure if it had changed for better or worse. Certainly, his time in front of that Oracle's cauldron had not prepared him for this reality, though he realized now he should have understood.

That in itself is what brings destruction...

He shook off the terrible clawing at his spine as he thought of the last words between himself and his mother, and slipped around an outcropping of crumbling stone to the right, until the northwest edge of the terraced mountain was at his right shoulder. The grey limestone still gave off a faint heat as he moved closer. When he was sure there was no one about, and that the deepening shadows would hide his cloaked figure well enough, he hugged himself to the side of the mountain. He pressed his ear to the stone, quieting his breathing, and listened.

The sound was so faint he could barely tell if it was his own imagination, but when he pulled his head away from the cliff face, still listening intently, there was nothing but the sound of the small river behind him and the rustling of a light wind through the olive trees, the giggles of the women washing their laundry lifting on the wind. He pressed his ear back to the rock. It was there. Soft. Like the mountain had a heartbeat, or perhaps lungs, drawing breath into itself and beating with a rhythmic, steady pulse. The mountain was not solid stone. Somewhere in there water from the sea pulsed a heartbeat through the stone, a spring of well-water from deep underground.

He continued north, following the uneven curve of the vertical lime-stone until he saw the shadows he was looking for. Just a small opening, barely wide enough for the darkness to gather inside, but it was enough. With some careful maneuvering and the sacrifice of some skin where he could not cave his chest any smaller, Sylviu squeezed into the small crevice, pushing further into the hollow that was too small to be called a cave, too cramped to be called a tunnel, but still, it was inside the skin of the mountain, inside the Cecropis' inner walls. He followed the sound of water until the passage opened around him, though he could not tell from sight, for everything was black and he only had his hands and his ears to guide him, along with that pull in his chest that he could not have ignored if he tried. He stayed still for a moment, breathing in the dank, musty air, the steady beat of waves somewhere below his feet and the insistent drip of water somewhere ahead telling him what he had heard from outside was correct. He pushed forward, feeling with his toes and his hands in the Stygian dark, until his boot scraped against stone. He tried to step around it, only to find his path blocked, and so stood on top of the stone. He felt forward, and hit another raised stone, and frowned, testing its stability under his foot. It was only when it happened for a third time that he understood.

Stairs.

Heart pounding in his throat, Sylviu climbed with swift precision de-spite the dark, his legs soon burning as each step took him higher, the air pressing down on him as he felt the weight of the entire rock citadel from above and all the pressure of this mission pressing on his guts from the inside. The pressure in his chest intensified. He could *feel* that he was close to finding what he had come for. When the rough wood of a door greeted his outstretched palm, he drew his sword, and a deep breath.

Even though he should be going back for the others, alerting Evandre and Ainippe and Percon, he was not going to wait any longer to make sure his mother was alright. He would not return to Themiscyra reeking of failure. He would find his mother, and Leandra, and the others. He had promised Pen he would. He would help her reignite the Flame she didn't even know he had extinguished, and he would be damned if was ever going to let her down again.

He lifted the latch on the door, and swung it open to reveal a luxurious bathhouse that rivaled any of Themiscyra's in both size and decadence. Sylviu stared, mouth agape. The women—no, not women, *girls*—stared back, all frozen in various states of nakedness, both in and out of the water. His frozen panic was shattered by the sound of one of the girls' screeching.

"*Sylviu!*"

He barely had tome to move his sword out of the way before a tiny, fierce, utterly astonished blue-eyed girl launched herself into his arms.

53

APOLOGIES

"I've never really said a proper thank you, Harp. And now I owe you an apology."

"What for?"

"Well," Penny said, eyeing the swelling, blackening bruise across his forearm with a pointed rase of her brow, "that, for starters."

Harp glanced down at his arm, then shrugged. "That wasn't you. That was The Tyrant."

He returned his focus to the thin bone needle and its trailing length of catgut poised above her jaw. She had already sat through his gentle cleaning of the wound, including the excruciating part where he had poured wine into it to clean it from infection, though she had been the one to ask for it. She had given him specific instructions every step of the way, and he had followed them without hesitation, surprising her with his lack of squeamishness as he discarded each bloody rag and took up the next. But now, his normally steady hands took on an unfamiliar tremor, and a sheen of sweat stood out on his brow. He moved the needle a fraction closer, touching her skin, but not piercing it. He took a deep, ragged breath as though preparing to push, but the needle did not move.

"Apologies for dragging you into all of this, then," Penny continued, waving a hand to indicate the tents aglow with lanterns as his men hunkered inside them, their outlines taking on a soft, fuzzed glow in the gray afternoon as the silently falling snow threatened to bury them by dark.

They had entered the foothills of the Rhodope mountains several days ago. The landscape had changed from gently undulating pastoral fields into craggy, unpredictable terrain, the granite outcroppings and thick forests, the deeply cut ravines full of rushing rivers slowing their progress, especially as winter began to take hold. The camp they had chosen the day before was well sheltered from the winds, but nothing could shelter them from the storms of snow and ice that would only become worse as the days went on, as they traveled further northwest. The only comfort the forbidding valleys and cold snow gave Penny was the knowledge that her father was closer with every step.

"Oh, well," Harp said, his eyes fixed warily on his own fingers as though they were live snakes. "Also not you. I volunteered, remember? Now hold still. I can't stick this needle into your jaw while it's flapping about."

Penny now fully doubted he could stick the needle in at all, but she sat obediently, head cocked awkwardly to give him the best vantage. His hand remained poised above the wound, until his breathing became shallow and quick.

"Here," she said, taking pity on him and holding out her hand. "Give it to me, and find me a mirror."

"No. I can do it."

"You don't want to."

"Of course I don't *want* to, Bella!" he hissed, waving the needle in front of her face with an angry jerk. "Why would I *want* to? It's going to *hurt* you."

Despite the burning along her jaw, Penny smiled, and covered his hand with hers. She pried his fingers open, a task that took more stubbornness than strength, and took the needle.

"Please. Find me a mirror. I never thought I was vain, but I would rather not have a scar as big and thick as an oak limb across my face."

"Bella, I can—"

"It's okay, Harp." She held his gaze, her fingers still covering his. "I have done this sort of thing on others for most of my life. I'm a trained *sivyeti*. Besides, I would rather hurt myself than put you through something so unpleasant. Just fetch me a mirror and hold it for me. Please."

Rubbing his arm across his sweaty head, then swearing as it reminded him how badly his wrist was bruised, Harp jerked to his feet and stalked out from the awning they sat beneath, headed for the tent he shared with General Mursilis. Behind Penny, the tent flap rustled, and Orithyia poked her head out, short hair spiking in multiple directions.

"Boy doesn't have the balls, eh? Want me to do it?"

"No," Penny said flatly, though she barely glanced at the woman. "Harp is plenty brave enough. He just doesn't enjoy seeing other people in pain. Unlike some."

She thought Orithyia's lips might have twitched in a smile, but the woman simply grunted and tugged the tent flap closed again, leaving Penny to sit and wait for Harp's return, her jaw still burning from the wine that had been liberally sloshed over the open wound. She was glad for any moments alone, or as alone as she could be surrounded by fifty men and a vicious old ha-mazaan. In the frenzied tension after her fight with General Mursilis, in which Harp was so livid she thought he might take up his sword and actually kill both Queen and General, and then in the sickening come-down after the rush was over, when the pain had set in and the realization that she had acted purely from instinct, from fear, from rage, and not out of any sort of self-control or honor, she had not had sufficient time to consider Orithyia's tactics. Once everyone had calmed, Harp had ordered Mursilis to submit to Penny's administrations, though only after unsuccessfully trying to force her to care for her own wound first. As she cleaned the General's wound, stitching it with the finest stitches even Marpe would have praised, and which would have to serve as its own apology, Penny had found plenty of time to ponder. So far, none of her thoughts were favorable to Sinope's Defending Queen. She was furious the woman had put her in such a dangerous predicament before she was ready, just to make Penny prove she could hurt a man if she needed to. She was even more furious it had worked.

Realizing her jaw was burning like a brand in the fire, Penny unclenched her teeth, and gave Harp a crooked, stiff smile as he made his way through the snow, peering anxiously at her face.

"Will this work?"

He held up a buckle attached to the end of a long belt. It was silver, and large for a buckle, but very, very small for a mirror. Penny sighed.

"It will have to."

He returned the stump opposite hers, rubbed the buckle against his woolen tunic to buff it into a high shine, then held it up. Penny grimaced when she saw her mottled reflection in the makeshift mirror. The red edges of the wound gaped open in a line as long as her forefinger, and just as thick. She thought she could see bone, but wasn't quite sure in the dim light and awkward, uneven reflection. At least it was clean, and most of the bleeding had stopped. Swallowing, her palms suddenly damp, Penny raised the splinter of needle to her face. She paused, breathing deeply to steady her hand as her eyes caught Harp's worried ones over the buckle, but suddenly a bulging wineskin was thrust between them.

"Drink this first."

Penny glared up at Orithyia. "No."

"You will need it for the pain, girl. I would offer to do the job myself, but these eyes are not what they used to be, and you don't want me sewing your lips closed by mistake. Tempted as I might be."

Those lips smiled as sweetly as Penny could manage with the sour taste of anger tainting her throat. "I need my hands steady and unencumbered by drink, so that my face does not look like yours when I am finished. No thank you."

Harp sucked in a breath. Bright eyes held hers for a long, tense moment, before Orithyia nodded, and withdrew the bag. "Have it your way."

The ha-mazaan did not go back into her tent, though, but instead set off toward the General's quarters, perhaps to offer him some of the same pain relief for his own wound and ease her own guilt in the matter. Penny wiggled her now even more tense shoulders to restore some flexibility back into her hand, and motioned for Harp to hold up the buckle again. She pinched the edges of skin together on her jaw, wincing, and lifted the needle.

"Bella, I think I should—"

She shoved the needle in. It burned sharply, but not as badly as she had expected. That is, until she pushed it all the way through, dragging the piece of catgut behind it. Fire burned through her face, into her ear, across her chest, then into her stomach, until she thought she might vomit, but she clenched her teeth closed and swallowed the bile down, breathed deeply through her nose. Then, she did it again. It was far worse the second time, and she quickly grew lightheaded. Harp kept the makeshift mirror as steady as he could, his musician's hands doing their best despite his obvious distress, and she wondered if he might vomit, too, out of sheer sympathy.

She was five stitches along, halfway done, her vision shifting between too bright and too dim as the pain began to make the blood rush in her veins, the way it did sometimes when she fought, when Harp said,

"Bella, I know you don't want to talk about this, but I need you to know that..." he broke off, and Penny paused after tugging the catgut too hard, allowing herself a few deep breaths until her vision cleared. She eyed Harp over the mirror, and his dark eyes shifted away, but then he straightened, and looked her squarely in the face. "I don't want you to take what I have to say the wrong way. Like I am...like I am one of those Achaeans."

She had just been about to push the needle through the skin a sixth time, but these words gave her pause. Her lips were pressed together, her breath dragging thinly through her nostrils, and she was afraid if she opened her mouth it would be to scream, so she kept silent, and waited for the nausea to pass. Blood seeped from the new wounds the needle made, dripping under the collar of her tunic in thin rivulets.

"I wanted to let you know that..er...I...well, I know you are supposed to fulfill certain requirements. To be Hearth Queen. And that...that maybe you can't. After the drink my mother gave you. But maybe you can. And one of these days you will need to find out. And that...er...well...ummm..."

She stared, her jaw throbbing with every heartbeat. Her lips were going numb from pressing them so tightly, and she dragged another deep breath, intentionally relaxing every muscle in her body as Orithyia had taught her, especially the ones in her jaw. Her skin felt hot, then cold, though she did not know if it was from the pain, or the garbled words of her friend. Harp gulped, and forged ahead.

"Er, time is...is of the essence, one might say. I've been told the ha-maza-ans have a time limit on these things, once the previous queen dies. So uh...so um, so, if you need to try, you know...I can. I'm not saying I *need* to. I mean I *would*. If I had to. Not if I *had* to. If you—"

"Harp."

His words ground to a halt. His breathing was almost as labored as hers, and his face betrayed the same panic she had seen when he thought Mursilis was about to cut her to pieces. She closed her eyes for a moment, focusing on her breaths, then returned her eyes to her reflection and shoved the needle through the wound a sixth time. The sharp burning had spread to her whole face, but she could not stop now. Three more stitches, each knotted tightly against her flesh. She poked the needle through a last time and tasted blood, but it was from biting the inside of her cheek. The catgut dragged and pulled, and there was so much blood on her fingers that she could barely see where to put the last stitch, but finally, the edges of the cut were together, and the worst of it was over. She stole a glance at his face while tying off the last stitch.

His beard had grown thick and full in their time on the road, giving him the appearance of a man instead of a gangly colt, but he was still every inch the satyr. His black eyes watched every movement of her fingers with intent worry, as though he could pull the pain from her wound with just the force of his will. She used her star-iron dagger to slice the end of the catgut as close as possible to her skin, then let her hands drop from her face, and tilted her chin for one final inspection in the silver buckle. Then, holding up a finger to indicate she needed more time before he could continue, she leaned to the side, turned her head away, and retched up the bile that had been pressing against the back of her throat the entire time.

Harp made noises of alarm, but Penny waved her hand, coughing and shuddering as the movements dragged at the stitches. When she sat straight again, wiping her lips carefully, Harp shoved his own wineskin into her hands. She tipped her head and opened her mouth awkwardly, painfully, and poured the terrible-tasting brew straight down her throat, only stopping when she needed air. When she lowered it, her head spun as much from pain as from the wine, but Harp's dark eyes were ever watchful, every steady in front of her, as they had been since that first day she had met him in the forest.

"Thank you," she croaked, handing the empty wineskin back to him. She swallowed, and let her stomach settle, hoping the wine would do its job soon. "For everything," she added softly, holding his gaze. "I...I don't know what my future is, Harp. If I cannot undo this vow I have sworn, then I cannot bring a child into this world knowing it will be cursed forever. But if I can..." she paused, searching his earnest, flushed face, and smiled gently. "If that is my destiny, then I shall accept your brave sacrifice to submit to my touch, and be honored."

His olive skin flushed to the roots of his hair, and he shook his head wildly. "I didn't mean it wouldn't be...I just don't want you to think..." he floundered to a stop, and Penny took pity on him. She reached out, her fingers still covered with her own blood, and he immediately grasped her reaching hand.

"You will never be like them. Like *him*, Harpalion. It is not in you."

His hand gripped her wrist with fierce urgency, as though they were searing a vow of fealty, the way queens and kings might do. Perhaps they were.

"No, it is not," he said, his voice once again steady, and sure. He shook his head, his eyes holding hers. "I never want you to think that is why I am here, Bella. I just want you to know I will help you in any way you need it. I will never be much with a sword and spear, despite Orithyia's teaching, so if there is another way I can help, and if that is what you want from me, then I will give it gladly."

"But it *would* be a sacrifice, yes?" she said softly.

His lips twisted, but his eyes searched hers with hopeful entreaty. He did not pretend to not understand. "I would not go so far as to say sacrifice, Bella. You are beautiful, after all. Even with that wound."

"But I am not who—or *what*—you...prefer."

He swallowed, and something like relief, or perhaps grief, made his mouth droop. There was a long silence before he answered. "No. But that has never mattered to my father." His eyes dropped to their clasped hands, which she did not let go.

"When we met, he was not just sending you after a horse, was he? He was banishing you for refusing to give him an heir, and securing his kingship. You only came back because you thought maybe I could be an answer to your problems. And now you are willing to give me an heir, to secure my throne, instead of his?"

Harp swallowed, but looked up again, his face stubbornly set, but also wary. "Yes. Mostly. The last part." He squirmed, but did not look away. "I don't expect you to believe me, but I did not take you to my father because I thought you...that you would solve any of my problems. That isn't what I wanted. I just thought you should not go alone to...to a village full of my father's men."

Penny smiled, believing him. She had suspected for some time that she was never going to be an object of this man's desires. She understood the way men looked at her, even more so after her encounter with Brekko, and there had never been any suggestion of that burning need in Harp's face when he looked at her. There had only ever been compassion, and curiosity, and perhaps something like affection, but never lust.

She considered the possibility of having a daughter by him. Of securing her place in Themiscyra's sisterhood as their Hearth Queen. A place she did not know if she would, or should, ever belong. She pictured the fierce women she had long since left behind, and some of those stolen on the Achaean ships. Sagitta and Toxaris and Molpadia, Melanippe and Cyra. She thought of poor Areto. All the women whom she now found herself missing with a fond longing that bordered on grief. She looked to the tent where Orithyia and General Mursilis sat outlined against the waxed canvas, their heads bent over a small table as they played some kind of strategy game the queen was so fond of. She had even grown fond of the irascible Defending Queen, despite how angry she was with the woman at the moment. The thought of never being a part of them, never fulfilling her Alsanti, brought a hollow despair to her insides that she had never before let herself feel. She had avoided thinking of it for a long time, ever since she had accepted that cup of snake-melon, but now, Harp's reminder of who and what she was supposed to be brought all that insecurity, that feeling of failure, and that undeniable longing to belong to someone, and to her own future, to the surface. She brought her attention back to Harp, who waited patiently, his hand still clasping hers.

"Hearth Queens are not supposed to reveal the fathers of their daughters, you know. My mother broke with tradition in letting me stay so long near mine, when I shouldn't have even known his name. When the fathers remain unknown, the Thrones remain secure from those who would seek to claim authority over the ha-mazaans. Not that any man ever could," she added bluntly. "What I am saying, is, your father would never even need to know."

"Well, the unfortunate part is that he would not care, if it was a daughter." Harp's words were matter-of-fact. Penny frowned, but Harp shrugged, his fingers warm over her wrist. "Only a son will matter to him. But the fact is, he does not deserve any child of mine to call him Grandfather, or carry on his name. So in that way, I would not want you to have a boy, as then I would have to claim him, and I would not want him to know the same fate I have known, if he was…if he was like me."

"Ah," Penny said, her voice sad. When she smiled again, it was full of sorrow, and also love. "No matter what, Harp, you will always be welcome with me, wherever I am. I would be happy to include any child of yours in that promise, daughter or son." But even as she said the words, her smile turned rueful, and she turned her hand to squeeze his. "I just can't promise that I will be in either Themiscyra, or Satra. I currently have no home to call my own, so I guess we can just be outcast together."

54

DOUBT

"If this small retinue is likely to intimidate this brother of yours, it won't be wise to bring the entire host upon him at once, and rouse him to violence out of defensiveness." Orithyia reined her horse around a steaming pile of dung one of the lead horses had left in its wake.

Penny wiped the back of her hand under her nose, which seemed to be constantly running in the cold. Even the queen appeared out of sorts in today's frigid weather. For once, Penny was not sorry for the woman's discomfort.

"My father's *bria* is high in the mountains, though there will be scouts throughout the lowlands. It may be best for me to continue on alone, and for the soldiers to remain below, as you say."

"I did not mean you'll go alone," Orithyia said.

"My father is—"

"Your father is a man, Penthesilea," the queen said, her voice flat with finality. "There is no reason to trust him, or this brother of yours."

Penny bit the inside of her cheek in an effort to keep silent. There was no point in arguing in her father's defense; the woman would not budge in her ideas about men, no matter how much honor Penny knew her father possessed. Still, Orithyia's insinuation that Thrax might not be overjoyed to see his daughter's return had been gnawing at Penny's thoughts the last three days. She resisted the urge to scratch at the stitches on her jaw as she mulled it over. They rode in silence a while longer, listening to the melody of harness and hooves, and the talk of men in front and behind, though all kept a respectful distance from the two women. It was only when Penny found her thoughts wandering up the long road to the *bria* of Perperikon, its flint grey stones sharp in her mind though she had not seen them for nearly ten years, that she ventured to ask another question, her voice coming out small and transparently hopeful.

"Do you think the oracle will actually release me from my vow?"

Orithyia glanced over at her from the other side of the road, where her horse was sneaking bits of dried autumn grass that poked through the snow. "I don't know," she said finally, and though it was not reassuring in the slightest, Penny was glad for her honesty.

"What will I say?"

"You will tell her the truth. That your mother forced you to—"

"My mother did not force me."

"She did not exactly teach you the different options you might have—"

"She did what she thought was best for me."

"If you could channel some of that stubbornness into your sword arm you would be much better served by it, girl," Orithyia said bluntly. "You will have to take your blinders off one of these days and see your mother was only doing what was best for *her*, and only she, and perhaps this oracle you swore to, knows why."

Penny pressed her lips together, but could not hold her tongue for long. "If the Oracles know so much, why would my mother not have had warning of what the Achaeans intended? If the Kebat did not warn anyone of such a thing, what good are they?"

"Who is to say they did not warn anyone? Specifically Antiope?"

"Obviously they didn't, or the Achaeans would have met our flaming arrows the moment their ships entered the Terme."

"Then why did Hippolyta send for my ha-mazaans that very first day?" Orithyia challenged. "I am told by your own women that Melanippe, too, was staunchly resistant to welcoming them, but her good sense was overruled by Antiope's vanity. This was not a problem with the Kebat, child. I think your mother knew exactly what she was doing, but something went wrong for the rest of you. Especially you, and every ha-mazaan now wandering the Otherworld, apparently including your mother."

A hot flush spread across Penny's chest, working its way up her neck until the words left her tongue hot and angry. "Are you saying my mother knowingly chose this fate?"

Orithyia shrugged, not meeting Penny's eyes. "I'm saying I would like to hear from your mother's own lips why she made you swear a vow that goes against everything a ha-mazaan lives for. Why she and her sisters are dead, and their city in ruins. I would like to hear why she drugged you and prevented you from Dreaming for your entire life in Themiscyra. But that will need to wait until we are together on the other side of the Gate, won't it? Right now, all I can say for sure is, Antiope died as she lived. Full of deceit."

Every breath burned Penny's lungs, and heat built up inside of her chest until she thought it might tear her apart. She could not draw her breath deeper or let it out fully, so it burned more, until her entire body became molten with rage. Her anger at Orithyia had only intensified since that morning with the General. Even if it had firmly convinced Penny she could face any man with the little courage she had, she had not forgiven the queen. The woman had to have known it would trigger her memories of being attacked by a man, and all the anxiety that came with those memories. Had used that knowledge to goad Penny's defenses into action. The fact that she had shown such little regard for Penny's feelings in the matter had built into a flame of slow-burning resentment in her, and now they flared into a full conflagration of fury.

"Would you cease this relentless campaign to malign my mother, you mean, leathery, *wretched* old hag? You're just jealous that my mother was beautiful and kind and loved by everyone, including men!" Penny was partly horrified, partly proud she had the nerve to say such things, but once the torrent of words began, an avalanche of hot coals tumbling over her lips, she could not hold them back. "No one has ever liked you that way, not even your own women, because you treat them like pig shit. Like they are disposable, and useless."

Orithyia's eyes were bright with their own fire, but Penny did not stop, and instead jerked Peyo to a halt in front of the Queen's horse, so she could direct the full force of her anger directly at the ha-mazaan's face.

"My mother did not betray her women for the sake of some man halfway across the world. She was already queen—twice over, in fact! She was queen beside my father, and she was queen beside her sister. And she would never have let me..." Her voice broke, and tears of anger closed off her throat. The queen stared at her flatly, without anger or even any acknowledgment of Penny's words at all, which only made matters worse.

"She had more honor than you have teeth, you *decaying* old bat. So don't ever speak to me of my mother again, because even if I cannot best you with star-iron, I can sure as the Goddess's fiery armpit burn your tent to the ground while you're *snoring* like a fat *boar*."

Seething with humiliation and frustration, Penny kicked her heels into Peyo's ribs and cantered ahead, weaving through the startled lines of men and horses, heedless of the tears on her face and their curious glances, or the fact that she had just threatened to murder Sinope's Defending Queen in her sleep. She turned her face away from Harp's curious stare and cantered past him, too, moving through the thickening fog until she reached the front of the line, where she reined Peyo into a fast walk behind the lead cavalry, grateful the men took one look at her face and let her be. She dared one quick glance over her shoulder, peering through the cold mist, but Orithyia had not followed. She felt a flash of shame at her behavior, but the anger was still there. She seethed alone, letting Peyo find his own way, mulling over Orithyia's words, and her own unkind response.

She should not have said those things, it was true, but the fact that the queen intimated that Antiope had known beforehand what the Achaeans would do to Themiscyra, to the ha-mazaans, to Penny...well, it was everything Penny had been trying to avoid thinking on her own. Nothing made sense. Why Hippolyta had sent for Sinope's ha-mazaans before the Achaean ships had settled on the shore made no sense, especially if Antiope had vetoed both Lyta and Melanippe in turning the ships away. Obviously, her aunt's suspicions had been aroused, and it was possible she had not only sensed danger, but also had forewarning from the Kebat in Themiscyra. But if that were true, Antiope would never have overruled her Defending Queen's orders. Would she?

It was Orithyia's constant questioning of Penny's oath that was most confusing, though. Why had her mother never wanted Penny to learn the ha-mazaan ways? Why would she not have wanted a daughter who could protect herself, rather than rely on everyone around her to do that protecting? Why had she gone so far down the path of hospitality as to welcome danger into their home, and make it inevitable that Penny would be hurt? *Worse* than hurt.

The fact that she now had this worm of suspicion eating at her heart, conflicting her thoughts about her own mother, made Penny sick with shame. Her mother had been captive to men, enduring only the Goddess knew what horrors before her death, and here Penny was being corrupted by innuendo, influenced by the jealous slander of an old hag. Only, Orithyia was one who had helped Penny, who had offered her advice and sanctuary in her time of need, and who had actively taken steps to ensure Penny could be free of the curse she had unleashed. She knew the queen was not alone in her suspicions of Antiope. Toxaris and Molpadia and likely many more held the same view, but there was no way to know the truth, when her mother's body likely lay at the bottom of the Zalapa, and the truth of the matter with her.

Penny did not know who to trust, or who to turn to. She only hoped her father would have wisdom on the matter, and that the Oracle she sought in her father's lands could explain some things that only the Great Mother seemed to know. And if Orithyia was right about Thrax, too, then Penny did not know what she would do. If her father loved her as little as Orithyia suspected, and was not willing to offer his help, Penny would be alone in the world, because she would not be returning to Themiscyra alone, childless, a failure as Ishassara for the Hearth Throne, and a threat to the ha-mazaan's very survival.

55

SATRA

The small army of fifty men and two women arrived at the narrow Perperishka valley, an undulating, sparsely forested river basin bordering Satra lands, on the eve of the full Frost Moon. The winds drifted fingers of ice over their huddled figures, their bodies small against the towering peaks surrounding the valley. Snow had begun to fall in earnest, making travel difficult and even treacherous through some of the higher passes. Penny was relieved to find the surrounding landscape growing familiar, recognizable by the twist of a familiar tree trunk or the burnt-out shell of one that had been struck by lightning when she was barely old enough to sit a horse on her own. When she alerted General Mursilis that they had crossed into Satraen lands, he agreed the valley bottom was a good place to set up camp.

For some reason, the man held a grudging respect for her after she had managed to stab him, though she was certain it would not be the case if she had not been so good with a needle and catgut, or at keeping infection from entering his wound. They had come to an understanding, though he still pressed her to the very edges of her limit on a daily basis, and merely grunted his approval whenever she made progress. Toward Harp, the man was more favorable, and in fact openly praised his achievements. Penny had noticed the change in Harp, too. He held himself with more confidence now, more ease when amongst the soldiers, but it was still at night, with his harp in his hands and his voice raised to praise the beauty of the stars that he came alive, that he became fully himself. Penny glanced at him now, her smile anxious, and he smiled back, though his fingers twitched on the reins. Lately, because of the wet weather, he had not been able to play the harp while on the road, but Penny was sure he would have calmed her nerves with a simple strum of the strings had he been able to.

"We may be here for two weeks, or two months," Mursilis said to Orithyia. "Your spies from the west will need to pass through this land if they follow you by road. It is as good a place as any to merge together."

Orithyia nodded her agreement, peering northwest toward the imposing Rhodope Mountain, and Perperikon. "Aye, as you say, General. Evandre best be here by the Cold Moon, though, else we will be waiting the entire winter in this valley, likely buried to our armpits in snow."

The man shrugged, and wiped beads of ice from his long mustache. "I can think of worse places to winter. My men will cut those trees for shelter and stables," he said, pointing to the eastern edge of the river, where stands of beech and ash, naked except for the frost clinging to their bark, stretched their thin arms toward the ivory sky. "If the girl's father is amenable, we will hunt the hills for food, and the horses will have plenty to graze on until the real snows fall. We will harvest as much as we can before then."

Penny listened to their plans with half an ear, her own eyes on the mountain ahead. She found the distinctive cut in the trees that indicated the road she knew would be there, snaking its way from the base of the mountain to the upper fortress. She was within a few hours' ride of her father, and her father's people. *Her* people. So why did she feel this pit in her stomach, as though every decision that had brought her to this place, back to the one person in the world she was sure she could count on, had been the foolish, *foolish* choice of a child? Everything in her wanted to ride in the opposite direction, and order everyone else to do the same. To abandon their quest for further help from this man who had once tossed her in the air like a squealing pig, only to catch her just before she hit the ground. Why had she thought the man who lived here now would be the same as then, after she had been gone for so long? It was foolish to think he would be. Foolish to assume he would want to see her again at all, just as Orithyia had said, let alone lend her his army.

Her eyes caught a movement among the trees at the edge of the mountain, in the cut line that separated the road from the forest. A moment later, a flash of silver among the grasping finger bones of the trees. She leaned forward across Peyo's withers, her focus sharp between his golden ears, until she was sure of what she saw.

"Orithyia, General Mursilis! Riders approach."

At once the soldiers formed ranks, with Mursilis in front, and when Orithyia nodded to Penny to follow her, she found herself beside the Eneti general. Her stomach knotted into a fist as the first riders emerged from the forest. The lead riders each carried a standard, their poles fit snugly into a ring on the edge of their saddle so that the rider only had to hold it upright. At the top of the first pole, the head of a wolf, its mouth gaping open to show the curved fangs, the ears permanently pricked. The emblem of the Dacii. The second pole was topped with a bronze hand, the thumb and first two fingers upright and slightly apart, the last two fingers curved inwards to the palm. It was her father's own standard; a real hand severed from a conquered enemy, forever embalmed in bronze casting, promising any future or perceived enemy that a personal meeting Sabazios would soon be their reward if they dared set their might against the Bessi priest and Satrean King. Penny's eyes scanned the riders for the familiar broad shoulders and red beard of her father, the knot in her stomach twisting tight at the thought of him being part of them, of their reunion happening before she was fully prepared, then tightening further when she realized he was not among the approaching men, and she must wait for his possible rejection even longer.

"It is my brother's people," Penny said to Orthyia's demands for details. "And a few from the Satrae. I don't see my father among them."

"Shall we ride to meet them?" Orithyia said, and nudged her horse forward without waiting for an answer.

Penny clicked her horse to follow, and the General did the same, waving a signal to his men to remain behind. The three of them were barely within arrow shot of Glinn's men when Orithyia reined in her gelding and looked to Penny.

"I think it would be best if you put your negotiating skills to good use from this point on. We don't need my mean mouth clouding the waters."

Penny opened her mouth to protest but Orithyia simply nodded her head sideways at the two riders splitting off from the other group to approach them, and Penny knew now was not the time to discuss the harsh words both had been avoiding since Penny had spoken them.

"Go on," the ha-mazaan said. "At the first sign of trouble, we will be launching our arrows. Don't forget, girl, you have a sword now. And you are allowed to use it."

Penny huffed a laugh at the thought of facing her brother or any of these men single-handedly, with barely more than two full moons of sword training under her belt, but she rode forward alone, straightening her spine.

The riders who rode forward to meet her looked familiar; one bore the wolf head of the Dacii, and one wore the checkered green of her own grandmother's tribe, his face a familiar square of ruddy complexion and close-cropped russet beard. Penny kept her eyes on that one as they drew closer together. She could see by the expression on the man's face that he was not expecting a woman.

"Hello, Cormu!" Penny called to him in her father's language. Her father's general and brother, her own uncle, crumpled his brow in confusion to hear his own language from an apparent stranger, and he peered at her face, the white sky behind her blinding his vision.

"Name yourself," Cormu called back, his eyes going to Orithyia and Mursilis several lengths behind her, then to the fifty mounted men behind them, their bows ready to draw at the first sign of trouble.

"I have two names," Penny replied formally, her tongue slipping into the language of her childhood as easily as an otter into water. "On the ninth day of my life, the Elders of Perperikon called me Penthesilea, as they sang songs of mourning for all that I would endure in this life, and wept to Sabazios for my suffering. But on the first day, my father, King Thrax, called me Bellatrix, for all that I would accomplish in his name. A beautiful warrior for his people. So I am known."

Cormu's mouth fell open in shock. She kept her expression carefully composed as his eyes searched her face, then her clothing, looking for the young girl of eight who had stubbornly refused to give up her bed with the leopards under the starry sky even when her uncle was sent to finally bring her inside. He did not see that child. He found a woman grown, though there was something in her face he must have finally recognized.

Her father's eyes, perhaps. Or her mother's hair, in braids tucked into her wide leather belt.

The second man with the wolf's head frowned at her. "Thrax's girl is in the east with the woman who took her, to be with the man-killers and the breastless women who eat their sons."

Penny bit her cheek to keep from laughing. She had heard these slurs before, of course, but to hear them spoken to her from her own people made the insults even more ludicrous.

"I was in the east, yes, with Antiope, the woman who was once your Queen, but I go west now. I seek the protection of Thrax's sword, and the hospitality of his family for those who accompany me." They could not deny such a request without impeding their own honor, she knew, but it was a stretch to think her brother would welcome her with open arms, let alone an entire army of foreign men and women.

"You bring an army to invade the lands of Glinn, son of Thrax, and ask for his hospitality?" the Daci said contemptuously.

Penny's stomach turned cold, and the knot in her belly tightened into a fist. *The lands of Glinn, son of Thrax...* Was her father already gone through the Gate? Had she come all this way, worried all this time, for nothing? The idea that he might be dead had never entered her mind. She sat stupefied for a moment, her tongue unable to utter the words that her mind was too fearful to settle on, until Cormu broke the awkward silence, his eyes still searching her face with a curious intensity as he responded to his companion's argument.

"Thrax has granted these lowlands to his son Glinn, for vineyards and winemaking, yes, but the king will welcome his lost daughter home to his highlands without question, I am sure."

The knot loosened, allowing Penny to breathe again in relief that her fears were unfounded, but the Daci pointed his chin at the men behind her, scowling.

"Why should Glinn welcome armed men to trample his fields and drink his wine? Your army has no business here, even if you are Thrax's daughter as you say."

"My brother should welcome this army because it is my own," Penny said, locking eyes with the man whose name she did not know, and who had disregarded the courtesies of hospitality in withholding it from her. "I am seeking kin who will help me find justice. In the meantime, I am seeking the hospitality of those who share my blood. This is not something even one such as Glinn can refuse without losing honor. If you deny me or my companions this, both you and my brother shall lose favor with Thrax, and with Sabazios, Son of Bendis, Who sees all deeds of men under the moon and sun. I will wait for your decision."

The Daci man's jaw clenched in anger, knuckles white on the ash pole of the wolf standard, but he knew she was right. He reined his horse in a tight circle and spurred it to a gallop, returning to his own small contingent. Cormu nodded his head with a slight smile and Penny smiled back across the distance, and they nudged their horses forward, closing the gap between them. When he was near enough, he swung down from his horse and strode toward her with the same grin she remembered from so many years ago. She dismounted, and immediately found herself swept into a hug that felt as though a bear were squeezing her ribs.

"Welcome home Bellatrix, daughter of Thrax," Cormu grinned, releasing her enough to hold her at arm's length with one hand on each of her shoulders, and Penny smiled back. "It is good to see you, Niece."

"It's good to see you, too, Cormu. Are you well? And my father?"

"Aye, I am well, girl, as is your father. Thrax hunts in the northern forest these last three days. He will be overjoyed to know his daughter has returned to him, and as a real woman now. And what a woman." Cormu's green eyes inspected her from head to toe, lingering for a moment on the short sword at her waist, then the line of fresh stitches along her jaw, but he only raised an eyebrow before saying, "I will send a messenger to him immediately. You will stay for a while?"

Penny hesitated a moment before nodding. "I will stay long enough to see my father, Cormu, but there is a task I must do here, and then another after I finish here. It is possible we will have an even bigger army joining us soon. I have come to...to ask for Thrax's aid, and his army, if he is willing and able."

Cormu's forehead drew into a worried frown, but he simply nodded, and gave her shoulder a hearty pat. "You and your people are welcome here for as long as you need respite, as you know, though only your father can command the armies. Come, bring your men, and we will be in the hunting camp by nightfall, sharing stories of how you come to lead an army of men."

When Penny shook her head, Cormu paused. "I will come alone, Cormu. The rest will stay here and wait for the others, though I would have Glinn's word they will be welcome to hunt in the forest and make camp without interference, or violence."

"Ah," he said, and smiled. "Just you, then, though be warned Imbrasus will continue his grumbling on behalf of you brother. Let's not waste time, young Bellatrix. I am most curious to hear your story, and my wife is going to be thrilled to hear everything about your time in the east with the man-eat...with the ha-mazaans."

56

THRAX

Penny remembered everything about her childhood surroundings quite differently than she was experiencing it now. Especially Glinn. To be truthful, she did not remember her brother very well at all, because she had barely known him as a child. He had certainly been less imposing, then. And everything else had been more grand, more opulent when she remembered it in her mind. Now it all felt foreign, and awkward, like a language she had once heard but had never fully learned. It felt nothing like home.

The tents that had once seemed vast and cavernous, holding intricately crafted trays and mirrors and braziers of beaten gold or bronze, some pilfered, some newly created, with every stretch of felt and canvas smelling of pine incense, now seemed cramped and crowded beyond capacity, with no room for a person to sit comfortably without being overshadowed by some thickly woven rug hanging from the poles. She sat as her host sat; cross-legged and stiff, her back braced by a thick horse-hair blanket that itched her shoulder blades and reminded her with every uncomfortable poke that, though this is where she had been whelped and raised, it was no longer her home, and she was not as welcome as she might have wished to be.

"And you wish us to help you?"

Glinn, nearly a full year younger than her, was already broad of shoulder and thick of limb, with a ruddy complexion after only a few years of being weathered by sun and rain and hard work. His thick, dusky red hair was plaited in twin ropes that hung on either side of a beard the same color, every braid wrapped with wide leather straps and secured by golden beads etched with the figure of Sabazios on a horse, whose hooves treaded on the head of a dragon. The only similar trait they obviously shared was their father's eyes, though Penny was beginning to think perhaps their shared love of silence was also inherited from their father. The serious, no-nonsense boy Penny remembered had grown even more sober and severe in his countenance in the ten years since she had seen him, and he regarded her now with contemptuous disdain that did not so much catch her off guard as it did exhaust her.

"I am asking for the help of my father's people, yes," she replied, wanting to shift her legs to allow some blood flow once more, but not wanting to give him the satisfaction of squirming under his forbidding stare. She stiffened her spine instead, the horse-hair blanket a welcoming discomfort that kept her rigidly upright. "I do not think it is too much to ask that my own kin aid me in a time of need."

Glinn grunted and tugged at his beard. "We owe no allegiance to you, or Antiope of the Amazons. She made her choice years ago, and so did you."

"I did not come here to listen to your whining, brother. I will wait in peace for our father if you have nothing civil to say."

"Our father whelped a frightened rabbit, it would seem, scared of words that cannot even hurt her."

"I was whelped to be a hunter, and a Bessi priestess, *and* a ha-mazaan Queen," Penny replied, raising her chin, "and you are probably no better with a bow now than you were ten years ago."

"Oh ho!" Glinn laughed without humor. "Let's go into the yard right now and see what kind of chance you stand against my axe, sister. I don't need a flimsy bow. I will cut you into fodder for the pigs before you can unsheathe your pathetic sword."

"You will feel those pigs' teeth rooting through your guts in search of yesterday's breakfast if you harm a hair on my daughter's head, Glinn son of Glannys."

"Father!"

Every intention of a poised, respectable reception fled as her father's rich, deep timbre filled the tent, followed closely by his dark auburn head as he bent under the heavy felt of the doorway. Penny lurched to her knees as Thrax unfolded his tall, broad frame, filling the space with his familiar, beloved, desperately missed presence. She flung herself into his arms with an unrestrained screech of delight, her worries of rejection flying from her thoughts.

"Oof!" he grunted with exaggerated dismay, but his arms were already tight around her shoulders and his body barely swayed from the impact of her full weight. "You're not as small as you once were to be flying at me so, Daughter."

Penny hugged him back, inhaling the sweet smells of pine and leather, the heady scents of horse sweat and the rolled leaves he smoked every night after a meal without fail, along with the peculiar, musky scent of his feline companions that incessantly marked him with their whiskered rubs. The strange mixture of it all that could only belong to her father, and that she had not known until this moment how much they had been missed. The smells brought back so many memories of them together. The memories ignited every anguished longing she had struggled to control, from the day she had left this place without saying goodbye, never knowing if she would ever see him again. But she was here, and his familiar arms, strong as the oak inscribed on the chain around his neck, were around her once more, assuring her she was safe, and missed, and maybe even still loved.

"What's this, then?" Thrax said softly, still hugging her tightly but one hand moving to support the back of her head, tugging at one braid. "Does the sight of your decrepit old father disturb you so much that you must cry about it?"

Penny laughed, as he had intended, but the tears flowed hot against her cheeks, soaking the front of his woolen tunic. She had not realized how much she craved her father's solid, dependable presence, and how much she feared she would never have it again. Now, after all these years, she could finally relax, could finally let her guard down, could stop pretending she was capable of everything, the perfect answer for everyone's expectations. She could just be. Her father would take care of everything. When she finally quieted, he pulled away to look into her face, his expression a mixture of concern and joy.

"Look at you," Thrax breathed, awe apparent in his voice as his eyes raked her tall, lean frame from head to toe and back again. He pulled her back in for another tight hug.

"It's good to see your face, Bella," he said softly. "I did not think I would ever see you again."

The wool of the green cloth and its fine embroidery at his chest were rough against the wetness of her cheeks as she smiled. She had almost forgotten what it was like to hear him speak his preferred name for her. She pulled away, though only enough to peer into his kind, weathered face as he smiled down at her. She had also forgotten how tall he was. Penny remembered him as huge, since she had only been a gangly, skinny child when she had last seen him, but even now that she was a woman, she still felt shrouded by the enormity of the man who was her father.

"You were the only one who called me that until recently. I've missed it," Penny said.

Thrax raised his eyebrows. "Called you Bella? Do they only call you Pigpen in Themiscyra, then?"

Penny sniffed and raised her chin. "Only you ever accused me of being messy, father."

"Because you are," Thrax said, eyebrows raised further in innocence. "Do you mean to say Antiope finally trained you to clean up after yourself? I won't be tripping over your blankets and tunics and pieces of pinecone artwork everywhere I walk now?"

"Does that mean I can stay?"

He peered at her with affectionate humor, but now there was an added gleam of consideration in his brown eyes. Her own eyes, mirrored back to her with infinitely more wisdom. The color of them was warm and rich, neither dark nor tawny but something in between, like aged copper, the shape of them square and wide, which on him served to quell his opponents with their forthright, piercing stare, but on Penny only gave the constant appearance of guileless wonder. Still, she had sought her father's memory many times in Themiscyra by looking for those eyes in mirrors and slow-moving streams, when the loneliness had overwhelmed her.

Somehow, he managed to raise his eyebrows another fraction as he considered her comment. With a hint of reproach, he said, "I did not think my hospitality towards my own daughter would ever be in doubt."

She wondered if his statement was meant for her, or for his son, who still sat at the brazier behind them, silent until now, but when Thrax looked over her shoulder with a warning gleam in his eye, she knew it was not for her. She relaxed, and smiled up at her father.

"Thank you, father. Truly." Penny hugged him again, quickly and tightly, before stepping away. "I have missed you."

"And I you, Bella," he said, smiling at her once again, but his eyes searched her face, resting on the stitches on her jaw. "I cannot wait to feast with you, and hear your story of what great fortune brings you back to me. Or," he continued, examining her eyes again, "perhaps you will tell me what troubles you face that give your eyes such sorrow, and brings you all this way with an army of men, and only one of your ha-mazaan tribe." He didn't wait for a response before turning to the doorway, holding the flap aside and motioning her underneath it.

"Come, daughter. We will go to my own tents. I think this is a story that does not bear waiting. Glinn," he said, as Penny ducked under his arm and into the crisp blue night, "see to a new tent for my Bellatrix, would you? And make sure she has plenty of blankets. I still don't believe that she doesn't make a mess of them when she sleeps, and I don't want her freezing to death before we can even spend a day hunting together."

The moment Penny emerged from the tent, a large furry head prodded at her hand, while an even larger furry body blocked her way. She halted, having little choice in the matter, and looked at them in wonder.

"Begri's cubs?"

Her father's favorite leopard had been well past her prime before Penny left Satra, so these had to be Begri's offspring. Thrax nodded, his hand going to the fur around his shoulders.

"Begri still watches over me, and you," he said softly, as his remaining leopards, his constant companions in battle, in hunting, and even in sleep, investigated every inch of her they could reach without standing on their hind legs. Penny remained as still as possible, only lifting her arms when one of them demanded to sniff the underside of her elbow.

"They remember you," Thrax said, smiling. "That one is Calla. Remember her?"

Calla inspected Penny's ribs with insistent pressure and a soft rumbling purr. "She moped for a full moon after you left, searching every hillock and copse for your warm hugs. As did I, I will add, though it was a lot longer than one moon. Indeed," he said softly, his eyes studying her face in the torchlight, "I never stopped."

Warmth spread through her, flushing her cheeks, and she smiled shyly. This man had once been so familiar, still felt familiar, yet he was virtually a stranger by now. But perhaps not as much of a stranger as Penny must be to him. The girl who had left him had become someone else entirely, and he had not been there for any of those changes. She wanted to apologize, to tell him she had never wanted to leave, to explain how often she thought of him and his deep voice singing her to sleep at night while these very cats curled their warm bodies against her, how everything had gone wrong, how she had failed to live up to the name he had given her, that she had not been a beautiful warrior when she needed to be the most. Her thoughts hammered inside her head, but they would not come out, and she met his smile with a pained silence.

"Come," Thrax said, sparing Penny the need to respond. He began walking towards the rising moon in the west, the white crescent crisp and slit like a cat's curious eye against the indigo sky. His two big cats immediately retreated from smelling her legs to follow their beloved master into the night, and Penny in turn followed them.

Glinn's tent sat near the center of the grounds, but her father's pavilion was tucked back against the base of the mountain, alongside the small, swiftly flowing river and well covered by the shade of the trees for the days when the sun shone bright. The rustling of late autumn leaves dried on the branch and rush of water drowned out the noises of the camp behind them, so that when her father lifted the tent flap and ushered her through, only the sound of water and trees speaking their slow lullaby made it past the heavy felt of the tent walls.

Thrax's tent held several rooms, each sectioned from the other with beautiful woven tapestries showing Satra's fierce and beautiful horses, some roaming free, some pulling chariots, some engaged in battle with their hooves and crushing teeth, all as white as the snow that blanketed this land in winter. The main room they entered was lit brightly with tall bronze and gold braziers, the base of each of them intricately detailed with the bodies of naked priestesses, along with horse and griffin, leopard and aurochs. Incense burned alongside apple and birch and oak, so that the air smelled thickly of the prayers Penny remembered chanting along with her father as a young child. The smell was so poignant, so powerfully reminiscent that more tears immediately sprang into her eyes. Through their glistening, she watched as both leopards stalked with lazy, deceptive indifference to one of the larger braziers to throw themselves at the base of it, where the heat was the most intense. They watched Thrax intently as he moved to the cushions piled on the floor, motioning for Penny to sit amongst them. When she had settled herself, he offered her a rug, the brightly colored checkered length of it a welcome warmth, though the interior of the tent was cozy and dry. Thrax stoked the fire to a bone-warming blaze before turning to her with a somber expression.

"Now, Daughter. Tell me why I Dreamed of you every turning of the moon for ten years, and I see you in that place, but you do not hear or see me? Tell me why, instead of your song and your laugh, those dreams are filled with blood and terror, and worse, your tears falling from the face of the moon. Tell me why there are shadows in your eyes that the very woman who took you away promised would never appear. And tell me," he said, his tone one of command as much as supplication, "why the woman I once called my lover, my queen, is trying to rebirth a prophecy she has already fulfilled long ago?"

57

RELEASE

Penny's thoughts spun like the tassels on the border of the tent's ceiling, twirling this way and that as they were buffeted by Thrax's words. She opened her mouth to answer at least one of his questions, but the answer to all of them made her throat close and words disappear into a fog of nothingness. By the time his last question registered in the fogged recesses of her mind, her hands automatically accepting the plate of food he offered, he was already settling onto a pillow opposite her, his expression one of expectant waiting.

"What do you mean, 'trying to rebirth a prophecy she has already fulfilled?'" She held the plate at an awkward angle as her muscles stopped working, the way a hind freezes at the scent of a wolf, an uncomfortable sensation working its way down her spine.

Thrax regarded her with a mildly reproachful look. "Are you not paying attention to your Dreams, daughter?"

Penny looked at her plate of food to avoid his searching gaze, tilting it upright at the last moment to save the food from falling. He had given her a chunk of dark bread, a wedge of hard, crumbly cheese and a pat of soft, ripe-smelling goat cheese, as well as a palm-full of tiny red berries and hazelnuts. Her stomach growled and her mouth watered at the sight of food that was not boiled grains in water, but she did not taste it. Instead, she lowered it to her lap, her eyes tracing the pattern carved on the edge of the wooden plate so she would not have to witness the disappointment on her father's face as she quietly confessed,

"I did not Dream for many years after I left here."

Thrax was silent for several breaths, but his voice was full of curiosity, not disappointment, when he asked, "You have much to tell me, Bella. I hope you will share. Tell me why you are here."

Penny took a deep breath, before straightening her spine and steeling herself for what she had come to do. She nodded, even more afraid to look her own father in the eyes at the thought he had already Seen what she was too afraid to tell him. There was another long pause, in which she was desperately trying to find the words to begin, to find the part of the story that was the beginning, without going all the way back to the moment she had hugged him in what she had not realized would be a final goodbye.

"I came to ask for your help, father. I would ask that you ride with us to Athens, and help me ...help me avenge my mother, and take back a daughter of Themiscyra who was stolen. There is much to tell you about that, and I will. But..." she bit her lip, and her eyes slid away from his.

"But?" he prodded gently, and she could feel the weight of his eyes as though they could see into the very heart of her. She squirmed at the thought of what he might see there, but it was time to tell him, to admit what had truly brought her here. There was no use delaying it any longer, even if it meant she would no longer have his respect.

"I have broken a sacred vow," she said, her voice small and scared despite how much she tried to be brave. Still, she did not look at him, though she no longer saw the food on her plate, either. She repeated the words, to ensure he understood. "I have broken the blood-sworn oath I made to harm none. And..." she swallowed, trying to rescue her voice, but it was being swallowed by thick tears. She pushed the last words out through a closed throat. "I cursed everyone around me by doing it."

She told as much as she could, and though at first it was hard to know what to say, as the story unfolded, the words came easier, and soon they poured out of her without thought or care, until she found herself once again at the door of the bathhouse, and she was washing the blood of Areto's birthing from her arms, and then Brekko was there with her.

When Penny's breathing became labored and her words faltered, Calla rose from her place near the fire and spread herself against Penny's left thigh, offering her back as a steady, warm support while Penny struggled to find a way to tell her story with any sense of dignity. She began to cry, and then shake, and she buried her hand in the soft fur of the big cat for comfort but she did not stop speaking lest she lose the ability altogether, and soon she was being suffocated by the humid air all over again, feeling everything, feeling *him*, feeling the way the knife had sunk into his belly the same as it would into the belly of a stag, how it had dragged and burned the muscles in her forearms to tear it upwards, how she had felt only relief as the light went out in his eyes, how the pumice could not scrape the feel of him from her flesh afterward but she tried anyway, how she wanted to stay underwater and never surface. How she could hear ha-mazaans outside, but they never came. Then she was in the Tower with the Flame, and the smell of smoke was in her nostrils though it could have been from the brazier's incense wafting upwards through the vent in the ceiling. She told how she had watched Theseus hold a knife to her mother's throat, then how she had looked on helplessly as her aunt was murdered, stabbed through the chest, Heracles tearing her zoster from her limp body. She told him of the Erinyes, and waking up to a Flame gone cold, further cursing her city, further condemning her. She told him about so many ha-mazaans laid on that beach, dead or dying. How she had learned first of her mother's kidnapping, then of her death, and more recently, of her supposed part in drugging Penny so that she could not Dream. She told him everything the Kebat had revealed, everything Themiscyra's oracle had instructed, as confusing as it all was. She told him of Harpalion's voice singing away her pain, and how she had drunk an elixir that meant she may never have children, may never be Hearth Queen, and now she was here and could not trust anyone, even herself, or her memories of her own mother. She told him of Orithyia's deal with her to become a true ha-mazaan. How learning to fight had given her a renewed sense of purpose, and a strength that Brekko had sought to steal from her, but she was sure it meant forfeiting her right to the Hearth Throne.

She told him everything that had brought her to this tent, pushing some words through strangling tears, some of them through burning anger, until finally, she was speaking of this moment, of her joy at finally being reunited with her father after missing him for so long, and she looked him squarely in the face for the first time since beginning the tale. His eyes were full of more pain and sorrow than she had ever witnessed in his rugged face, and the kindness there, the unfiltered, unshakable love, was finally her undoing. As her words came to an end, Thrax simply opened his arms, and Penny did not even think before crawling into them. He held her as she cried the last of her tears, though the hottest of them had already been shed, and the way he held her and stroked her hair, murmuring softly as both cats came to offer their solace on either side, their great heads butting into Penny and Thrax and their purrs rumbling loud in the tent, soothed Penny's spirit in a way she had been desperate for all this time.

Eventually, her weeping quieted, Thrax murmured against her hair, "I'm sorry, Bella. I'm sorry I was not there to protect you. I'm sorry you carry this pain in you. I'm sorry I cannot heal it. But if my love for you can be a balm on your wounds, know there is no vow you can break, no words you can say that will make me love you any less. I will always be proud of you. I wish I could undo what has been done to you, and to your mother, but I promise that whatever it is you would ask of me, if it is within my power, I will give it to you gladly."

She cried more, then, not knowing how she had longed to hear those words of support, of comfort. When she had quieted once more, she rubbed her cheek against the rough wool of his tunic, breathing in the scent of him, at once familiar and strange. The big cats still purred next to them, settled on either side of her legs as warm, bracing bulwarks. Penny reached out one hand to stroke Calla's back, and took courage from the feel of her thick fur under her fingers to ask what she feared the most.

"Are all of my people doomed because of what I have done?"

Thrax was silent for so long she knew what his answer would be. Slowly, though his arms resisted letting go, she pushed away from him, until the worried shadows of his eyes were clear. She searched his face, her apprehension returning.

Thrax met her eyes, his expression one of troubled unease. "You swore a vow by your own blood, sealing it with honey from the Mother Herself, and the fact you have broken it—even for the righteous cause of defending your own honor—means you are likely cursed by the Fates themselves, daughter. Once the Moirai unleash their Erinyes as punishment, they will never let you rest. Do you understand?" He waited for her jerky nod.

"But it is not for me to say whether or not your curse affects those around you," Thrax continued slowly. "There is only one who can tell you such a thing, or undo what has been done, as your Kebat has already said. I am still astonished Antiope knew where to find her, but...she was the best tracker I have ever known. I just wonder why she made you..." he broke off, shaking his head.

Penny stared at her hands. She had hoped her father would simply tell her it was alright, that she was merely entertaining childish fears and fantasies, that the dark shadow which haunted her waking and sleeping was not, after all, the consequence she so feared. She had always known her father would not lie to her, though.

"Tell me again, Bella, of what your Kebat said to you in her mountain cave. I would have the exact words, if you can remember."

Penny glanced up, frowning. "Marpe asked me for the same thing," she said. "Why is everyone so suspicious of her, needing her exact words? Surely she cannot tell a lie?"

Thrax shook his head, his expression guarded. "Oracles do not lie, Daughter. But be assured they will obscure the truth for their own ends."

"Their own ends? They are the Mouthpiece of Kubileya. Of Sabazios. What 'ends' do they have, other than to reveal Truth?"

Thrax laughed softly, a caustic tone to the sound that Penny was unfamiliar with.

"You may be surprised, Bella," was all he said, and then lifted his eyebrows expectantly.

Sighing, Penny repeated the Kebat's words, this time without the filter she had used for Marpe. Thrax rubbed a hand over his bearded face when she finished, and his sigh betrayed his weariness. When his golden eyes met hers, they were clouded with grief, and another, less distinguishable emotion that Penny could not quite decipher. Suddenly, her father stood, his swift, supple rise from the floor belying his age, and the two big cats were immediately at his side, leaving Penny to stare up in confusion.

"Come, Bellatrix," Thrax said softly, his hand extended toward her. As she took it, letting him pull her to her feet, he said, "Time for rest. Hopefully, your baths have been made ready, and your tent warmed for an evening of sleep, and healing. I will send Calla to stay with you, so that you are not alone, and in the morning, we will ascend to Perperikon. There is something there I must show you. Then, you will know that, though an Oracle may not lie, they certainly do not tell you enough of the Truth to make any sense of things."

58

PERPERIKON

Penny sank lower into the deliciously hot water until it sloshed over the high edges of the copper tub, relishing its heat on her skin, the smell of incense burning nearby, and the watchful eyes of Calla from the corner of the small tent. Eyes that reminded her of Harp's. After so many weeks of furtive bathing in frozen streams or cursory wipes with a damp cloth dirtier than her own skin, to have a bath, a *real* bath full of steaming, clean water carted in from the fire by her father's servants, was the most luxurious treat she could have asked for. Just as luxurious was the ability to be alone, with only the big cat for company. Peyo was close outside, his jealousy and distaste for the cat were a palpable thing. As much as she was delighted to be back with her father, and to have his assurance of love and support, telling her story in all its raw, brutal honesty had stripped away her last protective shield between her and the pain.

Now, everything inside of Penny felt exposed, raw, as though she had flayed the skin from her soul to let the wound there ooze out everything rotten. As painful as it was, she hoped it would be able to heal, now. She just needed to give it time. Time in her father's city, with her father's love and care, just as she had known she needed. She wondered what he had to show her in Perperikon. She pondered the possibilities as she bathed, and as she settled into the soft warm furs on the cot afterward, Calla's purring lulling her into an easy sleep.

The following morning Thrax ordered everyone, including Glinn, to strike their tents and return to their respective villages, whether or not they were finished hunting, his tone unyielding in the face of widespread resistance. Glinn grumbled loudly, blaming Penny with ill-concealed hostility, but she simply rested her hand on her sword hilt and made gnashing

343

motions with her mouth in his direction, reminding him that ha-mazaans were man-eaters with every clash of her teeth. He reddened with anger but said no more, and went about his work, leaving her to find Thrax and Cormu in order to begin to ascent to the *bria*.

The journey took the better part of the day, but thankfully the sun shone bright, and Penny's spirits were further buoyed as both her father and Cormu regaled her with tales of the last ten years and she did her best to tell them of her time in Themiscyra, and all the amazing exploits of the ha-mazaans she lived with. When the citadel at Perperikon finally came into view, Penny was stunned to see how small it was compared to what she remembered. Though the stone blocks making up the castle's outer walls were each big as an ox, the total circumference was only half of what Themiscyra's outer wall was, and the citadel itself was squat and flat, with short battlements of wood built into the top. For the second time, she realized just how grand her ha-mazaan city truly was. Or had been, before the fire. She remembered Theseus' awe as he had marveled at the palace's architecture, and now, his comments made more sense to her. In her mind, her father's home had been just as grand, but now as she returned to it with a perspective much changed, much broadened, she realized Perperikon may be the grandest fortification in all of Thrakia, but nothing would rival the home her mother had taken her to rule.

Thrax's mood visibly changed as they passed the citadel gates, though he greeted everyone with broad smiles of welcome. Penny thought they might stop to take a meal, or for the king to greet some of his resident wives, but instead, Thrax motioned for Penny to follow after him, away from the warm walls of the *bria*.

"Come, Daughter. Before the light is no longer with us."

He led her on foot into the outskirts of the village, to a small hillock where the grass was kept short by grazing goats, and where the earth had been smoothed into a perfectly circular mound encircled by a partially buried wooden fence, the wood planks tall enough that even the goats could not scale it. He walked the perimeter of the fence until he came to a small gate, which consisted only of a few boards he unlatched and lifted out of place entirely, as it did not swing open. He motioned with a nod of his head for Penny to go through, and she did, though her steps were wary and hesitant. Once on the other side of the fence, Penny saw that the mound was a barrow, and a familiar one at that.

"You used to come here all the time, when I was very young," Penny said quietly, remembering with sudden clarity the single, enormous boulder that marked the entrance. The carved stone acted as a lintel over a narrow passageway, a tunnel she knew led into the innermost chamber of the burial mound.

"Every changing of the seasons," Thrax agreed, then, more softly, "and especially on winter's solstice, when the sun shines Her light directly on her, as it will again very soon."

Penny looked at her father curiously, struck by the poignant sorrow in his tone. There was a faraway expression in his eyes as he stared at the barrow, but he made no move to go through the doorway and enter the passageway to the tomb she knew was inside.

"Her?" she asked instead, gently, lest she startle him from whatever reverie had taken him so far away, as though he were Dreaming right in front of her. His eyes shifted to hers, though part of him was still far away.

"Yes, Her," he said simply. "The woman I loved before all others. The woman who was Queen of Satra. The woman who was my first wife, the light of my life, so that all who came after her were mere shadows fleeing the light of her sun. The woman," Thrax said, his eyes finally returning to this place, to stare directly into Penny's with a sober, intent fire, "who was your mother."

59

Barrow-Tomb

Penny shrugged her shoulders to ease the uncomfortable tension building there, frowning in confusion as she stared at the mounded hill, the stone lintel of the doorway flickering with the shadows of her father's torch.

"My mother died at sea," she said slowly, wondering if her father had not been listening after all. "Did you See it in a Dreamtime, then, and make this place to honor her?" Then, she shook her head, denying the answer to her own question. "No, this place has been here since I can remember, even when Antiope was here..."

Thrax stared at her expectantly. As her voice trailed off, her mind busily searching for answers, Thrax said, "The Oracle never said your mother died at sea, Penthesilea." His tone was soft, gentle, but it was the use of the name she had never heard him use for her that caused the chill to seize her spine, and every bone in her body turn cold. "She said your mother had long gone through the Gate."

"Yes," Penny nodded impatiently. "I don't understand what difference these words games make when—"

"Antiope of Themiscyra is not your blood-mother, child," Thrax said gently, even as his hand took hold of her arm, his fingers squeezing to emphasize the words that would not take hold in Penny's mind. "She helped raise you, called you daughter, named you her heir, loved you, yes, all of the things a mother does for her own daughter, otherwise I would not have let you go with her. But she was not the one who gave birth to you. That woman lies here." He nodded to the dark entrance, and Penny's gaze followed, dragged there as one drags their limbs through rapid water. "Kleite was her name. She birthed you in my own tent, in my own arms,

346

in the shadow of a winter storm. But there was too much blood, and she did not live to see your face in the light of day. Just as she had told me she would not, when she made me promise to see your destiny fulfilled."

His eyes were staring into hers with earnest intent, his words gentle yet firm, sorrow and apprehension mingled together, but Penny still could not understand.

"But, Antiope..." was all her frozen lips and mind would utter, and her father smiled sadly.

"Antiope whelped a babe also, almost exactly one year later. She comforted me in my grief, and took a babe from me. A son, who never took a breath in this world, as his time in the womb was too short. He, too, is buried here, with the one who birthed you, and who loves you now from beyond the Gate."

Penny shook her head slowly, then more firmly, backing away from her father so that his hand fell away from her arm.

"My mother is Antiope. I am her Ishassara."

"Antiope has raised you and loved you as a daughter, and you are her Ishassara," Thrax agreed, his voice and eyes steady, implacable. "But she is not the one who birthed you, Bella. And she is not the one the oracle means when she says your mother has long gone through the Gate. There is more the Kebat did not tell you. That is why you are here."

The passage into the tomb was narrow, the whitewashed stone walls pressing in on her as she followed her father into the deep womb of the earth. Everything was intent on suffocating her. The walls. The darkness. The words her father insisted were truth.

Nothing made sense. Her mother was not her mother? Her real mother was dead? The only mother she had ever known had lied to Penny for her whole life? And possibly the worst part—her father had let Antiope take Penny from her home, from everything she loved, and live as a stranger among people who were not even her own kin? Penny could taste bile on the back of her tongue, held at bay by sheer force of will, but its bitterness was slowly creeping its way through the rest of her bones, mingling with the chill that seemed to have settled there permanently.

The flame on her torch flickered along with her thoughts, but her father's torch held steady ahead of her, his broad shoulders outlined against the darkness of the passageway. Even painted white, the narrow corridor was shadowed and small. When they reached the innermost chamber, the tightly fitted stone blocks painted red, Thrax stopped, and Penny waited silently behind him until he stepped to the side, making room for her to enter the small room beside him.

The chamber was small, a circular room barely three paces across. Everything was painted the color of blood, the color of life, to symbolize the dead's re-emergence with Sabazios in the next life, except for the domed ceiling encircled with figures of people and animals, including a leopard with a distinct black spot over its forehead. On a stone table, low against the wall opposite the entrance, red robes stitched with fine gold thread flowed over the sharp edges of stone. What had once been a body lay in gentle repose on the stone bed, but where the pillow of carved rock should have cradled a head, only a gold mask lay.

"She came to me from the northern lands," Thrax said softly, as though afraid of disturbing her slumber. He did not take his eyes from the figure on the stone bed, and neither did Penny. She did not know what she was feeling in that moment, could not feel much of anything but shock, so she simply listened to Thrax tell his story.

"We were both young, barely able to shoot our own bows, but my father needed to make a peace treaty with that kingdom, and betrothing his son to the Winter King's daughter was the only way to accomplish that. I fought him, not with my sword, of course, for I was not an absolute woolhead, but with my words, insisting I was of the Bessi, and should be allowed to Dream untethered to a woman here in this realm. But he would not listen." Thrax shook his head, and uttered a soft laugh, the sound tugging Penny's eyes from the mummified, headless body in the stone bed to her father's face.

"I fell in love with her the moment she walked into the tent. I think it was the way she smiled, so crooked and shy."

Thrax's eyes were far away, perhaps seeing the face of a young girl he once knew, even as he stared at the waxed body of the woman who had apparently been her mother.

"You have her smile," he said, finding Penny's pale face in the flickering dark. "I knew it when you were just a child, but seeing you again now, as a woman, your smile is what reminds me most of her."

He began to weep silently, his tears glistening in his copper beard in the torchlight. Penny suddenly felt as though she were intruding on her father's private mourning, and she did not know whether to stay or go. Something about his vulnerability made her own heart clench, but she was too overwhelmed, too in shock to know exactly what, or *who*, she should be mourning. She looked away from her father's pain, back to the figure on the bed, a stranger's skeleton. She stepped closer, inspecting the features of the golden mask, the wide almond-shaped eyes, the fine wisps of hair etched into the golden forehead, the strong, wide mouth that Penny recognized as her own even formed of metal. She tried to summon some kind of grief for this woman who had apparently birthed her, been her mother, but inside, there was only a hollow, resounding emptiness.

Everything she had been told about her life, about who she was, had been a lie. Every single person in her life had lied to her, deceived her, used her for their own purposes. And her father had *let* them. Had given her up without a qualm, sent her off to live with strangers, to be confined and controlled by people she had no relation to, all for the sake of keeping peace in his kingdom. She turned back to face her father, and even though his face still shone wet with tears, even though he watched her with loving, sorrowful tenderness, the only feeling she let rise inside the maelstrom of competing feelings within her chest was rage. The hurt behind it would be too much to bear at this point.

"*Why*? Why did you send me away? Why did you make me go with...with Antiope?"

Her father rubbed a hand over his face to clear the tears, then settled it on his beard, tugging the end of it sharply before answering. He met her eyes with a rueful grimace. "I did not *plan* to send you away, daughter. But Antiope could convince a stag to shed his antlers on the spot, or a leopard to step out of its hide and hand it over to her if she were feeling the cold on a summer's night. Plus, Kleite made me promise."

When Penny did not return his entreating smile in the ensuing silence, Thrax sighed.

"Antiope feared she would never claim her throne if she returned to her city without a daughter, and her womb had grown cold since the death of our son. It was give you up to her, or watch you suffer here, Bella. Or at the very least, live a life of obscurity. I had not yet made the changes I have since been able to make between our tribes, and our ways, especially when it comes to our daughters. Despite what Kleite and I had, I did not relish the idea of sending you to another man's lands in order to secure more men for battle, or more land for vineyards. Antiope promised that my beloved, courageous, beautiful daughter could one day be Queen of a powerful city, with all the freedoms she enjoyed. I thought you would be better off there. I thought it was the best way. And..." Thrax paused, his eyes returning to the figure lying prone before them. "And your mother, Kleite, she told me it was your destiny. She knew it was what our Dreaming had revealed, even though I didn't want to admit it. But she knew."

"What do you mean? What did she know?"

Thrax studied her face, choosing his words carefully. "Kleite was a Dreamer, like me. Perhaps it is why we loved each other so well. She saw you before you were born, Bella. She is the one who named you Beautiful Warrior, for she saw what you would become. She Dreamed of your courage, your strength. She dreamed of you in golden armor, with a crown of golden oak leaves, and a double-bladed axe and a sword like the one you wear now, leading an army of women in a fight for justice. And she knew...she knew she would die bringing you into this world. She just did not tell me that part until..." he swallowed, and his voice rasped with grief when he continued, "...until it was too late." He smiled, but it could not chase the sorrow from his eyes. "I named you Penthesilea, Mourned by the People, because I knew I would one day lose you, like I had just lost your mother. I just never knew how much I would mourn that loss, until the day Antiope took you.'

Penny did not look away this time as her father wept. Grief ate at her, but now there was a hungry anger tearing its way through the pain, devouring the confusion, and she could not shake its teeth from her soul.

"Except...I would never have been this warrior queen you say was Dreamed so long ago, Father. Not as Antiope's Ishassara. I was never going to be ha-mazaan with *her*."

Thrax frowned, bringing his grief under control to shake his head. "Antiope was one of the best warriors I have ever met. She was by far the best hunter I have ever, or likely will ever, meet. She trained you to ride and track prey from the moment you could sit a horse, well before you could walk. She assured me your city was full of women just like her, with no men to steer their course, or demand their daughters marry into foreign lands."

"Yes, Themiscyra is brimming with brave, strong women," Penny said, unable to keep the bitterness from her voice. "But Antiope was Hearth Queen, and her heir was never meant to wield a weapon, or fight, Father. As her Ishassara, I was meant to tend the Flame, and weave garments, and churn *kimiz,* and spit boars for the feasts, and pound drums and sing prettily when women died. And no, I would never be tethered to some foreigner, you're right. I would simply seduce as many men as I could in order to provide more daughters, more warriors, more queens to fight amongst themselves. So much better than the life of hardship you feared for me here, amongst my own kin, with you, my father. My *real* family."

The silence after her furious tirade was heavy, charged with pain, but even after releasing these pent-up accusations, expressing all the resentment they festered behind her breastbone, once they were free, Penny could not feel relief. Thrax merely studied her face in the torchlight, while the silent witness of her dead mother waited in the shadows.

Finally, he said quietly, "I thought I was doing what was best for you, Bella. I thought you would have a better life with her. With women who did not live by the laws of men. But...I see that I was naïve. Antiope did not tell me you would be restricted in such ways." He shook his head. "She assured me you would be safe. Liberated, free, unfettered by the rules our tribes place on women. She shocked me with some of her stories, even. Stories of women battling with griffons, of their feats of acrobatic skills on horses, how far they could shoot their strange bows. I even made her prove that last one to me, and she certainly was not lying about that."

Penny's lips twisted into a bitter simulacrum of a smile. "No, she was not lying about that."

"Did she teach you nothing of her people's ways, then?" Thrax asked.

Penny shrugged, staring sightlessly into the distant stone wall, as though it were a golden-pink sandstone instead of grey granite. "She taught me her skills with a bow, yes, though no one can match her with an arrow. Her sister Melanippe took the time to teach me some of their ways with a horse, but my duties to the Hearth always came first. There was little time for anything else. Antiope made sure of it. Just like she made sure I couldn't Dream after I left you. And now, because of her, I am cursed with a broken vow I never should have made in the first place."

Thrax was silent for a long time as the light of the torch flickered with its last flames. Finally, he said, "I cannot take back my choice, Daughter. Perhaps it was a mistake, to let you go. I certainly regretted it every day as I missed you. But Antiope cared for you as deeply as her own flesh and blood, and I cannot believe she would have ever done anything to harm you, no matter what others say." He approached her at the doorway to the barrow tomb, and laid a hand on her shoulder. The weight of it was both steadying and suffocating, as the walls of the small chamber pressed close on every side. "I only hope you can find the absolution you seek, and the freedom to live your life as you want to, daughter. Freedom is all I ever sought for you."

"Maybe freedom isn't what I needed, Father," Penny said, tears choking the words short. She could not keep her bitterness in check, and it stained every word she pushed past the lump in her throat. "All I ever wanted was to belong to someone. To *really* belong. To have a home, surrounded by people who love me. And *both* of you took that from me."

PART FIVE

THE NIGHT-BORN SISTERS

60

DEFENDING QUEEN

Eight riders rode hunched inside their waxed wool cloaks, cowls pulled low as the beginnings of another snowstorm rumbled from the low grey clouds from the north, and the horses' hooves slipped and skidded on mud frozen into ruts. Most members of the small caravan descending from the *bria* in Perperikon to Orithyia's camp in the valley bottom were accustomed to traveling in inclement weather, but there was one horse that was not best pleased with the circumstances. Peyo's ears drooped miserably as he stepped higher and more forcefully than necessary through every snowdrift that mounded across the narrow switchbacks leading down the steeper parts of the mountain. Penny did not mind giving extra attention to the horse, for, though Thrax and Cormu attempted to make pleasant conversation about everything from the administration of the salt mines in the south, to the silver and gold mines to the north, to the increasingly unpredictable weather of the last several years, and even the curious breeding of Peyo for his remarkable conformation and coloring, Penny had very little desire to talk.

Her dour mood was only outdone by Glinn's, who had immediately declined the invitation to meet Penny's military escort. Thrax had declared it was not optional, especially for a junior chieftan of the Satra, and family of a future queen, however. Penny had squirmed under the assumption she would have any claim to Themiscyra's Hearth Throne after learning the truth of her mother, while her half-brother remained committed to ignoring Penny in a way that only a seventeen-year-old male could. For that, she was only grateful, as it left her to her own tangled thoughts.

All she could think about were the lies. All those she had thought loved her, those she had thought she belonged to, who were supposed to belong to her, were in fact fantasies spun from a web of lies she had had no part in weaving, but which trapped her now in a suffocating cocoon of treachery and destruction. Liars and deceivers had decided her life for her, and their choices had led her to nothing but loss, and grief, and betrayal, and now she was without a home, without a mother, without a future, and without even her own honor to carry her forward. Truly, she had been cursed from the day of her birth. Born under the shadow of Death, only to be stolen away by a woman who had used her for her own ends, and now cast adrift in a sea of confusion and treachery.

Penny remembered with a wry twist to her lips that day in the orchard, telling Leandra of the ways of bees. It seemed a lifetime ago now, but her lesson on how bees chose their queen based on her fertility, how they were ruthless in their requirement for a queen to provide more daughters, and how very like the ha-mazaans their colonies were suddenly held an irony that made a short, bitter laugh escape her cold lips. Had everyone in Themiscyra known Antiope was barren? Had the ha-mazaans known Penny was not her blood daughter? She couldn't imagine why they would let a barren Hearth Queen continue to rule, if that was the case. No, it was very apparent that Antiope had kept her secret well, and anyone who had known was just as complicit as the woman she had once called her mother. The question that remained was who had known all along, and who she could trust now?

Her lips curling with bitter resentment, Penny was no closer to having a suitable response prepared for Orithyia's inevitable interrogation when the pennant flags of the Defending Queen's tent came into view in the valley bottom, now cast in white with winter snow come to stay.

"Remember what I said, Bella," Thrax's deep timbre interrupted her spiraling thoughts.

Penny glanced at her father, finding his watchful eyes fixed on her, a furrow of worry etched between his brows.

"I cannot keep such a secret from everyone forever, Father," Penny said quietly, glancing across the road to where the others rode in cold, glum silence. Thrax had assured her that, though Cormu had been there when Kleite died, and had stood watch for the burial of his nephew, Glinn knew nothing about the matter, and Penny would rather keep it that way.

"Orithyia is not a dull woman," she went on, "and I suspect at least some of the ha-mazaans—Marpe, for instance, our most senior atta and a *sivyeti* besides—already know the truth."

"Sivyeti?"

"Stitcher. Healer," she explained. "The women who practice the medicine of herbs and song for healing the ha-mazaan's wounds, and other sicknesses. She started as a *zizenti*, a midwife of birth and priestess of death. Now she sets broken bones and stitches wounds among the living. She is the one who taught me this," Penny said, running her fingers along the stitches in her own jaw, still sore, but thankfully not infected.

"Marpe has attended the birth of every child in Themiscyra since before she helped bring Antiope into the world, and she will likely be there for the next hundred years doing the same, if she has any say in the matter." Penny paused, her mouth a grim line as she thought of the *atta*. "She is also the one who drugged me for the last ten years, so that I could not Dream. Of you, or my real mother."

Thrax's mouth took on a grim look of its own. He had confirmed the herbs she had been fed as "medicine" the last ten years would sufficiently suppress her mind as to cut off access to Dreams. Dreaming was a sacred rite to a Bessi, and to cut one's Spirit off from access to that Otherworld was a crime against the very fabric of creation, against Sabazios Himself. In Satra, *zelas* was an herbal concoction administered as punishment for crimes against the Mother, and the main effects were to cut one off from the realm of Dreams, and therefore from power. Antiope must have taken that bit of wisdom home with her to Themiscyra, and concocted the same formula with Marpe's help. Thrax had been shocked to realize the depths of Antiope's deception and betrayal, but he had not ceased insisting the Hearth Queen must have had her reasons.

Penny knew her father had begun to blame himself for the events that had unfolded since handing her over to Themiscyra's Hearth Queen, and her words, spoken in hurt and anger, blaming him for letting her go, had not helped, but it was too late to take them back. The truth was, they were both victims of Antiope's manipulation and scheming, and the only thing left to them now was to rebuild their own foundation, together.

"In any case, perhaps you should wait before you tell them. Just for a time, Bella," Thrax said, as a shout from Cormu signaled approaching riders from Orithyia's camp. He held her gaze with steady assurance as they reigned their horses to a halt. "There are some matters that require more than just our thinking mind. Give it some time. Give me some time to find more answers. That's all I'm saying."

Penny chewed the inside of her cheek, but nodded. "I will try, Father. But you will see soon enough that Orithyia is not a woman. She is a force, and if she wants something, she will get it."

Thrax smiled. "This Defending Queen interests me very much. She is not looking for a husband, by chance?"

Penny's laugh was loud enough to startle the rooks from the nearby trees. She had no chance to answer, though, or assure her father Orithyia would never be interested in any man, as Harp's voice called out to her from the approaching riders.

"Bella!"

She was still grinning broadly when he dropped from his horse to lope over, heedless of General Mursilis' forbidding frown as he made his way past Cormu and Glinn and several Dacii standard-bearers, their wolf-head pikes dark shadows against the star-iron sky. Penny swung from Peyo's back and was immediately embraced by Harp, and though she stiffened for a moment in surprise, the next feeling was one of relief as his arms, stronger and more solid now that he had spent several months at weapons and athletics training, squeezed her tightly. She squeezed back, though they had never before shared such an affectionate moment, but then Harp pushed her away almost as quickly as he had hugged her, his eyes wide with chagrin.

"Sorry, Bella. Sorry. I—" he rolled his eyes at her father and the other men watching, his long curls wilder than normal and his thin face fully obscured by a thick beard, giving him a maturity that had not been there only a few moons prior. "I should not presume. I just—I missed you," he finished contritely. But then he focused on her face, seeing her smile, and his shoulders relaxed slightly.

"It's good to see you, too," she said, her heart warmed by his enthusiastic greeting. She gestured to her father as he dismounted to join them. "Harpalion, this is Thrax, King and Priest of the Satrae Bessi, and my father. Father, this is Harpalion, son of King Pylameneus, and grandson of Sinope's Hearth Queen. He is…" she paused, swallowing the words "my cousin", and finished with stilted words that made Harp peer at her curiously. "He is a cousin of Antiope."

The two men, of a height but in no way matched for build or strength or the undeniable air of authority that Thrax carried, grasped forearms in greeting.

"Bella has told me much of you. Especially how you helped her when she was in need, multiple times over," Thrax said. "I am indebted to you on my daughter's behalf, Harpalion son of Pylameneus, grandson of a mighty Queen. Whatever you may need, whatever you may want, if it is mine to give you, I will."

Harp ducked his head, and mumbled, "Nothing any decent person wouldn't have done."

Thrax smiled, his golden eyes studying Harp's abashed face. "Aye, perhaps. She also tells me you are a Singer. I would be honored to hear you play. You know there is one hereabouts who says he can raise the dead with his lyre? Orpheus, he is called. He holds theatre under the stars on each solstice. Perhaps we can hear him, as the winter solstice quickly approaches. I would be most interested to hear your thoughts on his technique."

Managing to look properly intrigued while also flushing red to the tips of his ears, Harp murmured an agreeable comment, before he turned to Penny.

"Bella, I have news from home you need to hear. Orithyia asked me to ride up the mountain and find you, and I was just about to leave."

Penny raised an eyebrow, her heart suddenly loud in her ears. "Are the missing ha-mazaans returned?"

Harp shook his head slightly. "Er—no. It's actually news from my father. He is furious—although when is he not? But this time it's about his taxes."

"His taxes?"

Harp grimaced, his fingers twitching so jerkily against his thigh that he tucked one hand under his leather belt and buried the other in his hair to scratch behind his ear before answering.

"His taxes due to Sinope, and now Themiscyra, have increased. Considerably."

Penny frowned. "Themiscyra only collects taxes from Galatae. We trade hazelnuts and honey and linen for Paphlagonia's mules, as agreed by Otrera years ago."

"Exactly," Harp said, his eyes flickering over Glinn and Cormu and the others, all listening politely but intently, before settling back on Penny. "Only, it seems that Themiscyra has a new Defending Queen, and she has made it her business to fund a military campaign, and those funds are apparently coming out of every city owing allegiance to either Sinope or Themiscyra. According to my father, even the cities who owe allegiance to Lykastia and Chaldesia have had taxes levied against their continued defenses."

The air seemed to have thickened with the low clouds, the sharp smell of snow stinging Penny's lungs. "New Defending Queen? So Cyra *has* returned?"

She tried to inflect the words with enthusiastic belief, with hope, but there was a cold dread building, and Harp's expression did nothing to dispel it, but before he could answer her, a voice said with cold finality,

"Cyra is gone."

Every head turned as one to watch the ha-mazaan approach. Penny met the queen's eyes with her best impression of confidence, the dread turning to ice in her chest as she felt the cold blue of Orithyia's gaze slicing into her, *seeing* her.

"Molpadia has taken up Hippolyta's axe. She has declared herself Defending Queen in Cyra's place. She is marching the ha-mazaans west as we speak. To Attica.

"She has declared war on Heracles and Theseus, and against all who stand in her way."

61

TRAITOR

"**B**ut..." Penny began, but she could think of nothing more to say. In the absence of authority left behind by the deaths of the queens, the loss of the Savaran General and its captain, the disappearance of the Ishassara for the Defender's Throne, and the deaths of so many seasoned warriors that fateful night, it made sense that Lyta's consort would take up the cause of defending Themiscyra's ha-mazaans. Still, Penny had not expected the ha-mazaans to have agreed to march their army west after they had already established it would do no good. Of course, that had been when it had only been Themiscyra's survivors. If all the ha-mazaans from every city were banding together...

"Can she do that?" Penny finished finally.

Orithyia came to a stop next to Harp, her bright eyes raking Thrax from head to toe, and his own eyes giving her the same treatment, though with far less contempt in his face. Orithyia's eyes slid off Thrax like water from a stryx, and returned to Penny.

"She can do whatever the ha-mazaans allow, hey? Someone has to run the place, and she's as good with spear and axe as Lyta. However, she could have waited a while before kicking Pylameneus in the shins, or the rest of the Hanassa villages. It certainly has not helped our cause."

The queen's earlier words niggled at her. "What about Cyra? Dia can't just call herself Defending Queen when Cyra still has the year to complete her Alsanti."

Orithyia grunted, casting her eyes over the rest of the men with Penny. "As I said, girl, Cyra is gone, and Molpadia at least is ready to live in that reality, even if you aren't. Are you planning on making introductions, girl, or do I need to do the task myself?"

360

Her mind spinning, Penny introduced Sinope's Defending Queen to the men, beginning with her father, who had not taken his eyes off the ha-mazaan, and ending with Glinn, who similarly eyed the queen, but with what Penny considered a more appropriate amount of trepidation.

"An honor to finally meet the ha-mazaan Queen who has done so much for my daughter, and whose fierce reputation precedes her," Thrax said warmly.

Penny eyed him askance, worried at his tone and wondering if his earlier comment about Orithyia looking for a husband had been in earnest, but the queen was even more brisk than usual in her reply.

"A pleasure, I'm sure. I take it we can count on your support when we march west, Thrax of the Satrae Bessi?"

Not appearing in any way offended, or thwarted, by the ha-mazaan's less than warm response, Thrax inclined his head. "Where my daughter calls me, I will go, and my men will follow."

"Hopefully they can keep up. They look fatter than my nephew's goats, and nearly as hairy," Orithyia said. She turned on her heel and stalked away, tossing a glance over her shoulder at Penny and gesturing impatiently. "Penthesilea, I will speak with you in my tent."

Penny hesitated, looking from the quickly disappearing ha-mazaan to her father's retinue, torn between obeying the queen and fulfilling the rites of hospitality her guests required. Thrax placed a hand on her shoulder. "You were right, Bella. She is a force."

His grin was wide, and Penny's mouth twisted wryly to mirror it. He gave her a gentle push. "Go on, then. No use trying to keep your tent flap closed in a hurricane. Best just go where the wind pulls you. Cormu and I will see to the men's shelter for the night. Perhaps Harpalion here will bless us with the sound of his music, and maybe even a hot bowl of gruel to warm our bellies, hm?"

As Harp rushed to fulfill Thrax's wishes, Penny hurried after Orithyia, ducking through the dark opening into the spacious tent, a much more permanent structure than what they had used on the journey to Thrakian territory, but still in no way opulent as Thrax's tents were. Orithyia's space was utilitarian at best, with a small cot against one wall, a simple brazier stocked with wood keeping the winter's chill at bay, and several stumps set out around a crude, misshapen table.

Orithyia gestured for her to sit on one crude log, and lowered herself slowly onto one opposite. She adjusted her zoster so that the attached sword did not drag on the ground, then stretched one leg closer to the brazier, massaging her knee in the warmth of the flames. Penny drew her own cloak tighter over her shoulders, as the fire's heat did not reach the far side of the table, and waited, but Orithyia continued to ignore her. The silence grew stiff, and Penny's heart thrummed in the tension as the secret she wrestled with seemed to grow inside of her with a life of its own. Despite Thrax's plea to keep the information to herself, Penny had already felt the weight of the queen's displeasure when she had confessed her pregnancy, and now she could not decide which was worse—confessing she was not the daughter of Antiope, and had no claim to Themiscyra's Hearth Throne, or keeping that knowledge to herself, only to have one of the ha-mazaans betray their knowledge later, and tarnishing the Defending Queen's trust in her.

The thought of Orithyia turning her back on Penny was enough to make her stomach flip queasily. She drew a deep breath. Her father was wrong. It would be best to have everything in the open, instead of pulling her under these relentless waves of guilt. She needed to tell her the truth. "Orith—"

"Molpadia has declared you one of her primary targets, girl. Right after she finishes with the man who killed Lyta. I thought you should know."

Orithyia's words cut off Penny's confession, stunning her into a brief moment of silence.

"*Me?*"

Orithyia sighed, and turned her attention from the flames. Her face looked worn and haggard, and Penny felt a new flash of guilt for all the trials she had put the woman through, dragging her halfway across the world when all she had wanted was to hunt and eat and watch other ha-mazaans ride to battle.

"Aye, you. She has declared war on those who murdered Hippoly-ta—Heracles and Theseus and every Achaean foremost, but names anyone hostile to Themiscyra as her enemy. Apparently, that includes every person born a man, and every person who threatens Themiscyra's sovereign refuge for women. According to her logic, that list invariably includes you, as she blames both you and Antiope for giving the Achaeans guest right. Unfortunately, she has also declared you an oath-breaker, and a traitor to the Thrones, and that is going to be a hard one to deny."

Penny's face grew cold, though not because she sat so far from the fire. So Molpadia knew about her broken oath? How did she know? *What* did she know? That she had killed Brekko? Or was she one of the ha-mazaans who had known Antiope's secret all along? Perhaps Molpadia knew the whole of it, after all. Her suspicions of Antiope had always been strong. Stronger than Penny had understood, before. But if Molpadia knew the truth, perhaps—

"Are you listening, girl, or are you in Dreamland?"

Penny snapped her focus back to the queen, meeting her scowl with an apologetic flush. "Sorry."

"I would rather not spend the day repeating myself, so please do your wool-gathering on your own time. I said, Molpadia learned you are training your sword against mine, with the intent on becoming a real ha-mazaan, and thus declared you an oath-breaker. She isn't very happy with me, either. She'll be even less pleased once she sees how good of a warrior you have become, I'm sure, and how much potential you still have."

Penny flushed at the unexpected compliment, a strange pride welling in her chest, but Orithyia was still talking.

"Either way, she has pronounced you unfit to pursue the Hearth Throne, because you have abandoned the care of the ha-mazaans when they were most in need, even though you were—are—their Ishassara. She says you should be completing your Alsanti, and finding a man to give you a daughter, but instead have abandoned your oath to the ha-mazaans. She says the punishment for these broken vows must be death. She even put a bounty on that belt you are wearing, offering a whole cart of star-iron to the woman who can cut it off of you."

Penny hugged her arm against the zoster at her waist until the metal discs bit into her flesh, the gesture hidden under her cloak, but Orithyia's brow raised as she detected the movement.

"I understand the rest, hey? But that piece of news about your zoster has had me wondering ever since Bremusa told me Molpadia's plan."

At Penny's blank look, Orithyia grunted again, and went back to staring at the flames. "At least we have some warning. Bremusa nearly rode her horse into the ground trying to catch up with us with the news from Sinope, so we have some time before Molpadia reaches us. Even if she can only raise a hundred women to her cause, it will take them a lot longer than it did us to travel here. We have plenty of time to prepare."

"Prepare for what?" Penny asked warily. "I am not going to fight my own people, Orithyia. That is not why I agreed to become ha-mazaan."

"Well, you may not have a choice, girl. Pylameneus sent his own envoy after General Mursilis, summoning him and the boy home with their men. He says he owes no more allegiance to Sinope other than the taxes that are already breaking him. So if Harp obeys his father, it will be you, and me, and whoever your father can spare. Unless, of course, you can offer Themiscyra's new Defending Queen proof that you are not, after all, an oath-breaker, and a traitor to your vows?"

62

ABSOLUTION

It was snowing heavily when Penny finally left Orithyia's tent, murmuring her excuses to the ha-mazaan that she needed to speak with her father, and ask for his support against the incoming threat. The clouds had thickened to the point of darkness, and the sun was already low in the sky, though it seemed to Penny that it had just breached the eastern mountains, but such was the brief light of day when the sun was swallowed by winter's darkness. From the far side of the encampment came the distinct strum of a harp, and Harp's voice raised in one of his favorite bawdy songs. The rich laughter of her father broke through the singing, and the pure joy in that sound made Penny smile, even as her heart squeezed with grief. She paused outside the tent where the men were drinking. A familiar smell permeated the air, thicker than the waterproofing beeswax on the tents and her cloak, more cloying than unwashed soldiers, darker than the oncoming night. It smelled of rotting flax and brimstone. The smell of her curse, a miasma that had begun to permeate everything around her, and would soon consume everything she was close to. It only took the sound of Thrax and Harp laughing together for Penny to know she could not go any closer. She slipped between the tents, moving in the opposite direction of their revelry.

She could not seek out her father, or Harp, just like she could not ask Orithyia to turn her sword against the women she was sworn to defend. The last thing she wanted was to ask anyone to fight a battle that was not theirs, against women she had already sworn to nurture, and never harm. Molpadia was not wrong in any of her charges, and no matter how much Orithyia had tried to convince her that the fight would be justified, that Penny had the right to choose her future, she knew she could not be

365

the cause of that kind of destruction. Not when there was another way. She needed to find the Oracle who could absolve her from her vow and release her, and all these people she cared about from the curse she had brought upon them. And if she failed, then she would surrender her life to Molpadia willingly. That way, this curse she carried would have no need to touch Thrax, or Harp, or Orithyia, or any of the ha-mazaans she had only recently come to realize that she loved with all her heart.

She would finish what she had come here to do, and only then would she perhaps take Harp up on his offer to fulfill her Alsanti before the next Sturgeon Moon. And if she could not absolve her vow and break this curse, then at least she could say she had tried everything possible to protect the ones she loved, rather than simply sit and watch them be consumed by the storm of her own making, the furious hurricane of Molpadia included.

Her course decided, Penny used the snow and the gloom to make her way to Peyo's shelter unseen. Peyo sensed the need for quiet, and hung close to her shoulder as she led him away from the tents, walking until they were well within the shadows of the naked birch trees before swinging onto his back. Then, she urged the stallion to a gallop, headed toward the tallest peak in the distant mountains, counting on the heavy snow to obscure their tracks before anyone could follow.

Thrax had told her what he could of the Oracle in the mountains, but he could only tell her so much about where to find her. He could not tell her where the cave was, insisting she would find the signs leading her there if she was meant to, as was the way for all who sought the woman's secrets. That cryptic message was the only map Penny followed, but it would need to be enough. If she failed at this, she failed every person who had helped her get this far. She failed her murdered aunt, and the sisterhood she had come to love, even though she now knew she had never belonged to them in the first place. She failed the woman she had loved as mother, who had kept so many secrets from her, told her so many lies that Penny was not sure she could trust anything from the last ten years, yet was the only one Penny had ever known, or loved, as a mother. She would fail Orithyia, and Harp, and even Thrax, thrusting them all into a war that was not of their own making. She would fail Leandra. It was the girl's face Penny kept in her mind as a brand of light, a warm beacon of hope, as the blizzard pressed close on all sides, blinding Penny to everything but the path directly ahead, and even that was unclear.

It took the full day to reach the foothills of the tall mountain, and the snow became a full blizzard, blocking out what little light remained. As the land became dense with rocks and trees, the snow deepened, and the stallion's long legs forged a trail where there was none, even as the blizzard blinded Penny's view of the trail ahead. When they could go no further, they rested. Penny dug through the snow to find dried grass for Peyo, and picked lichen from the nearby trees, which she fed him in the shelter under the roots of a giant cedar while the snow blanketed the earth around them. She wanted to make a fire, but there was no wood dry enough, so she tapped the horse on the shoulder and coached him to lie down. She huddled herself into the warmth of his belly, her waxed cloak hugged tight over her chest, and drifted into a fitful sleep against the rise and fall of his barrelled chest. Immediately, she fell into a Dream.

She walked along a cliff's edge, her hands feeling along the edge of the cold rock wall, a sheer drop of crumbling stone and scragged brush below her, where no horse could climb, and no human would dare to walk. As soon as she looked down, vertigo set in. Penny pressed herself against the cliff face. There was a soft light filtering from above, and when she looked up, the branches of an ancient pine towered high overhead, directly underneath the constellation of the Chalice in the sky. The pine's limbs were as thick as a fully mature tree's trunk, the needles hanging in round clumps from the ends of its branches were as long as her arm, forming great bulbs of spikes against the starry sky. The base of the tree was so wide that Penny was sure three horses could have stood abreast and not filled the inside of its trunk. Snow capped the outer edges of the giant limbs, but at ground level, because of the sheltering arms of the massive tree, the ground was only lightly dusted with snow. She could clearly see her tracks leading past the tree to the rock wall in front of her.

Penny jerked awake to Peyo snuffling in her hair. The shadows outside of their tiny hovel had shifted, though the sun had long since gone, leaving only the blue glow of the snow to light the world. Fat flakes fell to the ground with unrelenting quiet. The Dream clung to her as she adjusted to the silent world, the silhouette of the towering pine looming in her mind.

She had seen that tree before, as a child. The cliff face had been the last part of her journey with Antiope, before she had sworn her vow.

She only needed to find that tree, and she would find the Oracle.

They set off again. Penny urged Peyo onto a narrow path that led upward, letting his sure hooves find the best course, hoping she was not wrong about the direction. They climbed for some time, until the sky lightened to the color of Antiope's eyes, making Penny feel as though that woman watched their every step, judging her progress, disapproving of her intent. When they found the small stream, the edges of it lumped with snowy shapes hunched over its banks like grandmothers at their washing, Penny knew they were headed in the right direction. She remembered the way the water twisted under the overhanging rock on her left. She and her mother had drunk from this stream, its waters flowing full at the time with spring freshet. The cave, and Penny's absolution, was nearby.

They rested again at the edge of the stream while its gurgling soothed Penny's troubled mind. She drank her fill, the icy water making her shiver with cold, then let Peyo drink, watching his throat move and his golden eyelashes flutter as he gulped his fill. She was still kneeling at his feet when the stallion raised his dripping muzzle from the stream and screamed a shrill warning into the silent night. Penny lurched to her feet, unsheathing her sword and crouching into a fighter's stance.

Peyo bunched his hindquarters and hurled himself across the small stream in one easy leap, and for a breathless moment Penny wondered if he was abandoning her, but then he slid to a stop in a cloud of white, lashing the air with his front hooves, his teeth bared at the shadows in the trees. Penny looked around wildly for the Erinyes, expecting to see the writhing snakes and bat wings of the creature descending on them. Peyo's front feet returned to the earth with a thump, then hopped again as he tossed his head, squealing like s stuck pig. Gripping the sword tighter, Penny drew a deep breath, and followed the horse across the creek, barely making the jump without falling into the frigid, deadly water. She was just regaining her balance when the shadow emerged from the trees.

"Calla!"

Peyo's head snaked out at the big cat, but Calla slithered her lithe body out of his reach and, in one huge, utterly silent leap, bounded to Penny's side.

"Peyo, stop!" Penny called as the stallion prepared to run the cat down, and the cat snarled. Peyo reared again, furious, but he obeyed. Calla's eyes shone in the night, her huge body a dappled shadow against the snow as she butted her head against Penny's stomach, and began to purr.

Despite Penny's boosted confidence after the added companionship of Calla, they wandered on the mountainside for two more days, with the unrelenting snow and wind and cold freezing every hope Penny had of succeeding in finding her hidden target. How had Antiope found the cave with such ease? What had she tracked to lead them straight to it? Whatever traces the hunter had used to draw her onward were buried now under layers of snow and fog, and Penny despaired of ever finding her way back to the valley bottom, let alone the dark recesses of the cave. Who could even survive more than a few days in this hostile landscape, let alone live here permanently? What if that old woman was dead? She had been as old as this mountain ten years ago. There was a strong likelihood she was part of the stone itself by now.

Doubt and fear set their teeth in her soul as soon as food became scarce for Peyo, though the stallion ate the lichen she harvested without complaint, and forged up the increasingly hazardous trail and through the now sparsely populated fir trees with eager determination, every step a competition with Calla's silent passage along the narrow canyon of water. At least the cat could hunt prey on her own, but Peyo was reliant on Penny's care, and with the world blanketed in so much snow, with only sharp rocks under their feet when she dug down for grass, she felt sick with worry that she had led her companions into a hopeless dead-end.

Dusk was falling on the third day when she realized they were not only lost, but the cave was lost to her. She would not find it in this weather, and now, with so much white obscuring the path and even the guidance of the sun and stars blacked out, Penny feared they would not be able to find their way back again before the storm smothered their tracks, or buried their way out completely. Sick with desperation and failure, but knowing there was nothing else they could do when night was quickly falling, Penny resolved to turn back in the morning. She found a hollowed-out recess in the rock where the three of them had room to shelter for the night, and this time there were two bodies to keep her warm, though she was sure Peyo would rather have kicked the leopard over the side of the canyon than cuddle with it. Still, they came to some sort of tenuous agreement between them, Peyo's back to hers and Calla stretched out along her stomach with the luxurious ease only a cat could achieve, as though they were all warm and cozy under Thrax's tent, in front of his great braziers.

Despite the cold gnawing at her feet and hands, and the crushing sense of failure after having come this far, or perhaps because of these things, Penny slipped quickly into another Dream. Snow still fell from a twilight sky, but she was no longer on a mountain. She was walking on a darkened path, with no view of the way ahead, and when she looked behind her, the trail disappeared into blackness, dropping into an abyss, so that the only way to go was forward. There was no future here. No past. There was only a wide expanse of now, extending into eternity on either side of her. She felt dizzy with the vertigo of it, as though she were once again braced against the face of a cliff, unable to move up or down. She was spinning in place, with nowhere to go but *here*, and here was more full of terror than anything that had haunted Penny before, because here was nothing, and no one, only her, and the choices that had brought her here, lost and alone.

As the terror began to take hold in her mind, Peyo's solid presence nudged her shoulder, bringing her back to the present. This time it was Calla who padded slightly ahead, her svelte body pushing through the dark as though she saw a path where Penny could see only shadows. Unsure if there would be ground under her feet if she moved, Penny stepped forward tentatively. Solid ground met her foot, and she took another step after the cat, then another. Peyo glowed his golden light at her shoulder, but even as they moved, the path behind them faded. There was no way back, and the way ahead remained dark.

"Hope is always scarce when victory is near. Do not give up so easily."

Penny's breath caught. She turned to see her father walking next to her, his brown eyes watchful.

"You are not alone, Daughter."

"We are always watching over you, Bellatrix," another voice said, and Penny did not recognize it, but Thrax looked over Penny's shoulder to smile, his eyes shining with love. She followed his gaze, straining in vain to see the woman who spoke, and though she saw only a shimmering presence, she knew it was Kleite, her mother.

A lilting sound tickled her ears, drawing her onward. Though her parents said no more, she could sense they were still with her on the path, and it bolstered her flagging courage. She let herself be lured on by the leopard's sure footsteps and the music, to be pushed by the steady, unwavering presence of the stallion at her back, until the sound unfolded into a familiar deep voice raised in song, with the curiously alive strum of a harp lending commentary on every step she took.

"What are you doing here?" she said to the night, though she could not see anyone. The only reply was a trill of the strings and Harp's steady voice, strong and sure as it only ever was when calling forth the music. Penny felt the tightness in her shoulders easing, the thick knot of fear in her chest unwinding with every chord echoing in her mind. Penny's feet landed against the dark path with every driving beat of the music, quicker now, though she could see no better than she could before.

Soon the music faded, replaced by the steady susurrus of water. She glanced down at her feet and found she walked in water, with the mottled stones of the Terme bracing the arches of her feet, the swiftly flowing water in the shallows pulling her steps forward. Sylviu's eyes rose in her mind, the same color as those stones. His warm smile flashed in her vision, and she was sure she heard his voice, pitched low and gentle, urging her forward. Urging her to follow the river. She went where the water flowed, until the water turned to snow. The snow swirled, and Penny seemed to walk forever, but time passed differently in Dreams, she knew.

When Penny awoke, the world had changed.

The sky was clear and blue, and birds sang their hope for a new day. Peyo and Calla stood calmly in the cool dawn, their tails twitching with boredom, but not enmity. Scrambling to her feet, Penny emerged from their meager shelter to stare around her. She did not recognize any of the landscape. What had appeared in the dark blizzard to be an endless valley of snow and trees had opened into a crescent-shaped canyon in the broad light of day, though the lay of the land showed she had descended a steep ravine to get here, and she was positive they had only climbed higher and higher before finding a place to rest. Turning a slow circle, Penny swallowed. A pool of water, its edges rimmed with thick, untouched snow, without even a single track to show an ermine or fox might drink there, bubbled in the center of the hidden hollow. It trickled its way down the valley, creating the small creek Penny had followed up the mountain, but where she had last seen the water at the bottom of the steep and treacherous ravine, here it was surrounded by gently sloping banks.

Beyond the spring, directly in Penny's line of vision now that thick snow and fog did not block the view, the distinct limbs of an enormous pine reached its fingers towards the sky. Behind it, on the far side of the hollow, a cliff face, with a narrow path carved into the side of it, and a dark opening of a cave hidden in the shadows.

"Thank you," she whispered, not knowing if the spirits of those who had guided her to this place could hear her, and not knowing if she had indeed traveled here in a Dream, or if it was simply chance that she had spent the night directly outside of the oracle's cave. Either way, she was here.

Absolution was finally within her reach.

63

Spinner, Weaver

Peyo could not follow up the steep path, but Calla insisted on hugging Penny's every tentative step along the narrow path to the cave entrance. When she shouldered through the narrow opening, ducking her head under the stone lintel that had been nearly twice her height the last time she came here, the smell of incense struck her, along with something swampy, almost putrid. A small fire burned in a simple brazier, but it barely lit the room, and it emitted hardly any warmth.

"Enter, girl, but leave the Spirit at the door."

Penny pushed Calla behind her with a sternly whispered order to stay outside, doubtful the leopard would obey any commands, and squinted into the dimly lit room for the source of the voice. The last time she had seen the Oracle, she had been the oldest person, possibly the oldest living thing Penny had ever seen, if one did not count the oak and hornbeam in the forests. But the woman who perched entirely naked on the three-legged stool appeared younger than Penny herself, with cheeks rounded by fat and skin as smooth and soft and pink as a spring rose. Her breasts were small but firm, and her dainty, tapered hands flitted quick as sparrows across the skein of wool she held, her finely pointed fingers twisting what looked like shadows and sparks of firelight into a thread so fine it shimmered like a spider's web in the dew. Her hands did not stop their spinning when she turned her head to face Penny. Though her smile was sweet as honey, where there should have been eyes there was only blank skin, the sockets as smooth and unscarred as the woman's perfect shoulders. The sightless face stared into the very heart of her, as though searching her soul.

"You have your father's eyes."

Penny's skin prickled, but she forced her mind into calm, answering through stiff lips, "Yes."

"And his heart."

"Thank you."

The girl nodded, as though Penny had given the correct answer to a question she had not even asked.

"Why did you come here?"

She swallowed, though her mouth was dry. "I wish to absolve my vow. To make right what I have done wrong."

"Oh?" she said, her tone unbothered, barely even curious. "I see blood on your hands, and shadows in your soul. I hope you do not seek *me* out to heal these."

Penny's heart thudded down, the knot twisting in her stomach pulling tighter as she glanced around the small room. "I came to speak to the one I swore my vow to. I thought this was the place I would find her. Is she...is she dead, then? Are you her...er...successor? Who are you?"

The girl laughed, and the sound was fresh and young, like the first sprightly sprigs of grass after a long winter.

"I am Clotho, Spinner of Life and Teller of Tales. Who are *you*, that you would seek an audience with the Weaver of Worlds?"

Nonplussed at being asked her identity when the figure had just mentioned her father, Penny paused, before saying, "I am Penthesilea, daughter of Thrax of the Satrae Bessi, and..." she stopped, having never said the name out loud, but finally pushed on, "and Kleite, who named me Bellatrix." She paused again, wondering what right she had to call herself anything else, but finally, more quietly, she said, "I am Ishassara to Antiope, and future Hearth Queen of Themiscyra."

Clotho's hands flew, spinning light and shadow into thread, her wrists twirling the length of it so quickly onto the spool that it should have been twice the size as when Penny had first seen it, yet there appeared to be no more thread on that mound than when she had first entered the room.

"I do not see *you* in those words and names at all. Is that all you can tell me?"

Penny's mouth opened and closed like a landed fish. She shrugged, confused. "These are my names. They are who I am."

Those hands did not pause, as the eyeless face stared at Penny for many silent turns of the spool and thread. The rosebud lips curled down. "Penthesilea, yes. Mourned by the People, yes. This is the name the Bessi gave you, it is true, but do you deserve it? Do you? Do you think anyone will truly mourn you when you are gone?"

Penny's breath stuttered to a halt as those words hit her like a kick in the gut, but Clotho went on, heedless of the brutality of her questions.

"Kleite named you Bellatrix, she did, yes, yes she did, but are you brave enough, beautiful enough, to be what she named you? And Ishassara!" she sang, her voice trilling on the word, reminding Penny of Harp's music, but the woman's words were cutting her in a way Harp's voice never would. "Do you think you are savvy enough, kind enough, to be what the Queen of the ha-mazaans needed when she named you that? Are any of these things *you*? Are these things *all* that is you? *Who are you?*"

Stunned, Penny could only stare at that sightless face that saw every doubt, every insecurity she had hoped to forever keep hidden. The girl laughed again at Penny's stifled silence. This time, her laughter went on for a long time, echoing from the dark walls of the cave so loudly that Penny wanted to cover her ears, her own heart beating like a drum to the terrible music of it all.

The fire in the brazier abruptly dimmed, winked out, casting the room into complete blackness, but only for a moment. When the flames flared again, the figure on the stool was no longer the same, and the sound of the laughter, which had never stopped, turned dry as the crackling flames, until it was more of a wracking cough. Penny wanted desperately to turn and flee the cave, but her feet were rooted to the stone. She wasn't sure if her skin crawled, or if a breeze followed her through the open doorway and lifted the hair from her neck.

The young girl was gone.

A wizened old crone now hunched on the same three-legged stool, her skin shriveled and hanging from stark bones like limp sails on a ship. Her shrunken size was the only youthful thing about her. Hair as sparse and flat as the last blades of grass under a long winter's snow, and just as washed of color, hung in patches from her grey scalp, the skin painted with brown spots of age. Her gnarled hands, sparrow quick despite their twisted, skeletal fingers, passed a simple wooden shuttle through skeins of every color imaginable, and some Penny had never known existed, the shuttle trailing a thread as fine as a spider's gossamer web. It was the same type of loom Penny had once used what now felt like a lifetime ago, in Themiscyra's Moon Hall. Eyes with irises bleached of all color, so that even their pupils were white with cold ice, stared through Penny the same way the young girl's sightless face had. Eyes Penny had seen before, when she was a young girl.

"Who are you?" Penny asked fearfully. "*What* are you?"

The spotted hands did not stop weaving. The faded petals of what had once been a perfect rosebud mouth twisted into a gummy smile. The voice that answered was dry as an old husk of wheat, but the laughter was still there.

"I am Lachesis. Measurer, Weaver. I am the one whom you seek. The one to whom you swore a vow that should never be sworn. I told you it was not right, didn't I? I did, I did. And now you come here seeking to Unweave what has already been stitched into the fabric of time itself. Come, girl. See for yourself how your Thread has woven, and tell me how it is that it should be Undone."

Penny stared, uncomprehending.

"Come," Lachesis commanded. Penny went, her steps small.

"You can weave, eh? A nice, obedient Hearth Queen knows how to weave, knows how to read the Threads?"

Penny nodded, swallowing. Lachesis crooked a finger under her nose, drawing her eyes to the mounded folds of tapestry spread out on the table. It smelled of dust and blood and ashes, of rocks that have been dry for months now soaked by rain, smelling like the very core of the world and all its long ages. It smelled of leaves tight in the bud, and sap seeping from the cracks in an old pine. It smelled of crushed berries, the kind Antiope had once painted on her lips, and it smelled of musk, heady and male. It smelled of every memory Penny had ever lived, and her head swam with visions called forth out of the folds.

"Here it is. Your thread." Lachesis' bony knuckle pulled Penny's hand onto the tapestry, pushing her finger onto a plain yellow thread in the middle of the weave. Her skeletal hand lay atop Penny's, tracing the length of the thread until it was no longer yellow, until it turned ashen and black before it fell, loose and unwoven at the edge of the pattern, dropping into the shadows. Penny felt as though a hand were crawling up her spine. She shivered, and the woman jerked Penny's hand back to where it had started, then back further still, tracing the yellow thread this way and that, this way and that.

So many colors intertwined with the yellow. There was a blue thread intersecting the yellow, the two of them bound tightly together for most of their length. There were other colors as well. Brown and green and dusky red, all of them resonating under Penny's finger with a thrum of life, inside her heart. She knew they were the threads of others, Thrax and Sylviu and Orithyia, Harp and Antiope, Areto and Cyra and Sagitta. One thread, thick and gold, sprouted in the middle of it all, and Leandra's cloud of golden hair arose in Penny's mind. The threads of all the people she loved were woven together with hers, and the sight of it brought tears of awe to the surface.

"And here," Lachesis said, her voice taking on a purring quality as she spread the weft flat with one hand, guiding Penny's fingers with the other, until one finger touched a dull grey thread that ended in the middle of the weaving, directly beside the yellow one. "Here is the one you killed, after you swore you would do no harm."

Penny jerked her hand away and stared at the simple grey skein, her mouth going dry. Lachesis flipped the width of material over with a deft, practiced hand, as though the weave did not weigh more than her entire body, and pointed without hesitation to a spot on the back, though there were thousands of threads and several hundred knots to choose from. A small, neatly formed knot of grey linen, pushed tight against the weft so as to be barely distinguishable, marked the end of the grey thread.

"Right here is where your blade cut his thread. Poor boy."

Penny raised her eyes from the thread to Lachesis' face, anger surging hot and quick at the comment. "Poor boy? He raped me. He was going to kill me. I had no choice!"

"Pah," Lachesis said, but her voice was mild. "You had a choice, just as every person does. You chose to break a vow sealed with your own blood, and with honey from the Mother's own mouth."

"So I should have let him assault me? I should have just...just let him do what he wanted, without repercussion? I should have let him go, so he could help take the lives of more ha-mazaans? Is that what you wanted me to do?"

"It is not about what I want," Lachesis tsked her tongue, looking up from the folds of fabric with a frown. "It is what the Tapestry requires. Balance. Symmetry. Pull a string here, or cut it too short there, and there is a hole in the weave that lets the Shadow in. To simply change what is done, or to attempt to change what is to come, only tangles the threads of others, bringing destruction on the whole pattern. I told Antiope, who wanted to be Queen of the ha-mazaans, the same thing, but she thought she was so clever."

"When did you tell her anything? I came inside alone."

"You do not know as much as you think. But you can know this. Look." Lachesis dragged a finger along the yellow thread, over the uneven edge where the weave was incomplete, pinching the increasingly dark, dingy wool skein between her forefinger and thumb, pulling it taut. "Here is where your thread will be cut, just as I have measured. I have apportioned this thread according to your own destiny, giving you one year from the day of your broken vow to live. If this is what you seek to change, know that you come here in vain, Penthesilea of the ha-mazaans. Of the Dreaming Bessi. Of Nowhere."

64

ATROPOS

Penny's eyes were on the yellow thread, and the abrupt ending of the grey one, and, most of all, the sapphire blue cord that ran next to the yellow. Neither yellow nor blue ended near the grey one. A tremor of suspicion shook Penny from her stupor, and the oracle's words finally settle in her mind. One year. And she had already spent nearly half of it running from a curse that was slowly destroying everyone.

"If it is you that decides where the threads are cut, then all I am asking is that you give me time. At least enough to complete my mission. I need to bring Leandra and the others back. I need to reignite the Flame. Isn't that my destiny?"

"Perhaps. To lengthen a thread, another must be cut short, and properly knotted, or the Tapestry unravels. Is this what you want?" Lachesis smiled. "You are trained in the Craft. Surely you can find a Thread that will substitute for your own?"

Penny froze, staring down at the threads the woman pushed into her hands, deceptively innocuous as they twisted and whirled in the firelight.

"Go on, then," Lachesis purred, and she pulled Penny closer to the tapestry, laying threads into her hands that felt like they held the weight of the whole world. "Which thread will you cut short to lengthen your own? Show me, and I will summon my Sister, and you can be free to live as long as you wish. You are a Weaver. A Dreamer. It is in your power to make this choice, right now."

The skeins itched between Penny's fingers, prickling her flesh as she thought of all the lives she held. How easy it would be to snip one, two, all of them. The power one could wield if they controlled the destiny of every person to walk the earth. She pulled one thread through her fingers, dark green and strong, and as it slipped between her skin she saw in her mind's eye her father's face smiling down at her. She saw him hugging her close in front of the open flames of a fire, telling her tall tales of centaurs and monsters in caves, with the faces of women and the souls of Night and Shadow.

She felt another thread, dark orange and rough and thick, and instantly, Orithyia's blunt voice clashed in her mind, ordering Penny to move faster, fight better. Telling Penny she had done the right thing, in that bathhouse. Telling Penny she was stronger than she thought she was, when Penny had not thought she would ever have the right to call herself ha-mazaan.

Another thread, as mottled with color as the stones in the Terme, the same color as Sylviu's eyes. She thought of his smile, his quiet presence, always watching. She pulled that thread through her fingers with desperate longing, every twist and bump telling her its story, until she felt the pain from that day she had threatened him with her knife. She stopped before her hands could feel any further. She did not want to feel his anger, but most of all, she did not want a reason to think any of these threads were ones she could end. The fear she had struggled to keep at bay unfurled its black wings inside her mind, inside her heart. She flinched back, tossing the mound of threads back onto the table and into the shadows, and stumbled back from the table.

"No." Penny shook her head, taking another step back. "No, what you ask is not right. I will not sacrifice another to save myself. That is why I am here, didn't you hear me? Take my life, if that is what you are asking. But this curse has to end with me."

Lachesis tipped her head, her milky eyes somehow bright as they stared at Penny.

"Curse?"

Frustration burned in her chest, and underneath it, shame.

"The curse I unleashed. The curse that will be my death, just like you are saying. The curse that haunts me every night and day, so that I cannot even escape it in my Dreams. The curse that...that killed my aunt Lyta, and Areto, and all those ha-mazaans I see when I close my eyes, scattered on the beach....the curse that took Leandra into a den of vipers, where she has suffered Goddess knows what at the hands of those men for all this time. If she is even alive. The curse that…"

Penny began to cry, her throat strangling on the words she didn't want to say. "The curse that drove Sylviu away from me, and that killed the woman I loved as my own mother." She ended with a shuddering sob. "The curse that has brought death and destruction on everyone, so that I know I cannot ever love anyone again, or they will die, too. I do not care where my thread ends, but it is not fair that others must suffer because of me."

"Ah," the dry voice said after a moment. "Ah," the crone said again, then chortled in gleeful amusement, but she was still staring at her loom, and the pattern in front of her. "You think death is a curse? You are no longer so young to be so stupid."

The flames in the brazier roared, as though suddenly feeding their tongues on dry wood for the first time. Painfully bright light flared in the room, blinding Penny and scalding the tears on her face, searing her skin. She stepped back with a short cry, shielding her face with her arm. She thought she heard Calla's growl, and Peyo whinnied from the base of the cliff.

A whispering voice hissed unintelligible words, then there was another laugh, the same as before but deeper, as though echoing from the bottom of a dry, cavernous well. Penny lowered her arm enough to squint against the light, but the fire had gone completely, casting the whole cave into shadow. She shifted back another step, peering futilely into the darkness, the hair on the back of her neck raising further, every instinct screaming for her to flee. The shadows shuffled, shifted, creaked. Penny sniffed the scent that had been in the air when she first entered, of rotting vegetation and stagnant water. Of flax reeds soaking at the edge of a pond until their stems rot, and they are ready to be carded and spun into linen thread. The darkness deepened, the stale, rotten air drew closer, but even though she strained to see, there was only blackness.

From within that blackness, a single speck of light. It elongated, curved, until a crescent moon of sharp crystal hung before her eyes, and around the edge of it, the gossamer thread. Words that echoed with a multitude of voices thrashed through Penny's mind, so that she could not escape their sound.

"I am no curse. I Am Atropos. I Am Inescapable. I Am I, and We Are I, and I Am Us. I know the very step of the planets in their dance, the very chorus the stars will be singing when it is time for your thread to be cut. When your time comes to be called through the Gate, it will be Me who is there to greet you. What My Sisters spin and measure, I cut, unless another can be offered in your place. There is no other way to alter the time or day of your death, for it was measured at the Beginning, which is when I shall see you at the Gate. That is not a curse. That is destiny. *This* is a curse."

The leathery crackle of wings unfolded directly beside Penny's head.

She reached for her sword, but it was too late. One clawed hand gripped her throat while the other pinched the fingers clutching her sword hilt, until Penny felt the bones crush together. She wanted to cry out, but the fingers around her neck squeezed, and she could only choke under their unrelenting grip as they raised her from the floor as effortlessly as a dry leaf from water. The brazier flamed back into life. Penny kicked desperately as she dangled in the air, her free hand clutching at the Erinyes' claws. The creature laughed. Its hand squeezed tighter, the talons on the ends of its fingers carving into Penny's throat until blood dripped. A shiny black snake slithered the length of that bone-white forearm and reared its head in front of Penny's terrified eyes, while a crown of black snakes reared behind the Fury's skeletal face. Penny struggled with furious desperation, every muscle in her body straining to follow through on the months of Orithyia's tutelage, but she did not have the strength to break free.

The rattling voice hissed, and all the snakes opened their mouths to hiss with it. "We are Daughters of Nyx. Children Of Night and Shadow. We are Born before Light existed, and We shall go on when the Tapestry of this world has long crumbled into dust. We are Creators and Destroyers, All and One. We are Hope, and we are Vengeance. Is this the curse you are so afraid of, then?"

Penny could not answer for the hand choking her. The Erinyes pulled her close, so that she could feel the flickering forked tongues of the snakes testing her cheekbone, her jaw. Her vision was going dark for lack of air, the hand around her sword hilt going numb with the force of the creature's grip.

"Why so surprised, child? Is it truly such a shock to realize I am the one you have been seeking all this time? That I *am* our absolution?"

The creature dropped her suddenly, and Penny fell to the stone floor, gasping air into burning, tight lungs. She surged to her feet, finally lashing at the Fury with her sword, but the star-iron merely brushed through the Shadow's chest, its heart, its sharp-toothed, laughing maw.

"You should not be here, Daughter of Deceit. You seek what is not yours to find."

Penny shuddered, her sword raised protectively though she knew it had no effect, and said, "I seek only what I need, nothing more."

The Erinyes laughed again, though there was no humor in it. "What do you need, other than your just reward? What do you think you deserve, after everything you have done?"

"It has nothing to do with what I deserve. I *need* absolution, so that others do not suffer because of me."

"It has everything to do with what you deserve, daughter of Thrax and Kleite, and also of Antiope, the one who has tangled this weave so foolishly. You are a murderer, and an oath-breaker. You deserve to pay for your transgressions. You deserve to be punished. You deserve every suffering you have brought about by the perfidy of your own hands. Tell me you do not."

Penny swallowed hot tears as the Erinyes' words struck home, but there was an anger building in her chest, a seed of rage that had been planted the moment Brekko laid his hands on her, and its stem had only grown with every indignity, every unfair, harsh outcome at every turn since, until its trunk had become thick and rough with anger, its roots curling themselves around her heart, squeezing it into a painful new shape. She could not keep the fruit of that great tree inside any longer, and it spilled out in words of hatred, and bitter fury, but they were the truth.

"I had *every* right to claim justice for what he did to me. Only the darkest evil would ever think *I* should carry the punishment of a crime that was *his*, and his alone."

The Fury laughed, a shrieking, high-pitched sound that burned Penny's ears.

"You seek absolution for being an oath-breaker, and yet feel no guilt for breaking that vow." The creature hissed, spitting burning phlegm onto

Penny's skin. "You shake your head, as though you do not harbor the soul of a murderer? Come, show me there is not blood on your hands. Show me your soul is clean, and without blemish."

The creature transformed in an instant. Gone were the tattered black robes and the bulbous snakes, and in their place, the hulking, bronzed, sweaty face of a man too long at sea. Gone, too, were the cold stone and swirling snow of a winter mountain. Instead, there was the thick, hot, stiflingly close steam of the baths clouding the air, clinging to her skin. Penny stared, transfixed, as Brekko moved toward her through the steam. Her hand tightened on the hilt of her sword until it bit into her palm. She was alone with him all over again, and she could feel the fear crushing the hope from her lungs with every slow step he took toward her.

"Get away from me," Penny said.

"I only want to talk," Brekko's fat lips said.

Anger burned away the terror. She let every bit of rage pour out of her, lending speed and strength to her arm as plunged the sword straight into his heart without waiting for him to touch her, just as she should have done that day in the bathhouse.

"You had no right!" she yelled into his face, knowing it did not belong to him, but the Erinyes. She stabbed the shade of Brekko again, slashed again and again, but his face only smiled at her as blood poured over her hands.

"Maybe," his voice said calmly, as though he did not have holes through his lungs and throat. "But are you truly without blame? Is there not darkness in your heart?"

Again, the face changed. The mottled cheeks and thick, punctured chest became sharply chiseled cheekbones and strong jaw and copper hair brushing the broad shoulders of Deileon, his wide lips turned upward in sweet, seductive entreaty. Penny's knees nearly buckled as she adjusted to the awkward sway of a ship under her feet, and they became weaker still when she saw Leandra hidden behind the man she had once thought to welcome into her bed. Shame curled from her belly to her face, drowning out some of her frustrated rage. She tasted blood from her tongue, metallic and harsh, mixing its tang with salt from the sea, and it was bitter in her throat.

"What would you have done to me, Princess? Would you have kept your oath with me? Would you have kept the oath you swore to the Weaver of the World?" Leon's voice asked.

"I was only a child when I swore that vow."

"Do you not have a will of your own, then?"

Mutely, Penny stared back at his handsome visage, knowing it was a trick, but then he turned away from her, and raised his sword to strike Leandra. She did not hesitate. She lunged, arcing her sword with all the force terror and regret and guilt could lend her arm, burying the blade between his shoulder blades, deep enough into his spine to sever it before he could complete his deadly swing at the girl. He screamed. Reality wavered, faded to black.

It was night, and Penny knelt in front of her aunt's broken body. The stars winked cold overhead in a clear indigo sky. This time it was Molpadia who stared at her, her face twisted with the torment of her loss, dark eyes accusing.

"You are to blame for this, aren't you?"

"No," Penny said, but the word was choked with grief.

"Yes," the Erinyes said, though she spoke with the mouth of Molpadia, and those scarred lips curled when Penny shook her head.

"They came for Hippolyta's belt. Killed her for it. But they did not leave with it, did they?"

The breath went out of Penny's lungs. She raised a slow hand to the belt around her waist, her mouth agape as she realized the truth she had known all this time, but which her mind had never let her settle on, never acknowledge.

"No," Penny whispered. "*No.*"

The face of Molpadia was white with fury. "Hippolyta's belt would have protected her, could have given her a chance against that murderer's sword, but she gave it to *you*. A cowardly, useless girl, with no right to call herself ha-mazaan. It should have been you. It should have been *you*!"

Stunned, Penny could not think of a reply. The whole time, she had been wearing the zoster the Achaeans had come for. Her aunt had been killed for nothing. Guilt bloomed where before it had once been a tight bud, as she realized there was nothing she could say to her aunt's lover that would absolve her. Hippolyta must have known which belt they wanted. Antiope, too. They both must have known, and had said nothing, knowing who was wearing it. Penny thought back to her conversation with her mother the night before the battle, about keeping her belt on at all times, for her own protection. But she had not kept the belt on in the bathhouse. Maybe it had been her fault, like the Erinyes said. Maybe if she had obeyed her mother, Brekko would not have attacked her.

She knew the futility of this thinking, though. The what ifs and shoulds, all of the different choices that might lead to different outcomes. All of it futile.

Molpadia's dark eyes took on a blue hue, and her hair changed to the color of wheat at autumn harvest. Penny's breath caught to see her mother's beauty, at the sweetly upturned lips that she now realized were nothing like her own. She could not see herself in that face at all, though now she knew why.

"Do you expect me to believe you are so clean, so perfect, so blameless? You never obeyed me. How is it not your fault?"

Penny stared at Antiope's chagrined, disappointed face at a loss for words, until the anger returned, colder this time, and with the origin of her resentment in perfect view. She tasted bitter bile in her throat as she answered.

"*You* of all people cannot speak to me about blame. You took me from my people, from my home. From my family. You lied to me my entire life. You drugged me, kept me docile, forbid me to live with even the ability to defend myself. *You* were the one who insisted we welcome those ships, entertain those men, offer them guest rite."

Your mother is long gone through the Gate...

I told your mother nothing...

The Kebat's words gonged in her mind, their double meaning now clear and starkly obvious as a skim of ice on a lake. Penny grimaced a bitter smile to think of how the Oracle had told her the truth, but she had been playing a deceptive game in which Penny could only be the loser.

"I think you knew what would happen," Penny said suddenly, her rage making her lose sight of the fact this was not, in fact, Antiope, for the vision was too real, and the betrayal and pain Penny felt was too sharp. "I think you *knew*, and wanted to control things so they would still come out in your favor. That's what you do best, isn't it? Control and manipulate, and weave a web of deceit around everyone's steps according to how you think best?

"That's what you did with my father, wasn't it? Convinced him to give me up so that you could save your place on the throne. You never would have been queen without me. They would have found a new Hearth Queen, and new daughters for the Thrones, and you would have been *nothing*. So you took me from my home, and then you left me! *You left me!*" Penny screamed, her fury turning to untenable grief. "You left me to go off hunting with Theseus, and then you left me to clean up your mess, with a Flame gone cold and a city destroyed. *I* might have unleashed this curse by breaking my oath, but it was *your* fault. And I *hate* you for it." Penny began to cry softly, as Antiope's wide blue eyes simply stared through her soul, haunting her more deeply than any snake-rimmed shadow ever could.

"And now I...I am scared, and lonely, because you were the only tether I had to who I was, to who I was supposed to be, and now that is gone along with you."

The Fury's laughter was a dry rattle, like pebbles being shaken in a drum. Its shape shifted back into that of a snake-rimmed monster, and Penny cringed away, her tears blurring the creature into double the terror.

"You hold death and hatred and selfishness in your heart, but you think you do not deserve to be punished?"

It took a moment for its words to penetrate the fog of Penny's mind. The rage she had felt at seeing Brekko's face made a resurgence. She gulped her tears down, still gripping her sword.

"No, I don't."

Her words were quiet at first, but they strengthened with righteous anger as she went on.

"I don't deserve punishment for defending myself. I don't deserve punishment for defending anyone. So if you are going to haunt me for the rest of my life, or take my life as payment for a crime, it will not be done in the name of justice, if that is what you claim. It will be for an oath I never should have sworn, an oath which I will gladly break again and again to defend the people I love. If that deserves punishment, then so be it, but you should either finish the task now, or *leave me alone*."

Her chest heaved as she ended, and a frisson of icy dread snaked down her spine as the Erinyes gazed back at her, its dark eyes crying one single drop of blood to spill down its gaunt white cheek. She had gone too far in challenging a Night-Born sister, and now she would surely pay the price, but everything she had said was the truth. She did not feel any guilt about Brekko at all; the only regret she carried was that her actions had affected innocent women in Themiscyra, and all the consequences that had been unfairly visited upon Penny, and her unborn child.

The Erinyes curled its lips to reveal sharp teeth, a cruel version of a satisfied smile, and then, as suddenly as it had appeared, it was gone.

65

LIFE FOR A LIFE

Penny's whole body jerked, the way it did when jolted from a dream.

Lachesis was seated on the stool, weaving, with no indication she had ever been anything else than a Weaver of Worlds. Penny shifted her sword in a palm wet with fear, daring a quick glance behind her to the exit, but the crackling voice spoke before she could turn and run.

"My Spirit could have cursed you the moment you broke that oath, it is true, but the only thing you have been haunted by is your own trauma, your own guilt. I believe you may have finally decided to lay down that burden. Hmm?"

Penny swallowed, then shook her head, refusing to be played with. She gripped her sword tighter, wondering what the old hag was playing at.

"What do you mean?"

"I mean We are not the ones who hound your steps, though We have every right. This dark shadow you carry, the weight that suffocates you, is your own pain, and nothing to do with Us. If We had sought retribution for your broken vow, We would have taken it. It is not my Fury you struggle against. My spirit slumbers in Erebos. When We are unleashed on the world, you shall surely know it."

Though the words held a grim warning that made the hair on Penny's neck stand on end, she shook her head. "The Fury—*you?*—has haunted my every step since I broke my vow. It is not my imagination. It *is* real."

Ice-white eyes turned to her. For a moment Penny saw smooth, plump flesh over those hollow cheekbones, and overtop of that, a dark shadow, without form or shape, which hovered over the other two faces like shadows in the corners of a dream.

"The spirit of a Bessi Dreamer is strong, but if it goes too long unfocused, untrained, it becomes feral, and dangerous. It does, it does. It is much more than imagination, you are right. It is pain and anger made manifest in every drop of blood that lives in you. You are more than capable of haunting yourself, and have done since you broke that oath, but do not lay that blame at my door. I have no part in your suffering. If you wish to end it, there are plenty of threads alongside yours which will be happy to help ease your burden, if you would only let them."

Befuddled, Penny lowered her sword. She watched the gnarled hands pass the gossamer thread through the weft a dozen more times before she found her voice.

"What about the others? So many have died...my mother..."

"So arrogant, aren't you, to think you hold so many threads in your hand? Others have their own fates to find, and most have nothing to do with you. You have already declined to interfere with another's Thread, haven't you? It is not them you must worry about. It is yourself. The part of you who swore that oath is dead, and cannot be brought back. You must lay her to rest, and move into your future, for as long as that will last. Better yet, live Now. But if you do not accept who you truly are, and if you do not let others see who you truly are, you will never be free of that Shadow."

Penny swallowed, her limbs and eyes suddenly tired. It felt as though every purpose that had brought her here, driven her steps into this cave, had been pulled out from under her feet, leaving her spent and lifeless.

"And who am I? What future do I have, now that everything is destroyed?"

"Surely a girl with her father's heart, her mother's spirit, and the mind of the one who raised her would know that by now?"

Penny's thoughts flitted back and forth like the Weaver's shuttle. She knew less about who she was now than she had before entering this cave. A thousand questions floated to the surface, but there was one that had been gnawing at her the longest.

"Why did Antiope bring me here, then? Why did she make me swear that vow in the first place? Why did she not want me to be ha-mazaan?"

"Ah." The old woman nodded. "Finally, you seek something worth knowing. Come back to the Weave, and I will show you."

Penny hesitated, unwilling to return closer to the figure who changed her form as easily as the wind changes direction. Curiosity finally overriding caution, she moved with tentative, short steps, clutching her blade in front of her in case it was a trap, and the woman transformed into an Erinyes again.

One bony hand reached out, but it was not Penny she reached for. Lachesis began to gather the woven tapestry in folds, pulling it close before folding it in on itself in great lengths. The weaving on the table, or what showed of it, was deceptively small compared to what the oracle now brought forth, pulling the heavy weft with great tugs again and again, as though searching for a previous section of the pattern that was hidden in the folds of darkness on the other side of the stone table. Only, there were only shadows and stone on the other side, and the tapestry uncoiled out of nothing, until a great mound of cloth pooled at the oracle's feet. Penny's skin crawled as she watched, silent, until the old crone stopped pulling, and smoothed the fabric out once more, her hands caressing the folds into flat planes across the table. She pressed at the interwoven lines as though reading them with her fingerprints, her finger tracing gold and red and dark threads, and when she spoke, Penny peered at that clawed finger, the blurred patterns taking on vague shapes she could not quite recognize, as though hearing another language for the first time.

"It was because of me she made you swear that vow, you see."

Penny frowned down at the shifting pattern, trying to make sense of what was under the woman's fingertips, but these words made her look at the old woman's face.

"I told Antiope you would be her undoing."

"What do you mean, 'her undoing?'"

Lachesis' finger traced that blue line, before the yellow one began, the shapes of them finally taking form in Penny's mind. She could see the cold blizzard of snow high above the bonfire, the Elders of her father's council holding her high to Sabazios for her naming, while Antiope waited at the edge of the firelight, hope and fear both making her face shine like a torch in the night.

"Kleite died to bring you into this world, but she already had a plan, and so did Antiope. The day after your naming, ten days after your birth through the Gate of Death, Antiope brought you to me. She asked me if you were the answer to her prayers. If the prophecy given to her by my Womb-sister, the Kebat of Themiscyra, was now fulfilled."

"What prophecy?" Penny asked, and though she had thought this exact question many times in the past few moons, now that the truth was at hand, she dreaded the answer.

"Her prophecy of being Queen in East and West, of being a Mother to multitudes, just as she wished. Her prophecy that she would never hear her name uttered by a child of her own womb. Her prophecy that if she lay with a king and delivered unto him a son, and if she called forth a daughter from the Mother Herself, that the protectors of the Flame would continue their work in new lands, and new temples, with new names. She was also told that her son would be as dust beneath the hooves of his father's horses, that her womb would turn barren and dry as a desert, until such time as she would swear fealty to a man, and surrender her life to him. She was told her daughter, born of a foreign king, would carry on the ways of her mother's people, in lands beyond the sea, in times beyond our own, as mother of a new people. A people that will one day be the mightiest empire the world has ever known."

Lachesis shook her head, tsking her tongue at Penny's pale face.

"I assured her that her destiny did not end with you, just as it did not begin with you. But I also told her that because she sought to change the threads of her fate too soon, you would be both her salvation, and her undoing. I told her that though she called you daughter, loved you as her own, it would be by your own star-iron that she would meet her end. That when you learned the way of the sword and axe, you would raise an army against her. That her mantle would adorn your shoulders instead, and she would surely be brought low, with none whom she once loved able to save her from the fate she had chosen. I told her. I did. I did."

There was a hollow ringing in Penny's ears, like Harp had plucked an out-of-tune chord that would not fade. Her breath rushed out of her chest in one astonished word.

"What?"

"It is what Clotho saw," the oracle shrugged, but she was no longer old, her face wavering into a vision of plump flesh, eyeless sockets staring, hands now spinning a spool of fresh thread. "I told her the child she had already borne and the one she sought to claim as her own were not the ones of her prophecy. I told her she could not think to outwit the Moirai Krataia, We Who have already allocated her destiny. I told her that I had already sifted and spun her thread with all its colors, all its knobs and twists; that I, Lachesis, had already apportioned its length into the Weaving, and will hold it taut on the day that I, Atropos, cut it. I told her all these things, and still, she thought she could outwit Us. Manipulate Us. Alter the Weaving."

All three faces, young, old, indistinct, wavered in and out of existence as she spoke, so that Penny felt reality twisted with each turning vision. Nausea pushed bile from her stomach to her throat, and her knees felt as though she rode the waves of an undulating sea, but she swallowed it down, transfixed by the only continuous line holding all three visions aligned—that Thread in the oracle's ever-changing hands.

"She thought she could weave the pattern in a new way, make her thread longer, but she had nothing to offer as sacrifice to make it so. I asked," the oracle said earnestly, clicking her tongue. "I did ask, I did. But she would not give me what I needed. Instead, she brought you back eight years later, and made you swear an oath to never learn the way of the sword, to never be ha-mazaan, to never become the very thing that would be her undoing, while still fulfilling her own needs of returning home with a daughter. She thought it so clever, she did."

"What did you ask for?" Penny asked through numb lips.

The oracle smiled again, her gums black, and shrugged. "What do you think? The same thing I asked of you. I asked her for a life, in exchange for her own. A life for a life. But she refused, just like you have refused. She said she loved your father, and her sisters, and you, and everyone who might have been an equal trade. She said she had already sacrificed enough."

There was a darkness in Lachesis' tone, a malevolence that had not appeared until this moment, except for when the Shadow of the Fury was present, and Penny shuddered to hear it. It seemed as though the darkness itself twisted along the cavern walls, especially where the folds of tapestry had been pulled from, but when Penny looked directly at them, they remained still and cold, the rock unmoving. She was silent for a long while, listening to the painful thud of her heartbeat echoing in her ears.

She had come here looking for absolution, and instead, the trauma was multiplying, expanding. Hope seemed as far away as it had the moment her knife had sunk into Brekko's ribs.

"Then why me? Why did she not just leave me with my father, so that none of this would have been necessary?"

"Because she knew who you were. Kleite told her. Kleite knew, she did. She did."

"*Who* am I?" Penny demanded, frustrated to have the conversation come back to this. The One who was Three stared back at her, and at least two of those faces smiled.

"You, Penthesilea, will be the Mother to the motherless. Your heart will be the last hope of ten thousand men. This is what Antiope knew. This is why she wanted you. By the time she learned the rest of your destiny, it was too late. Antiope already loved you as her own. Her mind was already made up."

"What do you mean? The rest of my destiny?"

"That you will be the greatest ha-mazaan warrior to have ever lived, so that the bards will sing your name through the ages, telling the world of your deeds, and those of the one you once called mother. That your sword and spear and axe will release the Dreamers and the Guides from their prisons, casting them free onto a new ocean, full of possibility, and hope. That there will only be one who can match you in strength, he who can call down the spirit of my sister Lyssa, who can overcome you. He is the one who will help Me cut your Thread, on that day I have chosen.

"You, Penthesilea, were destined to be the last Queen of all the ha-mazaans. You are the one who will put an end to the reign of the sister-queens, killing them both to take the Thrones of Themiscyra for yourself. You are the one they will remember through the Ages, and it is this thread Antiope could not change, even though she tried."

66

SECRETS

Sinope's Defending Queen had eyes just like Antiope's, though there was an added hardness there, a bright star-iron that cut through Sylviu, and it only made his frustration grow stronger, his anger burn hotter. He was glad for it, though, because underneath those things there was now a terrible fear that threatened to tear him apart at the seams, and that fear was not for himself. It was for the one he had been forced to leave behind, and now, it was for Pen. So he focused on the Defending Queen's wrath to stoke his own rage, and smother that fear altogether.

"I sent my spies to bring me information, not to have an interloping son of Galatae put a spear in the chariot wheel, Sylviu. You could have jeopardized the whole mission!"

Sylviu stood his ground opposite Orithyia, his chest hot from both the fire burning in her brazier and the knowledge that she was indeed correct, that his actions and his promises to the people—*girls!*—inside that fortress had been rash, but he was beyond the point of being careful with either actions or words. Careful would not give his mother and the other ha-mazaans justice. Careful would not make anything right again, though he was well aware that nothing would ever be right again. Desperation had long since given way to fury, and now, to arrive here in this snow-filled valley of nowhere to find Pen had gone missing days ago, with no sign of where she might be, only made his anger heighten to the point of doing violence against the next person who stood in his way. At the moment, that person might very well be this leathery old queen who was well past her time to retire with the other attas.

"I was not going to just leave them there without some kind of hope," Sylviu ground out, though he could see from the corner of his eye Evandre trying to signal him to move on, let it go, but he was not in the mood for their political games. "And your *mission* seems rather compromised now that you've lost our future Hearth Queen, no?"

"Penthesilea is not the pathetic weakling you once knew, boy. She is more than capable of fending for herself, and it was her choice to run off into the wilderness. If she comes to an ill end, it is on her shoulders, not mine."

"Aye, no one seems to want to take responsibility for anything if it makes their Throne look weak. Must run in the family?"

He thought she might pull that sword on him, her eyes sparked so bright, but she merely bared her teeth in a cold smile, and nodded.

"Aye, Marpesia's blood runs hot in my veins, just as it did in Themiscyra's sisters. No doubt you felt the sting of Antiope's tongue once or twice, with your attitude, hey? Speak to me like that again, swineherd, and you will surely know the truth of how hot we can burn. Either way, when the girl returns, as I am sure she will, there is no need to be telling her what you've told me. She does not need that burden."

Sylviu shook his head once, sharply, and took a step forward. The air fairly crackled with tension.

"All you queens do is keep secrets. She should know the truth. All of it."

The thought of keeping any more secrets from Pen was enough to set his stomach roiling, but the ha-mazaan merely pursed her lips at him and stared, her stubborn resolve unshakable.

"Queens do not take advice from swineherds, any more than swineherds make decisions on matters of state, or war. What Penthesilea needs to know isn't your decision, just like—"

"Back to the topic at hand," Evandre cut in, casting Sylviu another warning look, "we will need Toxaris to bring what news she has from Lacedonia before we can make further plans."

Orithyia shifted her eyes from Sylviu to her General, and grunted. "That could be another two moons, at the least." Then she sighed, and her shoulders shifted. "We have no other choice, I suppose. We can't risk moving yet without a proper army."

"You already have a whole army at your command," Sylviu hissed. Evandre's eye roll and frustrated growl were loud beside him, mingling with approaching voices outside the tent. "Waiting another two moons could be too late. You aren't seriously going to sit on your asses the whole time, are you?"

"If Galatae wishes to march on Attica and take their vengeance, my boy, they are welcome to do so, but for as long as I am Defending Queen, my ha-mazaans will not be taking up men's bad habits of waging losing battles for an already lost cause. We will wait for Lacedonia's response, and then we will re-examine our plans. If they do not have the numbers we need, no ha-mazaan will be marching to their deaths, even for the sake of your ill-advised promises to girls you've no responsibility over. That will be your honor at stake, not mine."

"You—"

"Orithyia!"

The tent flap billowed open, cutting off Sylviu's white-hot curses he was about to unleash. All of them stared in varying states of shock as Penthesilea, cheeks white with high spots of red from exposure, hair wild and eyes alight with some strange flame, cloak crusted with ice and snow, burst through the doorway.

67

QUEEN OF ATHENS

The descent from the oracle's cave took nearly as long as the journey to find it, as Penny struggled to see any tracks in the snow leading to the hollow and the mountain spring. Finally, she simply chose a direction, not knowing where it would lead, and Peyo cleared a trail through the snow. Calla followed close behind, though not close enough that the horse could catch her under the chin with those sharp hooves. The worst of the storm had passed, but the two days of travel down the mountain were long and arduous, and, if anything, full of more confusion. Calla began to prowl in wider arcs in search of sufficient prey, and even the lichen was scarce for Peyo, though he dug what he could from the slopes of the foothills when they descended low enough. Then, as quickly as she had appeared, the cat was gone, seeking her own adventure in the forest.

Despite the hardships, the hunger, the cold, Penny barely registered the journey. She could not make sense of anything the Oracle had revealed, nor meld it with the reality she had already lived. Was her mother's death her fault, as the Oracle claimed? Had she somehow been her mother's undoing? She could see how perhaps Lyta's death had been her fault, if the zoster she was wearing had indeed been the one Heracles had come for. But if Molpadia had claimed the Defender's Throne, what did that mean for the prophecy? Was she supposed to fight Molpadia when that woman challenged her, and take over both Thrones? More importantly, in the very unlikely scenario where she was triumphant in such a battle, did she even want to be queen? She had never, ever considered the possibility of not being queen beside Cyra. She had no desire for power, no thirst for full control over the ha-mazaans. And how was she supposed to do any of that, and have a child to complete her Alsanti, in less than eight months before

398

Atropos cut her Thread? So what did it all mean? It was all too much, and so the landscape was one long, snowy blur of confusion as the three of them made their descent.

When the camp where Orithyia and the others waited came into view, dawn was shrouding the tallest eastern mountains in her rosy glory, Penny's stomach was clenched with hunger, and Peyo's boundless energy had slowed to a halting walk that tugged at Penny's heart.

"There will be clover and oats, and maybe even some figs soon," she promised wearily, and Peyo's ears flickered. "Or porridge, if that is what you prefer." She smiled when his ears pricked and his feet stepped higher.

Figures moved about in the morning mist, and four horses stood with their reins dangling when Peyo halted in front of Orithyia's tent. Light glowed from within the heavy canvas tent, the figures of five people vaguely outlined against the flame of the lamp. Two sentries stood outside, men from Harp's contingent, and Penny felt a momentary relief that he had not yet obeyed his father's summons. They eyed her first with suspicion, then with curiosity as she slid to the ground, forcing her knees not to buckle from fatigue.

"My horse needs food, and fresh, warm water. Please have someone fetch it immediately."

One of the men raised an eyebrow at her brisk command, but Penny did not wait to see if they would obey. She brushed past both of them to fling the tent flap wide, then halted.

Evandre and Ainippe stood next to the table, facing Orithyia. Another shadowed figure stood in the corner, barely visible in the low light, but she would know him anywhere. Sylviu's eyes locked with hers as the others turned to the doorway, their expressions sharp with concern.

Penny's heart thudded once, then clenched tight, before it pounded a heavy rhythm, like a mourning dancer's drum on the way to a burial. His face showed all the signs of hard travel, and there were new lines around his bearded mouth, but in his eyes, there was an anger she had never seen before. His expression could only mean one thing.

He had not found what he had gone looking for.

"Penthesilea!" Orithyia barked, though Penny thought she heard a measure of relief under the harsh anger. She dragged her eyes from Sylviu's searching ones to face the queen.

"You'd better have good news for me, girl, or else the search party—your father and Harpalion included—are going to have my full permission to roast you for our next stew when they finally return. What were you *thinking*, going off alone in a blizzard like that?"

Penny's tongue felt swollen and thick. She had not thought this part through. Had not thought there would be so many witnesses. What could she say? That there had never been a curse to break? That she had brought all of them here for nothing, except to learn she was not who she thought she was, *what* she thought she was, and that everything she had ever known about her past or pictured for her future was a lie? That she was supposed to be the end of the ha-mazaan sister queens, but not to worry, she didn't really belong to that role anyway, because her real mother was dead in a lonely hill some nineteen years ago, and she didn't belong anywhere, or to anyone? And oh yes, she would also be dead by the next Sturgeon Moon.

"I was born in a blizzard. Snow is part of my blood," she said finally, straightening her spine. Orithyia was caught off guard by such an answer, and for once, had no retort. Penny smiled tightly. "I have news, yes, but now is clearly not the time. What news do you bring?" She said this to Evandre, as the General regarded her with grim eyes.

Evandre glanced at Orithyia, her expression reluctant. Penny's wet cloak dripped loudly onto the carpet from the heat of the tent's brazier. She braced herself in that silence, preparing for the worst, trying to calm her breathing and her pounding heart.

Evandre's words were slow, cautious. "It is not good news, Ishassara." The ha-mazaan paused again, her manner abnormally hesitant. "We found only two of all the women taken from Themiscyra."

Penny swallowed through a throat raw after eating snow for a week, but the gnawing pain in her stomach was no longer hunger. "Who? Tell me."

Evandre glanced at Orithyia again, but the queen's lips were pursed.

It was Sylviu who answered.

"Leandra lives, just as you said." His voice was low, and gruff, and angry. On hearing Leandra's name, the surge of relief was nearly overwhelming, but it was a short-lived reprieve from the horror that had become her life, as his hazel eyes stared into her very soul.

"Leandra, yes. And your mother. All the other ha-mazaans are gone, probably drowned, my mother with them, but Antiope, wife of Basileus Theseus, Queen of Athens, traitor to Themiscyra and all of her kin, is doing just fine.

"She asked us to send you her love."

EPILOGUE 1

Athens, 3 weeks after the Sturgeon Moon, 1206 BC

Antiope climbed the last stair inside the dark hallway, Theseus' oxen shoulders blocking the light from the passageway ahead. Leandra was heavy in her arms, eyelids swollen from tears and fluttering in fitful dreams against her shoulder, rosy mouth slack with sleep. She held tight to the girl, and to her courage, and stepped over the stone threshold.

The room was opulent with tapestries and couches, braziers, baskets of knick-knacks and food, and most especially with young women—girls, in fact, though there wasn't the usual chatter or whispers and giggles of youth. They were silent, watchful. They perched on the couches and cots draped with richly dyed fabric, every one of them with hair the color of flax in its ripening season. They stared at Antiope and her armful of sleeping child, making no move to greet her or the man who surveyed them as one does a herd of cattle, sizing them up for the feast, eyes full of hunger.

One woman was older than the others, her pale skin no longer tightly stretched across mounded cheekbones, but lined with the writings of many days, the small stamps of time's stylus at the drying edges of her down-turned mouth. She approached, a willow-slip of a girl following, tucked behind the woman as though seeking the safety of her shadow.

Theseus turned to the woman and her companion, smiling. Always the same smile. Slick. Secretive. Sickening.

"Mother, how good it is to see you. I hope you have been well?" He did not embrace the woman, and she did not seek to embrace him. He held out a hand to Antiope.

"I would like to introduce you to your new Queen," he said without preamble, and his tone held something like pride, but perhaps something more deliberate, like a warning. "I have taken to bride the goddess Athena herself! Antiope of the Amazons. Mighty hunter, mighty warrior, mighty beautiful, wouldn't you agree? Wife, this is my mother, Aethra."

Antiope inclined her head, turning up her lips in what might have been a smile had she not been too tired, too wrung dry to make it convincing. "An honor, I'm sure."

Aethra murmured a polite greeting, her face a mask of disapproval, perhaps at Antiope's rudeness, perhaps at her son's choices.

Antiope shifted her gaze to the girl at Aethra's hip, a slender tree swaying in the shadows. She could not be more than ten or twelve summers, barely a season into her first moon-blood. Antiope waited for her captor to finish the introductions, but he was staring at the girl with undisguised hunger, and seemed to have entirely forgotten his new bride. His war prize. His assurance of peace against every ha-mazaan's wrath at his foul treachery.

"And this heavenly creature," Theseus finally continued, "is Helen, Daughter of Zeus himself, and the beautiful Queen Leda of Sparta."

Antiope peered closer at the girl as she moved out of the shadows. Her face was even more beautiful than Penthesilea's at that age, though she had many years of growing before her true beauty would unfurl. Her blue eyes were shy, and haunted. Her hair was the same red-gold as Lyta's.

Lyta. Precious, brave, doomed Lyta.

She hugged Leandra closer, a terrible dread seeping into her bones, though she had long thought they were already soaked through with horror. Helen of Sparta turned to Theseus, revealing her profile. Her belly bulged with the shape of a babe, though it was still many moons away from entering this world. Barely more than a child, yet already heavy with another, and Antiope knew with sick foreboding who was responsible for making the girl's belly swell.

Leandra stirred in her arms.

"Are we home now?" the girl mumbled, eyes blinking at the room of girls barely older than she was.

Antiope's arms tightened around Themiscyra's stolen daughter. She met Theseus' eyes, the fire in her finally returning after so many damp, despairing nights in the belly of his ship. Her lip curled as their eyes met.

"For now, Little Lion. For now."

EPILOGUE 2

Wilusa (Troy), Winter Solstice 1206 BC

Another dawn, another day closer to the Gate.

Molpadia lay under the frigid sky, the sounds of the camp coming to slow, methodical life around her, though she had barely slept. She rarely slept. She had no need of dreams or rest when very soon there would be an eternity for that. She watched the fingers of dawn caress the clouds into curves of strawberry and cream and gold, their promise of more winter storms in no way marring the visions they brought to mind.

She could see Lyta in everything.

She thought of the last morning she had spent with Lyta, when those same fingers of light had traced themselves over the perfect body of her soul's love. How she had been so naïve, so ignorant of the future that lay in store for them both.

After you, Little Marmot.

It was always supposed to be her, first. Not Lyta. And now there was so much to do before she could be with her again. So much to atone for, before she could face her queen without this terrible shame of failure.

One of the ha-mazaans called for the sentries to bring the horses in from morning pasture, to ready them for the day's travel, breaking the spell of the clouds. They were already within sights of Molpadia's next goal. She had already failed at the first, at catching Heracles and carving his beating

"

heart from his bull chest, but she could not let that drag her down, break her, though it nearly had. She would track that man until the end of his days, him and his offspring, and she would bring his legacy to a shuddering end at the edge of her axe. For now, though, reclaiming Lyta's belt from Antiope's girl, giving her the authority she needed to drag the rest of these straggling, resistant ha-mazaans west, and then watching that slick smile of Theseus' slackening in horror under her merciless blade would need to be enough.

When she had watched their lifeblood pool on the ground, heard their whispered pleas for mercy go unanswered, she would go through the Gate, and join Lyta in the Otherworld where she belonged.

And if anyone sought to stand in her way, she would happily take them with her, whether it was time for their Thread to end or not.

If you loved *The Night-Born Sisters*, or the first installment in *The Defender's Throne*, please consider leaving a review on Goodreads or Amazon, and sharing with a friend. Every positive word helps an author's sales, and means more than you know. I love keeping in touch with my readers, so find me online and say hello!
Keep reading for a sneak peek of The Last Hearth Queen, the third installment in *The Tapestry of Sword and Flame*.

Visit www.alessandrawoodward.ca to sign up of for the newsletter detailing all things ha-mazaan, including release dates, future book details, writing process, and more!

Excerpt from The Last Hearth Queen, coming 2024

"You enter this place without the protection of the Mother's blood, Sylviu, Son of Oistrophe. You must know Death has visited those with lesser crimes burdening their shoulders."

Sylviu paused to take in the giant of a woman standing naked before him, determined not to let her size, nor the Law he broke in entering this place, deter him.

"Why should my future be forbidden to me just because I am not a woman?"

"It is not for their futures that women seek me out, boy. It is for Seeing what Shadows and what Light lives in their heart of hearts. For finding what their soul truly desires. Is that what you have come to find out?"

"If that is what you give to the ha-mazaans, what you gave to my mother, then that is what I want to know."

The giantess studied him with those feline eyes, her dark tattooed face impassive in the eerie light of the crystal cave. Her thick lips curved in a slow, predatory smile, sending a shiver down his increasingly stiff spine. Finally, her deep voice commanded, "Then tell me what you think you desire—but be warned, if you do not give me the truest desires of your heart, what you find here will be a curse, not a blessing."

Sylviu did not need to think long. "I want to know my father. My mother said he was someone important. I..." Sylviu paused, unsure if he should say it all out loud, but she had demanded the truth. "I want to be someone important, too. To have some kind of impact on the world instead of being just a nothing swineherd in a hidden village of throwaways. I want to know if my father can help me with that."

The huge woman approached him, those carved bones on the ends of her braids rattling against each other until he thought it might be his own teeth chattering when she towered above him. At sixteen summers, he was no meek boy, but this was no ordinary woman, and he was already testing the Fates by seeking her out, especially without the guidance of a woman. But she did not seem to intend him any harm for his sacrilege; instead, he wondered if that was a glimmer of amusement he spied in her golden eyes. She held out a wide cup, gold with three lion's feet on the bottom, the smell of it putrid with swamp.

"Drink," she commanded.

Suspicious, Sylviu drank slowly, then finally tossed all of it down when his stomach threatened to heave the vile liquid back up. "Pah," he spat, screwing his mouth as he handed the cup back. The giantess stared at him with lion-eyes gone hard, and tipped a hand toward the cauldron.

"See your heart's desires unfold, Sylviu, Son of Scamander."

Sylviu stared. "You know who my father is?"

A black brow lifted, a mountain slope cresting above a lowering sun. Her fingers still pointed to the cauldron. Sylviu shifted his attention to the flames, their cold tongues sending chills of apprehension down his spine. Doubts about the wisdom in infiltrating the Kebat's cave were strong now. He had already broken the Law by stepping through that cleft, then again by looking upon the Kebat, and now that his desires hung in the air, thick with the taste of swamp on his tongue, he feared his sacrilege would cost him more than he had been prepared to pay...

ACKNOWLEDGMENTS

First and foremost, I have to thank my readers for your delightfully heart-warming response to *The Defender's Throne*. Without your enthusiastic clamouring for more of the story, *The Tapestry of Sword and Flame* series might not have taken shape quite so quickly, nor would *The Night-Born Sisters* have become a reality quite so soon. I know you are wanting more of Cyra and the others, and all I can say is, hold tight. There's a lot more of Penny's story to unfold, but rest assured other familiar faces will be seen again sometime down the road...

Thank you to my family, both blood and chosen, especially my mother, Isabel, and my sisters, Coralie, Paula, Kyla, and Holly, and all the Noots and Savages, for being the original source of inspiration for the ha-mazaan spirit, for the cheerleading during the rough phases of the manuscript creation, and for your continuous and unwavering support in everything I do.

Thank you to my street team at home and around the world, and my fellow crew at the bookstore— Debbie, Julia, Curtis, Sarah, Danya, Danika, and Jen—for reading first or final drafts, recommending my books to new readers and unsuspecting book clubs, listening to the dramatic woes of the writing life, and bolstering my creative process and daily life with your random conversations, feedback, humour, insights, and support. Thank you to the book clubs and readers who took a chance on The Defender's Throne, and gave me the inspiration and drive to share more of the ha-mazaans' story!

Thank you to my copyeditor and proofreader, Iulia, who works her magic on the final round of edits, and thank you to my amazing digital illustrator and cover design genius, TK, for the beautiful art and concept designs.

Last but not least, a huge thank you to my Alpha and Beta Readers, most especially Holly, Robin, Kyla, Susan, Sarah, Danika, and Erin. Your honest critiques, gentle nudges, inquisitive conversations, gracious kindness, and enthusiastic support mean all the world to a writer struggling in the storm of a first and second and fifteenth draft and so on. The story could never be as well-rounded or polished without your unique contributions, so thank you, thank you, thank you.

Alessandra Woodward lives in the Okanagan Valley of British Columbia, Canada, writing in the early hours of the morning, selling books during the day, and Dreaming at night alongside her *rhu-tasiyas*. She collects swords and books and stories that are too strange to tell anywhere but within the pages of a novel. Find her at www.alessandrawoodward.ca, and say hello.